Praise for *The Naked Baron*

". . . sweet and sexy Regency tale."—Maria Hatton, *Booklist* Top Pick!

"Naked and naughty—that's the kind of hero MacKenzie stakes her reputation on, and it's also the kind that readers adore. With their humor and heated love scenes, her books sparkle and light up readers' hearts. Her feel-good stories are just what we need."—Kathe Robin, *Romantic Times BOOKreviews*

"Caution: Reading *The Naked Baron* may cause spontaneous smiles and feelings of happiness!"—Connie, OnceUponARomance.net

"Sally MacKenzie may have penned her best 'Naked' book yet, raising the bar for the entire series. With unforgettable characters and blazing passion, *The Naked Baron* is a book to be savored over and over again."—Lettetia, SingleTitles.com

Praise for *The Naked Gentleman*

"Hilarity reigns as a queen of love and laughter crafts another 'Naked' book designed to keep you smiling. This delicious romance blends MacKenzie's hallmark humor with a cast of unforgettable characters and loads of sensuality."—Kathe Robin, *Romantic Times BOOKreviews*

"I laughed, I cried, and I enjoyed every moment of this fabulous love story."—Scarlet, RomanceJunkies.com

"What a great series! Funny, spicy, and romantic."—Jane Bowers, RomanceReviewsToday.com

Praise for *The Naked Earl*

"Naked, noble, and irresistible—who could resist one of Sally MacKenzie's heroes?"—Eloisa James, *New York Times* bestselling author

"Providing plenty of heat and hilarity, MacKenzie has great fun shepherding this boisterous party toward its happy ending; readers will be glad they RSVPed."—*Publishers Weekly*

"The latest in MacKenzie's delectably sensual 'Naked' historical Regencies series has plenty of sexy sizzle and charming wit."—John Charles, *Booklist*

"MacKenzie continues her delightfully humorous, sexy series with a nice and naughty 'Naked' hero who matches wits and wiles with an equally irresistible heroine in the author's typically touching style."—Kathe Robin, *Romantic Times BOOKreviews*

Praise for *The Naked Marquis*

"*The Naked Marquis* is an endearing confection of sweetness and sensuality, the romance equivalent of chocolate cake . . . every page is an irresistible delight!"—Lisa Kleypas, *New York Times* bestselling author

"With a delightfully quirky cast of characters and heated bedroom encounters, MacKenzie's latest 'Naked' novel delivers a humorous, sprightly romance."—*Romantic Times BOOKreviews*

". . . charming . . . funny . . . full of delightful characters . . . *The Naked Marquis* merits a place on the keeper shelves of readers of the traditional Regency and the spicier Regency-set historical romances alike."—RomanceReviewsToday.com

"*The Naked Marquis* is a delicious indulgence. Treat yourself!"—OnceUponARomance.net

Praise for *The Naked Duke*

"MacKenzie sets a merry dance in motion in this enjoyable Regency romp."—*Booklist*

"This is a funny, delightful debut by a talented writer who knows how to blend passion, humor, and the essence of the Regency period into a satisfying tale."—*Romantic Times BOOKreviews*

"Debut author Sally MacKenzie has penned a marvelously witty novel. . . . Readers who enjoy a large dose of humor will love *The Naked Duke*. The characters are charming, and the pace is quick. It is the perfect book for a cozy winter retreat."—ARomanceReview.com

The Naked Viscount

The Naked Viscount

Sally MacKenzie

ZEBRA BOOKS
KENSINGTON PUBLISHING CORP.

http://www.kensingtonbooks.com

ZEBRA BOOKS are published by

Kensington Publishing Corp.
119 West 40th Street
New York, NY 10018

All Kensington titles, imprints, and distributed lines are
available at special quantity discounts for bulk purchases for
sales promotion, premiums, fund-raising, educational, or
institutional use.

Special book excerpts or customized printings can also be
created to fit specific needs. For details, write or phone the
office of the Kensington Special Sales Manager: Attn.: Special
Sales Department. Kensington Publishing Corp., 119 West
40th Street, New York, NY 10018. Phone: 1-800-221-2647.

Zebra and the Z logo Reg. U.S. Pat. & TM Off.

ISBN-13: 978-1-4201-0254-3
ISBN-10: 1-4201-0254-0

First Printing: June 2010
10 9 8 7 6 5 4 3 2 1

Printed in the United States of America

For Beth and Dan—happy first anniversary

and

for Kevin—happy thirtieth!

Chapter 1

Edmund Smyth, Viscount Motton, tested the French window. It opened easily. *Tsk*. The butler was shockingly lax or, more likely, drunk as an emperor.

He pushed the window all the way up and stepped into poor, dead Clarence Widmore's study. The Parker-Roth ladies were currently in residence; he should drop a word in Parker-Roth's ear. Stephen would want to know his mother and sister were not being properly looked after. This was London, after all. Any sort of riffraff might try to break in.

Motton took a candle from the mantel and held it to the embers in the fireplace. It flared to life.

Of course, if Parker-Roth were living under this roof, he'd already know of the problem, but he couldn't fault the man for wanting to keep his own rooms. He'd like to do the same—the aunties were driving him mad. Winifred had arrived today with her parrot and monkey, so now all five of his paternal aunts and their pets were in residence. Zeus. Bedlam might be quieter than his town house at the moment. The worst of it was the women were convening to mount an attack on his single state. Aunt Winifred's arrival was especially alarming. She was a wily campaigner. He would have to be extremely alert until she returned to the country.

He surveyed the room. Damn, it would help if he'd been given a hint where to look. Searching through every book for this mysterious sketch of French spies the Earl of Ardley wanted would keep him here until tomorrow. The Parker-Roth ladies would not be out that long.

He opened the nearest book and ruffled its pages. If he wasn't Widmore's neighbor and hadn't been so damn bored, he would have politely—or not so politely—declined Ardley's request. The man was a pompous ass with a decidedly odd kick to his gallop. But when Ardley had cornered him at White's, he'd been in the doldrums. The jollifications of the Season were wearing very thin and even his extracurricular activities—tracking down and eliminating underworld vermin—were proving painfully frustrating.

If only he could discover the identity of the man behind so much of London's criminal activity, but he'd been stymied at every turn. Everyone knew the miscreant only as "Satan." He was beginning to believe the fellow was indeed the incorporeal spirit of evil.

He put the book back on the shelf and picked up another. Nothing about this little errand made sense. Paunchy, balding Widmore, a French spy? In all the years he'd lived next door to the fellow, he'd never once seen any evidence he was working for the French. Widmore had been odd—no question about that—but odd and treasonous were not synonymous.

Hell, if one were considering odd associations, Ardley's connection with Widmore would be at the top of the list. Ardley had been at Lord Wolfson's estate when Widmore had met his untimely end, landing bare-arsed on a nest of adders.

What Widmore had been doing capering about naked was not a question he wished to contemplate.

And why had Ardley associated with Widmore at all if he'd suspected him of treason? Or, more to the point, why did he suddenly care about a supposed sketch of some French spies when Widmore was dead and the war was long over?

He put the book he'd been examining back. He'd start with the desk instead. It didn't look promising—the wooden surface was as bare as a windswept moor—but perhaps something had got stuck in the back of a drawer or, better, perhaps there was a hidden compartment or two.

Here was something interesting. Most people did not decorate their work areas with an object about two feet high draped in Holland cloth. The white fabric billowed in the breeze from the open window, giving it a rather ghostly appearance. Unlikely it had anything to do with what he was looking for, but he'd leave no stone unturned. He plucked off the cloth . . .

Good God.

He stared down at a statue of the god Pan—a very, er . . . excited Pan.

Miss Jane Parker-Roth sighed as she closed *Frankenstein*. It was always hard to finish a book one enjoyed—it was like leaving a good friend. She'd pleaded the headache so she could stay home from the Hammershams' musical evening and read. Mama must have suspected her malady was feigned, but she hadn't argued, thank goodness.

She put the novel on the bedside table. One of the best things about coming to Town was the lending libraries. Oh, the Priory had an extensive book collection to be sure, but only a few were novels. Da had his poetry books; Mama had her art books; John and Stephen, her older brothers, had their horticultural books; but novels? No.

One would think a painter and a poet would have very liberal ideas on what their children could read, but such was not the case. Lucy, the baby, was already thirteen and had virtually memorized *A Vindication of the Rights of Women,* yet Mama still would not let her read even Miss Austen's stories. Lucy was a resourceful girl, however, and had managed to smuggle into the house an impressive assortment of novels.

Thankfully, Mama had given up on her when she'd made her come-out, and now, at the ripe old age of twenty-four, she could read whatever she wished, at least when she was in London.

What should she read now? She didn't want to start a new book immediately, but she liked to have her next selection ready. Anticipation added to the delight.

Hmm. She'd been meaning to read *Waverley* for the longest time. She was quite a fan of Mr. Scott's stories, but she'd never read his first. She glanced at the clock. It was far too early to go to sleep. She'd just slip downstairs and see if by chance the book was in the Widmores' collection. Perhaps she'd even take a quick look at its opening pages . . .

Jane climbed out of bed. Mama wouldn't be home for hours yet. Not that she'd been looking forward to the "infernal caterwauling," as she'd put it, of the Hammersham twins, but she'd been greatly anticipating seeing her artist friends. She'd surely go off into a side room with them and catch up on all the art gossip. She might not come home before the sun rose.

Jane put on her slippers. Her wrapper, unfortunately, was off to be washed—she'd spilled chocolate on it this morning. No matter. She'd only be a moment, and the servants were all in their quarters, celebrating the house-keeper Mrs. Brindle's birthday.

She stepped into the hall. As she'd suspected, it was deserted. She made her way toward the stairs.

If only she could spend all her time in London at the lending libraries and museums, but Mama had other plans, of course. It *was* the Season and she *was* still unwed. She couldn't plead a headache every night— Mama would have the physician at the door in a pig's whisker. The woman took her children's every twinge, every sniffle, very seriously.

She sighed. So Mama would drag her to as many society events as she could, hoping her eldest daughter would inspire undying ardor in some gentleman's breast.

Mama was living in air castles. When was she going to face the truth? This was her—damn. Jane grabbed the banister and stopped on the top stair. Could it be? She counted on her fingers to be certain . . . Yes, this was the beginning of her *eighth* Season.

She wasn't just on the shelf; she was stuck to it like a leaky glue pot.

Which was just fine with her. She started down the stairs. She'd met all the eligible—and some not so eligible—society gentlemen and had found them all completely boring.

Well, not all. There *was* Viscount Motton—six feet of elegantly attired muscle, with sapphire blue eyes, chest-nut brown hair, and a damn dimple in his left cheek.

Not that she'd noticed.

She snorted. The man certainly hadn't noticed her, or if he had, he only thought of her as John and Stephen Parker-Roth's younger sister. He'd never once asked her to stand up with him at any ball or assembly. She'd barely exchanged two words with him all these years.

Of course, he didn't attend many social events. He came—briefly—to the first few each Season and then vanished. And she'd wager she wasn't the only woman who'd made note of his habits in that regard.

She glared at a plaster cherub discreet enough to have avoided Mrs. Brindle's Holland cloths. Lord Motton didn't get dragged to every ball and breakfast, oh no. He was a man. He had the freedom to choose the path his life would take. He could stay on his estate like John, or go off to foreign lands like Stephen. When he finally decided it was time to start his nursery, he would just pick one of the many aristocratic girls displayed for his inspection on the Marriage Mart.

Faugh! A man's life was so much better than a woman's. Men could have adventures, while women must sit home, darning socks and tending children. It was not fair.

She reached the bottom of the stairs and looked around. There was still not a servant in sight. She'd just slip down the hall and into the study. With luck, she'd find the books in some discernible order, but given the general state of the house, she'd more likely encounter a complete hodge-podge. Oh, well. She had plenty of time to browse through the shelves.

She came to the study door, put her hand on the knob—and paused. Odd. She sniffed. Did she smell smoke? Only a trace, as if someone had just blown out a candle.

Ridiculous. She was allowing the gothic thrill of *Frankenstein* to cloud her thinking. This was present-day London. Nothing exciting ever happened to her.

She shook the silly, fanciful thoughts from her head and opened the door.

Her candle went out. Damn. She stepped toward the fire to relight it and felt a breeze. The French window was open. Why—

A strong arm snaked around her waist and a broad, naked hand clamped over her mouth. She was hauled up against a hard male chest.

Dear God! She swung her candlestick, but only managed to knock over the hideous statue of Pan on the desk. She couldn't turn and pummel the man behind her—he was too strong. But he *was* taller than she . . . She flung her weapon up and back this time and collided with something.

"Bloody—" The man took his hand off her mouth to grab for the candlestick. She drew in a deep breath. This was her opportunity. No one would hear her scream, of course—the servants were too far away and likely too drunk to come to her aid—but this miscreant didn't know that.

She yelled as loud as she could.

"Hell, woman, you just broke my eardrum."

"I'll break more than that, sirrah, if you don't release me immediately!" Odd, the man's voice had sounded educated and very faintly familiar.

He chuckled. "Who would have thought you were such a hellion?"

Hellion, hah! She hadn't grown up with two older brothers for nothing—and a younger brother as well. If he gave her just an inch, he'd be sorry. She screamed again and thrashed more vigorously.

"*Will* you stop that?"

"Not until you let me go, you—*oof!*"

He'd managed to twist her to face him. His left arm was now around her back, his right hand on the candlestick, and his mouth—heavens above!—his mouth was descending . . .

She gasped. The moonlight revealed his identity just before his lips touched hers.

She was being held and . . . hmm, well, kissed . . . by Viscount Motton.

Her fingers loosened and the candlestick crashed to the floor. Neither of them bothered with it. The candle was out. It wasn't going to set anything aflame.

The viscount was setting *her* aflame. She was surrounded by his scent—eau de cologne and leather and . . . him. His mouth covered hers, but she'd lost all desire to scream. No, her desire was headed in an entirely different direction. She felt boneless, like her knees would give out at any moment.

His lips moved, brushed hers, nibbled at the corner of her mouth, and then meandered over her cheek to a very sensitive spot on her neck just under her ear.

She'd never been kissed before . . . well, never like this. This was an entirely new experience—a *wonderful* experience. Mmm.

What was the man doing here? He lived next door—and yes, she'd occasionally tried to time her daily walks to catch a glimpse of him. Had he mistaken the house? Gone astray?

His mouth moved farther down her neck, his hands wandering lower to skim her bottom. Ohh. He was going *very* much astray.

Should she be alarmed? No, he must not mean her any harm. He knew her brothers, and he had an unblemished reputation.

Ohh. He was stroking her bottom now. Her nightdress was so old and worn, it was almost as if his hand were on her bare skin.

She'd dreamed of someday getting a dance with the man, of feeling his gloved hand on hers—and now . . .

They were quite alone. No one would know if she took advantage of this odd situation.

He'd come back to her mouth. Was that his tongue touching her lips? What would happen if she . . . ?

Ohh.

His tongue slid between her teeth. How disgusting! Hmm, well, it should be disgusting, but it was . . . not. Actually, once one got over the shock, it was rather wonderful. He tasted of brandy, and he filled her with wet heat.

Her mouth was not the only part of her that was very hot and wet. Her stomach . . . well, lower than her stomach . . . was embarrassingly damp—if she was still capable of feeling embarrassment, which she apparently wasn't—and throbbing. An odd hollowness opened there, wanting something . . .

She had three brothers. Her mother was an artist with more than one nude painting in her studio—she had never been shy about explaining things. Mama might not want her daughters reading novels, but she did want them to know certain facts of life. And Jane had been eleven when Lucy was born—she'd asked quite a few questions. She had a good idea what her body was aching for—and what part of Lord Motton's physique could provide what she needed. It had formed a hard ridge against her belly.

His hands were moving again, one still tracing the contours of her derrière, the other sliding up to . . .

Oh. Oh, heavens.

All rational thought fled as his fingers cradled her breast.

Motton was lost in a flood of sensation—the feel of this woman, so soft in his arms, her lovely curves unshielded by stays or layers of clothing; the taste of her sweet mouth under his; the smell of her skin, of lemon—

a hint of purity, of innocence—and the musk of heat and need; the sound of her small gasps.

She had been so feisty—so fiery—at first, but now she was yielding and feminine and thoroughly seductive. Fiery, but in an entirely different way. He certainly felt as if he were on fire—his cock was just about ready to burn a hole in his breeches.

He pulled her bottom closer, bringing her more tightly against his poor, straining member, but the pressure only served to stoke the flames higher. His other hand cupped one of her lovely breasts. It was firm, soft, perfect. It fit his palm as if it had been made for it. He ran his lips over her jaw as he rubbed his thumb over her nipple. The lovely woman in his arms gasped.

He chuckled and kissed her just below her ear as he flicked the hard little nub once more. She gasped again.

He almost gasped. Standing was becoming a bit of a challenge. Unfortunately the loveseat was far too small, but there was the desk. She'd thoughtfully cleared it of that obscene statue. At the moment he'd wager his cock was far larger than Pan's in any event.

She was running her hands down his back, spreading them over his buttocks, pressing him against her.

He cradled her jaw and returned to her mouth. Before he could plunge inside, she slipped *her* tongue tentatively past his lips and teeth. Ah. Who would have thought this girl would be so delicious, so responsive, so—

So virginal. So respectable. So closely related to two of his friends.

He froze. He'd actually been thinking of lifting Miss Parker-Roth onto the bare desktop, raising her nightdress, and—

Sanity came crashing back like a migraine. He straightened and jerked his hips back.

"What . . . what are you doing?" The soft little words were hardly more than a whisper. She sounded completely confused.

She looked completely seductive, but it was past time he started thinking with his brain and not his . . .

Long past.

He tried to push her gently away from him, but she wasn't moving. She wrapped her arms around his back and held on.

"Miss Parker-Roth—"

"Jane."

"What?"

"Jane. My name is Jane."

Had he known her Christian name? No. He'd never paid much attention to her, frankly. She'd been just another attractive item decorating the *ton*'s ballrooms—like a potted palm or a ficus tree.

Little had he known.

"What's your name?"

The question hit him in the gut. Surely she knew whom she'd been kissing? And rather more than kissing, actually.

He found he didn't at all care for the notion that he was just an anonymous male. "Motton."

She shook her head. "I *know* that. I want to know your *name*."

Ah, his Christian name. No one called him by that except the aunts. It felt rather . . . intimate to share it with her. "Edmund."

"Edmund."

She murmured it as if she were exploring how it felt on her tongue. Damn! He could not think of Jane—of Miss Parker-Roth—and tongues. Her tongue had been so sweet, so shy. He would dearly love to feel it on—

Think with your brain, Motton! He firmly detached the woman and stepped back out of her reach. "Miss Parker-Roth, it cannot have escaped your attention that we are in a dark room without a chaperone and you are in your nightclothes."

She grinned, the minx! "Yes, I know."

"I shudder to think what society would say were it to learn of this . . ." What? Scandal? Disaster? Monumental lapse in judgment? All of the above? "This situation."

And why wasn't Miss Parker-Roth having the vapors? Surely a gently bred miss should be in hysterics at the treatment she had just received. Not that she'd been struggling. Oh, no. She'd been a very active, a very willing participant.

She dimpled up at him. She did have a most attractive smile. "Oh, don't go all poker-faced."

It wasn't his face that was pokerish. If he didn't start thinking about something besides Ja—Miss Parker-Roth's—tongue and soft bottom and lovely breasts, he was not going to be able to light a candle and reveal his very impolite proportions.

Blast! His proportions just got even more shocking. Miss Parker-Roth had moved so her back was to the hearth. There was sufficient illumination from the fire's embers to reveal a tantalizing glimpse of her waist and legs and—

He turned away to step closer to the open window. It was suddenly infernally hot in the damn study.

"Society won't say anything because no one will find out," she was saying. "As you point out, there are no witnesses, and I'm not going to go blabbing about . . ." She paused, and he glanced back at her. He'd wager if there were enough light, he'd see her face had turned bright red. His eyes dropped. There was definitely enough light to see . . .

"I'm not going to blab about . . . about what we were doing," she said. "Are you?"

"No, of course not." He had to stop staring at her br— chest. He jerked his attention back to her face. "I am not a complete idiot."

"Well, then, there you are." Jane frowned. She was suddenly feeling very out of sorts. Here she'd just had the most wonderful experience of her life with the man she'd dreamed of for years, and the fellow acted as if he could hardly bear to look at her. He'd turned as prim and proper as . . . as her stiff-rumped brother John.

John, thankfully, was not in London with them this Season. He'd gone off to Baron Tynweith's estate. Odd, since the baron's parties were often disreputable, but John had said something about topiary when he'd left the Priory. Plants were John's passion—unlike Stephen, his *only* passion.

What was Lord Motton's passion?

Mmm. She'd like to taste a little more of his passion. Her dreams had not come close to the reality of it. Unfortunately, the man did not look at all willing to repeat his thrilling performance.

And now that she looked at him—really looked at him—she saw he was dressed most peculiarly. Every article of clothing he wore was black—black shirt, black cravat, black breeches, black stockings—and he had dispensed with a coat and waistcoat. Well, she'd vaguely noted *those* omissions when she'd been plastered up against him.

It was almost as if he wished to blend into the shadows. Why? More to the point, why was he here at all and how had he gotten in? Mr. Hunt, the butler, was at Mrs. Brindle's party.

He kept looking down at her chest. Had she spilled

chocolate there, too, when she'd had her accident with her wrapper this morning? She looked down.

Oh.

She darted behind one of the wing chairs. Thank God its back was high and she was not terribly tall. Damnation, if Lord Motton was truly a gentleman, he'd offer her his coat . . . he didn't have a coat . . . oh, bother.

He bowed briefly and cleared his throat. "Ahem, well, I must be going. Do pardon my intrusion. And, of course, my apologies for the . . ." He waved his hand vaguely. "For my behavior." He looked ready to go out the window.

Well, that answered the question of how he'd gotten in, but he certainly wasn't leaving before she got some answers.

She leapt back out from behind the chair and grabbed his arm. "Wait! You must tell me why you're here."

He frowned at her. "Miss Parker-Roth, please control yourself."

He sounded *far* too much like John. She considered uttering one of the very improper words she'd learned from Stephen, but she restrained herself. "I'll make you tell me."

He snorted, shook off her grasp, and turned. She latched onto the back of his shirt.

"Will you stop—"

"I have two older brothers, a younger brother, and two younger sisters. I know all about blackmail and coercion."

He didn't even bother to reply; he just pulled her hand off his shirt and kept going. She hurried after him, out through the French window onto the terrace.

"I'll tell your aunts what happened here tonight."

That got him to pause. "You wouldn't. You'd ruin yourself."

"Not if I tell your aunt Winifred—*she's* not such a high

stickler. I saw her arrive today with Theo and Edmund. Oh!" Jane covered her mouth with her hand, but her snicker still escaped. "She named the monkey after you, didn't she?"

Lord Motton sighed. Surely Miss Parker-Roth would not be so bold as to tell Winifred about this evening? If she did . . . well, Aunt Winifred was awake on every suit. She would immediately see a golden opportunity to push him into parson's mousetrap. And she would be right— he would be bound to marry Miss Parker-Roth if word of this encounter ever did get out. He couldn't be alone with a young, unmarried woman in her nightdress without of- fering for her. And they hadn't just been standing around discussing the weather.

He waited for anger to surge through him. He'd spent years avoiding marriage traps . . . but, to be fair, Miss Parker-Roth hadn't set out to trap him. He'd brought this on himself, not that he'd foreseen the risk when he'd agreed to search Widmore's study.

And kissing her *had* been extremely pleasant.

He didn't feel angry, he felt . . . he didn't know how he felt. Miss Parker-Roth was uncommonly attractive in that virginal nightdress with her hair in a long braid down her back. He'd like to spread her hair out over her shoul- ders and run his hands through it. It was a warm brown with hints of red.

Why had he never noticed her before? She must have been at all those dreadful society events over the years.

The answer was simple. He'd not been in the market for a wife, and John and Stephen's sister was not a suit- able candidate for dalliance.

"I'm waiting, Lord Motton."

And she was getting chilly. He could see her nipples peaking against her nightgown.

He'd like to make them harden for him . . .

"Come inside and I'll tell you as much as I know, which isn't much." He took her arm and turned her back to the study.

"I would advise you not to try pulling the wool over my eyes." She jutted out her lower jaw. She looked quite pugnacious.

He smiled briefly as he seated her in a wing chair and turned away to light the candles. He could easily bamboozle her if he wished—he'd had far more experience with deception than she, no matter how many brothers or sisters she had.

For some reason the thought of lying to Miss Parker-Roth sat like a rock in his belly.

He glanced back at her. She looked so pure, so beautiful sitting there staring at . . . her eyes were . . .

Good God! Miss Parker-Roth was studying his arse.

He turned to light some more candles. He could almost feel her gaze on his breeches.

She was going to have something else to study when he turned to face her if he didn't pull his wandering thoughts back to the subject at hand—which was . . . what?

Ah, right. Widmore's supposed sketch.

He lit the last candle and sat down quickly, leaning forward to shield his lap and any suspicious protuberance that might be apparent there. "I'm not trying to pull the wool over your eyes—I really do know next to nothing. The Earl of Ardley cornered me at White's this afternoon and told me Widmore had been a French spy—"

"*Clarence?*" Miss Parker-Roth gawped at him. "A spy?"

"I grant you, it does seem unlikely." He'd had almost the same reaction when Ardley had told him. Widmore had been fat and loud and . . . colorful. He'd wager the man was constitutionally incapable of moving unobtrusively. If Widmore *had* been a spy, he'd been a master of concealment. "But sometimes the best spies are those who seem the least likely."

"Oh." Miss Parker-Roth narrowed her eyes. "Are *you* a spy?"

"No, of course not." It was true. He'd never considered himself a spy, but if he'd ever been one, he wasn't one any longer.

Her expression did not change.

"Well, I may have done a little skulking about on occasion and a spot of listening here and there."

"Hmm. I don't suppose you'd tell me if you are a spy."

"I don't suppose I would, but I'm not."

"You're here."

"Merely on an errand for a"—no, he couldn't call Ardley a friend—"an acquaintance."

"Why isn't Lord Ardley doing his own skulking?"

He snorted. "Ardley?" The earl was fatter than Widmore had been.

Miss Parker-Roth laughed. "True, I can no more see Lord Ardley as a spy than I can Clarence Widmore." She shook her head and echoed his own thoughts. "If Clarence was a spy, why would Lord Ardley care about his activities now? The war is long over and Clarence is dead."

"Yes, but according to Ardley, Clarence sketched some of his fellow spies. That's what he wants me to look for. Such a drawing, if it exists, could be very useful in rooting out any traitors still lingering in positions of power." That was what had finally convinced him to take on this ridiculous mission. He wished to see all traitors brought to justice.

Yet something about Ardley, something in his manner or his voice had made him suspicious. Ardley wanted something, yes, but Motton would wager it wasn't a drawing of French spies.

Surely the man couldn't be stupid enough to think he wouldn't examine anything he found?

He leaned closer to Miss Parker-Roth. "Did you know Widmore well?"

"No. Mama knows his sister, Cleopatra. They are both painters, though Cleopatra paints flowers and fruit, while Mama paints"—Miss Parker-Roth suddenly turned red and cleared her throat—"other things."

"Ah." If the painting Stephen had hanging in his rooms was an indication of the bulk of Mrs. Parker-Roth's work, he understood Jane's embarrassment. Mrs. Parker-Roth appeared to have a fascination with nudes. "I see."

His eyes dropped to her nightgown. It was primly buttoned to her chin, but if he loosened that line of buttons . . .

He would like to see Jane nude, sprawled across his bed—

Damn it, he could not be entertaining salacious thoughts about this particular young woman. Such fantasies were totally inappropriate—and he had a job to accomplish before the servants or Mrs. Parker-Roth discovered him here. Mrs. Parker-Roth might be an artist, but she was also a mother. She would not look favorably on a man having a tête-à-tête with her nightgown-clad daughter.

"Are you familiar with the house, then? Do you have any idea where Widmore would have hidden a drawing?"

Miss Parker-Roth shook her head. "No, I'm sorry. We usually stay at the Pulteney Hotel when we come up for the Season. We're only here this year because Cleopatra is on her honeymoon and offered us the use of her house."

"I see." It had been too much to hope she would hold the answer to this puzzle. He looked at the crowded bookshelves. Zeus, he did not relish going through each one of those tomes. And Widmore could easily have hidden the paper elsewhere. Almost anything—the desk, a chair, a bed—

No. No thinking of beds with Miss Parker-Roth in the room. It would be . . . entertaining to search her bedchamber—

No bedchambers.

The truth was, anything could conceal something as slim as a sheet of paper.

"Didn't Lord Ardley have some suggestions as to where Clarence might have hidden the sketch?" Jane asked.

"Unfortunately, no."

She stood, which put his eyes on level with . . . gave him an excellent view of . . .

He shot to his feet.

"It sounds to me as if you are forced to look for the proverbial needle in a haystack," she was saying. "So I shall help you."

Help him? He caught a whiff of lemon and woman—which went directly to his groin. Blast. The only way she could help him was to lie down on the carpet and spread her legs.

He needed to haul his mind out of the gutter.

He'd have her lie on his bed instead—

Bloody hell! His imagination had never been this unruly before. He took what the women of easy virtue offered and left the other females—women like Miss Jane Parker-Roth—alone.

Miss Parker-Roth had pulled a book off the shelf. She opened it, turned it upside down, and shook it.

"What are you doing?"

She looked over her shoulder at him as she pulled out

another book. "Helping you. You'll be here all night if I don't." Nothing fell out of this book either. "You'll probably be here all night even if I do."

She was standing in front of the fire again. He could clearly see the curve of her breasts, the shadow of her nipples. If he looked lower, he knew he would see—

No, he would not look lower. He wrenched his gaze up to study the mantel. "You are *not* helping me."

"Of course I am—don't be so pigheaded. And why are you looking up there? Do you see something—*ack!*"

He'd grabbed her arm. He couldn't stand it any longer. "I said you are not helping me. You are going back upstairs to bed—"

Blast! She whirled to give him a piece of her mind, no doubt, and he stepped forward at the same time. Their bodies collided. Her soft, sweet body—her breasts and hips and belly against his hard . . . his rock hard, painfully hard—

Her tart, sweet scent enveloped him. She had tasted so good before. Her lips were just inches from his now. What harm could one small kiss do?

He bent his head. Just a small kiss. Just a brushing of lips. No tongues.

Just a small, good-night kiss . . .

Jane held her breath. He was going to kiss her again. She could tell. He had that intent, almost hot look in his eyes. He was staring at her mouth; her lips felt swollen, sensitive.

She tilted her chin, closed her eyes. Every part of her— even some shockingly embarrassing parts—tingled with anticipation. Waiting . . .

Would it be as wonderful as the first time?

Would it be better?

Would it—

She felt him move away. Her eyes flew open. His eyes were still hot, but with anger instead of seduction.

"You are going to bed."

"Huh?" She felt like a four-year-old being sent to her room with no supper for doing . . . what?

"You are going upstairs." He tugged on her arm. "Now."

"No." She dug in her heels, but she was no match for his strength. He dragged her toward the door. "You're hurting me."

He paused. "Am I really hurting you or are you playing one of your tricks on me?"

Lord Motton was a fast learner, especially considering he had no siblings. Best not to answer that question.

"My lord, you know you need help."

"I do not."

"You do."

He didn't bother answering; he just moved closer to the door. She had to do something.

They'd reached the Pan statue. It was in pieces—obviously the work had been a plaster cast and not the solid stone she'd initially supposed. Her foot sent Pan's mammoth member skittering across the carpet to slip between the legs of a small loveseat.

Had she seen something sticking out of the broken end, right before it had disappeared under the furniture? A piece of paper perhaps?

Excitement shivered up her spine. She had to get her hands on that penis.

Chapter 2

Jane threw herself toward the loveseat. Motton must have been startled by her sudden movement, because he loosened his grip.

That was all she needed. She'd learned early, playing with John and Stephen, to take any opening she was given. In a flash, she'd twisted her wrist and broken free. She fell to her hands and knees to peer under the loveseat, looking for the errant organ.

The Widmores' regular servants apparently were not much better than the temporary ones—the dust under the loveseat was easily an inch thick. Jane sneezed.

"What are you doing?" Lord Motton sounded extremely annoyed.

Jane spared him a glance. He looked extremely annoyed, too. "I'm searching for something."

"What?"

She grinned at him. "Pan's penis, if you must know."

"What?"

"Wait a minute." Her fingers brushed over something long and hard. "I think I've got it."

Motton stared at Miss Parker-Roth's delectable derrière. Had she just said she was searching for a . . . penis? His personal penis jumped at the thought.

What *was* the matter with him? He wasn't usually plagued by such inappropriate thoughts about young ladies. Of course, he wasn't usually treated to such a singular view of a young lady's nightgown-clad bottom. It would be so easy to catch the hem of her gown and pull it up to reveal—

No. This was Stephen and John's little sister who had the delightfully round, entrancing . . .

He pulled on his hair. "*Will* you come out of there?"

She grunted and started to back out. Her knee caught the fabric of her nightgown, stretching it tight across her lovely—

He clasped his hands behind his back and looked up to admire the ceiling molding.

"Look what I have."

He examined the object she was waving under his nose. It indeed looked to be Pan's once prominent penis.

"Er, yes, I see." He could not think of anything else to say. Surely she would not try to engage him in a discussion of . . . anything. "It appears poor Pan is somewhat the worse for wear."

Miss Parker-Roth shrugged. "I hit the statue with the candlestick when you surprised me. I should have realized then it was plaster and not stone, but I was thinking of other things."

"Yes, well." He could not afford to think about what a seductive armful a thrashing Miss Parker-Roth had proved to be. He considered picking the Holland cloth up from the floor and dropping it over her hand and the object she held. "I noticed you'd covered the sculpture."

She laughed. "Oh, no. Mama's an artist, remember? I'm inured to such things, but Mrs. Brindle, our temporary housekeeper, is not. I'm afraid she does not appreciate Clarence's work. The house is dotted with Holland cloth."

"Ah." There didn't seem to be anything else to say to that.

"But look here." She held the penis out again, her delicate fingers wrapped tightly around the hard length. It was a rather realistically rendered representation—if poor Pan were still connected to it, he'd be a very happy god.

His own organ let him know how delighted it would be to receive similar attentions.

Damn it, he could *not* be lusting after this woman. And furthermore, most proper young ladies would be swooning, not clutching a bodiless cock with such enthusiasm. "What is it?"

The lady blinked. His voice *had* sounded rather harsh, but, Zeus, he was sorely tried. She was standing there in her nightgown, for God's sake, totally naked under that flimsy covering. He knew exactly how her soft breasts felt pressed against his chest and how her bottom filled his hands. He'd tasted her hot, wet mouth, felt her tongue sliding over his, breathed in the musky scent of her desire. And she was standing there holding a fully engorged cock.

He should be lauded for only speaking harshly instead of doing what he'd really like to do—tear off that gown and bury his own cock deep inside her.

And he was sure he should be castrated for entertaining even for a moment such a shocking thought concerning the sister of two of his friends.

If he didn't get out of here soon, he was going to forget everything except she was a woman and he was a man.

"Look." She pointed to the organ's base where it had been attached to Pan's body. He forced the lust from his mind to examine the spot. Was that a corner of paper? He reached for it—

"No." Miss Parker-Roth snatched Pan's penis away, hiding it behind her back. "I found it; I shall look at it first."

Motton crossed his arms. "Well, look then."

"I will." Jane stared defiantly at Lord Motton; the viscount gazed blandly back. Finally, she brought the penis from behind her back. There was definitely a paper there. She grasped the corner that was sticking out and pulled carefully—she didn't want to tear it.

Lord Motton plucked a candle from the mantel as she spread the sheet on the desk and smoothed the wrinkles out. "It *is* a sketch. Well, part of one." Two sides of the paper were ragged—someone had obviously torn it. She bent closer to study the figures. They were jumbled together very oddly. What were they doing?

Lord Motton made a strangled sound and snatched the paper away.

"Hey!" She tried to grab it from him, but he held it above his head. "Give that back."

"No." The word was a verbal stone wall. Lord Motton looked exceedingly stony himself. His lips were pressed into a tight, thin line and his nostrils flared. "It is an inappropriate scene for you to view."

"It is?" Now she wanted to see it all the more. She looked up at the scrap of paper again. He was holding it too high; she'd never reach it. She could try grabbing his arm and pulling, but that had never worked with her brothers. Men were just too strong. "Why?"

"It depicts an orgy."

"Oh." She considered that. Yes, a few of the figures might have been partially naked, and they *had* been very oddly arranged. "I've never seen a sketch of an orgy."

"I should hope not."

She really, really wanted another look at that piece of paper. "I didn't realize you were a prude, Lord Motton."

"I am not a prude, I am merely cognizant of proper behavior."

"You *are* a prude."

He glared at her. She'd hoped by teasing him, she'd get him to relent and give her back the paper, but it was clear that wasn't going to happen. "Is it an orgy of French spies?"

"No." Lord Motton looked at the sketch, carefully keeping it out of her line of sight. "But I believe this is what Ardley was looking for. He's here in the picture."

"He is? What's he doing?" Jane hopped a little to see if she could catch a glimpse of the scene, but it was hopeless. If only she'd looked more carefully when she'd had the chance, but it had all been so confusing.

"Nothing you need to know about, Miss Parker-Roth." Lord Motton's tone was icy now. Oh, if only he weren't such a prig. He hadn't seemed so priggish when he'd been kissing her earlier.

"Do you recognize anyone else?"

"Yes."

She counted to ten. She'd kick him in the shins if she didn't know she'd only hurt her toes. "You know that's only part of the sketch."

"I'm aware of that fact."

"We should search for the other pieces."

"No, we should not."

"What? Why not?"

He shrugged. Miss Parker-Roth looked like she was ready to leap out of her skin. He was certain she was dying to snatch the paper out of his hands. It was completely inappropriate material for a woman such as herself to see, however. He glanced at it again. *Completely* inappropriate.

"I agreed to look for a drawing of spies, because I was persuaded it might be of some import to the well-being of the country. This"—he held up the paper and then folded it and put it in his pocket—"is merely evidence of peers behaving badly."

"Don't you think it must be more than that? Why would Clarence have torn it into pieces and hidden it away? And why would Lord Ardley be so anxious to locate it?"

"As to Ardley, I imagine he would find it extremely embarrassing if this were to show up in any of the London print-shop windows. He is anxious—very anxious—to wed the daughter of a cit, a Miss Barnett. Mr. Barnett is a Methodist. He would not wish to give his precious daughter into the keeping of a profligate."

"As well he shouldn't." Miss Parker-Roth looked horrified. "We must find some way to put a word in Miss Barnett's ear."

Surely the woman couldn't be that blind to the ways of the world? Though now that he considered the matter, he'd never heard of her angling for a title. "Miss Parker-Roth, if the woman weds Ardley, she becomes a countess."

"So? If she weds him, she's also saddled with a disreputable husband. At least Miss Barnett should be told of Lord Ardley's behavior so she can make an informed choice."

"The world doesn't work that way."

"*My* world does." Miss Parker-Roth glared quite fiercely at him. "We must find a way to let her know."

"We?"

"All right, *I* shall find a way."

"You can't tell Miss Barnett about the sketch—we don't even know that it depicts an actual scene." The thought of this impetuous woman spreading tales that could ruin Ardley's marriage plans caused his heart to seize. The earl was reaching point non plus. If he didn't wed Miss Barnett—and get his hands on her money—he was going to end up in debtor's prison. He might well lose his estate.

Ardley would not tolerate anyone—especially some young woman like Miss Parker-Roth—interfering.

"I can't not tell Miss Barnett. I can't let a fellow female fall into such a terrible trap."

"Miss Parker-Roth, you don't understand—"

"No, Lord Motton, *you* do not understand. I am determined to alert this poor girl." She stepped closer and poked him in his chest. "Can you truthfully say you'd let your sister, if you had one, marry Lord Ardley if there's any truth behind Clarence's drawing?"

Miss Parker-Roth was overreacting. Men—normal, decent men—did sometimes engage in behavior that women would not approve of. Orgies . . . well, perhaps not orgies. He had been compelled to attend an orgy or two in his days of skulking and listening, but thank God he'd not been required to participate. He did not at all care for the public nature of such an activity. Some things should definitely be conducted in private. In a bedchamber with a locked door and a soft bed . . .

And he should damn well *not* be thinking of any private activities with this annoying female, but he was, and in startlingly precise detail. Not as precise as he'd like, of course. He needed to get that nightgown off to see—

No. He would *not* see. He would not think of privacy and nakedness and Miss Parker-Roth.

He removed her finger from his chest. The woman was correct on one point. He would not want his sister, if he had one, marrying Ardley. "I—"

Blast! Was that the front door? And damn, he heard

steps in the hall. Miss Parker-Roth must hear them, too. She inhaled sharply.

"Mama's home early."

"Damn—" He swallowed his curse and took hold of her shoulders, holding her gaze with his. He spoke as authoritatively as he could, and having been raised to the viscountcy—having been the viscount since he was sixteen—he knew something of authority. "Miss Parker-Roth—Jane—you cannot, you must not tell anyone about this sketch. Not your mother or your brother or especially Miss Barnett. No one."

"I have to do something. I can't stand idly by while a young woman ruins her life."

He thought she was greatly overstating the case. Most women would put up with a lot to become a countess, but Miss Parker-Roth clearly believed Miss Barnett was in peril. He could feel the tension in her shoulders. "I'm not asking you to. I'm just asking you to wait until we can discuss this further."

"Jane, are you down here?" It sounded as if Mrs. Parker-Roth was just outside the study door.

He shook Jane slightly to emphasize his point. "Wait. Please?" He looked over at the door—the knob was turning. "I have to go."

"When will I see you?"

"At the Palmerson ball tomorrow night."

Jane watched Lord Motton slip out the French window and disappear into the shadows just as Mama came into the study.

"Were you talking to someone, Jane?" Mama removed her cape.

"Er." Jane was a terrible liar.

"Good heavens, what happened to poor Pan?" Mama stared down at the plaster pieces on the rug.

"I'm afraid I knocked him over." Jane clasped her hands to stop her fingers from pleating her nightgown nervously. "I came down for a book."

Mama smiled. "Finished *Frankenstein,* did you?"

Jane nodded.

"You were probably a little jumpy. And Mrs. Brindle will be happy. She did not care for Pan's, ah, exuberance."

"I hope Cleopatra will not be upset when she returns." Jane started picking up the biggest pieces and putting them on the Holland cloth.

"Oh, don't worry about that. I think Clarence went through a phase where he made a lot of those statues. If Cleopatra truly misses this Pan, I'm sure she can find another."

Jane paused. There were other Pans? "Oh? Do you know who has the statues?"

"No. Probably any number of Clarence's friends."

"Ah." She would tell Lord Motton tomorrow. She smiled at one of Pan's hooves. She was going to have a private conversation with Lord Motton tomorrow.

"What is so amusing?" Mama handed her Pan's horns.

"Nothing." Jane brushed off her nightgown and stood. "How was your evening? Were the Hammershams in fine voice?"

Mama snorted. "The Hammershams are never in fine voice. I spent the evening discussing oil paints with Hermione Littledon. She has developed a very interesting technique." Mama paused and frowned at the French window. "Did you open this?"

"Er, I was hot."

Mama closed the window tightly. "You must be careful. This is London, you know. You are no longer in the country. I don't mean to alarm you, but you never know what manner of riffraff might be hanging about."

"Ah. Yes. I'll remember, Mama." Was Lord Motton still within earshot? It would serve him right if he was. She glanced out the window, but it looked as if the terrace was deserted.

Mama was halfway to the door. "Coming, Jane? You can look for a book in the morning when the light is better. You need to get your rest."

"I do?" She wished she could catch one more glimpse of Edmund. Had he really been in this room, kissing her? It seemed like a dream now—but there were the shattered pieces of Pan to prove at least some of it had happened.

"Yes. The Palmerson ball is tomorrow night. Don't think I'll let you hide in your room with a book and miss that."

"Oh, I wouldn't want to miss the Palmerson ball, Mama."

"You wouldn't?" Mama looked momentarily delighted, but she quickly frowned, examining Jane closely. "Did I hear you correctly? You are actually expressing some enthusiasm for a society event?"

Jane shrugged and avoided her mother's gaze. "The Palmerson affairs always have excellent lobster patties."

"True." They left the study and climbed the stairs. "Though by far the best lobster patties are the Duke of Alvord's, you know, with their lovely flaky crust brimming with tender lobster . . ." Mama sighed. "Pity he's in the country this Season, anticipating the birth of his second child."

They parted in the corridor, Mama off to dream about the duke's lobster patties perhaps, and she—Jane grinned—if she managed to calm down enough to sleep, she'd dream of something, someone, much more delightful.

* * *

Motton should have heard the man the moment he'd left Widmore's terrace—would have if he hadn't been contemplating a certain annoying miss's behavior . . . and appearance . . . and taste. And wondering how other parts of her delightful person would look and taste and feel.

He hadn't been expecting to be set upon in Widmore's back garden, but that was no excuse, he thought, as he finally realized the thrashing in the underbrush was not some wayward animal. He was fortunate the fellow was so inept. Even a moderately skilled spy could have killed him five times over by the time he'd awakened to his peril. As it was, he sidestepped this fellow's attack easily and had the ruffian's arm twisted high up behind his back and a knife at the man's neck before the big lobcock realized what was happening.

"Are you alone?" Motton scanned the garden—he'd instinctively placed the wall at his back. He didn't see any other motion.

"Urgle." The man was shaking like he had the ague.

"Are you alone? You'd best give me the truth or I'll have your throat slit before anyone can come to your aid."

"Ah, ah, ah."

Motton looked down and saw an ominous stain spreading over the man's crotch. Wonderful. He must be a footman or a servant from the country. A denizen of London's stews wouldn't be such a milksop. "Who sent you?"

"Ooo."

Blast it! Surely the man's bowels wouldn't release as well? He wanted answers, but if he pushed the fellow too hard, the pudding-heart might swoon. He took his knife away from the man's neck and turned the fellow to face him, keeping a grip on his arm—and a safe distance from his breeches.

"Who sent you, man? Answer quick, and I'll let you go."

"But it'll mean my position iffen I spill the soup, milord."

"It'll mean your life if you don't." Not that he'd actually kill the fool, but clearly the man thought he would.

"Oh, please, take pity." The fellow clasped his hands in supplication; he was almost crying. "I has a wife and babe to support, I do."

"Then tell me who sent you—and why—and you're a free man."

"But 'er ladyship would throw me out—me and me wife and babe and—"

Motton held up his hand before the man could add half a dozen other dependents. "I don't suppose you work for Lady Farthingale?"

The fellow staggered, He was either an incredible actor or Motton's guess had hit the mark. "Aye, but please, milord, don't tell 'er I told ye—I didn't. Ye guessed."

"Just tell me why she sent you, and my lips are sealed." He'd give the man credit for loyalty, but more likely he was just too frightened and slow-witted to manage a quick answer. He brought his knife back to the idiot's throat to encourage him.

"She wanted a paper. Said ye'd have it after ye left that house."

Lady Farthingale must have spoken with Ardley—not surprising, in light of the drawing in his pocket. The two were apparently quite close.

"Lady Farthingale has let her hopes outrun her sense. There are hundreds of books in that study; countless places where a man might hide a thin sheet of paper."

"So ye didn't find it?" The man sounded worried.

"No, I didn't." And that was true—Miss Parker-Roth had discovered the sketch, not he.

"But what shall I tell milady?"

"The truth, I imagine. I didn't find it; you don't have it." He touched the edge of his blade to the man's neck and watched him pale again. "And you might want to suggest she stop her ill-considered efforts. Tell her Lord Motton would be extremely"—he pressed slightly on his knife for emphasis—"*extremely* upset if the ladies currently residing in Clarence Widmore's house are disturbed in any way at all."

"Y—yes, milord."

"Good." Motton wrinkled his nose. Damn, the fellow *had* soiled himself. He kept his knife clearly in view and stepped back. "You may go."

The man disappeared before he'd finished speaking.

Hmm. What was going on here?

He slipped out Widmore's back gate into the alley and back into his own garden, keeping a more attentive eye out for any problems this time. All was quiet, but until he understood what was afoot, he'd best put a few men on patrol. He'd hire one or two to keep watch on the Widmore place as well. He should have a word with Parker-Roth—Stephen would want to know if his sister and mother were in danger—but at this point he didn't know what to say.

He let himself into his study through his French window. He'd better secure this and all the other entrances to the house. He'd have Williams, his butler, look into—

"Where have you been, matey?"

Damn. He should have had Williams bar the door to his study.

"Yes, Edmund. Where have you been?"

He lit a candle and then turned to face his aunt Winifred and her large gray parrot, Theo. They were standing just inside his study door, looking at him most accusingly.

Theo kept turning his head, perhaps to determine if he looked better from one eye or the other.

He silently counted to ten. He was a grown man. This was his house. He did not need—he did not want—to explain anything to Aunt Winifred. "Out. I have been out."

Aunt Winifred sniffed. "*That's* obvious."

"Obvious. Obvious. Clear as the nose on my face."

He hated it when Theo turned supercilious. "You don't have a nose, Theo."

Theo fluffed his feathers. "Aw, don't be nasty, mate."

"Exactly." Aunt Winifred looked at him reproachfully. "It really is beneath you to argue with Theo, Edmund. He is only a parrot, you know."

"I *know*." He took a deep breath. He would not argue with Aunt Winifred either. "I thought you were going out with the other aunts to some musical evening."

"Oh, no. I wanted to stay home and be certain Theo and Edmund were settled in their new surroundings."

"Edmund." Motton looked cautiously around the room. He didn't see Aunt Winifred's monkey, but it could be hiding in the drapery. "Where is Edmund?"

"Up in my room. The poor thing was exhausted from our travels."

"Ah." Too bad the damn monkey couldn't stay exhausted. His house was already a bloody zoo with Cordelia's cat, Dorothea's two little yappy poodles, and Louisa's greyhound. Adding a parrot and a monkey was more than any man should be asked to bear. "I imagine you are tired, too. Are you off to bed then?"

"No." Winifred settled into one of his wing chairs. Theo perched on the chair back and glared at him.

His heart fell. He'd dearly love a glass of brandy, but then he'd have to offer Winifred something and chances were she'd take it and be here even longer. Perhaps if he remained standing, she'd be encouraged to come to the point quickly.

She came to the point immediately. "It's time you married, Edmund."

He sat down and poured himself a large brandy. To hell with good manners. "Married?" He cleared his throat. "Oh, there's plenty of time for that. I'm barely thirty."

"You're thirty-three, almost thirty-four."

"That's not so old."

"It is if you consider your history."

He took another gulp of brandy. What the hell could Aunt Winifred mean? He thought he'd been rather discreet in his liaisons over the years. "My history?"

"Well, perhaps I should have said pedigree. Your father's father didn't get an heir until his sixth child, and your father, though prompt in getting you, only had one child—though no one thought he tried to get any more."

"Aunt Winifred!" Motton rubbed his forehead. He did not want to discuss—he did not want to think about—his deceased parents' conjugal relations or lack thereof.

Aunt Winifred sniffed. "Well, the point is, we have no time to lose."

He had a sudden horrifying image of his aunt—all his aunts—supervising his wedding night. "I am quite capable of managing the issue—*every* aspect of the issue—myself." He looked her in the eye and spoke slowly and distinctly. "I do not need your help."

"Of course you need my help. Better mine than Gertrude's. She's already picked out Miss Elderberry for you."

"Aldenberry, Aunt. The girl's name is Aldenberry."

"Well, it should be Elderberry. She's only twenty-six, but she looks like she's forty-six. Scraggy, with no bosom to speak of."

"Aunt, please. You are putting me to the blush." He swallowed another gulp of brandy. Georgiana—George, as she was called by everyone—*was* painfully thin and angular. And dour. He'd never seen her smile, let alone laugh, in all the years he'd known her. How could Gertrude think she'd be an acceptable bride for him?

Simple. Miss Aldenberry had six brothers.

"Pshaw. I'm sure it takes more than a little plain speaking to make you blush." She tapped the edge of his desk. "You can be certain I set Gertrude straight. Men like breasts, I told her, the bigger the better."

He dropped his head into his hands. "Aunt."

"Dandy diddies, that's what ye need, matey. Big bubbies. Two—"

"Theo!" He and Aunt Winifred shouted simultaneously.

Theo hung his head. "Just having a bit o' fun, matey."

"Don't you have a Holland cloth or something we can drop over that bird's head to make him go to sleep, Aunt?"

"No. Don't be ridiculous." She glared at Theo. "I'll lock you up in the brig, sir, if you don't behave. Confine you to my room, you mark my words."

Theo ducked his head between his wings and turned away so all they saw was his hunched, feathered back. He looked suitably cowed.

Aunt Winifred nodded and then turned back to Motton. She tapped his desk again. "Now, about your marriage—"

"Aunt Winifred." He would try to look at her as sternly as she had looked at Theo. "I have already told you, I don't need your help. I don't want it; in fact, I'm offended—"

Aunt Winifred was not as easily cowed as Theo. She raised her hand to stop him. She now had more than seventy years in her dish, but age had hardly slowed—and had not dimmed—her will.

"Of course you don't need my help with the actual getting of an heir. What you need is someone to give you a good swift kick in the breeches to get you moving toward the altar. *That's* the aid I'm here to furnish."

Chapter 3

Thank God! The door closed securely behind Aunt Winifred and Theo. Motton blew out a long breath and poured his third glass of brandy. This one he could savor in blessed solitude.

His aunt had spent the last twenty minutes cataloguing every bloody girl on the Marriage Mart. He'd thought she would never leave.

He held a mouthful of brandy on his tongue and let the fumes fill his mouth. Why had she come to Town this Season? She'd left his marital state alone up to this point, contenting herself with an occasional pointed comment. Why suddenly appear on his doorstep now with a list of potential wives?

He swallowed the brandy. The answer was obvious. She was here because the other aunts had descended upon him. She'd been off with her friend Lady Wordham at Baron Dawson's estate celebrating the christening of Dawson's second child. Winifred considered herself an honorary grandmother as she'd been instrumental in bringing the baron and his wife—the former Lady Grace Belmont—together. But once she got wind that the other aunts were in London—well, she was not going to leave such an important task as selecting the next Viscountess Motton to her sisters.

It would be damn nice if they'd all leave that task to him, however.

He leaned back in his chair and chuckled. God, the look on Williams's face the other day when he'd announced the aunts—minus Aunt Winifred—in this very room. Well, it must have mirrored his. Horror, that's what he'd felt when he'd seen them all standing behind his butler. He was certain Williams had tried to park the ladies in one of the parlors, but the aunts clearly were having none of that. They'd probably surmised—perhaps rightly—that their loving nephew would have bolted out the back.

Aunt Gertrude, the oldest at seventy-six, hadn't waited for the poor fellow to get her name out. "Good Lord, man," she'd said, pushing past him, "I had your master's puke all over my shoulder when he was only days old. I don't think you need to announce me."

Cordelia, Dorothea, and Louisa had made various noises of agreement. At least they'd left their pets in the carriage; he hadn't been treated to *that* cacophony, too. They'd followed Gertrude like a flock of aggressive geese; Williams had given him a weak, commiserating look and fled.

He'd been trapped here, behind his desk—he wasn't quite bold enough to walk out on the aunties. Bold, hmm . . . brave was probably a better word. He'd be exiled from his house—hell, he'd be exiled from London . . . from England . . . if he tried such a trick.

He'd stood, of course, the moment he'd seen them. He'd heard the baby puke comment before; he very much hoped he could get through the interview without

Gertrude dredging up any other distasteful memories of his infancy.

"Aunt Gertrude . . . and Aunt Cordelia, Dorothea, and Louisa, what a, er, pleasant, ah, surprise. Are you in London for the Season?" he'd said.

"Well, we certainly aren't in London for our health." Gertrude had coughed and glared at him. "How anyone can bear to live in this filthy place is beyond me. I swear it can't get any dirtier each time I come up to Town, and each time I'm proven wrong again. How can you stand it?"

"Only with the strictest fortitude. The soot and noise are not at all what you are used to. I suggest you return to the country posthaste."

Dorothea laughed. "Nice try, Edmund. We didn't come up to see the sights, you know."

"Or attend all the balls and parties and other frivolous entertainments." Louisa had looked as though she'd bitten into a lemon. If she had a sense of humor, he hadn't yet discovered it.

"Ah. Then why have you come to Town, ladies?" He knew the answer, but he was hoping he might be mistaken.

He wasn't.

"To find you a wife, of course." Gertrude'd wrinkled her brow. "You ain't usually a lobcock, Edmund. Must be all this dirt—it's clogged up your brain."

He'd tried to laugh. He suddenly knew what it must be like to be a fox encircled by hounds. Death—or marriage—was beginning to feel inescapable. "I didn't know I needed a wife."

A colossally stupid thing to say—he'd recognized that the moment the words escaped his lips.

Gertrude snorted; Cordelia snickered; Dorothea laughed; Louisa merely rolled her eyes.

"You need an heir, Edmund." Gertrude had spoken

slowly as if she were addressing a complete slow-top. "So, of course, you need a wife."

"But I don't need an heir immediately. Not now. Not this year." He'd taken a deep breath. He was a grown man. The aunts could not force him into parson's mousetrap. "I have plenty of time for such things."

"You don't know that," Louisa said. "You could step outside this afternoon and be run down by a carriage."

"Thank you for the warning, Aunt Louisa, but I've managed to navigate London's highways and byways successfully so far."

"It's only a matter of time; London's traffic is dreadful."

"Yes, well, gruesome considerations aside, you still can't shilly-shally any longer," Gertrude said. "You're past thirty, aren't you?" She'd looked down her nose at him—a good trick as he was a half a foot taller than she.

"Ah . . ."

"You're thirty-three, Edmund," Louisa said.

"Exactly." Gertrude nodded. "We gave you an extra three years. *I* wanted to have this discussion on your thirtieth birthday, but Winifred persuaded me to wait."

Thank God for small favors.

"Where *is* Winifred?" He'd try anything to change the subject.

Aunt Gertrude just stared at him. "Away. Now about your marriage."

"Aunt Gertrude, I do not wish to discuss marriage."

"You must discuss it. There is no time to waste."

"Gertrude is right, Edmund." Cordelia had put a hand on his arm. "You know it took your grandpapa more than a dozen years to get an heir. And your papa, though fortunate to have you so quickly, had no other sons."

Gertrude'd snorted. "Well, there's no secret why *that*

was. I never understood why he married Dorcas. She was such a milk-and-water miss."

Louisa laughed. "It was crystal clear why he married the girl—he had no choice. He was caught with his breeches down, literally. And as it turned out, she was increasing with Edmund here."

"And she *was* very beautiful," Cordelia said.

"If you like china dolls." From her tone, it was clear Louisa did not.

Ah, yes, Motton thought, shaking his head to dispel the memory of the aunts' arrival, his father and his mother. He took another swallow of brandy. Theirs had been a marriage made in hell, not heaven. His father had been pushed up the church aisle just as the aunts seemed determined to push him.

He'd be damned if he ever let himself be trapped the way his father had been—though that had been partly his randy papa's fault. If the man hadn't always been ruled by his cock . . .

He took another swallow of brandy. His cock had been rather insistent over in Widmore's study just now. He hadn't done Miss Parker-Roth permanent damage, but if word did get out, she'd be as compromised as if he had.

Surely she wouldn't tell Winifred—that had to have been an empty threat.

Damn it all, he did not want a marriage like his parents'. He would rather have his title revert to the Crown. Papa had lived in Town, drinking and whoring; Mama had languished in the country, quacking her imagined ills with pills and potions. When Motton was sixteen, Papa died of apoplexy in his current mistress's bed, and then Mama took a touch too much laudanum to finally end her ills, real and imagined. No, he'd have no part of that kind of marriage.

He ran his hand through his hair. Why did he keep picturing a certain annoying neighbor? Hell, when Winifred had been listing all the young ladies of the *ton,* he'd been thinking only of Miss Parker-Roth. Winifred had mentioned her, but in passing—and he'd had to bite his tongue to rectify that oversight.

Was he completely mad? That would have been like waving a red flag inches from a bull's face.

He'd been amongst the *ton* too much recently—he was acting out of character. First he'd agreed to Ardley's ridiculous request, and now he was lusting after a respectable young woman. He might as well start looking for a comfortable cell in Bedlam. He needed to get away, avoid the jollities of the Season. He would—

No, he wouldn't. This time he couldn't disappear from the *ton*'s ballrooms as he had in the past. There were the aunts to consider, but more importantly, there was Miss Parker-Roth. She'd clearly taken the bit in her teeth on the issue of Miss Barnett; she'd run straight into disaster if someone didn't grab her reins. As he was the only person aware of the issue, the responsibility must fall to him.

And that thought should not be so damn pleasant.

He should tell Stephen, dump the whole blasted mess in his lap. Miss Parker-Roth was his sister; she was his responsibility, at least in the absence of her father or John.

But Stephen was leaving on another one of his planthunting expeditions in a day or two, this one to Iceland of all places. Didn't sound like the best spot to muck around looking for greenery, but then what did he know? He couldn't tell a rhododendron from a rutabaga.

In any event, all the arrangements had been made months ago, before John had gotten the crazy notion to attend Baron Tynweith's house party. Stephen couldn't delay his departure. John was supposed to come up to

London shortly, but not in time to keep Miss Parker-Roth out of mischief. It was unlikely her mother would keep an adequate eye on her.

This was not a job for a female in any event. Ardley had sounded desperate—and there was that bungled attack in the garden.

Motton frowned at his brandy glass. In his experience, amateurs were the most dangerous. Professionals knew how to achieve their goals unobtrusively and efficiently, but amateurs . . . They were so clumsy. Someone invariably got hurt.

He did not want Miss Parker-Roth getting hurt. He had no choice—he would have to make her his project.

And he was *not* smiling about it. She was certain to be headstrong and opinionated and defiant and completely annoying.

He leaned back in his chair. How had he overlooked the woman all these years? Yes, yes, he hadn't been in the market for a wife—and he still wasn't, no matter what the aunts thought—but he hadn't been blind, either. Had it just been the fact she was John and Stephen's sister?

He racked his brain, but he couldn't produce one clear memory of Miss Parker-Roth at a single society function. Had she spent all her time hidden away in the potted palms? Surely not. Yet how could he have so completely missed her beauty, her . . . animation?

It was a mystery, but there was no way he could ignore her now that he knew how she felt . . . and tasted. How much fire she had in her—

He sat up abruptly. Enough woolgathering. He should try to make sense of the mystery at hand—which was not Miss Parker-Roth, but the drawing in his pocket.

He spread it out on his desktop. It was only the top left corner of the sketch. Clarence had been good with his pencil, he'd grant him that. There was Ardley, breeches down around his ankles, a glass in one hand and a brandy bottle resting on Lady Farthingale's broad, naked bum, which was resting—well, resting was probably not the proper word—on Ardley's lap. Clarence had scribbled "Mammon" on Ardley's chair and had drawn a bubble, giving him the words "I've no farthings in my pocket; I'm in Farthing's pocket." Lady Farthingale's response was "La, my lord, you are so greedy! Have some more, do."

Lord Farthingale would not be happy. He might be in his seventies, but he was still a deadly shot. Ardley had bigger problems than Mr. Barnett's displeasure. And Lady Farthingale might find herself in unpleasant circumstances as well—word was the marquis was becoming disenchanted with his wayward wife.

Hmm. There was a naked knee to the right of Lady Farthingale's head and a slippered foot rested on the table by her elbow, the attached body presumably sprawled on the floor. At least two other people—and probably more—might be very interested in the other pieces of this drawing. In the bottom right corner, arching from one torn edge to the other, was a dark, shaded curve. It looked very much as if Clarence had torn the sketch so that some central image had been divided. He would need all the sketch pieces together to see what it was, damn it.

Why had Widmore torn the picture and hidden this piece? Where was the rest of the drawing? Who were the other actors in this orgy?

Too many questions. He hated not knowing who his enemy was. Hell, in this case he didn't even know how many enemies he had. The villain—or villainess—could be anyone from a duke of the realm to a scullery maid. How was he going to protect the aunts and the Parker-

Roth ladies? He would need to secure both his and Clarence's houses.

Impossible. He would have to move the Parker-Roth ladies into Motton House—they were no longer safe next door. It paid to be overly cautious until he knew what they were facing and, frankly, two more females in the house at this point would not make much difference, even though one of those females was the annoyingly fascinating Miss Jane Parker-Roth.

He took a sip of brandy and rolled it around on his tongue. He'd have the chit under his roof. In his home. In his bed—

No, not his bed. What was he thinking?

He shifted in his chair and spread his legs. His breeches were suddenly uncomfortable.

All right, it was clear—painfully clear—what he was thinking. It should be no surprise. He was a healthy male. He'd just had a pleasant, titillating, erotic encounter with the woman. Of course his thoughts had headed for the bedroom.

He had long ago learned to control his base urges. Miss Parker-Roth would not have to worry; he had no intention of trying to seduce her or to take any liberties at all. He was too much of a gentleman—and he did not want to find himself in his father's position.

Well, and he had too many aunts—not to mention Mrs. Parker-Roth—in the house as chaperones. He was tripping over them constantly. If he had any lewd inclinations, he would not have the opportunity to put them into action.

A pity . . . No! Excellent. Having the aunts about, in this case, was a blessing.

Now how was he going to convince Jane's mother that she and her daughter needed to move into his house? It was certainly an odd request. Mrs. Parker-Roth would want an explanation, but what could he tell her? He didn't want to discuss Clarence's artwork. The fewer people who knew about that, the better.

He would just have to take it up with Stephen. Stephen would understand without Motton having to spell out every detail—though on second thought perhaps he should confide at least some of the particulars. Stephen might have some useful insights. For someone so infrequently in England, the man was amazingly well-informed. He should have been a spy—he knew every last scrap of gossip.

Motton pulled a candle closer and examined the sketch again. Clarence had gone to a lot of trouble to hide it—or this part of it. Why? What was its significance?

Was it some kind of elaborate joke—or had Clarence felt endangered? Given his odd method of death, perhaps the man had had good reason to be concerned for his safety.

He had heard whisperings of a new group, a sort of hellfire club, but he'd heard those rumblings from time to time over the years. He'd thought the most recent rumors merely the boastings of some bored peers who'd held a few wild parties. Perhaps he should have listened more closely. Once in a while such drunken revelries took a darker turn. Still, neither Ardley nor Lady Farthingale struck him as the type to be involved in violence.

He rubbed his temples. He was beginning to get a headache. He couldn't come to any conclusions until he found the missing pieces of the sketch and saw the completed picture. How the hell was he going to find a few scraps of paper in all of London? Blast it, Clarence could have scattered the pieces all over England—all over the world for that matter.

No, that didn't make sense. Widmore must have wanted the sketch found or he would simply have thrown it away. Perhaps he was overlooking some clues in the drawing.

He examined the scrap of paper once more. Could he identify the room, maybe puzzle out where the orgy had occurred? The wallpaper was a vaguely floral pattern. It didn't look familiar, but that proved nothing. He'd be hard pressed to describe the wallpaper in his own house. There was a window with equally nondescript curtains. Hmm. Clarence had drawn the view from the window—a garden with a rather careful rendering of some flower. It had to be a clue. He would show it to Stephen. The man traveled the world looking for exotic plants; surely he'd be able to identify something growing in English soil. He would just— Wait a moment.

Behind the flower, drawn small but clearly visible, was . . . He pulled his magnifying glass from his desk drawer and held it over the area to be sure. The figure leapt into focus. Yes, it was what he'd thought.

In the garden was another lusty Pan.

Mama leaned forward and touched Jane's knee. "Are you feeling quite the thing, dear?"

Jane pulled her attention from the carriage window and her effort to will the conveyance to move faster. "Yes. Of course. I'm fine." Mama had been giving her sidelong glances ever since this morning when she'd asked what time they were leaving for the Palmerson ball. "Why do you think I'm sickening?"

Mama furrowed her brow. Jane furrowed hers back.

Mama laughed. "Because I have never in all your Seasons, with the possible exception of your very first ball, seen you show the slightest interest in society events. Yet today you've been unable to sit still. From the moment you got up, which was earlier than usual, I might add, you've been checking the clock, drifting from room to room, looking out the windows"—Mama gave her a dreadfully knowing look—"most often the one facing the walk in front of Viscount Motton's house. If I didn't know better, I'd say you were almost beside yourself with excitement."

"I am not!"

"I didn't think so. That's why I asked if you were feeling quite the thing."

"Of course I am. I'm fine." Jane bit her lip. She would not pull caps with Mama. "Excitement is not a sign of illness."

"No, but since you are never excited about balls, I decided your agitation must be due to some other cause."

Silence was surely the best reply. Jane shrugged and looked back out the window.

Thankfully, Mama let the subject drop. Jane felt Mama's eyes on her and had to struggle not to add a few more protests and explanations. She had a tendency to natter on when she was nervous or challenged, and she definitely did not want to reopen this subject. She would only get herself into further trouble if she did.

She gritted her teeth and kept her face turned firmly to the window. In a few moments—though it felt like an eternity—she heard Mama sigh and shift position. She shot her a quick glance. Mama was now directing her attention out the other window, thank God.

Jane went back to watching the people and carriages passing on the street—and to wishing the coachman would hurry along.

Perhaps she *had* been looking forward to this evening's gathering rather more than usual. It was no surprise. For once she had something to anticipate beyond standing among the potted palms listening to the pompous—and the portly and the priggish and the pedantic—old peers prate on about completely boring topics. Tonight she would converse, at least for a short time, with Viscount Motton.

She had lust— She had *admired* him from afar from the moment she'd first seen him at her come-out. She'd been so silly back then—she'd been only seventeen and in London for the first time. Her head had been stuffed full of fairy tales, even though she had three brothers and knew very well that men rarely, if ever, bore any resemblance to the storybook heroes who slew dragons and rescued maidens. Real males were far more likely to tell the maiden to rescue herself, they had a cricket match to play.

But Lord Motton had looked very much like a hero when she'd seen him standing by the windows at her uncle's town house—and she'd felt a bit like a damsel in distress. Uncle Rawley had never accepted Mama's marriage to Da—he'd thought his sister should not have thrown herself away on an untitled poet. His wife looked down her elegant nose at her poor little niece. And it didn't help that her cousin Hortense, who was also making her come-out, was tall and blond and beautiful— everything Jane was not. She'd felt like a small brown mouse creeping into the ballroom in Hortense's shadow, afraid someone might notice her and chase her out with a broom.

Mama had forced John and Stephen to come to the ball and dance with her—or, better, persuade their friends to do so. Stephen had complained bitterly and had spent most of the evening in the card room, but John had morosely done his duty. She'd just joined a set with one of his horticulturalist friends, who was droning on about some obscure weed, when she'd seen Lord Motton. He'd been alone, aloof, and so damn handsome her heart had literally lurched. She'd *wanted* him—dear God, how she'd wanted him. She'd ached with it—and he hadn't even acknowledged her existence. He'd danced once with Hortense and once with some other girl and then he'd left.

She rested her head against the carriage window and sighed.

"Are you *sure* you're all right?"

"Yes, Mama, I'm fine."

All that Season and every Season since, she'd watched for him. It was no longer something she could control. She knew whenever he walked into a room—she felt it in her heart. Her eyes were drawn to him like iron filings to a magnet.

And every single Season he ignored her.

Until last night. He hadn't ignored her last night, had he? No, he'd taken shocking liberties with her person— and she'd like him to take more liberties at his earliest convenience.

She was twenty-four. She'd allowed a few gentlemen to kiss her over the years, more out of curiosity than anything else. The experiences had not been gratifying. Ha! At best they'd been boring; at worst, disgusting. She still shuddered when she thought of Lord Bennington. She must have had one too many glasses of champagne the evening she'd allowed him to escort her into Lord Easthaven's shrubbery. Ugh! That kiss had been so slobbery, she'd had to mop her face with her handkerchief afterward.

But Lord Motton's kisses . . . mmm. Just the brush of his mouth had sent unsettling sensations coursing through her, but when he'd slipped his tongue between her lips, she had felt so, well, *full*—though another part of her had suddenly felt very, very empty.

Dear God! She felt empty—and damp—just thinking about it. A little shiver of . . . something ran through her at the memory.

"Are you cold, Jane?"

"What?" Stupid! She had to control her emotions more. She did not want to have Mama watching her all evening.

"Are you cold?" Mama's voice held a note of worry. "I'm certain I just saw you shiver."

"No, I'm not cold."

"I didn't see how you could be. I am perfectly comfortable." Mama scowled at her. "You *must* be ailing. Here I thought you wanted to stay home last night to read, but you were indeed feeling poorly. You looked fine, but I know looks can be deceiving. You should have told me you really felt unwell. I will have John the coachman turn the carriage around immediately."

"No!"

"Jane! Why are you shouting?"

Jane took a breath to get her voice under control. If she wasn't careful, Mama would have her back in bed in a pig's whisker with the covers pulled up to her chin, a hot brick at her feet, and a bowl of steaming gruel waiting to be forced down her throat.

"I'm sorry, Mama. I truly am perfectly healthy—and I am quite content to attend the Palmerson ball." Content? She was dying to go. She *had* to see Lord Motton tonight. And she needed to speak with him about that sketch, of course.

"Well . . ." Mama looked her over carefully. "I don't know, Jane. I think you are a trifle flushed."

"I am *fine,* Mama."

"I don't want to take any risks with your health. There will be plenty of other balls—the Season is just beginning. I think it would be prudent to turn back—"

"Mama, please." Another deep breath. She could scream with vexation, but that would upset Mama even more. What she couldn't do was tell her about her burning desire to see the viscount . . . How could she explain this sudden fascination without revealing their scandalous activities in Clarence's study? Not that her interest was sudden. A seven year infatuation could not be called sudden, but she suddenly had the opportunity—the promise!—of seeing and conversing with him. She could not—would not—let this chance slip through her fingers.

Perhaps he'd even wish to take a stroll in the garden. He might well. He certainly wouldn't wish to discuss that sketch in the ballroom where anyone could overhear. And when they found themselves in the darkened shrubbery . . . Well, one never knew what might happen.

"You're flushing again." Mama reached to give the coachman the signal to turn around.

Jane lurched across the space separating them to grab Mama's arm.

"Jane! You're behaving most peculiarly." Mama tugged her arm free.

"We are almost at Lord Palmerson's, Mama." Thankfully that was true. "It would be silly to turn back now."

"But if you're ill . . ."

"I am *not* ill." Mama looked unconvinced—not surprising, as even Jane had to admit she was behaving like a Bedlamite. "But if I feel ill, I promise I will alert you immediately."

Mama glanced from Jane's face to the window and back again. "Very well, since we are almost there." The carriage stopped just as Mama spoke. They had joined the long line of coaches waiting to disgorge their passengers at the Palmerson town house. "But you do promise you'll let me know the moment you feel at all unwell?"

"Yes, yes, I promise." Jane looked out the window herself. How many carriages were in front of them? Too many. She wanted to get out of the coach immediately to avoid further conversation with Mama—and to get into the ballroom more quickly. Could she suggest the footman let down the steps here?

No, of course not. That wasn't done—scrambling out of the conveyance in such a helter-skelter fashion. Mama would haul her back inside and instruct John the coachman to drive directly to Bedlam. She must strive for some patience.

She took a deep breath and sat back. She tried to appear calm—and ignore Mama's concerned gaze. The damn coach moved at a snail's pace when it moved at all.

Finally they reached the front door and joined the long line of elegantly attired men and women making their way slowly up the marble stairs to the ballroom. The sound of all the conversation was deafening. Was Lord Motton somewhere in the crush? She looked around as casually as she could. There was no sign of him. He must be in the ballroom already, waiting for her. Her stomach fluttered. If only the people ahead of her would hurry up.

It took forever, but finally they were announced. She stepped into the ballroom and surveyed the crowd. Surely Lord Motton was watching for her. He wouldn't come up to her immediately, of course—that would be too obvious. They didn't want to focus the *ton*'s attention on them. But she would glance around, so she could see where he was and drift in his direction. Then it would look as if they met by accident.

She frowned. Where was he? She looked again, scanning each corner of the room.

"Come, Jane, we need to move on," Mama said. "We are blocking the entry." She gave Jane a surreptitious push.

"Yes, Mama. Of course."

Damn it all, unless the viscount had suddenly turned invisible, the blasted man was not in the ballroom.

Chapter 4

Where was Lord Motton? Damn it, he'd definitely said he'd talk to her at the Palmerson ball tonight. She hadn't imagined that; she remembered it quite distinctly. He'd said it right before he'd slipped out Clarence's window.

"I understand you are, er, staying at the, ah, Widmores' house, Miss Parker-Roth?"

"Oh." Jane jumped and got pricked by a palm frond. She'd forgotten that Mr. Mousingly—or the Mouse, as the wags called him—was standing next to her in the foliage. He was a very forgettable gentleman—short and thin, with slightly hunched shoulders, large ears, and light brown hair that had retreated to the back of his head. "You startled me."

The Mouse's brow furrowed. "I don't know how I could have. I've been standing here for the last ten minutes. Or fifteen. Yes, I do believe it's been fifteen. But I'm very sorry if I startled you. I didn't mean to. I'd never startle a woman. I'd never startle a man, either, at least not intentionally. I—"

"Yes, yes, I'm sure you wouldn't startle a flea, Mr. Mousingly, and you wouldn't have startled me if I hadn't been woolgathering."

"Er, woolgathering? Ah. I'm very sorry to have interrupted your thoughts then. I'll just stand here quietly until you are finished, shall I? Unless that would startle you, too?"

Jane wanted to scream, but that would certainly startle the attending *ton*. Heavens, they might think the Mouse was doing something to provoke her scream. How absurd. She giggled.

The Mouse frowned again. "Did I say something to amuse you, Miss Parker-Roth?"

"Oh, no, it was just a stray thought. Please, disregard it."

"Very well." The Mouse nodded and continued to look at her as if waiting for a crumb of cheese.

What did the man want? He'd said something to start this silly exchange. Oh, right. He'd asked where she was staying. What an odd question. Why did he wish to know?

"Did you ask if we are staying at Widmore House?"

The Mouse nodded, looking suddenly eager. Odder and odder.

"We are. Miss Widmore—now Baroness Trent—is off on her honeymoon, and poor Mr. Widmore—"

The Mouse heaved a gusty sigh redolent of garlic. Jane eased back a step or two. "Yes, poor Clarence. He's gone aloft, hasn't he? So tragic." He cleared his throat. "He was an artist, you know."

"Yes. A sculptor."

The Mouse nodded. "But he also drew, ah, pictures. Did you know that?" His small—his *beady* little eyes blinked at her. His expression was meek, deferential—mouse-like—but she'd swear she saw a spark of something else in his gaze.

Good God! Could the Mouse know about the sketch? Could he be *in* the sketch?

The thought of Mr. Mousingly participating in an orgy was both ludicrous and appalling.

"I believe sculptors often draw their subjects before they begin work on statues," she said.

The Mouse shook his head. "But Clarence drew pictures. Scenes. Er, details."

Jane took another step backward. "I'm sure he did. Few artists work solely in one discipline. My mother paints, but she also draws." Could she steer the conversation away from Clarence? "Mr. Widmore's sister is a very accomplished painter, you know. She's—"

"Have you seen any of Clarence's sketches lying about?" The Mouse stepped closer; Jane stepped back once more—and onto someone's foot. She heard a grunt of pain as two gloved, male hands steadied her.

"Oh! I'm so sorry. Please excuse me." Jane turned quickly and almost bumped into an elegant black waistcoat embroidered with silver threads. She looked up. Viscount Motton smiled down at her.

Oh, my. Her heart slammed into her throat, and her mouth turned as dry as a field in the middle of a summer drought. He was so *close.* She drew in a deep breath and inhaled his scent—clean linen, eau de cologne, and . . . male.

He'd been incredibly handsome last night, but he was impossibly handsome now, dressed so elegantly in waistcoat, coat, and cravat.

"L—Lord Motton."

"Miss Parker-Roth." His gaze was so intent. He made her feel as if she were the only woman in the room. No, more than that. As if everything else—the orchestra, the *ton,* everything but the two of them—had faded away.

His eyes grew sharper, hotter. What was he going to do? She held her breath . . .

He dropped his hold on her and stepped back.

Oh. She wanted to cry with disappointment or frustration or . . . something. But the extra space between them freed her from her stupor. Awareness and sanity rushed back.

They were in the middle of Lord Palmerson's ballroom, and she would have kissed the viscount right there in front of half the *ton* if he'd offered her the opportunity. Good God!

"Well, well. If it isn't Motton and my little sister."

Her head snapped around. Damn! Stephen was sauntering toward them, a glass of champagne in his hand. She hoped he hadn't noted her stupefaction. If he had, she'd never hear the end of it.

"Stephen." She tried to smile. He was her favorite brother most days. John tended to lecture her far too much, and Nicholas was still up at Oxford—and still too young and full of himself to be pleasant company.

But Stephen was not her favorite brother this evening. "You *should* be surprised to see me. You were supposed to stop by Widmore House and escort Mama and me to this ball, you know."

If Stephen had arrived as he was supposed to, she wouldn't have been subjected to Mama's worried gaze. It would have been a much pleasanter trip—as long as Stephen hadn't made note of her distraction. On second thought, she'd take Mama's worry over Stephen's teasing any day.

"I do know, and I give you my deepest apologies." Stephen bowed slightly, looking properly contrite— except for the teasing light in his eyes. "But I see Mama managed to drag you here without my help."

Jane laughed. She could never stay angry with Stephen. "Yes." No need to mention there'd been no dragging involved. She angled a glance at Lord Motton. Fortunately, he was looking at Stephen, and Stephen was now looking at . . . Oh, she'd forgotten Mr. Mousingly. The man was still lingering amidst the greenery.

"What are you doing hiding in the palms there, Mousingly?" Stephen asked.

The Mouse executed a small, jerky bow. "I, ah, was just having a pleasant, brief, er, conversation with Miss Parker-Roth when Lord Motton arrived."

"Oh? And what were you discussing?"

Heavens, Stephen's voice had an edge to it. What did he think she'd be discussing with the little man? She opened her mouth to tell him to stop being absurd, but the Mouse was already speaking.

"Nothing. Just this and, er, that. I was on the point of leaving, actually. If you'll excuse me?" The man bobbed his head and darted off through the palms without giving them the opportunity to reply.

Stephen snorted. "What were you doing hiding in the foliage with that rodent, Janey?"

Why did Stephen sound so accusatory? She looked at Lord Motton; he was frowning as well. "I was not hiding with the man. I was standing here, and he came up to speak to me. Things like that happen at a ball."

"Don't be saucy with me, sister mine. I know what happens at balls. And let me ask you this—at how many balls have you seen the Mouse?"

"I don't know. I don't pay attention to the man. He's very forgettable."

"I can tell you how many," Stephen said. "None. Zero."

"What do you mean? I see him everywhere." He'd been in Town for at least as many Seasons as she had.

"Everywhere but balls." Stephen shot a significant look at Lord Motton. The viscount's face was carefully blank.

The men obviously knew something they weren't sharing with her. How annoying. She snapped open her fan.

It was getting infernally hot in here. "So are you going to tell me why he doesn't go to balls?"

Stephen shrugged, but he wouldn't meet her eyes. "He doesn't dance."

Lord Motton made an odd noise that sounded like a laugh turned into a cough. Jane scowled at them both and plied her fan faster.

"Zeus, Janey, are you trying to start a gale in here? You're going to blow us clear across the Channel."

She'd like to blow Stephen *into* the Channel. Perhaps she'd just break her fan over his head. She hated being kept in the dark. "What aren't you telling me?"

"Nothing." Stephen pointed his finger at her. "But here's something I *am* telling you—stay away from the Mouse."

Jane pointed her finger back at him. "Don't be ridiculous. He's harmless."

"Oh, no he's not." Stephen glared at her.

Lord Motton cleared his throat. "If I may interrupt this little sibling squabble?" He turned to Jane. "I do believe your brother is correct in this case, Miss Parker-Roth. You should most definitely avoid the man."

"Why?" Trust the men to band together.

"Because," Lord Motton said, "I have evidence someone—or several someones—are taking a marked interest in Clarence Widmore's work."

"Oh?" This was interesting. "Who besides Lord Ardley?"

The viscount looked as though he was grinding his teeth, but Stephen was the one who hissed at her. "*Will* you keep your voice down?"

"What, the palms have ears?" But she did glance behind her. No one looked to be within earshot.

"Precisely." Stephen's eyes narrowed. "What exactly was the Mouse chatting with you about?"

"Er . . ." Oh, dear. Perhaps Stephen and Lord Motton did have a point. "Clarence and, well, his drawings."

"That's odd. Clarence was a sculptor mainly," Stephen said.

"Right. But he also drew." Lord Motton reached into his pocket. "I was looking for you tonight partly to show you this."

He handed the scrap of paper over to Stephen. Jane tried to steal a look, but Stephen was careful to shield it from her. His eyebrows shot up and he gave a low whistle. "I guess old Clarence did draw once in a while. That's Ardley and Lady Farthingale."

"Obviously. And you'll note this is only part of the full sketch," Lord Motton said. "There must be other members of the *ton* depicted."

"Like the Mouse?" Jane asked. That was the only logical explanation for the man's questions.

Lord Motton nodded. "He's not in this portion of the drawing, but, yes, it would seem so. Do you have any idea who else might be involved, Stephen?"

"No, sorry. I've heard rumors about a new club—well, not new, precisely. More an old club that's changing. No one will say much—never more than a word or two, and then whoever is speaking stops, looks around, and changes the subject."

"Damn." Lord Motton glanced at Jane. "Your pardon, Miss Parker-Roth."

Jane waved her hand dismissively. "Please, my lord, don't regard it."

He smiled briefly and then turned to point something out to Stephen. "What's that, do you know?"

Jane tried again to see the drawing, but Stephen held it up, out of her sight.

"It's a rather well-done rendering of *Magnolia grandiflora*."

Stephen handed the sketch back. "Clarence was obviously very talented in a number of areas. He could easily have drawn for *Curtis's Botanical Magazine* had he wanted to."

"I see." Lord Motton put the paper back in his pocket. "And do you happen to know where I could find one of these plants?"

Stephen laughed. "You might try the garden here. Last time I looked, Palmerson had an excellent specimen."

"Really? Then I think we should—"

"Why, look who's here!" Lady Lenden came up in a rustle of silk and a choking cloud of lily of the valley, Lady Tarkington behind her. She appeared completely unaware that she had just interrupted the viscount. "Lord Motton and Mr. Parker-Roth! How wonderful. We don't see enough of you gentlemen, do we, Bella?"

"No, indeed. I believe this is the first time I've laid eyes on you two all Season."

Jane rolled her eyes. It was not as if the women had had many opportunities to encounter Lord Motton and her brother—the Season was barely underway.

Lady Tarkington tapped Stephen on the arm with her fan. "Are you just back from foreign climes with crates full of exotic plants, sir?"

Neither of the women had yet even blinked at Jane. Had she vanished? She looked down. She could still see herself. She reached out to brush one of the palm fronds. It moved. So she hadn't turned to vapor and disappeared.

"No, Lady Tarkington," Stephen was saying, "I've been here since the Season opened; I suppose our paths just haven't crossed."

"Ah, well, we will have to fix that, won't we, sir?" Lady Tarkington dimpled up at him.

Stephen shrugged. "Unfortunately I leave shortly for Iceland."

"Oh, dear. What a tragedy! What can we do, Lydia?"

"I don't know." Lady Lenden put her hand on Lord Motton's arm and stroked it. "You aren't going away as well, are you, Lord Motton?"

Jane had never liked Lady Lenden, but she truly detested her now. The woman had just passed her thirtieth year. She was forty years younger than her husband, the earl, and had done her duty promptly, presenting him with his heir and spare in the first three years of their marriage. She had been amusing herself with other men ever since. It was common knowledge her third child, a daughter, was the product of her liaison with Mr. Addingly.

Lord Motton removed his arm. "Not from London, but I'm afraid I must leave this little group. I was just about to ask Miss Parker-Roth to stand up with me for the next set." He turned to Jane. "Would you care to dance, Miss Parker-Roth?"

Jane grinned at him. She had lov—admired him for years, but he'd just risen even higher in her estimation. "Why, thank you, yes, my lord. That would be very pleasant."

"Miss Parker-Roth?" Lady Lenden laughed. "I'm so sorry. I didn't see you standing there among the palm fronds."

Was the woman blind? Jane nodded and smiled politely. She could afford to be gracious—she was going to be dancing with Viscount Motton in a moment.

"Yes, Miss Parker-Roth, how nice to see you." Lady Tarkington had a slight edge to her overly sweet voice. "We made our come-out together, didn't we? Seven—no, I suppose it's going on eight Seasons ago, isn't it?" She laughed. "Dear me, and I've been married to Tarkington six years already—how time does fly!" She paused, adopting a vaguely pitying look. "You never did marry, did you?"

A host of replies occurred to Jane, but she realized they would all make her sound like a harridan. She had sisters, though. She knew how to play this game. She smiled as pleasantly as she could. "I haven't sworn off the wedded state, Lady Tarkington. I just have not been as fortunate as you in finding true love."

Ha. Tarkington was a fat, old, ugly spider of a man, whose only redeeming feature was his title.

Lady Tarkington's smile turned brittle. She was clearly trying to think of a suitably caustic rejoinder she could sugarcoat sufficiently so the men wouldn't notice its acidity. Lady Lenden came to her assistance.

"Time marches on, Miss Parker-Roth, as I'm sure your looking glass has told you. Not all of us can wait for love."

Jane raised her eyebrows and looked Lady Lenden in the eye. "I know, but I do admire how you're making the best of things."

Lady Lenden and Lady Tarkington both sucked in their breath; Stephen turned his sudden bark of laughter into a cough.

Lord Motton smiled briefly. "If you'll excuse us? I believe the next set is forming." He took Jane's hand, placed it on his arm, and directed her toward the dance floor before the ladies could recover from her effrontery.

"Are we actually going to dance?" Miss Parker-Roth looked surprised when they did, indeed, join the couples gathered on the ballroom floor.

"I think it advisable, don't you? We did tell the ladies that was our intention. No need to further ruffle their feathers." Ah, excellent. A waltz. He put his hand on her back. She blushed and dropped her eyes to his cravat.

She was such an intriguing mix of fearlessness and

timidity. She'd stood up to those two harpies just now without any apparent hesitation, and she'd certainly been brave—and bold—last night. He grinned as they moved through the opening steps. Definitely bold. Could he persuade her to be even bolder?

He glanced over the room—and happened to meet Aunt Winifred's eye. Damn and blast. He looked away immediately, but the damage had already been done. Winifred was sure to have noted his expression, which, given his thoughts at that particular moment, must have been markedly lascivious.

"I don't like either of those women," Jane was saying. "I never have."

He directed their steps so fat Mr. Clifton and his partner were between them and Aunt Winifred. Were the other aunts lurking about the room somewhere? He'd thought one of their ancient beaus had escorted them to Miss Welton's musical evening. "They are not especially popular."

Miss Parker-Roth snorted at his cravat. "Oh, yes they are."

"Excuse me?"

She finally looked up at him. "Admit it. They are quite popular with the male members of the *ton*."

He choked back a laugh at Jane's innocent double entendre. Yes, those particular ladies had had frequent intimate contact with many of the *ton*'s male members, though not his. "Why do you say that?"

She shrugged. "I've watched men watch them. As Lady Tarkington so kindly pointed out, I've endured more than a few Seasons. You must have noticed Lady Lenden, in particular, has two exceedingly large—"

Miss Parker-Roth's sense of decorum finally caught up with her tongue. She flushed violently.

He couldn't resist the temptation. "Yes? Two exceed-ingly large . . . ?"

She frowned fiercely. "You know."

"I do?" He'd danced them into a less crowded spot where they were less likely to be overheard.

"Yes. You *are* male."

"Ah." He was suddenly feeling exceedingly male— almost painfully male—and the sensation had nothing to do with Lady Lenden or Lady Tarkington. "But I confess I'm not entirely certain what you're getting at. Two arms? Eyes? Br—"

"Yes!"

"—ows?"

"No!" She blew out a sharp, short breath. "You are being purposefully obtuse."

"I am?" Miss Parker-Roth was just about emitting sparks.

He had a sudden overwhelming desire to see what kind of sparks the lady could emit in his bedchamber . . . in his bed . . .

Oh, Zeus. Aunt Winifred was arguing with Aunt Gertrude and gesturing in his direction. He swung Miss Parker-Roth through a turn that put them behind a sturdy pillar.

"Yes, you are," Miss Parker-Roth was saying. "I have brothers, Lord Motton. I am familiar with the male thought processes. John may not show much interest in fe-males unless one is speaking of botany, but Stephen . . ." She rolled her eyes. "You know Stephen is called the King of Hearts."

"He *is* a very accomplished card player." And his skill with cards was one reason he'd got that nickname. Motton was not going to discuss any other possible rea-sons for the moniker with Stephen's sister.

Miss Parker-Roth gave him a very long, skeptical look. He smiled blandly back at her. It was past time to redirect the conversation.

"Miss Parker-Roth, I assure you I am not an admirer of either lady—nor is Stephen, for that matter."

"Then why did they come rushing up to you like that?"

"Hmm. That is an interesting question." Why *had* the women sought him out? He could understand them looking for Stephen, even though Stephen had long ago made it clear he did not dally with married women. Stephen *was* the King of Hearts. Women found him devilishly attractive for some reason. But women, as a rule, did not flock to Viscount Motton. Oh, he'd had the occasional pleasant liaison, but he'd never had Stephen's success. And he'd never been interested in furthering his acquaintance with ladies of the *ton*.

A young cub and his giggling partner galloped toward them, and he pulled Jane close to avoid a collision. Her breasts brushed his waistcoat; he breathed in a light scent of lemons. His unruly cock responded immediately.

The music had better not end soon. Aunt Winifred's eagle eye would be sure to note the bulge in his breeches.

Apparently, too apparently at the moment, he was now interested—very interested—in furthering his acquaintance with one particular lady of the *ton*.

"I don't know why they accosted us." Perhaps he was wrong; perhaps it was only Stephen they'd been seeking. He glanced over at the palms. Stephen had left—probably to lighten some peers' pockets in the card room—but the women were still there, talking furiously to each other, their lips shielded by their fans, their eyes . . .

Damn. They were watching him, ready to pounce the moment the set was over. Now he had to dodge the harpies as well as the aunts. Perhaps *he* would hide in the foliage.

Speaking of hiding and foliage . . . "Why were you in the greenery with the Mouse?"

Jane scowled at him. "I wasn't in the greenery with the Mouse."

"No?"

"No."

"Miss Parker-Roth, you were speaking to the man when I arrived."

"Well, yes, I was. But I wasn't in the foliage *with* him." Lord Motton looked extremely displeased. His eyebrows had shot up and his mouth was twisted as if he'd just bitten into a lemon—or had had a poker shoved up his . . . ahem. "I was there, and he just came along and started talking to me."

"About Clarence's drawings."

"Y—yes." She had been so focused on Lady Lenden and Lady Tarkington, she'd forgotten about the Mouse. Their conversation had been very odd. Well, the fact that they were having a conversation at all had been the oddest part; she could not remember a single time during her many Seasons that she'd exchanged more than a brief greeting with the man. And then there'd been the subject matter they'd been discussing . . . "I do think the Mouse knew about Clarence's sketch. How do you suppose he found out about it?"

"That is the question, isn't it?" Lord Motton was frowning now. "Or one of the questions." He spun her through a turn. "But perhaps more importantly, why is he—and Lady Lenden and Lady Tarkington, I suspect—so interested in it?"

"Yes." Jane considered those issues—or she tried to consider them. It was very difficult to concentrate on anything other than Lord Motton. He was so close. She could see the very faint shadow of his beard and the tiny laugh lines at the corners of his eyes and his mouth. And she was surrounded by his scent; she breathed in deeply and let it fill her lungs.

The music wrapped around her, weaving its magical spell. She and Lord Motton moved together so effortlessly, and his hand on the small of her back was both comforting and tantalizing. She never wanted the waltz to end, but it would end all too soon.

"What are you going to do next, my lord? We must do something. I have not forgotten Miss Barnett's peril."

He brought her a little closer. Lovely. "I am not so concerned about Miss Barnett's peril as yours, Miss Parker-Roth. You must be very careful."

"Oh?" A thread of alarm twisted through the warmth she felt at his obvious concern.

"Yes. I plan to speak to your brother about the situation."

Her brother wasn't going to be much help. "You know Stephen is leaving for Iceland, and he can't change his plans at this late date. Too many arrangements have been made."

"I realize that. I'm sure he'll agree to entrust you—and your mother, of course—to my care."

"Oh." Excitement coiled in her gut. What exactly did that mean? At a minimum she would be seeing much more of Lord Motton.

She bit the inside of her cheeks to keep from grinning.

He swung her through one last turn. As the music ended, she glanced across the ballroom. Lady Lenden and Lady Tarkington were glaring at her. She tried not to smirk at them.

She would definitely like to know if they appeared in

Clarence's drawing. "Are you going to look for another piece of the sketch tonight, my lord?"

Lord Motton nodded. "Yes. As you heard Stephen say, Clarence drew a picture of some flower. As soon as I return you to your mother—"

Jane grabbed Lord Motton's sleeve. "Oh, no. You are not dumping me with Mama. I'm coming with you."

"But Miss Parker-Roth—"

"You need me, my lord. How else are you going to find the *Magnolia grandiflora*?" She grinned. She had him there. "I may not be a plant expert like John and Stephen, but I couldn't live in the same house with them without picking up some basic facts."

Lord Motton snorted. "I do not need you, Miss Parker-Roth. I can look for the flower myself. As your brother said, Clarence was extremely detailed in his drawing."

She should let the arrogant man wander around the garden all night, but Lady Lenden and Lady Tarkington were coming their way. If he went out in the dark alone, he wouldn't be alone for long.

"That would be an excellent plan, Lord Motton, except for the fact that *Magnolia grandiflora* doesn't bloom for another month or two."

"Oh." Lord Motton's expression of dismay was comical. "I see. Well then, I shall look for the leaves. Clarence drew those, too."

"My lord, it is dark in the garden and to an untrained eye, many leaves look the same."

"Well . . ."

"And furthermore, you cannot be so unchivalrous as to abandon me to those two harridans."

"What?" He looked in the direction Jane indicated. Lady Lenden and Lady Tarkington were now only twenty yards away.

"Nor do you want to find yourself alone and unprotected in the garden should either of them try to compromise your virtue."

He laughed. "Too true. You win your point, Miss Parker-Roth. Come on."

He put her hand on his arm and they stepped out into the darkness.

Chapter 5

Motton glanced around the terrace. There were only a handful of couples in evidence, and all appeared much too engrossed in their own conversations to pay any attention to him and his companion. Good.

Especially good as Miss Parker-Roth apparently had no awareness of the need for artifice. She strode directly toward the stairs to the garden, tugging him along as a leashed hunting hound might pull his master to his quarry.

He pulled back, put his hand over hers, and murmured by her ear, "Slowly. We don't wish to encourage an observer to wonder what we might be rushing into the foliage to see . . . or do, you know."

"Oh." She stopped and shot a slightly panicked look at everyone on the terrace.

She would make a terrible spy. He urged her toward the balustrade. They could pause a moment there and observe the garden from above before descending and following one of the paths. As far as he could tell, the other couples were still uninterested in their activities, but a few minutes spent chatting would cause most people to lose any trace of curiosity they might have.

Unfortunately, it would do nothing for the curiosity he was certain was raging in the ballroom. The aunties and the *ton*'s gabble-grinders were probably speculating wildly at this excursion with Miss Parker-Roth. Not that there was anything scandalous in escaping the heat and crowd of the ballroom for a few moments' respite on the terrace, or even in strolling along the garden paths, enjoying the evening air. Many men engaged in such activities; he'd just never been one of them.

After tonight he would have to keep his distance from Miss Parker-Roth until the gossip dissipated.

His stomach—and another organ—sank at that thought.

He scowled at the stone railing. Damn it all, what was the matter with him? He had never reacted this way to a female, or at least never since his salad days. The only organ that should be stimulated at all was his brain—his poor, muddled brain. There was a puzzle that needed to be solved and, given the number of people expressing an interest in Clarence's artwork, the solution must be important. He could not afford to waste any time lusting after the woman at his side.

"The *Magnolia grandiflora* is over there," Jane said, gesturing to the left. "You can't see it from here, but if you follow that path, you'll come upon it."

There was something about Miss Parker-Roth's voice that went straight to his—damn. He rested his hands on the balustrade, a better location for them than the one he'd prefer—Miss Parker-Roth's breasts. "I'm impressed with your detailed knowledge of Palmerson's garden."

She glanced up at him and shrugged. "This *is* my eighth Season. I've been dragged into Palmerson's garden many times." She snorted. "I know every society garden in excruciating detail."

"Oh?" Her words stabbed at his gut. Good God, was he jealous? This situation just got worse and worse.

She scowled. "Yes, but not in the way your tone suggests. My older brothers are known to be very keen on plants."

"Ah." He bit back a grin. Calling John and Stephen "very keen on plants" was rather like saying the Archbishop of Canterbury was very keen on religion. "I take it you don't share your brothers' enthusiasm?"

Jane's nose wrinkled. "No, though unfortunately everyone assumes I do. I've been dragged into more bushes by more mad botanists than I care to count." Her delectable lips turned down. "I might as well have been in the foliage with my brother John. The men were certainly as staid and boring as he is."

What did that odd note in her voice mean? Did she wish to do something . . . interesting in a garden's greenery? A jolt of pure lust shot through his body to lodge in the obvious location.

Focus, Motton, focus. Think about the puzzle. Clarence's sketch.

"I'm quite sure Stephen doesn't discuss botany when he takes a female into the foliage," she said. "He's the King of Hearts, after all."

He was quite sure Jane was correct. He made the mistake of glancing down at her. She was looking somewhat wistful.

No, he must be mistaken. Miss Parker-Roth was a well-bred, *virginal* young woman. She could not wish to frolic in the foliage. He, however—

No, no frolicking. Just serious searching. All work; no play. Finding the next sketch piece—that was all he should be thinking about.

"Miss Parker-Roth, you shock me."

She muttered something that sounded like "Too bad."

Bloody hell. This trip to the terrace had been a major error in judgment. He should return to the ballroom immediately. He was far too aware of the woman at his side.

Aware? Ha! That was like saying a burning man was aware of the fire's heat.

He *was* burning. All last night, he'd dreamt of her—her fearlessness when he'd first grabbed her, her yielding softness when he'd kissed her. The taste of her mouth, the feel of her body, the scent of her arousal. The bold way she'd stared at his arse when she'd thought he wasn't looking. Her obvious intelligence and humor . . .

He wanted to take her into the bushes and do far more than discuss the plants or look for a statue. He wanted to kiss her and touch her and have her dress up around her waist, her back to a sturdy tree, and his—

No, no. Was he completely mad? As, er, stimulating as that thought was, the girl was a virgin. He'd never had relations with a virgin, and his married friends were far too discreet to discuss the subject, but other men were not discreet at all. If even half of what they said was true, he'd want a soft bed and a locked door for his first time with—

He *was* insane. The only way he'd get Miss Parker-Roth between his sheets would be to marry her.

He waited for panic to hit; the choking, suffocating feeling one must get when sinking in quicksand.

Nothing. He felt nothing . . . Well, not nothing. He still felt lust. Apparently at least one of his organs was willing to pay any price to bury itself deep in Miss Parker-Roth's lovely body. It swelled even further at the thought.

What *was* the matter with him? Just the word "marriage" had always turned his entrails to ice, but tonight the notion made him feel anything but cold. Hell, if he'd had any ice inside him, it wouldn't just melt, it would turn to steam.

He was over thirty. He needed to marry sometime. Why not now? Why not Miss Parker-Roth? His marriage would make the aunts happy . . .

He wasn't seriously thinking of marriage, was he?

He gripped the balustrade. He should bang his head against the nice, hard stone to see if he could knock some sense into it. He should flee back to the ballroom—

He couldn't go back to the ballroom. He needed to see if one of Clarence's obscene statues was lurking in Palmerson's garden and, if it was, get the pornographic piece of paper from its penis. Good God.

The situation was absurd—and getting more so. Unless he missed his guess, he heard Lady Lenden's obnoxious voice behind him, which meant there was no time to waste. He grasped Jane's arm and urged her toward the stairs.

"If everyone thinks you are plant mad," he said, "no one will be the least bit surprised at you dragging me into Palmerson's garden." And if they detoured into the bushes . . . No. He would only be going into the bushes if they found Clarence's statue. He did not have the luxury of dallying in the greenery with Miss Parker-Roth.

"I suppose you are correct," Jane said. "I—"

"Have you seen Lord Motton, Miss Peddingly?"

Jane paused. That was definitely Lady Lenden's voice.

"Will you hurry up?" Lord Motton took another step. He was almost bristling with impatience. "You don't want those two harpies to trap us here, do you?"

She glanced over her shoulder. Lady Lenden and Lady Tarkington were indeed talking to Miss Peddingly and Mr. Bodrin, a pair of besotted bird-wits. The two had met at the first event of the Season and had spent every moment since their introduction gazing into each other's eyes.

Prinny could have pranced naked over the terrace and those two would not have noticed. She and Lord Motton were safe for the moment, but the man was correct. There was no time to lose.

"Right." Jane picked up her skirts and hurried down the last few stairs, turning to almost run down the path. The *Magnolia grandiflora* wasn't far.

"Oh, look." Lady Tarkington's voice carried in the night air. "I think I see Miss Parker-Roth."

"Damn!" Lord Motton muttered the curse rather vehemently behind her. "Ah, your pardon, Miss Parker-Roth. I shouldn't have—"

She waved her hand to cut him off. "I have three brothers, my lord. I have heard worse." The tree should be just around this bend . . . ah, yes, there it was. It was a fine specimen, but it wouldn't provide enough leafage to hide them from the pursuing ladies. However, there were some splendid bushes just beyond the tree.

"Come on." She grabbed Lord Motton's hand and darted off the path. "I think we can hide back here."

Fortunately there was a narrow break in the line of shrubs so they could get through without tearing their clothes or collecting too many stray leaves and twigs. One branch did catch her bodice and scrape along her skin. It left a long scratch just above the neck of her dress. A thin line of blood welled up.

"Oh, bother. I don't have a handkerchief. May I borrow yours?"

"Ah."

Lord Motton sounded very odd, as if he had something stuck in his throat. She glanced up at him. He was staring at her chest. Had he never seen blood before?

Perhaps she could blot it with her glove. It wasn't very much blood, though she would rather not stain—

Lord Motton caught her hand before she could deal with the scratch. "Allow me," he said. His voice still sounded odd—husky. Perhaps he needed a glass of water. Unfortunately she had none to offer him here in the bushes.

His handkerchief looked startlingly white in the darkness. Surely it wasn't terribly visible? "On second thought, perhaps you should put your—"

He put his arm around her shoulders and turned her so his body shielded hers.

The tiny part of her brain that remained rational applauded his instincts. The women would have a much harder time spotting them now—his black-clad figure must blend perfectly with the night. Most of her brain, however . . . Hmm . . . Did she have a brain? Thought, rational or irrational, appeared to be impossible. Feelings overwhelmed her; she was surrounded by Edmund's heat and scent. Her heart started to thud so, she half expected to see her chest move.

He was so close. His coat sleeve was slightly rough against the tender skin of her neck and shoulders. Her nipples peaked; the place between her legs began to throb in union with her heart.

Oh! He touched his handkerchief gently to the scratch. He'd removed his gloves. She stared at his fingers; they were strong and dark against the white of the cloth, the white of her skin. They moved slowly, gently, from her collarbone down to the swell of her left breast.

She stopped breathing. A shocking, wonderful, wicked thought slipped into her frozen brain. What if his fingers moved lower? What if he pulled down her bodice and his soft lawn handkerchief touched her there?

God should strike her dead right here in Lord Palmerson's garden for thinking such scandalous thoughts.

What if his lips replaced his handkerchief?

Her nipples tightened into almost unbearably hard little points.

"Does it hurt?" His whispered words slid over her cheek.

"Yes." Yes, it hurt—they hurt. How did he know? She hadn't known nipples could ache like this.

Idiot! Think! Edmund wasn't talking about her nipples; he was talking about her small cut. She must gather her wits before she did or said something completely mortifying. She could hear Lady Lenden and Lady Tarkington muttering to each other—the women were still looking for them on the path. If they found her with Lord Motton, the scandal would be horrendous. She'd be forced to marry the viscount immediately.

Perfect!

No, not perfect. Forced marriages were never good; becoming the latest course in the *ton's* gossip feast would be disastrous. Lord Motton, in particular, would hate all the giggling and whispering. Well, and she would hate it, too.

She should be alarmed. She was in immediate danger. She needed to act sensibly, to detach herself from the man so they would not be found in the leafage together—and certainly not as together as they were at the moment.

Why couldn't she feel alarm?

Apparently there was no room in her aching, throbbing body for alarm, or thought, or anything but this hot, drenching need.

His fingers were now hovering right above her gown's neck. What if she arched a little? Would that encourage him to move lower? Perhaps a moan . . .

"I think the ladies have moved on."

"What?"

"I think the ladies have moved on." Motton forced himself to straighten and step back. Thank God the ladies had left. He'd been about to do something very foolish with Miss Parker-Roth. He wadded up his handkerchief and stuffed it in a pocket. Something very foolish indeed.

She would have let him, too. He could tell. She'd been standing so still. Hell, she'd been almost panting.

Why shouldn't he touch her? She was not a young girl. She must have stolen a kiss or two in a garden sometime over her seven Seasons. What harm could one more kiss do?

But he would not have stopped at one kiss. He knew that. He might not even have stopped at two kisses. He might not have stopped at all.

She was not *that* experienced. He'd wager she was not very experienced at all, even given her seven Seasons. She had not acted experienced in Clarence's study. Enthusiastic—yes; experienced—no.

She was a gently bred young woman. She was the sister of two of his friends. She was . . .

Beautiful. Entrancing. Attracted to him.

And not available for dalliance. He could only have her if he married her—and he was not prepared to make that decision here in Palmerson's garden. Especially as he had Clarence's sketch, something far more important—or at least more pressing—to consider.

The girl was staring at him as though he were speaking Hindi. "Miss Parker-Roth, Lady Lenden and Lady Tarkington have returned to the ballroom. They are no longer looking for us."

"Oh." She still appeared to be seriously bemused. He felt an odd mix of annoyance and pride. They did not have all night to search for Clarence's statue. Anyone might come along and interrupt them—and with so many people interested in the sketch, he could not rule out the possibility that someone else might find the next piece of this puzzle before they did. There was no time to waste. They had the advantage—at least, he thought they had the advantage—but nothing was certain. They needed all the pieces to fully understand what they were dealing with. He needed Miss Parker-Roth to focus on the problem immediately.

Still, it was more than a little flattering to think he'd caused the prickly woman to be so distracted, and by doing something as simple as attending to her small scratch.

Of course, he'd been rather distracted by his actions as well. She had such perfect skin, such lovely breas—

Focus. "This would be a perfect time to locate that tree, Miss Parker-Roth. Do you have any idea where it is?"

The woman looked at him as if he were a complete cod's-head and then laughed. "It's a good thing you aren't trying to do this by yourself, my lord."

He frowned. "Why do you say that?"

"Because you obviously don't know a magnolia from a mulberry. We walked right past it when we left the path."

"What?" He looked back through the bushes at the tree Jane indicated. There was nothing especially remarkable about it—and there was certainly no obscene artwork lurking under its foliage. "Where's Pan?"

"Not there. I can't think Lord Palmerson would put that god in such a public location, can you? Imagine how the debutantes and their chaperones would react. There's not enough hartshorn in England to revive the swooning masses."

Blast it all, she had a point. "But I could have sworn . . . I mean, the sketch was very clear . . ." Damn. He'd been so certain Clarence had drawn the flower as a clue. What the hell was he going to do now?

Miss Parker-Roth extended her hand. "Let me see it. Perhaps I'll notice something you missed."

"I can't let you see Clarence's sketch."

She scowled at him. "Why not? You need help, don't you?"

"No."

Miss Parker-Roth snorted.

He couldn't argue with her. Of course he needed help—just not hers. "I can't show you Clarence's drawing."

"Why not? I may not be an expert in botany, but I'm obviously more versed in the subject than you are."

"It's not botany, but biology that's the issue."

"Biology? What do you mean?"

Surely she knew the answer to that question? She had gotten a glimpse of the paper in Clarence's study. "Miss Parker-Roth, the sketch is extremely pornographic. It is not fit to be seen by a young, unmarried woman such as yourself."

The woman actually rolled her eyes. "My lord, I appreciate your chivalry, but if you believe the drawing can tell us where the next statue may be, I think we need to sacrifice my tender sensibilities. I assure you I'll be able to withstand the shock. My mother is an artist, after all."

"And I assure you your mother does not draw pictures like these."

"Perhaps not, but they *are* only pictures. It is hard to imagine how they could do me any permanent harm."

"No?" The word was sharp in the quiet garden. Light glanced off Lord Motton's tightly clenched jaw. "Not all harm is physical."

"I know that." Did the man think she was a child? Anyone—especially anyone who'd survived seven London Seasons—knew gossip and innuendo could fell a person as surely as a bullet.

"Innocence is precious," Lord Motton said. "Once lost, it cannot be recovered."

The man *did* think she was a child! How patronizing. She should—

She bit her lip hard and listened to the words again as they echoed through her memory. He hadn't said them easily. He hadn't sounded condescending; he'd sounded pained, as if he spoke from bitter experience.

What innocence had he lost, and when?

"I understand that, too, my lord." She spoke more gently than she would have. "But that doesn't change the fact that you need my help. Finding the next statue is important, isn't it? We can't just give up."

Lord Motton's lips tightened further into a hard, thin line, turned down sharply at the ends. He clearly wanted to argue with her, but just as clearly realized he had no reasonable argument—and no alternative. Finally he emitted a short, resigned sigh.

"Very well. Please do try not to look at the rest of the sketch." He pulled the scrap of paper out of his pocket and handed it to her, pointing to one corner. "There's the flower. If you look closely behind it, you'll see the statue."

"Yes." The light was very dim. She moved closer to one of the lanterns Lord Palmerson had hung throughout the garden for his guests. There was Lord Ardley and Lady Farthingale. What were they—oh, my! She was . . . he was . . .

Was that possible?

Jane felt her face burn so, she feared it was brighter than the lanterns. At least Lord Ardley and Lady Farthingale appeared very jolly about whatever they were doing.

Lord Motton had thrust his hands in his pockets. He looked very gloomy. "The drawing must be of some other garden." He shook his head. "When Stephen said

Palmerson had one of these trees, I thought— But it would be too dam—demmed easy if the statue were here, of course. Do you know any other gardens I might search?"

"You are not searching gardens by yourself; I thought we had already established that." She turned from the graphic biology to examine the botany more closely. There was nothing to indicate Clarence was trying to illustrate an actual view from one of Lord Palmerson's windows, so the placement of objects to one another was probably irrelevant. Still, if the statue was here, it would make sense it was near the magnolia.

"We should go back to the ballroom. Your mother will notice your absence."

She put her hand on Lord Motton's arm to stop him. "No, not yet." The statue would have to be hidden from the path; if it wasn't, the gabble-grinders—and thus all the *ton*—would know about it.

Where could one hide an obscene statue? The *Magnolia grandiflora* must be a hint.

He plucked the sketch out of her fingers. "Miss Parker-Roth, it's time—"

This spot, behind this line of evergreen bushes, would be adequate, but the lantern's presence indicated it was not remote enough. Where were the bushes even bushier, the foliage denser, the— "There!"

"What?" What the hell was the woman up to? She ignored his proffered arm, gathered her skirts, and strode through the darkened greenery toward an unsightly mass of dense vegetation. Blast it! If she wasn't careful, she'd end up tripping over some damn root and sprawling face-first in the dirt.

He took off after her—and had to grab a low-hanging branch to save himself from measuring his length in a patch of Palmerson's weeds.

"Bloody hell—" He untangled some ivy from around his ankles. He wasn't much interested in greenery, but if *his* head gardener ever let any of his plantings run wild like this, the man would be explaining himself or finding a new position.

He straightened and looked back at the path. With all the noise he was making, it was a wonder the entire ball-room wasn't lined up watching him, but no, he was still alone. Very alone. Where had Miss Parker-Roth got to? Ah! He saw the corner of her dress just before it was swallowed up by the shrubs.

He hurried after her, minding his feet this time, and shoved his way through the bushes into a very small clearing by the back garden wall. The moonlight illuminated Miss Parker-Roth, both hands on Pan's prodigious penis. She glanced over her shoulder and grinned.

"Look—it twists off." She gave the penis another couple turns, and the plaster organ came off in her hands. She reached into the open end, pulled out a folded piece of paper, and held it up. "Aha!"

"Splendid. Now give it to me." He reached for the paper, but Jane snatched it behind her back.

"I found it. I—"

"My lord?"

Jane's heart stopped. Her eyes flew to the spot where Lord Motton had pushed through the bushes. There was no discernible gap, no sign of anyone, but she could hear someone clearly. The man could not be very far from their hiding place.

Edmund leaned close and whispered by her ear. "Quiet. With luck he only saw me. I'll get rid of him."

She nodded to show she understood. Then he moved, sliding out of the clearing much more quietly than he'd entered and from a different section of the shrubbery.

"My lord?" The whisper came again, a little closer now. Jane looked around. There was no place to hide. She jammed the paper down her bodice, sliding it all the way under her breasts, and grasped the penis securely in case she had need of a weapon.

"Lord Motton?" Dear God, the man must be just on the other side of the bushes.

"Yes?" That was Edmund's voice. He sounded farther from the clearing than the whisperer. How had he managed that? "Thomas, is that you? What is it? What are you doing here? I thought you were watching Widmore's house."

Watching Widmore's house? Edmund had set his servants to spying on Clarence's house? On her and her mother? Oh! She felt a jolt at the betrayal and then a wave of anger.

She'd just tell him exactly what she thought of *that* effrontery.

She took a step and paused. Wait. There was no need to advertise her presence in the greenery. Lord Motton's servant might be trustworthy—or he might not. Why risk adding grist to the gossip mill? She would just—

"I was, my lord. Me and Jem saw two men slip in the back, from the terrace."

"You didn't try to stop them, did you?"

Not try to stop them? Lord Motton had told his servants not to stop housebreakers?

"No, my lord, we did jist as ye said. We watched and waited. Jem followed them when they left and I came fer ye."

"Good work. Now go back and watch until I get there."

Jane took a sustaining breath and tried to hold on to her temper. John could be very high-handed on occasion, but at least he was her brother. He might—*might*—be forgiven for thinking he had some right to dictate to her; though, as she had pointed out too many times to count, their parents were still very much alive. If her own father didn't object to her behavior—even though Da was admittedly lost in the intricacies of his newest sonnet most of the time—or her mother (who also tended to get a bit lost in her creative endeavors), it was most certainly not a brother's business to insert his nose into her affairs. But Lord Motton! He was merely a neighbor—no, he was a housebreaker himself! On what grounds did he think to govern her actions, to spy on her *and* Mama and allow riffraff to invade Clarence's house? It was the outside of enough.

Finally the servant left, and Lord Motton stepped back into the clearing. He opened his mouth to speak, but she was not about to let him order her around. She poked him with Pan's penis. He was lucky she didn't smash it over his head.

"What the *hell* is going on, my lord?"

Chapter 6

Lord Motton glared at the penis and then glared at her. "Will you put that damn thing away?"

She flourished Pan's member like a sword. "I will when you tell me what is going on."

"If I knew that, we likely wouldn't be standing here in the greenery with *that*." He seemed especially affronted by poor Pan's disembodied phallus. "You'd best put it back on the statue."

"Why? I didn't replace the . . . er . . . I didn't do that with the Pan in Clarence's study."

He gave her a look that clearly indicated he considered her intelligence on par with a grasshopper's. "That Pan was shattered. I imagine you threw all the pieces out."

"Oh. Well, yes."

"This Pan, however . . ." He gestured at the statue. It did look suspiciously incomplete. "I think—I hope—we're the only ones who know where Clarence hid the sketch pieces. That gives us a huge advantage. But if any of the people who've shown an interest in the drawing were to stumble upon this statue . . . Well, even a complete bird-wit might be able to figure out where the papers might be found. And the other searchers, if they are indeed part of whatever group Clarence was illustrating, might have a much better idea where to find the other statues."

"I see your point." Jane felt about as bright as a drunken grasshopper as she surveyed the gaping hole in Pan's privates. Why hadn't such an obvious problem occurred to her? Probably because she hadn't the experience listening and lurking that Lord Motton had.

She sighed and stooped to screw Pan's penis back into place. "Mama thought Clarence had made many of these Pans, so there could be a number of decoys scattered around Town."

"Ah."

The viscount sounded very odd. She glanced up as she finished turning Pan's phallus. He was staring at her hands, a strained look about his eyes. She actually saw him swallow. She'd swear his color was heightened as well, though it was admittedly hard to tell in the dim light of the clearing.

She wiggled the penis and tugged on it. It appeared to be securely fastened. She gave it a final pat and straightened. Lord Motton was actually running his finger around his neck, as if his collar and cravat were too tight.

"Are you feeling quite the thing, my lord?" Perhaps his high-handedness was all due to being in queer stirrups. "You look overheated."

"Er." He cleared his throat. "I'm, ah, fine, but we should definitely return to the ballroom. The gossips will be starting to talk."

"Lady Lenden and Lady Tarkington certainly will." Jane had never been a topic for the gabble-grinders before; she found she did not care for the prospect, especially when the speculation would include Viscount Motton.

"No, I don't think the ladies will be quick to bruit this about. They will not want to direct any attention to their activities, even in this tangential fashion. Whatever we are dealing with has been carefully hidden from the *ton* for some time."

"Right." Jane allowed Lord Motton to hold back the bushes so she could leave Pan's clearing without adorning herself with more leaves and twigs. She took his arm when he offered it. Her anger had dissipated.

"Getting back to Thomas's report," he said as they started strolling back to the main path.

Perhaps her anger hadn't dissipated. "Yes, let's get back to that. Why did you set your servants to spy on us?"

He frowned down at her. "They weren't spying; they were protecting you."

She glared back at him. "Oh, really? Then why did they allow thieves to enter Clarence's house?"

"Because they knew you were here with me. I assure you, if you'd been home they would have alerted me and half a dozen of my footmen."

"Hmph. That still doesn't make me feel very secure." She stopped to untangle her foot from a vine. How would she ever be able to sleep in her bed at Widmore House again? To think she'd been bored and wanting an adventure! Adventures were quite overrated.

And why hadn't she felt this disquiet after Lord Motton had appeared in Clarence's study uninvited? Perhaps she'd best not consider that question too closely. "Who broke into the house?"

"I don't know yet. I'm hoping Jem can discover the answer."

"What about the servants? Was anyone hurt?"

"No. The intruders kept to the study; the servants were all in their quarters, since you and your mother were out."

"Ah, well, that's good, then." Things could have been worse. But still, strangers had been in the house . . . Her stomach twisted. "I think . . . I mean, I'm not certain . . . I doubt I can bear to stay . . ."

"You won't be staying in Widmore House another night."

"Oh." She felt a tremendous wave of relief. She didn't have to worry about the intruders returning. She'd be safe. She'd be . . . where? There were no suitable houses standing vacant. The Season had begun; everything was full. She and Mama would be lucky to find rooms in even a second-rate hotel.

They reached the main path and turned back toward the terrace. She looked up at Lord Motton.

"But where will we stay? Do you think we should return to the country?" Oddly, that thought wasn't appealing.

His expression brightened, but then he frowned and shook his head. "No. Normally I would suggest that, but until we know what's afoot . . ." He blew out a long breath. "I think it best you stay here where I can keep an eye on you."

She did not care to be viewed as a chore or an assignment. "You must know my father does not keep a house in Town. In past Seasons we've taken rooms at the Pulteney Hotel, but I'm sure that isn't possible now. We might be able to move in with one of Mama's artist friends—"

"You'll move in with me."

"What?" She stopped dead in the center of the path.

"Good God, woman, will you keep your voice down? We don't want the entire ballroom rushing out to see if you're being murdered."

Jane knew her mouth was agape, but there was no helping it. She was too busy trying to grasp Lord Motton's meaning to bother with something as minor as a dropped jaw.

He wanted her to move into his house. Eat at his table. Sleep in his bed—

Heat flooded her, provoking enough awareness to prompt her to finally close her mouth. Not his personal bed, of course—not the bed he was currently occupying. Simply one of the beds he owned.

She was having some difficulty breathing. Her stomach was somersaulting in a truly scandalous fashion. Ha! Her most scandalous reaction was happening a bit lower than her stomach.

To be in bed with Edmund . . . naked . . .

"You needn't look so shocked." He was scowling at her. "My aunts are all in residence. And your mother will be there as well, of course. We will be more than adequately chaperoned. The society cats will have nothing to sharpen their claws on."

"Yes. Of course." But once the aunts and Mama were asleep . . . She opened her fan and waved it in front of her face. It was exceedingly warm this evening.

She should not be considering sleeping chaperones and nocturnal assignations. Lord Motton saw her as an annoying responsibility, that was all. He was not interested in reenacting any of the activities they'd—*she'd*—enjoyed in Clarence's study. No. Of course not. She was being absurd.

Lord Motton offered her his arm again and she laid her hand on it. They resumed their progress to the terrace as if nothing out of the ordinary had just occurred—as if she weren't suddenly burning with lust for the man.

As if she didn't have part of a pornographic sketch stuffed in her bodice.

She'd forgotten about that in the heat of her anger . . . and other emotions. She glanced down. Nothing showed. Nothing should show—she'd shoved the paper in as far as she could. She felt it pushing up against the underside of her right breast.

"I'll speak with Stephen," Lord Motton was saying. "He'll agree with my plan."

"Oh?" Her stomach sank a few inches. He sounded so matter-of-fact, as if he were discussing the storage of a valuable necklace or painting. And if Stephen agreed with him . . . Stephen might be the King of Hearts—he might be exceedingly nimble at getting in and out of ladies' beds—but when it came to her, he was very much the protective, straitlaced older brother. He would never countenance anything that would expose her to un-wanted—or wanted—attentions of a lascivious nature.

"Yes. It's unfortunate he's leaving the country so soon, but he knows I am perfectly capable of safeguarding you."

"Ah." Was he going to lock her away in the attic then?

"I can't post an adequate guard on two houses, so moving you and your mother into my home is by far the best course of action. My men know how to protect Motton House, and should anyone manage to slip by them, I will be there to deal with the problem. You will be perfectly safe."

She did not want to be locked away. "But you'll need my help."

He frowned down at her. "Your help?"

"Yes." Why was he looking at her as if she'd just es-caped from Bedlam? "You would never have found either part of Clarence's sketch without me."

He grunted. "The first incident was an accident."

"An accident that wouldn't have happened if I hadn't entered Clarence's study."

"Perhaps."

"Assuredly. Come, Lord Motton, be truthful. You would not have smashed the statuary if I hadn't surprised you."

"*I* didn't smash the statuary."

"My point exactly." The minx grinned up at him.

He laughed reluctantly. "All right, I admit you had a hand in discovering the first part of the sketch, but I'm sure I would have found the second if I'd spent more time studying the drawing."

She raised her eyebrows. "So you say. I disagree, but we'll never know for certain, will we?"

"No, but—" Wait a minute. They *had* found the second part of the sketch. Where was it? He'd seen Jane pull it out of Pan's penis, but he hadn't seen where she'd put it. Thomas had arrived just then, and he'd been distracted by that and then by his concern for Jane's safety—and her mother's as well, of course. How could he have so completely forgotten about the drawing? Damn. Was he losing his touch? He'd never been so careless before. "What did you do with the paper? Is it in your reticule?"

They'd almost reached the terrace, so there was enough light to confirm that Jane blushed. "No," she said. "It's not in my reticule."

"Then where is it?" Why was she embarrassed? And, more to the point, where had she hidden the sketch if not in her reticule? Good God! A terrible thought punched him in the gut. If he'd been distracted by Thomas's arrival, perhaps she had, too. He stopped her, but had enough self-control to keep himself from grabbing her shoulders and shaking her. "You didn't lose it, did you?"

She scowled at him. "Of course I didn't lose it. Do you think I'm a complete widgeon?"

Frankly, he didn't know what to think, but he had a well-enough developed sense of self-preservation not to say so. She looked as if she was capable of slapping him soundly, and while he could defend himself easily, he didn't care to entertain the *ton* with the spectacle of Viscount Motton grappling with Miss Parker-Roth.

Grappling in private, however . . .

Where the hell had that thought come from? "Of course I don't think you a widgeon. Just give me the paper. I'll put it in my pocket."

She turned even redder, if that was possible. "I can't give it to you."

"Why the blood—why not?" Good God, if she had lost the paper, they'd never discover whatever Clarence's secret was. It must be important, since half the *ton* were apparently quite anxious to discover it as well.

Damn. If Stephen was correct and the secret had some connection to a hellfire club . . . Ardley, the Mouse, and the ladies were not real threats, but there must be other people involved who could be very dangerous indeed, especially if they became frustrated or desperate. It was not inconceivable that Satan himself had a role. "Are you completely certain you haven't lost it?"

"I haven't lost it." It sounded as though Miss Parker-Roth was speaking through clenched teeth. Well, he felt very much like clenching his teeth—or gnashing them—too.

"So where is it?" He managed to speak slowly and not raise his voice . . . very much.

"In a safe place." She wouldn't meet his eyes. That must be a bad sign.

"What safe place?" All right, now he *was* yelling. He took a breath and tried for control. "If it's not in your reticule, where can it be?"

She mumbled something.

"Miss Parker-Roth—" Damn. He *had* to lower his voice. He just hoped he hadn't attracted the attention of anyone on the terrace. "Miss Parker-Roth, you are not making any sense. We have spent all our time in the garden. Where is this safe place?" Another thought intruded. "Good God, you didn't stick it back in Pan's—that is, you did get it out of the statue, didn't you?" The girl couldn't be so harebrained she'd left the sketch behind, could she?

John and Stephen were bright—rather more than bright—but he didn't know their sister. Mrs. Parker-Roth had an admittedly odd reputation—perhaps lunacy ran through the distaff branch of the family.

She was glaring at him now. "If you must know," she hissed, "it's in my bodice."

"What?" He couldn't help himself—his gaze dropped to her dress. Well, not her dress precisely. To her . . . he bit his lip.

She had such lovely small breasts. He remembered with a jolt of painful clarity how they had felt through her nightgown in Clarence's study. He'd love to touch them now without any distracting cloth in the way; he'd love to lift them out of her dress and run his fingers over her smooth, silky skin—

He jerked his attention back to her face. "Oh. I see, er, that is, ah, you can show me them—I mean *it*—you can show me it when we get to Motton House."

She lifted her chin. She was remarkably flushed. "Perhaps I won't."

He was definitely dealing with a lunatic. "No, I must see them—*it*—immediately. Er, that is, soon. This evening. When we can be private—ah, I mean when we don't have a terrace full of the *ton* staring down at us." On further reflection, perhaps he was the mad one. Reality as he'd always known it was especially elusive this evening. "I expect I'll be able to discover the identities of a few other members of the *ton* who are involved in this situation, and I'm hoping Clarence has drawn another clue that will lead me to the third Pan."

"Lord Motton, you say 'I' and 'me' as if you are intending to continue this search by yourself. I thought we had already addressed that issue. You need my help."

Now what was the matter with her? "Your help? I don't believe I agreed to your help—and I don't need it."

"You don't need it?" She almost spat the words. "As I said before, you would never have found anything without my help. I expect to be included in every step of the search. We will look at the sketch together and solve the puzzle as a team."

"My God, you *are* a Bedlamite!"

"Ooh!" For a split second he truly did think she was going to slap him, but she stamped her foot instead and then thrust her index finger into his waistcoat. "You are the biggest coxcomb I have ever had the misfortune to meet." She poked him to punctuate each characterization of his idiocy. "You are a colossal cod's-head"—poke—"a beef-witted, mutton-headed clodpoll"—poke—"an unbelievable—"

He believed he'd had more than enough of her spleen. He captured her hand against his chest. "Miss Parker-Roth—"

"Lord Motton"—she waggled the index finger on her free hand in his face—"I will not give you this piece of the sketch if you do not give me your word you will include me in all your efforts."

Did she intend to force him to her will? She obviously did not know him well. "By God, woman, you are trying my patience. Surely you must know I can have that piece of paper from you whenever I choose."

"Oh, really?" She narrowed her eyes and jutted out her chin in a distinctly challenging fashion. "I should like to see you try."

"You would, would you? Well, then, Miss Parker-Roth, I'll just—" Blast and damn! He'll just what?

He couldn't help it—his gaze dropped back down to her bodice. It would take but a moment to spear his fingers in between her lovely, rounded . . .

Mmm. A moment was far too short. Once his fingers touched her skin, he would not be thinking of bits of paper. He'd be thinking of touching and kissing and tasting and licking and sucking.

Her bosom had turned a lovely rosy shade. She drew in a sharp breath and made her tempting bodice rise, her delightful breasts swell.

One of his organs was swelling to uncomfortable dimensions.

"Er." Her voice sounded breathy and uncertain. His eyes flew back up to her face. Yes, her bravado was gone; she looked adorably confused. A slight bit of intimidation might be an excellent notion—only to remind her that she was a woman and so weaker than he. She needed to be guided by him—protected.

He stepped a little closer so their bodies were almost touching. "Shall I take it from you, Jane? Now?"

"Er . . ."

Did he see a shadow of fear in her eyes? She should fear him—he was dangerous. But he didn't want her to fear him. He wanted her to lov—

Damn and blast. His head snapped up and he took a quick step backward. What the hell was he thinking? Aunt Winifred must have addled his wits with her talk of marriage.

"I, ah"—he swallowed—"that is, well . . ." What should he say? What *could* he say? He should apologize for causing her discomfort, but hell's bells, she was causing him discomfort—acute discomfort—at the moment.

Thank God his nether region was in deep shadow. And the shock of his behavior with regard to Miss Parker-Roth was working rapidly to decrease the size of his . . . problem. "I didn't mean—"

"What didn't you mean?"

Motton's head snapped around. Stephen was striding up the path from the terrace.

Miss Parker-Roth jumped back. She caught her heel on her hem and started to fall; Motton caught and steadied her. "Must you sneak up on people, Parker-Roth?"

Stephen snorted. "You were only surprised by my arrival because you were far too focused on my sister." Stephen frowned at Miss Parker-Roth. "As you were far too focused on Motton here, Jane. The idiots on the terrace were getting quite the eyeful. What were you thinking?"

"Ah." Miss Parker-Roth shrugged. "Er."

Stephen's eyebrows shot up. "Damn it, Janey, you don't have a tendre for Motton, do you?"

Miss Parker-Roth closed her eyes as if in pain. "Stephen, when do you leave for Iceland?"

Stephen laughed. "Friday. And yes, I do realize I shouldn't have said that."

"Thank God for that," Motton said. It was definitely time to change the subject. "Stephen, I was going to come looking for you. There's been a break-in. It's time to move your sister and mother to my home."

"You must be exhausted." Lord Motton's Aunt Winifred—Miss Winifred Smyth—grasped Jane's hand and patted it in a comforting fashion. Miss Smyth had just accompanied Jane to a lovely bedroom painted a very restful shade of blue. It could have been painted bright orange; restfulness was not a state Jane was going to achieve anytime soon.

"I don't know what I am." Jane gently detached herself. She was too agitated to be comforted; she was too agitated to stand still. She wandered over to the dressing table. Lily, the maid she and her mother shared when they came to Town, had dumped all Jane's things in a mishmash there, complaining vociferously all the while how London was such a heathen place that ruffians would break in to a gentleman's house.

Clarence's study had looked horrible—books torn and scattered everywhere, the drawers of his desk pulled out and thrown on the floor, anything breakable smashed into hundreds of pieces. "How could anyone be so destructive?"

"They were obviously looking for something, my dear, and had little time to find it. They had to choose the most expedient method. And of course they did not care about Clarence's things. They might even have enjoyed destroying them, I suppose." Miss Smyth shrugged. "I can understand how men who live in desperate situations, in the darker parts of London, might have little patience for such fripperies as books."

"Books aren't fripperies."

"They are if you've no money for food or shelter."

Miss Smyth was right, of course. And Jane wasn't naïve. She might come up to London only for the Season, and travel only in the wealthy parts of Town, but she knew there was plenty of poverty and despair here. She'd just never encountered its existence so forcefully.

She shuddered. She did not wish to encounter it again. What would have happened if she'd been in the house when the men had broken in? True, no one was hurt, but that thought wasn't very reassuring. If she'd come upon these men in the same way she'd stumbled upon Lord Motton . . . well, the outcome would have been vastly different.

Perhaps she was wrong to insist Edmund include her in the search. Perhaps she only wanted an adventure when it was in a novel and she could skip to the last page to be sure all ended well.

No, she was not so poor spirited . . . was she?

Miss Smyth was by her side again, putting a hand on her arm this time. "Don't worry, Jane—I may call you Jane, mayn't I?"

"Yes, of course." At this particular moment, Miss Smyth could call her the Queen of Sheba for all she cared.

"Please don't worry. You are very safe here, you know. Edmund will take good care of you." She smiled. "And the villains weren't after you, were they? They were after something of Clarence's." She patted Jane's arm. "I don't mean to offend your mother—I know Clarence's sister, Cleopatra, is her friend and I think Cleopatra seems perfectly nice—but Clarence . . ." Miss Smyth shook her head. "I always felt there was something not quite right about Clarence." She shrugged. "With luck, the miscreants found whatever they were looking for and are done bothering anyone."

"Mmm." Jane nodded noncommittally. The housebreakers had *not* found what they'd been searching for— the newest piece of that puzzle was still poking into the underside of her breast. Given the interest she and Lord Motton had provoked at the ball this evening, she'd say her safety was very much in question.

"But in an excess of caution," Miss Smyth was saying, "and because we truly are full-up, what with all the aunts in residence and now you and your mother, I've put you right next to Edmund"—Miss Smyth gestured toward a door that obviously connected this room with its neighbor—

"so if you become alarmed or . . . upset during the night, you need only call out and he can be in to help in an instant." She gave Jane a rather sly grin. Jane would swear Miss Smyth had more than a touch of mischief in her eyes. "Doesn't that make you feel more secure?"

"Ah." It certainly made her feel more . . . something. She stared at the connecting door. Edmund's bed was on the other side. And tonight Edmund would be in that bed.

Did he sleep naked?

Damn. She squeezed her eyes shut. Where had that thought come from?

"I'll take you down to Edmund's study, shall I? I'm sure you could stand to have a nice glass of brandy, and Edmund did say he needed to speak with you as soon as you were settled."

"Oh." The thought of seeing Lord Motton in the flesh—no, not in the *flesh*—made her stomach flop around like a dying fish. "I should see how Mama—"

"Your mother is fine. She's not easily upset—she did raise six children, didn't she? Though I suppose the two youngest girls can't be considered raised quite yet, and Nicholas is still at Oxford."

"Y—yes. When he isn't being sent down."

"Precisely." Miss Smyth tugged on Jane's arm and directed her toward the door to the corridor. "I must tell you, Jane, that I've always admired your mother's strength of character." She grinned as they stepped out of Jane's room. "And I should also tell you at the moment she is down in the drawing room with all the other aunts. I can assure you most sincerely you do not want to subject yourself to the aunts right now. Edmund is definitely the better choice."

"Oh." Yes, she would agree with that. Lord Motton's aunts—especially en masse—would be very intimidating.

Stephen had obviously thought so. He'd fled as soon as he'd seen her and Mama safely moved in.

And she did need to talk to Lord Motton. She still had the sketch piece in her dress. She'd intended to remove it when she got to her room, but Miss Smyth had not given her the privacy to do so. It would have been very hard to explain why she was fishing around in her bodice or why she'd needed to hide the paper there in the first place. She would just have to attend to the matter when she reached Lord Motton's study.

Unless, of course, Miss Smyth was intending to stay and chaperone them, but surely Lord Motton would not permit that. He would want to discuss the sketch, and he couldn't do that with his aunt present. No, Jane was sure to be quite alone with him—with all his aunts and her mother just a few rooms away.

"I'm sure Edmund has worn a path in the carpet, Jane," Miss Smyth said as she stopped in front of a door. "He is most anxious to see you. I wonder why." She waggled her eyebrows.

"Ah, er, we merely have some business to discuss." Good heavens, did Miss Smyth think there was something of a romantic nature afoot?

She did. She waggled her eyebrows some more and then winked. "I bet you do."

"No. Ah, that is, we have *business*. Things of a business nature. Important topics . . ." She couldn't have Lord Motton's aunt believing that she and he . . . that they . . . oh, blast. Her relationship with the viscount was odd, to be sure. Complicated. But romantic? No. Not romantic, though she wished . . .

No, no, no. She did not wish . . . anything!

Miss Smyth smirked at her, and then pushed open the door. "Miss Parker-Roth is here, Edmund."

Chapter 7

"Do you have the paper?"

Jane frowned at Lord Motton. A few pleasantries would have been nice, or at least a token show of concern. She *had* just had the house she'd been staying in ransacked. Well, not the entire house, of course—just Clarence's study. It would have been much, much worse, now that she considered the matter, if the reprobates had invaded the room she'd been staying in, pawing through her clothing, throwing her books and sundries everywhere . . .

Her fingers tingled; her palms felt clammy. She struggled to take a deep breath—

"I'm sorry, Jane." Edmund's arm was around her shoulders. She leaned into his warm hold. He felt wonderfully solid in a world that was suddenly out of kilter. "I didn't think. You've been so pluck to the backbone in all this, I forgot how upsetting the break-in must be for you."

His voice was gentle, kind, understanding—and it made her burst into tears. His other arm came up to pull her against him; his hand cradled her head as she wept all over his waistcoat.

How mortifying. She never fell apart like this. John and Stephen had taught her early on that tears were a disgustingly weak, girlish response to any problem, but try as she might, she could not stem the flow. Edmund must be completely appalled.

"Shh," he murmured by her ear. His hand massaged the back of her head. "Things will be all right, Jane. You're safe here."

Damn. A fresh spate of tears overcame her. Was she ever going to stop these ridiculous waterworks? She—

She felt his lips brush her cheek.

Oh! Her tears dried up as if he'd found the spigot and turned it off. She sucked in her breath. His lips were moving from her cheek to her . . . She turned her head, so her face was no longer buried in his waistcoat. His lips touched her eyelids, moved down . . .

She tilted her head back, and his mouth found hers.

Ah! His lips were firm, warm, male—she felt surrounded by his strength. His tongue slid deep into her mouth, filling her slowly and thoroughly. He tasted of comfort and brandy.

He smelled of brandy, too, and eau de cologne. She opened her mouth wider; his tongue moved leisurely through it, as if he had all the time in the world to discover every one of her secrets. She should be alarmed, but she was not. She wanted him to know her, just as she wanted to know him. She was happy to be kissed—and to kiss him—forever.

Except she couldn't. Sadly, her nose was still stuffy from her tears. Breathing was becoming a rather insistent need. She made a small sound of regret and pulled back.

He let her go immediately, as if she had suddenly burst into flames. She did feel exceedingly heated, but not to the point of singeing anyone. She blinked up at him. He looked horrified.

"Forgive me." He stepped back so quickly she was afraid he might trip. "It was unconscionable of me to take advantage of you like that."

"Ah." Her wits were too scattered for her to form a coherent reply. Saying he had not taken advantage of her—or that she wished him to take much more advantage—seemed too bold. Perhaps he had just kissed her out of pity and then been overtaken by his male instincts. Surely he would have expected a well-bred woman to have struggled or at least protested in some way. She felt herself flush. "Er, well, I am not usually such a watering pot."

He straightened his waistcoat and cleared his throat. Her gaze followed his hands and then dropped a little lower. Damn. Her heart sank. If he'd been moved by passion, he had clearly got over it. His breeches were as smooth as a lake's surface on a windless day.

He turned away abruptly and took refuge behind his desk. Oh, God, did he think she was going to attack him? This just got worse and worse.

"No, of course you aren't," he said. "I am sure it was just the shock of all that has happened." He cleared his throat again. "But about the sketch—I hate to be so single-minded, especially when you have suffered such a fright, but I do think the sooner we solve this mystery, the better. Do you have the paper with you?"

"Yes, of course I do." She could still feel it under her breast, only it seemed to have shifted a bit, perhaps due to the amorous gyrations of a moment ago.

"Splendid." Lord Motton extended his hand. "Let's have a look."

"Ah, well, you see I haven't had a chance to remove it from my bodice."

Lord Motton's eyebrows shot up and his eyes dropped to contemplate her bosom. She kept her hands from flying up to shield herself from his view only by the strongest exercise of self-control.

"If you will turn around, my lord, I will retrieve it."

"Yes, indeed. Of course." Motton turned and contemplated the red and gold brocaded curtains. Were they starting to look a trifle shabby?

He tried very hard to ignore the breathy little scrambling sounds coming from the woman behind him. What was taking her so long? It should be the work of a moment to reach—no, he would *not* think of where she was reaching. Still, it could not take that long—

"Lord Motton?"

Jane's voice was thin and tight, as if she might be on the verge of tears again. "Yes? Is it safe for me to turn around? Do you have the paper?"

"Yes, you may turn, but no, I don't have the paper."

He spun around, ready to jump down her throat for being so careless, but he swallowed his spleen the moment he saw her face. She looked miserable.

"I mean," she said, "I have the paper, but I don't."

"Excuse me?"

She turned as red as a furnace. "It's stuck."

"Stuck?" She couldn't mean . . . he looked back down to her bodice. It was in some disarray. The neck was crooked and a bit of her shift was sticking out.

"Yes."

He had never seen a human blush so hotly. He was half-afraid she would spontaneously combust.

He was feeling rather hot himself. Only one solution presented itself to his admittedly randy intelligence . . .

well, intelligence might be a bit of a misnomer at the moment. Lust was reducing his meager thought processes to their most basic, bestial, instinctive level. He cleared his throat. "Ah, normally I'd call one of my aunts in—or your mother—to help, but I don't believe we wish to have anyone else aware of our quest."

Jane was staring at a point midway down his chest. "I understand that."

"Ah. So, er, shall I, ahem, assist you?"

It was not possible, but she turned even redder. "Yes."

"Very well." He stepped around the desk. Jane had best not look down at his fall now. If she were redder than red, he was bigger than . . . He'd never felt so enormous. Perhaps his member had been inspired by Clarence's Pan. "Did you stick it between your shift and your dress?"

"No." Jane's eyes closed, and she whispered the words. "It's between my shift and . . . me."

"I"—he cleared his throat again—"I see." He looked down at her lovely bosom. He would have to reach in and touch . . . have her silky skin, her beautiful, round . . .

He was only getting a bit of paper out of her clothing. This was not a seduction. Jane was a gently bred young woman, the sister of his friend. A virgin. He should make the process as brief and dispassionate as possible.

Dear God, how the hell was he going to manage that?

Perhaps he could try to imagine he was a physician. Doctors must be able to treat women's bodies as, well, merely bodies.

He took a deep breath and looked down at Jane's lovely, soft—

All right, so pretending to be a physician wasn't going to be possible. He would just have to grit his teeth and get the job done. "Where exactly is the paper? Under which breast?"

"The right one." Jane was staring at his waistcoat again. "I think when I . . . when we . . . ah, just now when you and I—" She let out a long breath and scowled at his clothing. "When you kissed me, I think I moved so that the paper slipped down a little under my s—stays. I might be able to get it out myself, but I'm afraid I would tear it."

"We can't tear it. We might lose a crucial piece of the puzzle."

"I *know*." She frowned fiercely at one of his buttons. "Will you just get on with it?"

"Very well." He couldn't merely thrust his fingers into her dress; as she said, they couldn't risk tearing the paper. He would have to look at what he was doing . . . what he was touching . . .

Jane darted a glance at the door. "Will your aunt Winifred—or one of your other aunts—come looking for you? I'd hate for them to walk in just as you were . . . you know."

Winifred was not one to lay traps. She might be considering Jane for the role of viscountess, but she would not be so crass as to try to surprise them in an awkward moment. Still, it always paid to be cautious. "I don't believe you need worry, but I'll lock the door just in case."

"You must be very accomplished at getting women out of their clothes," Jane said as he secured the door. She was still standing stiffly exactly where he'd left her. The sooner he got this over with, the better. "You must be an expert at seduction."

"No, not really." He tried to smile reassuringly. It was true he wasn't much in the way of separating women from their dresses, but when he did . . . well, he was discovering the task was far easier when seduction *was* involved. Then he had an eager, pliant woman in his hands, not one who was staring at him as though he were a poisonous snake choosing where best to bite her.

He did not want to frighten or disgust her, but he suddenly realized he did not want to bore her, either. He wanted to give her at least a taste of seduction—but how to do that when she was scowling at him?

"Perhaps it would help if you closed your eyes and thought about something else?" he said as he approached her again.

"What should I think about?"

"I don't know. Something pleasant."

Her brows edged down even farther so they almost met above her nose. "I shall count to one hundred. Will that give you enough time?"

He laughed. "I suppose it depends on how quickly you count. You aren't planning to count aloud, are you?"

Her chin jutted out. "Yes, I believe I will. It might hurry you along."

"It might make me nervous, and then I won't be able to manage the deed." His fingers already felt thick and clumsy.

She snorted. "I can't imagine that."

"It's true."

"Hmph." She rolled her eyes and then closed them. "One."

He smiled. Perhaps he should have some fun with this. He would see if he could seduce her a little—he had been having some luck with that just a few moments before. She had been so eager and soft when he'd been kissing her.

Instead of turning her to reach the buttons on the back of her dress, he pulled her gently forward, up against his chest, and reached around to slip the top few free.

"T—two."

He stepped back and eased her dress down to reveal her chemise and stays.

Her breath caught and she bit her lower lip. "Three."

His breath caught as well. He could see the darker shadow of her nipples behind her thin shift. And now . . . Ah.

He slid his fingers over her lovely soft skin. It would be sacrilegious to hurry. His thumb, all on its own, rubbed over her sweet nipple, causing it to pebble instantly.

"Ooh." Jane wobbled. He slipped his arm around her to support her.

He needed some support himself. Fortunately, the desk was right at his back. He leaned against it, spreading his legs to brace himself.

Mmm. Jane fit delightfully between his thighs. He nestled her up against his aching member, then bent his head to look for the paper—and to kiss her rounded flesh. She arched back to give him easier access to her bosom. If the paper was there, he should see it clearly—once he took the time to look.

He circled her nipple with his tongue and listened to her small, breathy pants—she'd stopped counting. He cupped her breast and suckled; she moaned. He could spend all night worshipping her body—his throbbing cock wished most sincerely, desperately even, to pay its respects immediately—but he had ventured here with a specific purpose. An important purpose . . .

What was it?

Oh, that's right—the sketch. He had to find the sketch.

He kissed his way to the place where her beautiful body and her chemise met her stays. There was nothing there. He ran his fingers back and forth, gently lifted her breast, and looked again . . . no paper.

"Jane, love, the sketch isn't here."

"Huh?"

Her eyes were unfocused, soft with passion. He couldn't resist—he kissed her again, flicking his thumb over her nipple as he did so. Her hips bucked between his thighs and his cock twitched with frustration. If only he could . . . But he couldn't.

He lifted his head. Much as it pained him, he would have to stop teasing her so some sanity could filter back into their brains. "Jane, there's no paper caught under your stays."

"Mmm, kiss me again." She reached for his face; he leaned back, dodging her grasp.

"The paper, Jane. What happened to the paper?"

"I told you—it's under my breast."

"No, it's not."

She frowned. "Yes, it is."

He traced the line of her stays. "It's not here, Jane."

Her frown had deepened to a scowl. "Of course it's not *there*. It's under my *right* breast. I said so in the beginning."

"Ah." He grinned. "So you did. And I suppose that would be your right, not mine." He shifted her in his arms and ran his fingers along the underside of her right breast. Yes, here it was. He eased the paper free and stuck it in his pocket.

"Oh, no, you don't." Jane struggled to detach herself from Edmund's embrace. "You aren't going to hide that paper from me. I'm going to help solve the puzzle." Anger and annoyance flooded her until she almost choked on them. Good. They were much safer emotions than the confusing sensations she'd just experienced. She understood anger and annoyance. "Take that paper out of your pocket. We are looking at it together."

"Jane—"

"Don't 'Jane' me." She wiggled free of his hold and

stepped back. For some reason her chest suddenly felt quite cool. She looked down. "Dear God!" Her bodice was almost at her waist and her breasts . . .

She whirled around, stuffing herself back in her chemise and yanking up the neck of her dress. "See if you are as good at buttoning as unbuttoning."

She was going to die, she was so embarrassed. What had gotten into her? She'd behaved like a light-skirt, a fancy-piece, a . . . a . . . dolly-mop. What must Lord Motton think of her?

She felt his fingers slowly doing up her buttons. How could his touch feel so ordinary on her back, but so very, very extraordinary—torrid—on her breasts? It was as if lightning had flashed from his fingers to her nipples and on to her—she swallowed—to *that* part of her.

And when his mouth and tongue had, well, *feasted* on her— She covered her mouth to muffle a moan. She had been mindless, mad, willing to do anything—*anything*—to prolong that drenching pleasure.

He'd been taking her body somewhere wonderful, pulling her tighter and tighter with each touch, as if she were a harp string he was tuning. She was sure when he'd brought her to the perfect tension, he would have plucked her and she would have exploded in a clear, vibrating note.

But instead he'd distracted her with that stupid paper, so now she was just . . . tense. Unfinished. Her breasts still felt overlarge—oversensitive—and *that* place was still throbbing.

"There you go. I've done up all the buttons. Does everything feel, er, secure?"

She adjusted her bodice slightly. "Yes, thank you." She had better put the activities of the last few minutes behind her. Yes. That's what she would do. Ignore what had just happened. She had important business to attend to.

Someone had wanted Clarence's sketch so desperately, he—or she—had trespassed and destroyed Clarence's property.

She turned back to Lord Motton, but she couldn't quite meet his gaze. "Let's look at that paper."

"No."

"No?" That did cause her eyes to fly up to meet his. He was looking damned mulish. She could be mulish, too, when circumstances called for it. "What do you mean, no?"

"If it is anything like the other piece of the sketch we've found, it is not at all appropriate for a gently bred woman to see."

She flushed and raised her chin. "I believe I've just proven I'm not quite so gently bred. You needn't treat me like some blasted hothouse flower, my lord."

He laughed; he couldn't help it. She looked so adorably prickly and defiant and embarrassed. "Do you think you can rival the Cyprians now?"

She flushed redder and raised her chin higher. "Yes."

"You are wrong. You are nothing like them, Jane."

"And I suppose you know many of them *intimately*." She bit her lip and looked slightly abashed for a moment, but quickly recovered her glare.

"No, but I know more of them than you do." He'd consorted with a few Paphians in the past. Truth be told, he'd always found those encounters somewhat flat and vaguely distasteful—not unlike his feelings after choking down a meal in the low taverns he'd frequented when he'd been skulking about in London's underworld. The action temporarily assuaged a physical hunger, that was all. It satisfied his cock, not his mind or heart.

Mind and heart? Gad, he sounded like a bloody poet. But it was true. Jane made him feel passion that wasn't merely physical nor, perhaps, temporary.

A good thing, since it looked as though he'd be marrying her. He couldn't treat John and Stephen's sister as he just had and not step briskly into parson's mousetrap. Hell, Stephen would probably have already served him his bollocks in a bowl if he'd any idea what had just transpired.

"Lord Motton, the sketch, please." Jane held out her hand; she'd clearly decided to pretend the last few minutes had never occurred.

Should he let her see this portion of Clarence's drawing? It was certain to be as pornographic as the other. On the other hand, the sketch was surprisingly light-hearted—and he found the thought of sharing the pictures with her strangely arousing.

Not to mention the fact that she looked as if she'd gladly take his penknife from his desk and remove his bollocks herself if he didn't hand over the drawing immediately.

"Very well." He opened the square of paper and flattened it on his desktop. He heard a little squeak. "Are you certain you want to examine this picture?"

Jane nodded. This was the upper right corner of the sketch. Two women were dancing on a table, their dresses—if that's what they were supposed to be—merely sashes around their waists. Everything—*everything*—else was exposed, and they were touching each other in a very odd fashion.

"Oh! Is that Lady Lenden and Lady Tarkington?"

Lord Motton leaned closer so his arm brushed against hers. "I believe so. Now we know why they were so interested in us this evening."

"They were interested in you."

His lips curved slightly, his lips that had been so recently fastened around her— No! She drew in a sharp breath. She would not think about where his lips had been and what they'd been so busy doing.

He lifted an eyebrow, the scoundrel, and gave her a very knowing look. "Are you warm, Miss Parker-Roth? You look a bit flushed."

She sniffed and ignored him.

He grinned. "And they were not interested in me; they were interested in getting their hands on this paper."

"They certainly have their hands in peculiar places." Peculiar? Rather more than that. Lady Lenden was touching Lady Tarkington's bosom, and Lady Tarkington was touching—

Jane averted her eyes from the ladies' activities, only to encounter an equally odd drawing of Mr. Mousingly. Clarence had written "Moloch" across the Mouse's thin chest.

"Moloch? Mr. Mousingly is anything but warlike. Just look. The man behind him has him trapped . . . oh." The man's hands were on the Mouse's—Jane felt herself flush. "Who is that?"

Edmund's voice was harsh. "Walter Helton."

She looked at Mr. Helton more closely, carefully avoiding his hands' activities. Clarence had drawn him so thin as to be almost skeletal, with a long sharp chin and nose, horns, a tail—and no breeches. It looked very much like Mr. Helton and the Mouse . . . She gaped up at Edmund. "That's a capital crime, isn't it?"

Edmund, frowning down at the picture, shrugged. "Beelzebub is a master at avoiding punishment."

"Beelzebub?"

"His nickname—from Milton's *Paradise Lost*. He's been implicated in countless crimes, but he always manages to wiggle free—or, rather, rumor has it Satan frees him."

"What?" Lord Motton looked completely serious—grim, even. "Good heavens, surely you don't believe that?

I mean, I suppose I do believe in Satan, but only in a general sort of way. I don't think he directs people's actions, and I certainly don't believe he intervenes in the British courts."

"What are you talking about?" The viscount looked at her as though she were a lunatic. "Satan is a nickname, like Beelzebub."

"Oh. Yes, of course." How foolish of her not to have realized that. "What is Satan's real name?"

He looked back at the sketch and scowled. "No one knows. He could be a duke or a dustman."

"No one knows?" Perhaps she wasn't the foolish one. "So why do you think there is such an individual? Couldn't Mr. Helton be working by himself?"

"No. Helton doesn't have the connections or the intelligence to carry off most of what he's been charged with. He definitely has someone telling him what to do."

"Oh." She looked down at the drawing, too. Now that she had gotten over the shock of seeing such scandalous goings-on, she noticed something else. "What's this?" She pointed to a dark arch, almost like a monk's cowl, on the torn edges of the paper. In the shadow under the cowl, Clarence had drawn two small, very sharp-looking horns, but the head to which they were attached—or, more importantly, the head's face—must be on the other parts of the drawing.

"It looks like—Zeus!" There was barely controlled excitement in Edmund's voice. "I think Clarence may have drawn a portrait of Satan, and if he has . . ." He straightened, looking almost exultant. "Once I have the entire picture, I'll be able to identify the man at last."

Once *he* had the entire picture . . . Edmund wasn't back to excluding her, was he? "When *we* find the other parts," she said. "Where do we look for the next section, do you think? Did Clarence give us another clue?"

His brows snapped down. "*We* don't look anywhere, Miss Parker-Roth. With Satan involved, it is far too dangerous for you to be involved any further. Satan is not to be trifled with. He's thought to have a controlling interest in the worst brothels and gambling hells in London, if not in England. He kills with impunity."

"Kills?" Surely Edmund was exaggerating.

"Yes, Jane—kills. This is not someone like Ardley or the Mouse. The man has an extensive, highly disciplined criminal network—and discipline among thieves and murderers is maintained by sheer terror. The fact that no one knows his name is proof he rules with an iron fist."

"Oh." Suddenly this adventure was far more complicated than saving Miss Barnett from a dreadful marriage— but that didn't mean she was going to turn into a pudding-heart. "Well, you can't face this miscreant by yourself. You need my help."

Chapter 8

"I do not need your help." Edmund started to fold up the sketch, but Jane slapped her hand down on it.

"You do, too."

Edmund stared at her, his face incredulous before his brows snapped down again and his look turned stony. "No. Disabuse yourself of that notion immediately."

"But—"

"The situation is far too dangerous. Good God, Jane, Satan would squash you like a bug."

That was an exceedingly unpleasant thought. "What makes you think he won't anyway?" She wasn't a fool or foolhardy, but she'd rather do *something* than wait patiently for Satan's heel to come down on her neck.

"He has no reason to connect you with the sketch."

"No? Are you certain? You know the Mouse approached me at the ball this evening, asking if I'd seen any of Clarence's drawings."

"Perhaps the man merely admired Clarence's artistic talent."

"You don't believe that, my lord. Clarence was a sculptor. Sketching was not what he was known for."

Lord Motton's face was impassive; he clearly was not

going to admit she was right. "Perhaps the Mouse was confused."

And perhaps you are grabbing for straws. "Oh, please! Besides the fact the Mouse appears in the sketch, the way he asked the question was telling as well. He was very secretive and repulsive."

"The Mouse is often secretive and always repulsive."

She refrained from rolling her eyes, but just barely. "Even if my encounter with the Mouse was unrelated to Clarence's drawing, there are a host of other connections. I'm staying in Clarence's house—or was until now. Lord Ardley sent you to look for the sketch, and suddenly, after years of not acknowledging my existence, you spend time with me this evening—a lot of time if anyone was paying attention, which Lady Lenden and Lady Tarkington certainly were."

"I realized you existed."

Jane raised a skeptical eyebrow. "You hid your awareness very well then."

"To my regret."

She did roll her eyes then. The viscount had better not try to distract her with sweet words. "And now you take me and my mother into your house."

"I'm your brothers' friend."

She couldn't stand it. She poked the man in the chest. "Don't be obtuse. There is something important about this sketch, and a number of people are suddenly very anxious to find it. I for one would like to know *what* I am dealing with even if I can't know *whom*."

Jane had a point, but the thought of Satan having any interest at all in her made his blood run cold. "I'll stay away from you. I'll make it clear you are only a houseguest. You'll go everywhere with your mother or my aunts. And you most definitely won't look for the other Pans."

Jane poked him again; he caught her hand to save himself from further attacks. "If anyone was watching," she said, "they saw you show Stephen the first bit of Clarence's drawing at the ball when I was standing there, obviously part of the conversation."

Bloody hell, she was right about that. How could he have been such an idiot? "There's no reason for anyone to remark on that. It was a very brief event. The chances someone noticed it are minimal." He tightened his hold on her hand. That was a lie. If people were purposely watching him, they would have noticed, and if Satan was indeed involved . . . well, the man left nothing to chance.

Jane's eyes widened and her face paled. "Dear God, Mama is Cleopatra's friend. These people may think she knows something—she may be in danger as well."

He put his hands on her shoulders. "Don't worry. I'll have men watching both of you whenever you're outside this house. You and your mother will be safe."

"If this Satan is as evil as you say he is . . ." Jane shook her head and took a deep breath. "I don't believe you can guarantee anyone's safety, my lord."

Damn it, she was right, of course. But he had to find a way to protect her. If anything happened to Jane—

Anger, fear, and frustration roiled his gut. "If you stay in the house—"

She shrugged off his hands and reached for the sketch. "I can't stay in your house forever."

"Er." Damn. He had a sudden vision of her doing just that, her belly big with his child. What the hell was the matter with him?

"The sooner we find out what this is all about, the

better. There really is no time to waste." She studied the sketch. "Do you have the other piece?"

"Yes." He'd never thought of having a child with a woman before. A child suckling at Jane's breast . . .

Her eyes flashed up to meet his. "So? Are you going to get the other piece or simply stand there like a great looby?"

Damn. Think with your head, not your cock, Motton. "I have it here." He pulled it out of his pocket. Jane made an exasperated sound and laid the pieces together on the desk.

"I do wonder why Clarence tore the drawing and hid the pieces in different places," she said.

"He was probably afraid. I tell you, Satan is not a person to be trifled with."

Jane shot him an annoyed look. "You have made your point, Lord Motton, but no matter how you try to frighten me, you are not going to persuade me to go hide under the bed."

Oh, damn. Why the hell did she have to mention beds? And why the hell couldn't he keep his randy brain under control? He should not be thinking what he was thinking—having Jane naked in his bed.

She turned back to the sketch. "Clarence definitely drew a figure in the center of this. The two pieces fit together perfectly. It does look like a person's head—a person in a monk's garb, hunched over so his face is shadowed by his hood." She pushed her hair back out of her face. "Unfortunately we'll have to find the other pieces to learn the person's identity."

"Ah, yes. Indeed." He'd love to see her hair spread over his pillow—

"Look, there's another Pan." She pointed to the corner over Beelzebub's left shoulder.

Motton wrenched his mind from lascivious images of Jane and beds. "I see it." He took out his magnifying glass and held it over the area. This Pan was just as excited as the others—if anything, his phallus looked even more impressive. The statue appeared to be in a room with a black-and-white tile floor. Behind it were several framed pictures. Had Clarence drawn a copy of this sketch? He moved the magnifying glass to get a better view.

No. Only one drawing was clearly rendered and that was of a half-eaten apple and two lopsided pears.

"That's one of Cleopatra's paintings," Jane said. She grabbed the glass and pushed him aside. Her breast pressed up against his arm. She smelled of lemon—sweet, but tart. "That tile looks familiar." She shifted so her bottom pushed up against his hip. Was she trying to drive him mad with lust? No, she seemed oblivious to her effect on him.

"Oh?" He tried to focus through the fog of lust clouding his brain. "Can you tell where it's hung?" If Clarence kept to pattern, that would tell them the next Pan's location. "It's not one of the rooms in Widmore House, is it?"

Jane shook her head and a few errant wisps of hair floated briefly across his face. The lemon scent intensified.

Focus, Motton. You are not going to write a treatise on Miss Parker-Roth's hair.

"No, I don't think so. See, he's drawn all these other paintings as if they were in a gallery."

"Hmm. So could it be the Royal Academy? Is it Somerset House?"

"No, I'm almost certain Cleopatra never exhibited there. It's a bit of a sore point with her. In fact, she was complaining about the academy the last time we saw her, just before she went off on her honeymoon."

"All right, so if it's not the Royal Academy, where is it?"

Jane straightened and looked at him. "It must be the private gallery Mama and a few of her friends set up on Harley Street. She dragged me there once. I think at least one of the rooms has a black-and-white tile floor."

"Splendid." Motton folded up the sketch pieces. "Give me the street number and I shall go there tomorrow."

She was frowning again. "I will not. If you go, you will go with me."

Why did she have to be so pigheaded? "Miss Parker-Roth, we discussed this. With Satan quite possibly involved, it is far too dangerous for you to participate in the search any longer."

She stuck her damn little nose in the air. "I'm not aware that we discussed anything, Lord Motton; you merely blustered about like a misguided male protecting a weak little female."

He wanted to shake her. "And what is wrong with protecting females? You are most definitely weaker than I am." And if Miss Parker-Roth didn't start acting sensibly, he would be delighted to give her a demonstration of his strength. He could easily immobilize her and have his wicked way with her if he wanted to. Which he didn't, of course. Well, not without her enthusiastic cooperation.

"Nothing, exactly. It's the condescending, patronizing, superior attitude that goes with it. The feeling that because you are physically bigger and stronger than I am, you are also more intelligent." She snorted. "More intelligent? Ha. Why deal with roundaboutation? Men far too often treat me as if I had feathers for brains."

He smiled in spite of his annoyance. "Surely your brothers never made that mistake?"

She grinned at him. "Not more than once. I was not shy about correcting them, even if it required a good wallop with a hard object."

He would like to have seen Jane trying to educate John and Stephen—and the younger brother as well. "I understand that, Jane, but *you* must understand this situation is completely different." Maybe if he tried again, the message would get through her hard head. "I cannot stress enough how dangerous Satan is."

"Oh, you've frightened me quite well, my lord, but that won't deter me. And it will cause less comment if I appear at an art gallery than if you do. My mother *is* an artist."

"And you always accompany her to the galleries, correct?"

"Er, well, perhaps not." Damn, he had a point.

"How many times have you taken in our artists' offerings, Miss Parker-Roth?"

"This Season?" The man was going to make her grovel, wasn't he?

"Yes."

"Ah, well, this Season has barely begun. I still have plenty of time to view a gallery or two." Perhaps she could still wriggle out of this bind she'd got herself into.

"All Seasons, then. How many times since your comeout have you attended any sort of art display with your mother?"

Blast, he had her. "I can't recall."

He raised his eyebrows. "The truth, Jane."

"Oh, very well. I went with her once to the Royal Academy and once to the Harley Street gallery. I have enough of paintings and pictures at the Priory. I don't need to stare at more art in London."

The damn man smirked and crossed his arms. "So your attending the gallery will be as odd—odder, actually— than my doing so. I am quite the connoisseur, I'll have you know."

He was quite the unconscionable prig. If there were a

Pan handy, she'd bash him over the head with it. "I am not going to let you go alone. You know you need my help; you are just too stubborn to admit it."

"I do *not* need your help." He was gritting his teeth again.

"You do, and if you don't take me with you, I will go on my own."

The thought of Jane looking for the sketch by herself turned his blood to ice. She had no experience with villains; she couldn't even begin to understand the precautions she should take. And if it truly were Satan he was dealing with, he couldn't afford to split up his men, having some guard Jane and others watch his back. "Don't be ridiculous."

"You may rage at me all you like, but unless you intend to lock me in a dungeon or tie me to my bed, I am going."

Tie her to her bed . . .

Focus.

He scowled at her. She scowled back and raised her chin. She clearly did not intend to let herself be persuaded—or bullied.

He knew when to throw in the towel. "Very well, you win." She tried to repress her grin of triumph, the minx, but she wasn't quite successful. Well, he was going to demand some concessions in return. If she insisted on being involved in this, he would insist on keeping a very, very close eye on her. "But to keep you safe, I need to stay by your side—so I shall pretend to be courting you."

"What?" Jane lifted her hand to her chin to ascertain her mouth wasn't hanging open. Courting her? What did he mean by that? Yes, they'd just engaged in some rather heated exchanges, but that wasn't courting, that was Lord Motton taking what she had shamelessly offered him. He was a

man. He wasn't going to turn down such opportunities. Even her brother John had a mistress.

Not that Lord Motton would ever cross the final line with her—of course not. But, well, men were just very different from women.

And she must not forget he'd managed to ignore her for more than seven years. She might have been longing for him, but he had definitely not been doing the same for her.

"It's not so shocking," he was saying. "I think the *ton* will believe it. As you point out, I spent a good bit of time with you tonight. People may already be speculating about my intentions. The aunts certainly are." He grimaced. "They have made it their mission to see me wed."

"Ah." Now she understood. "So this playacting is for your benefit as well."

"Partly, I suppose. But it is mostly for your safety." His expression was serious. "Even though you scoff, Jane, you do need protecting. You've never dealt with a black-hearted bastard like Satan. You can't handle him."

She tilted her chin. Lord Motton was back to frightening her—and he was doing an excellent job—but she refused to be frightened. "And you can?"

His face went from serious to chilling. "I can."

"Ah." Her heart was suddenly pounding in her throat. Perhaps she would be a little frightened . . .

The doorknob rattled.

"Eep!" She slapped her hand over her mouth to muffle her squeak. Was that Mama? Lord Motton might find himself more than pretending to courtship; he might find himself forced up the church aisle.

"Try not to look quite so guilty," Lord Motton murmured as he walked past her to open the door.

Not look guilty? Ha! She *was* guilty. She was alone with

a man in a locked room, which was bad enough, but when one considered what she'd been doing with that man—

Oh, dear God. She looked down to be certain her dress was where it belonged.

"Aunt Winifred and Theo. What a . . . surprise," Lord Motton said. He stepped aside so his aunt and her pet could enter.

At least it wasn't Mama—though perhaps this was worse.

"Awk!" Theo turned his head to examine Jane and then flapped his wings, sending strands of Miss Smyth's hair flying around her face. "Something's rotten in Denmark."

"Theo, please!" Miss Smyth's eyes met Jane's and then dropped to consider Jane's bodice. Jane clutched her skirts to keep from shielding her breasts from the woman's scrutiny. Surely Miss Smyth didn't look disappointed that Jane's clothing was not in total disarray? "I'm certain there's a perfectly reasonable explanation why Edmund had his study door locked, Theo." Miss Smyth smiled at her nephew. "Edmund?"

"Yes, Aunt?"

"Would you care to elucidate?"

"No."

Dear God, why wasn't Lord Motton concocting a plausible explanation? Did he *want* his aunt to think the worst? "Ah, you see, Lord Motton and I . . ."

Lord Motton raised an eyebrow. Damn. Jane tried again. "Lord Motton and I were merely . . . we were just . . . we had some business of a private nature . . ."

Lord Motton turned back to consider his aunt. "You are the one who escorted Miss Parker-Roth to my study, Aunt Winifred, and then left her unattended. I find it hard to fathom why you seem so concerned with the proprieties now."

"You had asked to speak to her, if you will remember. I got the impression you had a matter of some import to discuss. And I didn't think poor Jane was up to spending time in a roomful of aunts." Miss Smyth raised her eyebrows. "But I did not lock the door."

"I did need to speak to Miss Parker-Roth, and I didn't wish to be interrupted."

Miss Smyth snorted. "I would imagine not."

Lord Motton merely stared at his aunt. Jane stared at the floor.

Miss Smyth waved her hand. "Oh, I suppose it doesn't matter. I'm certainly not going to spread any tittle-tattle."

"Tittle-tattle." Theo examined Jane. "Tiny titties. Bitty bubbies."

Jane felt herself flush. She knew she didn't have an especially impressive bosom, but she certainly didn't need a rude parrot bringing her deficiencies to Ed—to everyone's attention.

"Theo!" Miss Smyth glared at her parrot.

"Aunt"—Lord Motton almost spat the word—"control your pet or I'll be using his feathers to stuff pillows."

"Pillows!" Theo reared back. "Shiver me timbers! Ye won't be makin' a pillow out o' me."

"I will if you don't mend your manners, you obnoxious bird."

"Edmund, it's beneath your dignity to argue with a parrot."

"Right. I won't argue." He looked Theo up and down; Theo sidled closer to Miss Smyth's head. "Perhaps I'll make him into a feather duster instead of a pillow."

"Jiminy!"

Miss Smyth shooed her pet away from her hair. "Theo, much as it pains me to say so, you have indeed merited some punishment, but Edmund would never really pluck you."

Lord Motton leaned toward Theo and bared his teeth. "Don't bet on it."

"Lord a mercy, save me, save me!" Theo flapped his wings so vigorously he knocked some of Miss Smyth's pins askew, causing her coiffure to list drunkenly.

"Edmund, you are not helping matters." She tapped Theo on the beak. "Now apologize to Miss Parker-Roth, sir. Your behavior has been beyond boorish. I am very sorry to say I am ashamed of you."

Theo ducked his head. "Aw, Theo's sorry. Theo's sorry."

Miss Smyth looked at Jane again. "Please forgive Theo, Miss Parker-Roth. He *is* a bit of a birdbrain on occasion."

"Er, yes, of course. Do not give it another thought." It was past time to change the subject, but Jane couldn't think of a new topic to save her soul.

"And, in any event, Theo is wrong. You have a very nice bosom"—Miss Smyth smiled—"as I'm sure Edmund has been telling you."

"Ah." She was going to spontaneously combust from embarrassment. There was no question of it. She closed her eyes and felt the heat sweep through her. She must be red as a beet.

"Aunt!"

"Well, you wouldn't want Miss Parker-Roth to get the wrong impression, Edmund. Young women can be very sensitive about such matters."

Poor Jane looked miserable, and any further conversation with Aunt Winifred and Theo would just add to her misery. "I believe it's time for Miss Parker-Roth to retire. You can see she's fagged to death."

Aunt Winifred clicked her tongue. "Edmund, you are

as bad as Theo. Wasn't I clear? A gentleman should never make disparaging comments about a lady's appearance."

He took a deep breath—he would not shout. "I'm not making disparaging comments; I'm stating the obvious."

"Obvious. Ob—"

He glared at the parrot. "Don't push your luck."

Theo snapped his beak shut and hid his head under one of his wings.

"Miss Parker-Roth has had an exhausting day," Edmund said.

"Indeed." Aunt Winifred nodded. "That's why I came to see why you were keeping her from her bed."

Had Winifred stressed that last word? He would ignore it. "Miss Parker-Roth, are you tired?"

Jane sighed and nodded. "I'm afraid I am rather."

"Then I shall escort you to your room. Where have you put her, Aunt Winifred?"

"In the blue bedroom."

"Ah. The blue bedroom." He was going to strangle his aunt.

"Yes. I thought that would make her feel more secure. I told her if she felt alarmed during the night, she need only call out and you would come and assist her—didn't I, Miss Parker-Roth?"

"Y—yes." Jane sent him an uncertain glance.

He would like to reassure her, but he was too angry. The thought of sleeping next door to Jane, knowing she was in the viscountess's room, connected to his by a door whose key had been lost years ago . . . well, sleeping would very likely not be something he would do much of.

"You *will* assist her if she is disturbed in the night, won't you, Edmund?"

Strangling was too kind an end for Aunt Winifred. He forced his clenched teeth apart. "Of course."

"I really—there's no need—I'm perfectly fine," Jane said. "And if my current bedchamber is inconvenient, I'm sure I can share my mother's room."

"No, no, your bedchamber is fine." Aunt Winifred patted Jane's hand. "You've suffered quite a shock to your nerves, dear. You must allow Edmund to ease your . . . distress." She grinned and waggled her eyebrows. "Men have to be useful for something, don't you think?"

And what the hell did his elderly, virginal—Good God, surely Winifred was virginal?—aunt mean by that comment?

He didn't want to know.

"Shall we go, Miss Parker-Roth? Aunt?"

"Oh, you two run along. I believe I'll have a word with Gertrude before I find my bed."

"Very well. Good night, then." Motton nodded and then guided Jane out of the study.

"Your aunt must be completely scandalized," Jane said. Thank heavens Miss Smyth hadn't arrived earlier when her dress had been down around her waist.

Lord Motton looked down at her, one eyebrow raised. "Did she appear scandalized?"

"N—no. Not exactly."

"Not at all. Apparently Aunt Winifred has decided you will make an excellent viscountess."

"What?" Jane's stomach clenched. Lord Motton must be revolted by the situation. "You're joking, aren't you?"

"She's put you in the viscountess's room."

"Oh." Her stomach lurched and then clenched tighter. "But there's nothing to that. She told me the house was very crowded with all your aunts here."

He snorted. "There are plenty of bedrooms. No, Aunt Winifred is a master tactician. She used the same ploy a few years ago at one of my house parties, putting Alex

Wilton and the former Lady Oxbury in adjoining rooms."
He laughed. "Worse, she forced Lord Kilgorn to share a
very small bedchamber with his estranged wife."

"Oh? Well, her ploys succeeded. Both those couples
have growing families and are rumored to be very un-
fashionably in love." And would Miss Smyth's efforts be
as successful in this instance? Jane wondered.

Heavens! Where had that thought come from? How
absurd.

"Perhaps I should apologize for Aunt Winifred's actions at that gathering," Edmund said as they started up
the stairs. "I think your brother John suffered as a result."

"Why? What do you mean?"

"It was right after that party that Lady Dawson—then
Lady Grace Belmont—jilted John at the altar."

Jane sighed as they reached the top of the stairs. "It
was quite horrible, being in the church that morning and
waiting and waiting for Grace to appear, but I've always
believed it was for the best. I never thought John and
Grace well matched. The betrothal was all Grace's father
Lord Standen's doing. John went along because he
wanted a patch of Standen's land for his roses—not the
best reason to enter a marriage."

"Hmm. John is a bit of a madman when it comes to
plants."

"A bit?" Jane laughed. "I'd say so." They stopped in
front of her door. "I think Grace's defiance in that instance was what finally persuaded Lord Standen to ask
Miss O'Neill to marry him—something he'd have done
long ago if he weren't such a stubborn, prideful man. The
idiot just couldn't stomach the thought of a poor Irish
cottager becoming the Countess of Standen."

"And now she's given him his heir."

Jane laughed. "And perhaps a spare. Had you heard she's said to be in the family way again?"

Edmund gave her a very intent look and she felt herself flush again. Damn her tongue—how could she have spoken so boldly?

She put her hand on the door—the door that opened to a room that was connected to Edmund's . . .

"My lord, I am sure you mistake your aunt's intentions. Miss Smyth barely knows me."

He snorted. "Miss Parker-Roth, my aunt would have been a great asset in the war against Napoleon. She is far better at gleaning intelligence than any mere spy. I am quite certain she knows everything about you—maybe even things you don't know yourself."

"Oh."

"Indeed." He reached past her to open her door. "Sleep well."

"Thank you, my lord." She stepped over her threshold. "Pleasant dreams."

As she was closing the door, she could swear she heard him mutter as he continued down the corridor, *"Not bloody likely."*

Chapter 9

Jane stopped on the breakfast room's threshold. Damn. All Edmund's aunts except Winifred were seated at the table, consuming toast and tea—and kippers and kidneys, judging from some plates. Whatever happened to having a cup of chocolate in bed?

No one had yet seen her. She'd just back out quietly—

A black-and-white cloud erupted from underneath the table, resolving itself into two energetic poodles that flew over to yap and jump around her skirts. So much for exiting quietly.

An angular aunt, her gray hair pulled back into a tight bun, peered over her glasses at her. "Don't linger in the doorway like that, Miss Parker-Roth. Come in, come in." She turned to frown at a plump woman whose hair was as wildly curly as the dogs'. "Dorothea, will you get control of your animals? What must Miss Parker-Roth think?"

Miss Parker-Roth thought she'd much rather deal with the dogs than the aunts. She bent to pet the black poodle, and the white one butted in for some attention, too.

"Helter, Skelter, come to mommy!"

The dogs glanced at Dorothea and then started licking Jane's hands.

"The poor woman can't enter the room without tripping over your dogs, Dorothea." This aunt had sharp features and tight braids. "You don't see Diana behaving in such a hurly-burly fashion, do you?" A brown-and-white greyhound lay on the floor by the woman's chair. It looked briefly at Jane, yawned, and dropped its head back onto its front legs.

"At least my dogs are full of frolic, Louisa." Dorothea sniffed. "Diana has about as much fun in her as those dusty, dry books you're always reading."

Louisa sniffed back. "Diana is to your plebian animals as my Latin texts are to your novels."

The last woman at the table laughed. "I'm sure Miss Parker-Roth is very tempted to skip her breakfast now that she's been treated to all this squabbling." She gestured with a ring-bedecked hand. "Do come in and join our festive gathering, my dear."

Helter and Skelter had finally had their fill of her and had gone back under the table—well away from the superior Diana—so Jane could finally approach the buffet. She chose an egg and some toast. She suspected she'd need some sustenance to get through the next few minutes.

"Here, come sit next to me, Miss Parker-Roth," the woman with the rings said. "I don't have any pets with me—my cat is still upstairs, the lazy thing—nor do I have *A List*." She looked significantly at the angular woman.

"Ah." Jane glanced at the woman, too. She did, indeed, have a long, numbered list, written in what looked to be a very neat hand, and she was tapping a pencil against the table as if she was anxious to begin crossing things off. She frowned at Jane over her glasses. Jane sat.

Where the hell was her mother? Hiding in her room, most likely. She must have known there'd be an aunt inquisition. And where was Winifred?

It was more than a little disconcerting to realize she actually wished for Winifred Smyth's company.

"Finally." The angular woman looked past Jane to the door. "You're late—and thank God you left the pets upstairs."

Winifred had arrived. The poodles shot back out from under the table to greet her. Dorothea leaned over to confide, "I was going to call my dogs Salt and Pepper because of their colors, of course, but dear Edmund thought Helter and Skelter were more appropriate names."

Louisa snorted. "Those weren't the first names he suggested, if you'll remember. He—"

"Louisa!" The angular woman glared over her glasses. "We do not need to air all our dirty linen, I believe."

Louisa shrugged. "I suppose you're right, Gertrude."

"Of course I'm right." Gertrude looked back at Winifred, who was now heaping her plate with toast and ham and kippers and kidneys. Obviously a convocation of her sisters didn't diminish her appetite. "Will you hurry up, Winifred? We need to get started."

Winifred looked over her shoulder, a slice of tongue dangling from her fork. "Why don't you introduce everyone, Gertrude? I bet you haven't done that yet. Poor Jane probably hasn't a clue who's here." She chuckled. "Except Edmund's many aunts."

Gertrude flushed slightly and adjusted her glasses. "Very well. A good suggestion." She looked at Jane. "My apologies, Miss Parker-Roth. I am Gertrude Smyth, the eldest of Lord Motton's paternal aunts. He has aunts on his mother's side, of course, but we don't need to consider them."

"Except in regard to their number," Louisa said. "He has five aunts on that side, too, so a total of ten aunts—and no uncles."

"Indeed." Gertrude nodded. "There is a shocking dearth of males on both sides of the family, which is of great concern to—"

"Finish the introductions, Gertrude." Winifred winked at Jane as she sat down next to her and then tucked into her breakfast.

Gertrude sighed. "My apologies again. Cordelia"—she indicated the woman with the rings and the absent cat, on Jane's other side—"is the second oldest. Winifred, whom you've already met, is the middle aunt. Dorothea is next and Louisa is the youngest."

"Except for George," Louisa said. "George, Edmund's papa, was the youngest."

"Exactly." Gertrude pointed her pencil at Jane. "And that's the problem in a nutshell."

Jane swallowed her mouthful of toast. "Excuse me? I don't quite—"

Winifred speared a bite of tongue. "The point is, Jane, it took my father six attempts—well, probably significantly more than six attempts, of course. I do believe he was in Mother's bed—"

"Winifred!" Gertrude almost shouted.

"Oh, Gertrude, you're such a dry old stick."

"Proprieties, Winifred, proprieties." Louisa came to Gertrude's defense.

Cordelia laughed. "Whatever Papa did or didn't do, Mother conceived five times before they managed to do it right and get an heir."

"So you see there is no time to lose," Gertrude said. "The odds are not in Edmund's favor."

"The odds? What odds?" Jane asked. Were these women completely mad? "What are you talking about?"

"Babies, Jane. Boy babies." Winifred shrugged. "Heirs."

Gertrude leaned toward Jane. "Edmund is getting old."

"Old?" Cordelia laughed.

Gertrude waved her hand in Cordelia's general direction. "Well, not *old*. Not decrepit, of course. A normal man would still have plenty of time, but given Edmund's pedigree . . . there's no time to waste."

"He needs an heir," Louisa said, "and, if history repeats itself, he'll need to work hard to get one."

Winifred spat her tea back into her cup. "Oh, my, yes. He'll need to work *hard,* poor thing."

She looked at Cordelia and the two of them went off into gales of laughter.

"Will you stop that?" Gertrude glared at them. "This is no laughing matter. You told me last night, Winifred, that Miss Parker-Roth here might be our best bet, but she is not so young herself." She turned her attention to Jane. "How old are you?"

Jane felt her jaw drop. How rude! She knew she wasn't a debutante, but she found she didn't care to be lumped in with the octogenarians. "Twenty-four. And what do you mean, best—"

"Tsk." Gertrude shook her head. "*That* old?"

"Gertrude!"

"Winifred, you know age is something we must consider."

"Yes, it is something we must consider," Winifred said. "But you don't have to be so Friday-faced about it. Dorcas"—she glanced at Jane—"that was Edmund's mother, was twenty-six when she had Edmund, two years older than Jane here."

"But . . ." Jane tried to get a word in, but no one was paying any attention.

"And Edmund was her first and only child." Gertrude tapped her pencil again.

"That doesn't signify," Winifred said. "You know George only gave it a go once. You knew Dorcas."

"Why he ever married her . . ." Dorothea shook her head. "She was a wet rag if ever there was one. A deuced hypochondriac."

"You know why he married her," Louisa said. "She was increasing."

"Excuse me," Jane said firmly, "but I don't understand why you are having this discussion with me present. I am not a member of your family."

"Yet." Winifred smiled. "There was last night in Edmund's study."

"*Nothing* happened in the study." Jane felt herself flush. "Nothing m—much."

All the aunts stared at her, various degrees of speculation in their expressions.

Oh, damn. Where the *hell* was Mama?

"Good morning, ladies." Lord Motton appeared at the breakfast room door. "Am I interrupting?"

"No!" Jane said.

"Yes!" the aunts said.

Helter and Skelter shot out from under the table.

"Gentlemen!" Lord Motton spoke firmly. "Sit."

The dogs sat, tails beating a tattoo on the floor, tongues hanging from their mouths, looks of doggy ecstasy on their faces.

"Well done." He bent to scratch their ears, and then looked up at the ladies. His eyes stopped at Jane; he smiled slowly.

Damn, anyone might think he was in love with her, he'd managed to adopt such a besotted expression. Jane glanced around. The aunts looked at Lord Motton and then at her.

"Miss Parker-Roth," Lord Motton said, "would you care to take in the exhibition at the Royal Academy?"

All the aunts grinned at once.

"Well, that was setting the cat amongst the pigeons." Jane looked over at Lord Motton as he gave his horses their office to start.

He grinned at her. "Why do you say that?"

She rolled her eyes. "You know your aunts are here to find you a wife, and given your father's and grandfathers' failure to produce a suitable quantity of male offspring, they are concerned about the succession. They think you should start work on filling your nursery immediately. Singling me out for this excursion gets their hopes up."

"So they want me to start work on my nursery *immediately*?"

Jane flushed. Edmund could look quite lecherous when he'd a mind to. "Don't be ridiculous."

He sent her a sidelong glance. "I don't know. I don't want the aunties in a pother. Perhaps I should get right to business." He waggled his eyebrows at her.

"Behave yourself, my lord. We are in an open carriage with your tiger behind."

Lord Motton glanced back. "Close your eyes, Jem."

"My lord!" Jane refused to look at Jem. He was a wiry young man about her brother Nicholas's age, at a guess. He could probably imagine Edmund's intentions far better—and in much more detail—than she could. Blast. He was probably wondering why she hadn't soundly slapped his lascivious employer's face. At a minimum she should have had an attack of the vapors.

She raised her chin and tried to sound as prim and

spinsterish as possible. "I must ask you to conduct your-self with more decorum, Lord Motton."

"Now that sounds deadly dull. What if—"

"Milord!"

Lord Motton's expression changed instantly from teasing to alert. "Yes, Jem?"

"We're being followed. I recognize one of the men from the break-in last night."

"You do?" Jane started to turn to get a look at this villain, but Edmund's hand shot out to stop her.

"No, Jane. We don't want them to realize we're aware of them. I don't believe we're in any danger at the moment"—he smiled at her—"but when we reach the academy, stay close to me, just in case." The smile slid back into a leer. "Very close."

Her heart was pounding in her throat, and this man was making salacious suggestions. "How can you take this so lightly?" She wanted to turn around and look, but she forced herself to face forward.

Edmund's expression turned serious. "I'm not, Jane. I'd never take lightly anything regarding Satan. I've sent men ahead to our destination, and I've stationed one or two along our route as well. We'll know if we're in any danger well before anything happens, so we can avoid trouble—and if we can't avoid it, we'll have friends nearby to help."

"Aye, milord," Jem said. "I jist saw Thomas take off runnin'. He must have recognized the man, too. He'll let Ben and the rest know."

"Excellent." Lord Motton encouraged his horses to pick up their pace.

Jane watched his hands on the reins. He was so confi-dent. He could step off the cliffs of Dover with her, assuring her they'd land safely, and she'd believe him. She was clearly an idiot.

"I could try to lose them," he was saying, "but I think it's best if they believe we've no notion they're there. Why should we be the least bit suspicious? We are merely on a pleasant outing to view some paintings and perhaps enjoy a little flirtation."

Jem almost successfully muffled his guffaw, but it was a near thing. His ears must smart from holding in the noise.

Jane sniffed. "I do not flirt, my lord, in case it has escaped your notice."

"You don't?" Edmund raised an eyebrow. "Perhaps you should try it." He pulled back on the reins. "Here we are. Jem, go to their heads, if you will."

The viscount swung down from the carriage and came around to help her alight. He murmured in her ear as her feet touched the walk. "I don't flirt much myself, you know."

Jane snorted. "Liar. You flirt constantly. You're flirting now."

He was smiling, but his eyes were serious. "When have you seen me flirting in society's ballrooms?"

"I haven't seen you in many ballrooms." She stepped past him. "I assume you do your flirting in other, less public locations."

He laughed. "Oh, *that's* not called flirting."

"Lord Motton!"

He put her hand on his arm and smiled down at her. "We will practice our flirting skills together."

Damn it, her stomach was fluttering again. "Flirting with me will stir up the gossips, you know."

"I hope it does. I want to throw Satan and his hounds

off our scent, so they think we are together simply to enjoy each other's company."

Jane clutched Lord Motton's sleeve. "Do you see the man who was following us? Is he still there?" She started to turn her head to look, but he stopped her.

"Tsk, Miss Parker-Roth, please remember—you're supposed to have eyes only for me." He lifted her hand and kissed it, effectively sending all thoughts out of her head. "Don't worry. I have my people on the watch for trouble."

"I'd feel more confident if I knew whom I needed to avoid. I—"

Edmund brushed a strand of hair off her face. "You'd probably stare at the fellow so intently even a blind man would know it. I think it safer if Satan thinks our association is purely romantic—which he will not do if you go searching behind every painting and potted plant for a villain."

She took a deep breath. "All right, you may have a point."

"Of course I have a point." He started walking toward the entrance. "One reason I wanted to attend this exhibition was to have society—and Satan—see us together. The sooner the *ton* take note of my courtship, the better."

"Ah." Courtship. Blast it, now her heart was behaving erratically as well. This was all playacting—she must remember that.

"And the added advantage of this particular excursion is it starts people thinking we are interested in art, so they won't remark on it when we visit the Harley Street gallery. I spoke to your mother this morning and learned it is only open on Thursdays."

"I see." Did Mama think Lord Motton was courting her

daughter? Oh, dear. That could be very awkward. "Did Mama find your question, er, odd?"

He shrugged. "Not that I could discern. She's an artist. I assume she thinks everyone should want to tour any available gallery."

"But . . . she didn't find it remarkable that you would be interested in escorting me?"

"Hmm. You know, I'm not sure I mentioned you."

Of course he hadn't. He was a man. Men, in her experience, didn't mention lots of interesting details, and the details they did mention often weren't interesting at all. It wasn't as if he needed Mama's permission to escort her. She was twenty-four—not a young debutante. "Where was my mother this morning, by the by? She certainly wasn't in the breakfast room helping me stave off your aunts!"

He laughed. "She's wilier than you—or perhaps just more experienced with my aunts. She had chocolate in her bedchamber. I caught her in the corridor shortly before we left—perhaps when you were fetching your bonnet."

Just as Jane had suspected. "That is what I am going to do tomorrow."

"I'm not sure that would be wise. If you do, I'll wager Aunt Winifred will remark on your absence and point out your room is right next to mine—"

"She wouldn't!"

"She would. And she'd go further to remind all the aunts that the key to the connecting door has been lost for years."

"It has?" Damn, she knew she was blushing. She cleared her throat. "So the door is locked?"

Edmund's lips slid into a slow smile. "Oh, no. It's unlocked. Permanently."

"Ah." So the viscount could come into her room—and she into his—at any time and no one would know. She shivered.

How was she ever going to get any sleep?

"Cold?"

"Oh, no. I'm fine." She hoped she wasn't blushing again.

He smiled, but thankfully didn't comment. They'd reached the entrance, and Motton handed the old man at the door their admission fees.

"Thank ye, milord." The man grinned, revealing a large gap where a few of his teeth were missing. "Iffin I may say so, yer lordship, yer lady's portrait could be 'ung 'ere, she's that lovely."

He slipped the fellow an extra coin for the compliment. "I couldn't agree more."

They strolled into the big room. The light streaming in from the high windows cast a halo around Jane's figure and burnished her rich brown hair, making the red in it gleam. The man at the door had been right—Jane was beautiful. Someone should paint her portrait and hang it on the walls here.

Though perhaps not here. Here the walls were infernally cluttered, as usual. Paintings were hung from rafters to floor with no space between them to slip a shilling edgewise.

"You know that man just wanted the vail, don't you?" Jane asked.

"Hmm?" Her eyes were the same shade as her hair. How had he not noticed that before?

"I'm sure he must say that to any male he thinks he can gull, even those escorting the veriest crone." She snorted. "Actually, now I see he spoke the complete truth. Look at the woman in that portrait. She must be eighty if she's a day—and she couldn't have been attractive in her youth."

He took Jane by the elbow and turned her to face him. "I will not have you denigrating yourself. The man was completely correct. You *are* lovely."

Her jaw dropped and her eyes widened—and then she blushed and laughed. "You're blind, my lord."

He shook her arm slightly. "No, *you're* blind, Jane."

She shook her head and looked away. "You're the only one ever to say I'm at all out of the ordinary."

"Am I, Jane, or am I the only one to insist you hear me? Has no man told you how beautiful you are?"

She snorted. "My brothers surely never have."

"Of course they haven't—they're your brothers. But you've survived all those Seasons—you can't persuade me not a single man has complimented you."

"Well . . . perhaps, but it was idle flattery. I am quite aware I am not a diamond of the first water, my lord."

"You are not in the common way, that's true, but you *are* lovely." For some reason it was important to him she believe his words. "I would not say so if I didn't think it. I do not deal in Spanish coin."

"Oh." Her cheeks were very red. Good. "Well, er, thank you then." She was obviously uncomfortable accepting the compliment, but at least she did so, albeit grudgingly. "Now come look at this painting with such a very amusing cat."

He followed her from painting to painting, commenting on any that caught her attention, but giving them hardly more than a cursory look. He was far more interested in Jane, in her changing expressions, the range of emotion in her voice, the play of light over her hair.

He forced himself to pay some attention to their surroundings. He couldn't rule out the possibility that one of the other gallery visitors was a threat. Thankfully, the room wasn't crowded. A scattering of people sat on benches to study the paintings hung near the floor or to rest their sore feet; two men in a corner passionately debated the brush technique in a portrait of an old woman; another fellow trained his quizzing glass on a landscape featuring a shepherd, a sheep, and a mostly naked nymph. Motton's men, stationed around the room, tried to blend in and look more interested in the paintings than the people.

A woman came in with two small children, a girl of about seven and a boy who could not be much older than five. It was immediately apparent to everyone present that she'd made an extreme error in judgment in selecting the exhibition as a suitable outing for her charges.

"I wanna go to the park." The boy did not bother to lower his voice.

"Yes, dear, but we went to the park yesterday."

"I wanna go to the park!" The volume increased. The boy crossed his arms and stuck out his lower lip.

"But I've already paid our admission, dear. Now come look at this darling kitty."

The boy planted his feet solidly in place. Nothing and no one was going to move him. "I hate kitties. I wanna go to the *park*."

At this point the young girl joined the fray to ill effect. "You are such a baby, Oliver."

"Oh, dear," Jane murmured. "I'd offer to help, but . . ."

"Indeed." Motton eyed young Master Oliver. The lad's face was rapidly assuming the hue of a ripe apple. "Nothing is going to help this situation except departure—either theirs or ours."

"I am *not* a baby!" Oliver had an excellent set of lungs.

"You are!" The girl put her hands on her hips and chanted, "Baby Oliver, Baby Oliver."

Oliver yelled and lunged, grabbing a fistful of the girl's

hair; she shrieked and burst into tears; their mother, if that was who the older female was, merely wrung her hands and tried to make soothing noises.

"Now, Oliver, dear, do stop that. We'll go to the park next. Juliet, sweetheart, you know ladies don't scream . . ."

"I am going to scream if we don't go now," Motton muttered. Jane gurgled as if she was repressing a laugh while he directed her toward the exit. Most of the other visitors had the same idea.

"That poor woman was overwhelmed," Jane said as they stepped back into the sunshine. "But I suspect she has spoiled those children terribly."

"Or perhaps they are just evil little beggars." Where was his carriage? He consulted his watch. They'd stayed a far shorter time than he'd planned. Jem should be back with the coach in five or ten minutes; in the meantime it was a beautiful day for a short stroll. He put his watch back and started down the walkway with Jane on his arm.

She tilted her face up to catch the sun. "Oh, no, I don't believe they are evil."

"You don't?" He considered her. "You're a disciple of Monsieur Rousseau and John Dryden then?" He snorted. "Noble savages. I'll grant you those children were savages, but I have serious doubts about the noble part."

Jane shrugged. "All children have their disagreeable moments."

"Ah, but do they ever have any agreeable ones?"

"Of course."

They walked along in silence. Motton contemplated the notion of children. He had to have at least one—an heir—but, frankly, children made him nervous. He had no experience with them.

He watched an elderly woman cross the street.

Children had made his mother nervous, too. No, not

children—him. An active young boy was far too upsetting to her delicate constitution. And his father? His father had felt his job was done once Motton had successfully taken his first breath.

But Jane . . . She had brothers and sisters. And her parents, unlike his, seemed to enjoy their progeny.

What would it be like having children with Jane?

"What's that noise?" Jane asked.

"What?" He listened. There was a rattling behind them. More than a rattling now—a rumble. It was getting closer . . .

He whirled around. A man on a bright yellow dandy-horse, one of those damn newfangled velocipedes, was hurtling down the walk straight at them.

Chapter 10

"I don't know why you had to grab me like that. We must have presented quite the spectacle, sprawling on the ground." Jane allowed Lord Motton to lift her down from the carriage.

She was a mess. Her bonnet was squashed sideways and her hair was halfway down her back; her dress was muddied; her hem, torn; and her gloves would simply have to be thrown out. Lord Motton was not in much better sartorial shape. "I don't know what my mother and your aunts are going to say. It looks as if we've been wrestling in the dirt." Which they had been.

Thank God the day wasn't windy or her skirts might well have been up around her ears. As it was, the London passersby were treated to a shocking display of ankle and, yes, leg.

"The man was going to hit you, Jane." Lord Motton sounded slightly sulky. Oh, dear.

"I know, my lord. I'm sorry to be ripping up at you so. You were very kind to watch out for me." Jane couldn't keep a little testiness from creeping into her voice. This had been one of her favorite bonnets. "But I believe I could have stepped out of the way to safety by myself."

Lord Motton frowned. "I'm not certain of that. This was not a case of a runaway dandy-horse. That fellow was aiming at you."

"Now, don't be ridicu—"

"I am not being ridiculous. Did you note he kept going? He never paused to inquire about your welfare or render assistance."

"Well, of course he didn't stop—he couldn't. That was rather the heart of the problem."

"I don't think so." He escorted her up the walk to the front door. "In fact, I wonder if that woman with the beastly children wasn't part of the plot."

"Oh, for heaven's sake, now you truly are allowing your imagination to run wild. It was just an unfortunate mishap. You know the sudden prevalence of these dandy-horses is leading to a number of pedestrian accidents. Surely you've read about it in the papers."

"Yes, but—"

The door swung open. Williams stood there, looking far from his usual precise self—apparently sartorial disaster was in the air. The butler sounded little like himself either.

"Oh, my lord, I am"—he coughed and obviously tried to get himself under better control—"it is fortunate you have returned. There is an Incident in progress involving the Animals."

"Oh? And I assume Aunt Winifred's monkey is at the center of it?"

"Indeed, my lord. I—"

A tremendous crash emanated from the drawing room, quickly followed by a chorus of barking and shouting. A large orange cat shot out of the room and across the entry, followed by Edmund's aunt Cordelia moving faster than Jane would have thought possible.

"Come here, Kumquat, love." Cordelia smiled briefly as she caught sight of them. She pushed her cap back out of her eyes. "Hallo, Miss Parker-Roth. Edmund, you might wish to look into the drawing room, especially if you have any knickknacks there you value. Winifred's monkey is at it again." She frowned at their clothes. "Or have you already been in? I don't believe I saw you there."

"We just got home," Edmund said. "But I shall attend to the, er, situation immediately."

"That is a very wise idea. Kumquat and I are going to retire to our room until things calm down—that is, if I can find Kumquat. She does not care for such hurly-burly goings-on." She pushed her cap back again. "Please excuse me."

Cordelia hurried off in Kumquat's wake, while Edmund, muttering under his breath, headed for the drawing room.

"If I might be so bold as to say so, Miss Parker-Roth, you might wish to follow Miss Cordelia's example," Williams said, "and retire to your room until the Incident is over."

Jane smiled reassuringly, she hoped. "Thank you, Mr. Williams, but I believe I'll go along and see if I can be of help." With luck no one would notice that her attire was at sixes and sevens *before* she entered the room, and so would attribute her dishevelment to whatever was occurring there.

She cracked the door open and was met with a blast of sound—barking, screeching, squawking, and shouting. She slipped inside just as Edmund yelled, "Silence!"

This worked on the women and even the dogs and parrot, but had no effect on the monkey. It screeched at Edmund from the mantel and then picked up a small porcelain dragon and flung it at his head. Edmund caught it.

"I say, well done!"

"Shut up, Theo." The viscount didn't even glance Theo's way.

"Edmund, your language!" Gertrude glared at him.

"But Theo is correct," Winifred said, clapping. "That *was* well done. An excellent catch."

"What I *want* to catch is your blood—"

"Edmund!" Gertrude said. "There are ladies present."

"—blasted monkey."

"And speaking of the presence of ladies, you are presenting a dreadfully shabby appearance." Gertrude frowned. "Why is your coat torn?" Her frown deepened. "And you have mud on your boots and breeches."

"I must say"—Mama had strolled over to whisper to Jane—"life is never dull in Lord Motton's household."

"Not when the aunts are in residence at least."

"It quite takes me back to when all you children were young."

Jane grinned. "And you never let us have a monkey."

Mama gestured at the destruction around them. "For obvious reasons."

The room did look as if a whirlwind had passed through it. Three occasional tables lay on their sides, figurines and other trinkets spilled over the carpet, and an upended footstool rested on its cushion, legs in the air like a dead bug. A shepherdess's head lay by Jane's foot; she bent to pick it up and saw its headless body under a loveseat. She righted one of the tables and put the shepherdess pieces together.

Diana barked one more time and then returned to her place at Louisa's feet, apparently of the opinion Lord Motton could handle the situation without her help. Helter and Skelter, however, had recovered their usual exuberance and were leaping about, yapping as if Edmund had never spoken.

Theo squawked, flapping his wings. "That's the way, lads. Show the little bug—"

"Theo!" Lord Motton and Winifred shouted at the same time.

Theo snapped his beak shut and dropped his head. "Aw, Theo's sorry. Theo's sorry."

The monkey, now swinging from the curtains, was wearing a red leather leash around its middle. If it could be lured close enough, it could be captured relatively easily.

"Aunt Dorothea," Lord Motton shouted over the din, "I think matters would be improved if you'd take your dogs elsewhere."

"That's what I was telling her before you arrived, Edmund." Louisa stroked Diana's head. "They even provoked Diana to raise her voice."

"Your precious Diana would have barked at the demmed demented monkey even if Helter and Skelter hadn't, and you know it." Dorothea glared at Louisa.

Louisa glared back at her sister. "I know no such thing. Diana is a perfectly behaved lady, aren't you, beautiful?" She made kissing motions at the greyhound, and Diana licked her face.

"You know, Jane," Mama said, "I love my daughters, but I was always glad I didn't have all girls."

Jane heard a scratching on the door and opened it. Mr. Williams stood there, a cut-up apple on a tray.

"Cook believes the beast might be lured into captivity with food," he said.

"Excellent idea." Jane took the tray and closed the door. "Lord Motton, your cook has sent up some treats to entice the monkey closer."

"Treats?" Theo flapped his wings. "Theo likes treats."

"Don't you dare." Lord Motton scowled at Theo and then strode over to take the tray from Jane. "Thank you." He turned back to his aunts. "Dorothea and Louisa, I must ask you and your dogs to leave. Now."

"But—" Dorothea began.

"Edmund—" Louisa said.

"Now!" Lord Motton's tone brooked no arguments.

"Oh, very well, but I don't see why I have to leave." Louisa sniffed. "Diana is not creating a rumpus like Dorothea's animals."

Edmund just stared at Louisa, brows raised. She stared back, then blew out a short, sharp breath and departed with her greyhound, their noses tilted in the air at identical angles.

Getting Helter and Skelter out the door took a good deal more effort, but finally they and Dorothea left as well.

"Thank God," Lord Motton said as the door shut behind them. "Now, let us see if we can capture this beast."

"I don't know why you don't call him by his name, Edmund," Winifred said.

The viscount merely glared at his aunt.

Mama leaned over to murmur in Jane's ear. "What is the animal's name?"

"Edmund."

"Pardon me?"

"You heard correctly, Mama. Miss Smyth named her pet after the viscount."

"Oh."

"Here, Aunt," Lord Motton said as he handed the tray with the apples to Winifred. "I imagine the monkey is most likely to come to you."

Winifred wrinkled her brow. "Yes, of course, but he does sometimes take exception to Theo."

"Then give the bird to Edmund." Gertrude wrinkled her nose. "His attire is in such deplorable disarray, a few feathers—or worse—won't make a difference."

"That's a splendid idea. Here, Theo, go to Edmund now."

Lord Motton's expression was somewhere between disgusted and appalled. "Can't you just put the parrot on the back of a chair?"

"I don't 'put' Theo anywhere; Theo chooses to alight where he wishes." Winifred looked at Lord Motton quite reproachfully and then turned to the parrot. "I know Edmund is not being terribly hospitable at the moment, Theo, but I do need you to move to his shoulder, if you would be so kind."

"Awk," Theo said, fluttering over to land on Lord Motton. He examined the viscount through one eye and then the other. "Scurvy dog."

Lord Motton was moved to reply, "Anytime you'd care to leave, I shall be happy to show you the door."

Winifred laughed as Edmund the monkey leapt down to grab an apple slice. She grabbed his leash. "The moment you find a wife, Edmund, you can wave a fond farewell to all your aunties." She turned to wink at Jane. "So I suggest you not waste any time."

Jane waltzed around Lord Easthaven's ballroom with Baron Wolfson. Apparently Lord Motton's interest in her at the Palmerson ball had woken the *ton*'s male bottom-dwellers to her charms. The decrepit, the spotted, the corseted, the padded—they were all desirous of dancing with Miss Parker-Roth. She had not sat out a single set.

To be fair, she had also danced with Lord Motton and a few other presentable gentlemen, but the bulk of her partners had been like Baron Wolfson—far from prime catches on the Marriage Mart. Truthfully, she was surprised the baron even knew there was a ballroom in Lord Easthaven's house; she'd only ever seen him in the refreshment room, drooling over the lobster patties.

And speaking of lobster patties, Lord Wolfson might consider cutting back on his consumption. His dimensions must rival Prinny's. At least the size of his belly ensured he kept her at the proper distance—and the farther from him she was, the better. The man smelled of garlic and dirty linen.

She glanced up at his fleshy face. His eyebrows bore a startling resemblance to graying moths, his nose tended toward the bulbous, and his lips were unpleasantly thick.

He smiled. His teeth were yellow and crooked.

She dropped her gaze to consider his cravat pin. That was far more attractive, if a trifle gaudy—a ruby, surrounded by delicate gold filigree. Quite distinctive—

"What?" Jane jerked her attention back to the baron's face. What had he said? Something about Clarence's house . . .

His mothlike eyebrows jumped to the top of his forehead and his fat lips pulled into a disgustingly oily, expectant smile. And those teeth—she returned her gaze to his cravat. "I'm sorry, my lord, I was woolgathering. Would what be possible?"

"A private tour of Widmore House, of course. Just the two of us." The moths did a little jig on his forehead.

"Excuse me?" The man wasn't expressing an amorous interest in her, was he? She might be twenty-four and stuck to the back of the farthest, darkest, dustiest marriage shelf, but surely he didn't think she was so desperate she'd consider any sort of connection with him? He was thirty years her senior, besides smelling of garlic and dirty linen. "I'm not staying at Widmore House any

longer, my lord. There was an unfortunate incident—
someone broke into the house—and we decided it wasn't
safe to remain in residence."

"How terrible." He sounded suitably concerned, but
something in his expression—something about the look
in his eyes—was not quite right. He looked almost . . .
predatory.

Old fat Lord Wolfson? Was she daft? Perhaps she'd had
too much champagne.

She blinked and looked again. It must have been the
flickering candlelight. Now he looked perfectly ordinary.

"Was anything taken, Miss Parker-Roth?"

"No, I don't believe so. But of course I'm not familiar
with the house and its contents—Mama and I had only
been there a few days."

"I see. And where are you staying now?"

She felt an odd sense of relief. If Lord Wolfson were
truly interested in her, he'd already have discovered all the
details of her living arrangements. The temporary Widmore servants had certainly not kept their tongues between their teeth. "Lord Motton lives next door and is a
friend of my brothers John and Stephen. He very kindly
took us in. All his aunts are in residence, so two more
females are hardly noticed."

The moths jigged again. "Oh, I'm certain Lord Motton
notices *your* lovely addition to his household."

"Er . . ." Something about his tone made her long for
a nice hot bath. Thank God the music was drawing to a
close. "Ah . . ."

"Jane!"

She had never been so happy to see her brother. "You
know my brother Stephen, don't you, Lord Wolfson?"

"Of course." He inclined his head. He looked like a
completely normal, if unattractive, elderly peer. There

was nothing lascivious or unsettling about him at all. Stephen would think she'd lost her mind if she told him she'd been concerned.

"Wolfson." Stephen nodded back and turned to Jane. "Dance with me, will you?"

"Of course." Stephen didn't usually seek her out—she *was* only his sister—so he must have a reason. And she was delighted to be free of Lord Wolfson. The man bowed and moved off.

"Not showing a lot of taste there, Jane," Stephen said.

She made a face at him. "Women don't have the freedom men have, you know. I can't very well go ask a gentleman to stand up with me."

"Yes, but you can decline, can't you? Have a torn flounce or some such thing?"

The music started—another waltz. Good. They would be able to converse without interruption.

"I can't suddenly develop problems with my attire every time Lord Wolfson approaches—that would cause comment." She frowned, the niggling doubt resurfacing. Stephen knew almost everything about the *ton*. Did he know something particular about the baron? "Is there a reason I should avoid the man?"

"Good taste isn't enough?"

"If good taste were the determining factor, I wouldn't be dancing with you."

"Now, Janey, half—or more—of the women of London would sell their—er, that is, they'd be delighted to dance with me."

Unfortunately, Stephen was probably correct. He was revoltingly popular with the ladies. "If they only knew you as well as I do."

He laughed. "You need to stop holding all my youthful follies against me." He grinned. "Though, given the chance,

I'd still put a toad in your sewing kit. You screamed so loudly and just about jumped out of your skin. I still laugh when I think about that."

"At least Mama made you clean up all the spilled threads and needles after you'd captured the poor animal—and I was happy enough not to have to work on my sampler that day."

"See, I did you a favor then."

"Perhaps, though I could have happily strangled you for the fright." She frowned at him. "Not that I was afraid of the old toad, of course. It was the surprise that got my heart to pounding."

"That's what you say. I'm not so sure." He grinned. "I should have brought a toad with me tonight and tested your theory." He chuckled. "Though I suppose you were just dancing with a toad, weren't you?"

She decided not to dignify that observation with an answer. "So why did you want to talk to me? I do assume you weren't dying to dance with your sister."

"Well, of course not. Gad, what do you take me for? Another Byron?" Stephen swung her through a turn. Even though he was her brother, she'd admit he was an excellent dancer. "No, the reason why I sought you out was merely to tell you good-bye. My departure has been moved up. I'm leaving on the first tide in the morning."

"Ah." Jane swallowed her disappointment. She was used to Stephen going off to foreign lands, but she still hated to see him leave. He was experienced and planned carefully, but no amount of planning could guard against storms or other natural disasters. And now, with the odd events at Widmore House . . . well, she felt a bit aban-doned. "Be careful."

He grinned, cocky as usual. "Of course—I always am." He frowned. "And you be careful, too. I would rather not leave right now, but it can't be helped—and John will be in Town as soon as the house party he's attending ends." Stephen laughed. "Can you imagine staid old stick-in-the-mud John at one of Lord Tynweith's gatherings? Mama thinks he's more interested in a female than the foliage for once. Amazing."

"I hope he is interested in some lady. He needs to get over Lady Grace's jilting."

"True. What's it been? Three years? Surely by now he sees what a mistake that marriage would have been."

"One would hope so, but John can be so stubborn."

Stephen snorted. "That's a bit of an understatement. When John makes up his mind, it almost takes a royal edict to get him to change it." He looked a little annoyed. He and John had probably had more than one disagreement even as adults, as they worked together in a fashion— Stephen gathered plant specimens for John. "But I didn't ask you to dance to discuss our pigheaded brother— I wanted to tell you you can rely on Motton completely while I'm gone."

"Ah." Just the mention of the man's name made her heart beat faster.

"I'd feel a lot more concerned—hell, I'd strongly urge you and Mama to return to the Priory—if Motton wasn't in London to take charge of you. I do trust him to be able to keep you both safe. He's capable of handling anything that might come up. He's a good man—a regular brick."

"Oh?" Her damn heart was still thumping so she could barely speak. If Stephen had any idea how much she was enamored of Lord Motton, he'd laugh so hard he'd fall on the floor here in Lord Easthaven's ballroom.

"Yes. He's responsible, levelheaded, intelligent." He gave her an odd, speculative look. "Are you going to marry him?"

"What?" She stumbled, and Stephen had to haul her up to keep her from falling on Lord Easthaven's ballroom floor. Apparently Stephen didn't find the notion of some connection between her and Lord Motton so laughable. But to assume she'd be considering marrying the man . . . where had he gotten that idea?

"Getting a little clumsy in your old age, Janey?"

She glared at him. She was too angry to speak.

Stephen grinned. "So, *are* you going to wed Motton?"

Of course she wasn't going to marry the viscount. For one thing, he hadn't asked.

"That's the gossip, you know." Stephen's eyes followed a young woman in a scanty bodice and then came back to her. "And it would be a good decision. I mean, you aren't getting any younger. Twenty-four is a bit long in the tooth. Don't know what else you could be waiting for."

She hadn't thought she could get any angrier, but she'd been mistaken. She really, really wanted to kick Stephen in the shins—or higher.

He laughed. "Good thing I mentioned this while we were dancing, eh? You look ready to darken my daylights."

"How perceptive you are—about some things."

"Right." The music faded, and they slowed to a stop. "And don't think I didn't perceive how you looked at Motton when he came upon you at Palmerson's ball."

"Ah." How she'd looked at Lord Motton? Damn. She hadn't really been that obvious, had she? "I don't know what you mean."

He smirked at her. "Don't try to cozen me into thinking you don't have feelings for the man, Janey. That horse won't run."

She gritted her teeth and tried to smile in case anyone

was observing them. "You are a cabbageheaded, cork-brained, coxcomb, Stephen."

He waggled his damn eyebrows. "Methinks the lady doth protest too much."

Jane could only manage a strangled sort of growl in response.

"Throat dry, sister dearest?" He put her hand on his arm and ignored her glare. "I know all that capering around makes me thirsty. Let's repair to the refreshment room and see if Easthaven has anything worth the effort of lifting a glass for." He winked. "And maybe we'll even stumble upon the viscount there."

She was definitely going to kick him.

She should be happy. Lord Motton's plan was to convince the *ton* he was courting her—apparently he'd been extremely successful already. She just hadn't realized how much his sham courtship would bother her, especially as he'd managed to fool her own brother.

She would not consider that Stephen was talking about *her* sentiments, not Lord Motton's.

As usual, once they reached the refreshment room, all the women present—and a few who had trailed after them from the ballroom—converged on Stephen. In short order Jane found herself pushed to the fringes of a crowd.

It was no more than what she'd expected. She'd had seven full Seasons to observe how silly the London women could be around her brother. The men of London must celebrate every time Stephen left on one of his expeditions.

She went over to procure a cup of punch and examine Lord Easthaven's culinary offerings. Thankfully, Lord Wolfson wasn't haunting the refreshment table, though the thin, annoying Mr. Spindel was. He peered at her over his spectacles.

"Have you sampled the lobster patties, Miss Parker-Roth?"

"No, Mr. Spindel, I haven't."

"Then I must warn you before you do—they look appealing, but at Lord Easthaven's last event I discovered they can have unpleasant effects on one's digestion."

"Oh?" She did *not* want to talk about Mr. Spindel's digestion.

Mr. Spindel nodded very seriously. "Yes, indeed. I confess, though I know it is a touch indelicate"—he dropped his voice—"they gave me wind. It was most uncomfortable until I managed to—"

Could she manage to tip the punch bowl over and stop Spindel's discussion of his digestive disturbances? No, it looked to be too large and heavy. Perhaps she should just grab the ladle and whack him over the head with it? Again, no. She might be able to make the toppling of the punch bowl look like an accident, but wielding a ladle as a weapon, satisfying as that would be, could only be construed as intentional—and might even be alarming enough to distract the ladies clustered around Stephen from their adoration.

"Yes, well, that is indeed most unfortunate. My sympathies."

"Thank you. I just thought I should warn you in case you were contemplating having any. They may not offend your system, but you never know. I've found it pays to be cautious."

"Yes. Of course. I'll keep that in mind."

"Now, I *can* recommend—oh, hallo, Motton."

Jane spun around and almost collided with the viscount.

"Good evening, Spindel." Lord Motton put a steadying hand on the small of her back. She felt his touch as if it burned through her dress, branding her. Her stomach shivered. It was a very good thing she'd not sampled the lobster patties.

"I hope you don't mind, Spindel"—Edmund's tone sounded like he didn't care whether Mr. Spindel minded or not—"but I've come to ask Miss Parker-Roth to dance." His voice was so much deeper than Mr. Spindel's thin whine.

"No, no, of course, my lord. You go right ahead. We were just discussing digestive issues, weren't we, ma'am?"

"Digestive issues?" Lord Motton raised an eyebrow.

"Mr. Spindel was cautioning me about Lord East-haven's lobster patties."

"Indeed I was." Mr. Spindel's Adam's apple bobbed earnestly. "And I'll caution you, too, my lord. Ingest them incautiously and you might well find yourself breaking wind at the most inopportune moment."

Jane swallowed a giggle. Was there an opportune moment for such an activity?

"Ah, yes. Thank you for the warning." Lord Motton's tone was as dry as the Sahara. "Now, if you'll excuse us?"

"Yes, yes, go along. Enjoy the music. Can't say I see the point in prancing around the room myself, but there you have it." Mr. Spindel smiled briefly and then turned back to continue his surveillance of the refreshment table.

"Why the hell—your pardon—why in the world did that buffleheaded lobcock come to a *ball* if he doesn't dance?" Lord Motton guided her out of the refreshment room.

"He's hungry, I suppose." Jane laughed. "At least, unlike Mr. Mousingly, he's only interested in the food."

Lord Motton frowned down at her. "We can't assume that."

"Oh, come, my lord, can you imagine Mr. Spindel involved in anything but eating? Haunting the refreshments is all he does at any event he attends. It's a wonder the man is so thin. He must be host to a tapeworm." She noticed they were skirting the dancers. "Where are we going?"

"To the terrace. I need a private word with you."

"Oh?" He was far too high-handed; he was almost dragging her to his destination. People were looking at them and whispering. She should protest, but she was much too delighted at the prospect of a few minutes alone with the viscount.

What did it matter if people talked? According to Stephen, they were talking already. She must have set every tongue to wagging with her disappearance into Lord Palmerson's shrubbery with Lord Motton. The added detail that she was now staying under the viscount's roof, even with the chaperonage of her mother and his five aunts, was merely extra spice to the chatter broth. Well, she was twenty-four—far from a debutante. Let the gabble-grinders talk.

However, they should probably slow their progress somewhat. Lord Motton's single-minded speed was not only causing eyebrows to rise, it was making them vanish into hairlines. She pulled back, and he reduced his pace from a quick stride to a brisk walk.

"Come on. I don't want to be overheard," he muttered, as they stepped outside. He led her to the terrace's farthest, darkest corner and turned her so her back was to the balustrade. He used his body to shield hers from any curious passersby and put his hands on her shoulders. He stared down into her eyes.

"Jane, Thomas found the yellow dandy-horse that almost ran us down. It had been tossed in a rubbish heap just blocks from the academy."

He felt her try to shrug; his hands held her shoulders

down. "Perhaps it was damaged and the owner threw it away in a fit of pique," she said.

He wanted to shake her—she was taking this all too casually. Clearly she did not believe she was in any danger. "No, dandy-horses are too precious. No one would just throw one away, unless that person had stolen it to use once—to run us down."

"That's ridiculous." Jane's voice wavered slightly. Was he frightening her? Good. She'd certainly frightened him. When he'd looked around Easthaven's ballroom and had been unable to see her, his heart had seized in his chest.

"You need to be careful." He shook her slightly to emphasize his words. "You cannot wander off like you just did."

Her eyes widened. "I wandered off?"

"Yes. You left the ballroom."

"With my brother." She looked at him as if he had escaped from Bedlam. Perhaps he had. He certainly felt mad. "I went to the refreshment room with my brother."

Hearing her say it, his fear did sound irrational. What could happen to her in Lord Easthaven's refreshment room with Stephen nearby?

It *was* irrational—but he was still afraid. He had to convince her of the danger. If he knew she took the threat seriously, he could relax a little.

She grinned at him, a cocky little expression. "Do you share Mr. Spindel's fear of the lobster patties?"

The damn saucy wench! How dare she dismiss—belittle!—his concern? He was not some bloody little worm like Spindel.

His grip tightened and she sucked in her breath. He was hurting her. He didn't want to hurt her, but he wanted to do something. He relaxed his hold, but anger, frustration, fear, and, yes, lust still flooded his veins.

He couldn't hit her, as he would if she were a man. He couldn't shake her until her head flopped on her neck. He couldn't shout at her here on Easthaven's terrace.

He did the only thing he could do. He kissed her.

It wasn't a gentle kiss; he was too consumed with pent-up emotion to be gentle. He wanted to force her to believe him, to promise to be cautious and alert at all times. He wanted to keep her safe, to guard her, to make her . . . not afraid of him, no, but compel her to bow to his superior strength and experience.

He didn't frighten her. She was startled, yes. He felt her stiffen; her mouth hardened and her hands moved to his chest to push him away.

He wouldn't allow her to push him away. He'd—
God.

She changed her tactics. She softened against him, and her fingers slid up to tangle in the hair at the nape of his neck.

It wasn't surrender, it was seduction—and he was completely and utterly seduced. His anger, his fear and frustration, his lust coalesced into a red haze of need that blinded him to all but her taste, her touch, her scent.

Her lips parted, letting him into her moist heat. His hands slid down her back to pull her hips tight against his hard, aching cock. He wanted her naked and under him on a soft bed, but he'd settle for anything he could get, even if it was only—

He jerked his head up. Bloody hell! Had he actually been thinking of throwing Jane's skirts up around her waist and taking her against the balustrade on Lord Easthaven's terrace with half the *ton* just steps away from them?

"What?" Jane looked disoriented by his abrupt movement. She also looked delightfully debauched. Her eyes were dreamy, out of focus; her mouth, soft; her lips, open; her breath came in little pants; her lovely bosom heaving slightly.

She blinked. Her gaze sharpened and she smiled, tugging on his neck and tilting her chin. "More."

The word, dark and feminine and tempting as sin, shot straight to his groin.

He forced himself to step back, breaking her hold. The night air was pleasant, but the inch his movement inserted between them felt as chill against his heated skin as an ice bath—which was precisely what he needed.

His voice sounded far harsher than he intended. "See? A ball can be a very dangerous affair."

The sting of her hand on his cheek actually felt good. It knocked a modicum of sense into his overheated, randy brain.

Chapter 11

"Lord Motton is taking a marked interest in you, Jane."

Jane stopped fidgeting with the bow on her bonnet and met her mother's beaming gaze in the mirror. Oh, dear. Mama was making wedding plans already. "He's just interested in art."

Mama snorted. "That's not what the gossips were saying at the ball last night. That's not what his aunts are saying—or my own eyes are telling me."

Jane looked back at her bow and fussed with it some more. "I'm sure he also wishes to escape his aunts."

"He could escape them just as easily—no, more easily—by retreating to White's."

Mama shouldn't get her hopes up. She hadn't been on the terrace last night when her darling daughter had left the imprint of her hand on the viscount's face.

"He is merely being a polite host." She glanced at her watch. How long had she been sitting at her dressing table? She never spent hours perfecting her appearance, yet here she was, obsessing over a bloody bow.

She was supposed to be downstairs. Lord Motton must be checking his own watch, wondering what was keeping her.

And what *was* keeping her? An acute case of cold feet. She squeezed her eyes closed, but opened them quickly. Better focus on this stupid bow. Her fingers were not normally so clumsy.

Fingers . . . dear God! How could she have been so stupid as to have slapped Lord Motton last night? True, the man had been an idiot—getting angry that she'd gone with Stephen to the refreshment room would be completely infuriating if it weren't so ridiculous. And then he'd taken outrageous liberties—but she'd just about begged him to do that. She hadn't struggled at all. Hell, she'd pulled his head down to her, hadn't she?

How *could* she have been so bold?

"He's being far more than a polite host," Mama said.

"He's being kind to his friends' sister then."

She should have been frightened. Edmund was far stronger than she—she'd felt that clearly when he'd put his hands on her shoulders. She'd been trapped, completely at his mercy.

But she hadn't been frightened. She knew he wouldn't hurt her. He might break her heart—*would* break her heart come the end of the Season, or sooner, when they solved Clarence's puzzle—but that was her fault. She wasn't guarding her heart carefully.

She made a face at herself in the mirror. Did she regret not being more careful? No. The pain, when it came, was just the price for all the pleasure she was learning now. And oh, his kisses were *so* full of pleasure. The feel of his lips on hers, his tongue deep in her mouth, his hard body pressed so tightly to hers . . .

Lord, she was going to spontaneously combust with embarrassment . . . or something else. *Why* had she slapped him—and hard, too? He'd had to stay on the terrace long after she'd left, waiting for the mark of her fingers on his cheek to fade.

And now she was going to visit this art gallery with him. Spend a number of hours in his company . . .

Even if he didn't hate her, he must be heartily wishing her at Jericho.

"Perhaps Lord Motton *is* merely being kind and polite, Jane," Mama said, "though I don't for a moment believe that. But why are you accompanying him? I almost fell over in a dead faint when you went to the Royal Academy. I've never known you to take an interest in art." She raised her brows significantly. "I've certainly never been able to make you do so."

"Um." She couldn't tell Mama the next piece of Clarence's sketch might be in the Harley Street gallery. If it weren't for that—

No, she wouldn't fool herself. Even if she and Edmund weren't searching for another piece of the sketch, she'd be eager to go on this excursion because it meant more time with him.

She glanced at the door—the *unlocked* door—connecting their rooms. She'd tossed and turned all night . . .

"I suppose I'm just not an . . . interesting enough companion, mmm?" Mama said.

Jane hunched a shoulder and avoided Mama's interested gaze in the mirror. She should hurry with her toilet just to escape Mama's chatter.

"What gallery are you visiting today, Jane?"

An easy enough question. "The one on Harley Street."

"What?" Mama's jaw dropped and her eyes looked ready to start from their sockets. She turned white as a ghost. Whatever was the matter?

Jane leapt up to grab her hands. "Mama! You look ready to swoon. Come, sit down."

Mama stumbled to take the chair Jane had just vacated. "Harley Street?" she said faintly. "Did you say Harley Street?"

"Yes. I don't see—" Good God! Mama couldn't be in Clarence's sketch, could she?

Impossible. Mama was completely devoted to Da and had been for the thirty-odd years they'd been married. And even if she hadn't been so devoted, she spent very little time in London. There must be something else behind her odd humor. What?

"You really shouldn't go to the Harley Street gallery, Jane. You wouldn't like it at all."

"Don't be silly, Mama." She didn't expect to like it— or, she expected to like it as much as she liked any art gallery. "Lord Motton has already made his plans. He said he even asked you the other day what the gallery's hours are."

"Yes, he might have, but I didn't think he meant to take *you* there."

Of course Mama would not think a handsome peer would be taking her plain-looking daughter anywhere. Jane straightened.

"I'm going, Mama," she said. She just hoped she didn't sound as nervous as she felt. "I daresay Lord Motton is impatiently waiting for me downstairs."

Mama dropped her head into her hands and moaned.

"I'll send Lily up to attend to you. I'm sure you'll feel much more the thing once you've had a bracing cup of tea and perhaps a nap."

"Ohh." Mama's hand darted out and grabbed Jane's wrist.

"What is it?"

"Tell Mr. Bollingbrook—he'll answer the door at the gallery, though you may have to wait for him to get there, since he'll likely be painting in the studio." Mama paused and took a deep breath. "Tell him you are my daughter. But I'm sure he'll recognize you. I did drag you there a few years ago, didn't I?"

"Yes, I—"

"Right. Tell Mr. Bollingbrook who you are. But as I say, he's sure to recognize you—he's got a painter's eye for detail, of course, and a good memory—and tell him that I said he must close the blue room." Mama finally met her eye. "You must remember that particularly— close the *blue* room. Do you have that?"

"Yes, of course, but—"

"Good. I'm off to lie down." Mama pushed herself to her feet. "Do have a pleasant visit. Just avoid the blue room. Believe me when I tell you you do not want to view that room."

"Yes, I—" She was talking to air. Mama had already left.

What the hell was in the blue room?

Motton tried to concentrate on his horses—there seemed to be an inordinate number of careless drivers on the roads today—but his attention kept wandering to the woman by his side. He couldn't decide what to say to her.

"Are you comfortable?" Not very scintillating, but Jane *was* squirming around in her seat.

"You asked me that before," she said.

He had, but she didn't need to point it out.

He pulled the horses up a little to avoid hitting a damn high-perch phaeton. The idiot driver had taken the turn from Brook Street with nary a glance in his direction.

"Eek!" Jane grabbed the side of the curricle and his arm. "Will you be careful?"

Bloody hell, that was just too much. "*I* wasn't the one being careless."

She threw him a quick look and then stared straight ahead again.

He felt his teeth set and his jaw tighten. Why did the woman have to be so damned prickly? He only wanted to keep her safe.

And he could start with keeping her safe from himself.

Damn. He forced himself to take a deep breath and relax his jaw. He knew he owed her an apology—had known it from the moment he'd dragged her onto Easthaven's terrace. He'd tossed and turned half the night composing the damn thing.

And the other half of the night he'd lain stiff as a board—and hard as a rock—harder than Pan's plaster penis, wondering if he could concoct some excuse to use the bloody connecting door.

"Miss Parker—"

"My lord—"

"Damn." What was the matter with Londoners today? Now a flower cart had toppled over. If his team wasn't so well trained—and if he wasn't such an excellent driver—they might have toppled over themselves.

"Well done, my lord," Jem said from his tiger's perch.

"Thank you, Jem." Was the woman next to him going to congratulate him on his handling of the ribbons? Of course not. "Are you all right, Miss Parker-Roth?"

"Barely. I almost ended up on the pavement that time."

He would not snap at her. She'd had a bit of a fright— as had he. Silence was the best policy. If he didn't say anything, he would have nothing to regret.

How was he going to impress upon her the need for caution? If she was right, they would find another part of the sketch at the Harley Street gallery and be that much closer to solving the puzzle—and perhaps discovering Satan's identity. Things could only get more dangerous.

He heard a sigh and glanced over at her.

She met his eyes and smiled briefly. "I'm sorry for being so snappish, my lord. I didn't sleep well last night."

Wonder of wonders—an apology of sorts! And now it was his turn. "I hope I wasn't the cause of your insomnia."

Bloody hell—she flushed. He *had* been keeping her awake. It was only fair, as she'd definitely been disturbing his slumber. He directed his gaze back over his horses' ears. "And I need to ask your forgiveness for my behavior last night on Lord Easthaven's terrace. It was unconscionable. I heartily regret it."

"You do?"

Damn, did she sound hurt? No, it must be his imagination. "Of course I do."

They traveled along in silence for a few moments. They were almost at Harley Street.

"Do you regret all of it?" she asked in a small voice.

"What?" He swiveled his gaze to stare at her. She was plucking at her skirt. She glanced up at him, and then went back to examining her dress.

"Do you regret all of your behavior last night, or is there some of it that you"—she cleared her throat—"don't regret?"

"Er . . ." What the hell was her point? He had a very bad feeling he was going to be in trouble no matter what he said. "I sincerely regret causing you discomfort."

"Oh. Well, that's all right, then. I didn't feel any discomfort"—she shrugged—"except after we got home and I couldn't get to sleep."

"Ah." He would have overshot Harley Street if Jem hadn't spoken up. He took the turn less skillfully than he liked. "You did slap me, you know. That gave me the distinct impression—both literally and figuratively—that you were unhappy with me."

"Oh. Yes. Well." She glanced at him again, a bright flush covering her cheeks. "I do apologize about that. I should not have resorted to violence, but you can be extremely infuriating. I do not like being taught a lesson in such a fashion."

"Taught a lesson?" He'd been teaching her a lesson? No. The lesson he'd most like to teach her required a locked door and a nice soft bed.

"You know—about being cautious."

"Ah, yes. Cautious." She should be far more cautious with him, but he wasn't about to say that. In fact, an insistent part of him would like to urge her to throw caution to the wind.

He shook his head in a largely vain attempt to dislodge his lust. He needed to focus on the subject at hand. This was the perfect opening to stress the danger of their situation—the danger that had nothing to do with soft beds. "You *do* need to be cautious, Jane. Things could get even more dangerous if we find"—he didn't want to mention their goal, even though he trusted Jem—"what you think we will."

"I'm sure we'll find it." She smiled and then looked off to the right. "Oh, see. There's the gallery."

Lord Motton pulled up and gave Jem the reins. Then he swung down and went to help Jane. As soon as her feet touched the pavement, she strode up to the gallery door and rapped soundly with the knocker. Nothing happened.

The viscount took the knocker from her and pounded harder on the door. They waited. "Your mother said the gallery was open today, but only a deaf man could not have heard my knock."

"Mama also said Mr. Bollingbrook might be in the studio painting. I'm sure he'll be here shortly."

Lord Motton huffed impatiently and clasped his hands behind his back. "I don't care for this exposed position."

"What?"

"We are standing here on the street for anyone to observe. It is not safe." He looked at his watch. "We'll give this Bollingbrook fellow a few more minutes and then we are leaving."

"Oh, for God's sake, will you—"

The door swung open. A hunchbacked bald man in a smock glared up at them. He had a long green streak across his forehead and a blue splotch on the side of his nose.

"What do you want?" he snarled. "Speak up. Paint's drying. I've got no time to waste."

"Mr. Bollingbrook?" Jane spoke quickly before Lord Motton could vent his obvious spleen.

"Aye. And who are you?"

"Sir—" The viscount looked as if steam were going to emerge from his ears. Jane stepped in front of him and raised her voice.

"Jane Parker-Roth, Cecilia Parker-Roth's daughter, and—"

"Oh." Mr. Bollingbrook nodded and stepped aside so they could enter. "Why the hell didn't you say so in the first place?"

"Now see here, sir—"

Mr. Bollingbrook was already walking away. "Close the door behind you," he said over his shoulder. "And you can let yourselves out when you're done."

Jane made the mistake of looking up at Lord Motton. His expression was an interesting mix of anger and stupefaction. She slapped her hand over her mouth, but couldn't muffle her giggle completely.

He looked down at her and joined her laughter. "That man is very odd."

Jane shrugged. "He's an artist."

Lord Motton pulled the door firmly shut and took her arm. "Your mother is not odd."

"She can be when she's deep in the midst of creating." Jane let Lord Motton direct her into the first room, which was painted a muted yellow. This gallery had originally been a town house, so, unlike the Royal Academy, the paintings here were hung in a series of regular-sized rooms. She glanced around. No Pan. Damn.

"Life at the Priory is very interesting when Mama has a new painting and Da is in the middle of writing a sonnet," she said. "Poor John. He often had to act as father and mother for the younger ones, because Mama and Da were off communing with their muses."

They strolled past a painting of a bored-looking child with a large, ugly dog.

"John has always struck me as very serious," Motton said. "Perhaps it's his nature to take charge."

"Perhaps. Or perhaps he had to become serious to deal with the chaos around him." Jane glanced up at Lord Motton. "Were you a serious child, my lord?"

"Yes, I suppose I was." There had been nothing to be lighthearted about in his youth.

"You don't have any brothers or sisters, do you?"

"No, nor any parents any longer." He forced himself to smile. "But plenty of aunts."

Jane smiled back at him. "Definitely plenty of aunts—but they don't live with you normally, do they?"

"No, thank God." He inspected a rather pedestrian depiction of a fruit bowl. "I would probably strangle them in short order if I had to spend more than a few weeks with them."

"But you love them."

It wasn't a question. And Jane was right—he did love his aunts, no matter how maddening they were. They—especially Winifred—had provided the occasional bright spots in his mostly grim upbringing.

They wandered into the next room, this one a light green. He did a quick survey. No Pan. Jane stopped to study a misty painting of the Thames.

What would it have been like to have been part of a large family like the Parker-Roths? To have numerous sisters and brothers and parents who liked their children and one another?

His parents had been completely disinterested in his existence. No, that wasn't strictly accurate. They definitely wanted him to keep existing, else they'd be put to the great inconvenience of getting another heir. But as long as he kept breathing, neither his father nor his mother had much cared what happened to him. His father was too busy whoring in London; his mother, too enamored of her pills and potions and other quackery.

He'd always wanted a brother, or even a sister, but he'd learned early on—it was probably one of the first lessons he'd learned—that there was no point in hoping for the impossible. No one got to choose his family.

He looked down at Jane, who was now frowning at a painting of a fat cherub and an emaciated hermit. He couldn't choose his birth family, but he could choose a wife and make a new family with her. With Jane?

The thought was seductive.

"I suppose we should hurry along, shouldn't we?" she said. "We aren't really here to admire the artwork."

"Shh." He glanced around. Fortunately there was no one else in sight. Still, the hard floors and walls would carry the sound. It was possible, though unlikely, someone else was in the gallery. "We don't want to raise anyone's suspicions," he murmured by her ear. Mmm. She smelled of lemon.

She raised her eyebrows and looked around the deserted room.

"Remember, it pays to be cautious." If he leaned just a little closer, he could brush her cheek with . . .

Cautious. He was supposed to be cautious—and alert. He took Jane's arm again and urged her into the next chamber.

She stopped on the threshold. "This is the blue room." Her voice sounded odd—almost shocked.

He looked at the walls. Yes, they were painted blue, but it was a pleasant enough shade. "What's the matter?"

"Mama told me to avoid the blue room. She was quite adamant about it."

"Oh?" He looked around again. It was just another room with paintings. No sculpture—no Pan.

"Yes." Jane walked into the room—she was apparently not the most obedient daughter. "Something about this room—oh, no!"

"Jane!" What the hell was the matter? Jane was staring—gaping, really—at a large painting. She turned bright red, then deathly white. Then she made a strangled sound and ran for the nearest exit. There were two closed doors—she jerked one open and disappeared through it.

"Jane!" He looked at the painting that had so disturbed her. Yes, it was of a naked man, but half the paintings in the gallery depicted the human figure in partial or total undress. Jane was not a prude—she'd certainly not reacted with such consternation when she'd encountered the Pan statues, and they were far more salacious than this.

He stepped closer and examined the work more carefully. This man looked to be older than most of the gallery subjects—in his late fifties, perhaps. He was reclining on a sofa, facing the viewer, one hand supporting his head, the other resting on his left knee. His legs were flopped open—and the artist did not believe in fig leaves.

Hmm. Motton focused on the face, since obviously he'd not be acquainted with any of the fellow's other body parts. The man did look oddly familiar. He'd swear they'd never met, but something about him . . . Was it the eyes? The shape of the face? The painting reminded him of—

Good God!

He looked—yes, the work was signed: C. Parker-Roth. This must be Jane's father.

Oh, damn. He'd best see how she was—if she wasn't already halfway home. He frowned. Surely she wouldn't have left without him? He strode toward the door, threw it open—and almost collided with Jane.

"It's a closet," she said.

"I see that. Are you all right?"

She nodded. "It was just a shock seeing Da that way. I mean, I've been in Mama's studio at home—though I usually do avoid it—so I probably saw that painting while she was working on it." Jane turned bright red. "Well, not *while* she was working on it, obviously—while Da was actually, er, posing. They lock the door then, thank God." She took a deep, shuddery breath. "I just wasn't expecting to see it in public, if you know what I mean."

"Yes, and your mother must have known, too, since she told you to stay out of this room. I do think she should have told you explicitly what the problem was though, so you weren't taken unawares."

"I suppose she should have, but Mama is oddly reticent about some things. She probably didn't want me to know the painting wasn't still tucked away in her studio." Jane shook her head. "I wonder if Da knows? Though perhaps he doesn't mind. Men are different from women, are they not?"

"Er, yes." He'd not care to have his cock on display for anyone and everyone to gawk at, but—he looked over Jane's shoulder. What was that in the shadows? Something white . . .

Jane straightened her bonnet and sighed. "I think I am ready to return home, if you don't mind. I must have misinterpreted Clarence's drawing, though I was so certain—"

"Jane."

"What? Are you going to let me out of this closet or not?" She felt very . . . she wasn't certain how she felt. Embarrassed. Annoyed. Confused. Would it have been better if she hadn't been with Lord Motton?

What was she going to say when she saw Mama—or Da?

"Look behind you, over by that ripped canvas."

She sighed. "Oh, very well." She turned and scanned the shadows. There was a stool, a ladder, a broom, a broken frame . . . ah, and there was the canvas and beside it, barely visible, something white, something that looked like a hard round knob, just like the head of— "Pan's penis!"

She lunged and grabbed the knob, pushing the old canvas out of the way. Pan grinned up at her. "I was right—he *is* here." She grasped his member with both hands and turned. This penis came off more easily than the one in Lord Palmerson's garden, probably because it hadn't stood out in the rain and the wind and the dirt for who knows how long. She reached down inside, slid out a folded paper, and held it up triumphantly. "Lo—"

Lord Motton clapped his hand over her mouth. "Shh. Listen."

She listened. Footsteps, coming toward them.

The viscount pulled the closet door shut. "Give me the paper."

She didn't want to give up her prize, but it was suddenly so dark, she was afraid she'd drop it. It was probably safer in his pocket. She felt for his hand—it truly was pitch black in the closet—and gave him the sketch. She heard rustling—he must be putting it in his pocket—and then his hand found hers again. He pulled her to the very back of the closet.

"Ow." She stubbed her toe on something hard. "How can you see where you're going?"

"*Will* you be quiet?" Lord Motton hissed in her ear. The words tickled; she had to swallow a giggle—and how she could even consider giggling in such a situation was a mystery. They might be discovered at any moment—and she did not care for enclosed, dark spaces in the slightest.

Apparently being enclosed with a large, warm man made the situation more bearable.

"I have excellent night vision." He was still whispering in her ear. She'd like his lips to move to her cheek and her lips and— "We'll hide as best we can behind the canvas and other debris. Hurry." He pulled her down with him.

"Ohh." She lost her balance, knocking something crashing to the floor and landing on top of Lord Motton.

"Oof." He flinched. His hand pushed her knee away; it had landed between his legs . . . high between his legs . . . maybe on a very sensitive spot.

"I'm so sorry." She tried to scramble off, but his arm came around her to clamp her against him.

"Be still." He shifted a little so his body now shielded hers from the door—she thought. She really couldn't see her hand in front of her face. "It's all right. You didn't hurt me."

He must be telling the truth or else he had superhuman

control. She'd never forget the time she'd accidentally hit Stephen in the crotch with a cricket ball. He'd fallen to the ground writhing in agony, unable to utter a word—but the look in his eye told her she'd best not be within sight when he recovered.

"Oh, er, I'm glad. I really am so sorry."

"Don't give it another thought."

"Are you certain you aren't hurt?"

"I'm fine."

She nodded and tried to quiet her breathing. "Do you think they heard the thing I knocked over?"

He actually chuckled! "Unless they're deaf, they did."

"Ohh, damn."

"Shh." He cupped her head and pressed it against his chest. How could he be so calm? His heart was beating slowly and steadily, as if he were sitting in the drawing room, while hers was trying to leap out of her body. It was a wonder the people in the gallery couldn't hear it, too.

Oh, God. What was going to happen when they opened the door and found her? How was she going to explain being sprawled on a closet floor, tangled up with Lord Motton like this? She'd—

The doorknob rattled. Oh, damn, oh, damn, oh, damn. She bit her lip to keep from making a sound. She must be still, like a statue. So still—

The door opened.

"I swear I heard something, Albert."

Her head jerked up. "That's—"

Lord Motton's mouth came down on hers, cutting off her words—and any desire to speak or think or worry about the fact that her mother was standing just a few feet away.

Chapter 12

"It was probably a rat." That was Bollingbrook's voice. Motton kept one ear cocked as he explored Jane's mouth. Kissing appeared to be the most efficient way to keep her quiet—as long as she didn't start moaning. He must guard against that. He truly would prefer Mrs. Parker-Roth not find them in this particular position.

"A rat! You have rats here?"

"This is London, Cecilia. Of course we have rats."

There was a scraping noise and some cursing. "Damn ladder."

"Well, you've something in the way." It sounded as if Jane's mother bent over. "What in the world is this?"

"Looks like a mammoth prick, don't it?" Mr. Bollingbrook sniggered. "I know you've seen one before—that's why you're here, ain't it? To cover up John's—"

"Yes, yes, but one doesn't usually have a disembodied penis rolling around the closet floor."

"It probably fell off Pan—maybe that was the noise we heard."

"Pan?"

"One of Clarence's randy gods. You remember when he made all those statues?"

"Of course. Cleopatra was sure he'd run mad."

"He stuck me with one—and I stuck it in this closet the moment the front door hit his arse. Here, give me that."

Bollingbrook must have flung the penis to the back of the closet; something hit Motton on the shoulder. He flinched. The damn thing was hard; he'd have quite a bruise. Thank God it hadn't hit him in the head.

There was more scraping and grunting.

"Do you want me to help you with that, Albert?"

"I can manage the blasted ladder. You have the sheet?"

"Yes, of course. And some wire. It will be a simple matter to hook the wire over the frame and cover the painting. I do it all the time at home."

"I'll bet you do."

More scraping and cursing. Motton broke the kiss. There was now enough light to see Jane's face clearly. "Shh," he breathed. "They've left the door open."

Jane nodded, and he turned slightly so he could look over his shoulder. Good. They were completely hidden.

"I tried to get here as quickly as I could once I discovered Jane was coming," Mrs. Parker-Roth was saying, "but I had the devil of a time getting a hackney. I was hoping I'd run into them in one of the other rooms. You're sure Jane and Lord Motton have not seen the painting already?"

"I have no bloody idea. I didn't follow them around like some damn stray dog. Here, steady the ladder, will you?"

"But where are they?"

"I don't know. Maybe they've already come and gone." Bollingbrook's voice sounded like it was coming from higher up; he must have climbed the ladder.

"I made a point of instructing Jane to tell you to close this room."

"Well, she didn't tell me. Here, hand me the sheet."

Motton heard the swish of cloth and a little fumbling sound. "All right. Now I have to move the ladder. I'm not going to risk breaking my head. Why the bloody hell did you have to make the painting life-sized?"

Mrs. Parker-Roth let that comment pass. "I *do* hope Jane didn't stray in here."

Bollingbrook grunted. "How long do you expect me to leave this drape up?"

"It would be safest if it stayed in place until we return to the Priory."

"You want me to cover a painting for the rest of the Season? Why even bother to leave the bloody thing hanging? Art was meant to be seen, Cecilia."

"Yes, but—"

"I know—I'll use it to raise money. Charge people a penny a peek, shall I? John would find that highly amusing."

"Oh, I know the situation is absurd, but how was I to guess Jane would suddenly take an interest in art?"

Bollingbrook chuckled. "More likely she's taken an interest in that buck who came here with her. She was gazing up at him like he was a bloody god."

Jane moaned; Motton pressed her face gently against his chest, muffling the sound. Had Jane really looked at him that way?

"It would be an excellent match," Mrs. Parker-Roth said. "I was beginning to lose hope Jane would find a suitable man. She can be rather critical, you know."

"Well, the specter of spinsterhood causes many a maiden to lower her sights."

"Lord Motton is a viscount, Albert. There's no lowering involved."

Bollingbrook snorted. "It wasn't the man's title your girl was making eyes at, Cecilia. The fellow has an

excellent set of shoulders and no need for false calves."
He chuckled. "No, I suspect she's as lusty a lass as you are."

"Albert! You have no way of knowing if I'm lusty or not."

"Heh. I've seen John's expression in this painting, haven't I?"

"Oh!"

Jane moaned again. Motton rubbed her back, but truthfully he was having a hard time not laughing.

"If you ever get lonely when you're in London, Cecilia, you may call on me."

"Albert Bollingbrook, you know I am completely faithful to John!"

"Yes, I know, more's the pity. He's a lucky man. Now, can I put this bloody ladder away and get back to my own painting?"

The voices came closer. Motton ducked in case they looked in his and Jane's direction.

"Yes, of course, Albert. I'm sorry to have disturbed you. Thank you very much for your help. You're sure you haven't seen Jane and Lord Motton in this part of the gallery?"

There was a scraping sound again as Bollingbrook put the ladder back. "I told you—I let them in and then I went back to work. I imagine they wandered through and went off to their next destination."

The door closed, cutting off further eavesdropping and plunging them back into darkness.

"We'd better wait here for a while until your mother has departed," Lord Motton murmured.

"Oh, yes." That would be truly horrid—to escape detection only to stroll out of hiding straight into her mother's arms. She closed her eyes—not that she could see anything with them open—and rested her head against Lord Motton's convenient chest. "Thank God they finally shut the door. When I heard Mama's voice, I thought I would die. My heart literally stood still."

She felt a chuckle rumble under her cheek. "That *was* a bit of a surprise."

"A surprise? It was more than a surprise—it was . . . it was . . ." She couldn't think of a word strong enough to convey what a complete and utter disaster it would have been—would be—to have Mama discover her hiding in a closet with Lord Motton. "How did you remain so calm?"

She felt him shrug. "What good would panicking have done?" He chuckled again. "Cursing or crying or bounding about in this enclosed space would have led to our certain discovery—besides not being very manly."

She chuckled, too. "True, but you seemed completely unconcerned."

"Oh, I wasn't that. Before I knew it was your mother, I was very concerned indeed."

"Why *before* you knew it was Mama? I would have thought Mama was the last person you'd want discovering us." Jane opened her eyes, lifting her head to look at him. Damn. She still couldn't see a thing. He was just a disembodied voice.

Well, obviously not disembodied. She rested her head back on his chest. But it was disconcerting not to be able to see his face—his eyes and his mouth.

Mmm, his mouth. Would he kiss her again? Could she encourage him to do so without being completely brazen?

She shifted slightly. Perhaps she shouldn't try to engage him in any more amorous activities. Her hip was starting to ache from lying on the hard floor, and she was getting a cramp in her neck. She shivered. It was cold, too.

"I was more concerned we'd be trapped here by Satan or one of his minions. Compared to that, your mother is not a threat at all." He rubbed the back of her neck right where the cramp was and pulled her closer. Mmm. He was so large and warm. "I might fear your father a bit, though. I don't suppose he'd care to find me with my arms around you."

Perhaps she could bear this position a little longer. His fingers felt so good—firm, but not too firm. "I can't imagine Da leaving the Priory for London."

"Surely he would if he thought some blackguard had injured his daughter?" Lord Motton sounded rather stern and disapproving. "He loves you, doesn't he?"

"Oh, yes." She had no doubt about Mama's or Da's love. Their attention, yes—she often doubted she had their attention—but their love? Never.

"Then I'm certain he'd ride ventre à terre to bring me to justice. He'd probably beat me to within an inch of my life before forcing me up the church aisle into parson's mousetrap."

Lord Motton sounded amused rather than appalled by that scenario.

"Er, perhaps." Da would be more likely to write a scathing sonnet, but perhaps she was wrong. Lord Motton *was* male; he should be more intimately familiar with the male mind.

"I think we've probably waited long enough," he said. "I'll wager your mother is gone and Bollingbrook is deep in the arms of his muse. Unless you think your mama might linger to look for you?"

"No, I imagine she's left."

"Then let's go. Jem should be back with the curricle." Lord Motton stood and helped her up. She clutched his hand.

"I can't see anything, it's so dark."

"Hold on to me. I won't let you stumble." He started to walk away, but she pulled him back.

"I mean I can't see *anything.* It's like I'm blind." She heard the panic in her voice and tried for a lighter tone. "I don't want to slip on Pan's—er."

"Don't worry. Bollingbrook flung that to the back of the closet."

"How do you know?"

"It hit me."

"Oh. Well, I still might trip on something else. There's a lot of . . . rummage in here."

"There is, isn't there? Here, give me your other hand." He took it and wrapped them both around his waist. "Just hold tight and follow me—step where I step. I won't let you fall."

"All right." She clutched him, his belly hard and flat under her fingers. She rested her cheek against his back as he picked their way safely to the door.

"Wait," he whispered, loosening her hold. He stepped out of the closet, partially closing the door.

She had to bite her cheeks to keep from panicking. At least he hadn't closed the door entirely. There was some light in the little room. She took a deep breath and let it out slowly.

In a moment, he opened the door wide. "Come on out. There's no one here."

"Thank God." She scooted out of the closet. "I must look like I've been dragged backward through a bramble bush."

Edmund grinned at her. "Oh, I wouldn't say that; however, you do look as though you've been cleaning out a very dusty cupboard."

"Oh, dear." She put her hand to her hair; it felt as if half her pins had come out. "I must be a complete mess."

"You could never be a mess, complete or otherwise."

The right corner of his mouth turned up in a half smile, and his eyes had an odd, smoky look. "But you *are* a bit dusty."

"I'm certain I am." Her skirts were covered with lint and cobwebs. She brushed off everything she could reach. "Can you see to my back, my lord?"

"My pleasure." He ran his hands over her shoulders, waist, and skirts, tracing her outline—especially her derrière—rather more closely than necessary.

"Ah, thank you."

"I'm not certain I got everything." He grinned wolfishly down at her.

"I'm sure it will do." She looked at him repressively. He was still grinning.

"Very well." He offered her his arm. "Shall we depart, or did you wish to examine more of the paintings?"

"No, thank you. I have seen more than enough."

"You don't wish to peek under that drape?" Mrs. Parker-Roth and Bollingbrook had done an excellent job of covering up Jane's naked father.

She glared at him. "*No.* Thank you." She strode out of the blue room without benefit of his guidance.

He caught up to her. "Your mother is to be commended for her dedication to your father."

"Why? What do you mean?"

He shrugged. "Not every woman would decline Bollingbrook's offer."

Jane stopped and wrinkled her nose. *"Bollingbrook?"*

"Ah, so you think your mother's answer might have been different if a different gentleman had been asking?" The thought disappointed him, though why it should was a mystery. Mrs. Parker-Roth was beyond the age where she could present her husband with a cuckoo. If she wished to amuse herself when she was away from home, that was her business. She came to London every year for the Season while her husband stayed home. They probably had an arrangement. At least they spent the rest of the year together, which was more than his parents had done.

"No, of course not. Mama would never—" Jane twisted up her face as if she'd bit into a lemon. "She'd never do that with anyone but Da. Don't be ridiculous."

"There's nothing ridiculous about it. You've been in Town long enough to know such things are quite common."

"Not with Mama. Not with Da." She frowned at him. "Er, I don't mean to pry, but . . . well, your aunts said something, but I didn't completely understand . . . ah, that is, I take it your parents did not have a happy marriage?"

He snorted. Not have a happy marriage? Hell, they hadn't really had a marriage at all. "My father had a string of London mistresses. My mother stayed in the country and spent her days in bed, but with medicines, not men."

"Is that why you don't have any brothers or sisters? Because your mother was ill?" Jane touched his arm gently, her eyes full of compassion.

Blast it! How stupid could she be? He shook off her hand and turned to stare at a pack of hounds tearing a fox to pieces. The painting suited his sudden mood perfectly.

"My mother's ills were all in her mind, Miss Parker-Roth. I don't have any siblings because my parents detested each other."

"No. They must have been in love in the beginning. Why else would they have married?"

He snorted again. She really was naïve. "They married because my mother's father found my mother naked in my father's bed at a house party."

"Oh." Jane flushed. "Then they were in lust."

"No, they were not. My mother wished to be a viscountess, and my grandfather wanted to get rid of the last of his six daughters. I'm sure he was delighted to trap a viscount, but I suspect he would have taken a chimney sweep."

"Couldn't your father have refused to marry your mother?" Miss Parker-Roth actually sounded angry on his father's behalf. Silly girl. "He should have stood up to them all. He was innocent."

"Not so innocent. My father was never one to decline an invitation. When my grandfather and half the house party opened the door to his bedchamber, the first thing they saw was his naked arse pumping—" What was the matter with him? There was no need to be crass. "Suffice it to say, there was no question that my parents needed to marry. Fortunately from my father's perspective, I arrived nine months later." He smiled without a touch of humor. "As long as I managed to keep breathing, dear Papa could disport himself as he wished in as many London bedrooms as he could gain entry to."

Jane was frowning at him. "How do you know any of this is true, my lord? The only ones who know with certainty are your parents, and surely they never said a word to you."

He brushed a strand of hair from her face. She was so sweet. He hadn't realized how innocent she was. "They said many words, my dear. Did I not say they hated each other? My father told me the tale each of the few times he saw me. Even when I was a child and far too young to understand his meaning, he recounted the story of my conception, always ending with the admonition to be careful not to die so he wouldn't be forced back into my mother's bed."

"That's terrible." She looked furious, her brows meeting in a fierce frown. "What a terrible way to treat you. Why didn't your mother stop him?"

"Why would she? She wanted him in her bed as little as he wanted to be there." He shrugged, vaguely surprised at how much the sordid memory still hurt. "I heard her side of the story as well, in graphic detail—and since I was forced to live with her until I escaped to school, I heard her story rather frequently. I came not to take her animosity personally. She didn't care for me, but then I think she didn't care for young boys—or males— in general."

Were those tears in Miss Parker-Roth's eyes? She had far too tender a heart—and he had no heart at all. "I'm sorry. You didn't ask for that."

"No, but . . ." She took out her handkerchief and blew her nose. "That's horrible."

He didn't want her pity. "I had it no worse than many children of the *ton*. Your family is unusual. I take it your parents' union was—is—a love match?" He offered her his arm, and they started walking again.

"Yes, indeed. Mama met Da at her come-out ball, and it was love at first sight. They are still very attached to each other." She flushed. "We all avoid Mama's studio when she's painting Da. She often gets, ah, distracted." She glanced up at him. "You saw the painting."

"Yes." He'd never met the senior Parker-Roth, but if his wife believed at all in realism, then Bollingbrook was right. Parker-Roth's painted expression bespoke a man well satisfied.

And had Bollingbrook been right about the other, too? *Had* Jane looked at him as if he were a god? He hoped so.

Many women admired his title and pocketbook, and many found him physically attractive, but he'd never had a woman care about *him*. Did Jane? Once they solved

Clarence's puzzle and were free of Satan, he intended to find out.

They reached the gallery's front door and came upon Mr. Bollingbrook standing in the entryway, straightening a painting. His eyebrows shot up.

"Where have you two been?"

"Observing the art." Motton kept his voice level, but he'd wager Jane looked extremely guilty. He could tell by Bollingbrook's expression he'd win his wager. She really would make a terrible spy.

"I see." Bollingbrook smiled in far too knowing a manner.

Damn it, there was no way he could challenge the man without wading deeper into the quicksand of speculation. "We enjoyed our tour—"

"I'll bet you did."

"But, sadly, we must leave." The sooner, the better.

Bollingbrook nodded and looked at Jane. "Your mother was here."

"Oh?" Jane cleared her throat. "Indeed? I'm sorry we, er, missed her."

"One wonders how you did. The gallery is not that large."

Poor Jane was being led to slaughter.

"It is odd, isn't it?" Motton said. "But there you have it. Don't know how it happened. Thank you again for your hospitality." He took Jane's arm and dragged her out the door.

"Do come again," Bollingbrook said as he waved good-bye.

Lord Motton helped Jane into his curricle and took the reins. He started the horses down Harley Street toward Mayfair.

"Thank you." Jane sighed. "I had no idea what to say to Mr. Bollingbrook."

"Then don't say anything. I learned early on that silence is often the best response. Make your interrogator work for an answer."

"That is very wise." But so hard to do—at least for her. John, Stephen, and Nicholas had no trouble playing mumchance, and even her sisters could be mute as fish if doing so would save them from Mama's wrath, but she always let the cat out of the bag. Stephen would never let her in on any of his most exciting adventures, because he said Mama was sure to get every last detail from her. It was most annoying.

Lord Motton had let a bit of the cat out of the bag just now. Poor man—how could he have borne growing up with such heartless parents? Anger coiled tight in her gut. If they weren't dead already, she would cheerfully strangle them. They might hate each other, but how could they have taken their spleen out on a defenseless little boy?

Jane gripped the side of the curricle tightly and glanced at Lord Motton. He kept his eyes on traffic. A good thing. Carriages crowded Harley Street as they made their way down to Cavendish Square, and masses of people traversed the walkways. There were so many more people in London than the country, and so much more noise.

She sucked in her breath as another curricle cut them off, almost clipping their wheels. The grays faltered, tossing their heads, but Edmund kept his hands steady and settled them down quickly. "Well done, my lord."

He smiled briefly. "Traffic seems worse than usual. Anything happening in Town today, Jem?"

"No, my lord."

They turned down Henrietta to New Cavendish Street

and then to Oxford Street. More carriages and carts and
riders pressed around them, but Lord Motton looked as
calm as if he were driving his pair down a deserted country road.

They had just passed Park Street when disaster struck.

"My lord! Watch on yer left."

"I see it, Jem."

A woman had spilled her cart of vegetables. Turnips
and potatoes bounced and rolled everywhere. Traffic
ahead of them slowed; people shouted; the woman threw
choice epithets right and left. Lord Motton reined in and
glanced over at Jane. "Unfortunately, it looks like—"

Two large, mangy dogs darted out of an alley, barking
and snarling. They went right for Lord Motton's team.
The horses, already spooked by the screaming people and
vagrant vegetables, bolted.

"Hang on," Lord Motton shouted.

Jane was too terrified to make a sound. She clutched
the side of the curricle as tightly as she could, but with
every bump, she flew up out of her seat. She watched the
horses' hooves squash a turnip. If she didn't keep her place
in the curricle, she would be under those hooves or the
hooves of one of the other horses on the crowded street.

She squeezed her eyes shut as they shot between a
phaeton and a hackney. Dear God, how had they missed
hitting them? She glanced back to see both drivers shouting at them and making very rude gestures.

It was a testament to Lord Motton's consummate skill
with the ribbons that they made it down Oxford Street at
breakneck speed without crashing. When they got to
Hyde Park, he urged his team through Cumberland Gate
and down the gravel carriage way.

The dogs had stopped chasing them, but the horses still

refused to slow. "Hang on," Lord Motton said again. "They'll tire soon. I'll get them to—blast!"

"What?" Jane looked ahead. "Oh."

Old Mrs. Hornsley and her poodle were coming toward them, taking the air in Mrs. Hornsley's ancient barouche. Mrs. Hornsley's coachman was older than she, stone deaf, and more than half blind. He drove sedately down the middle of the road.

Lord Motton did the only thing he could—he swung his team onto the grass. They thundered up a small rise, brushed past some bushes, and—thankfully—started to slow. Jane let out a long sigh of relief and relaxed her death grip on the curricle. A mistake.

The wheel on her side of the carriage hit something hard; she heard an ominous crack and her seat shifted abruptly. She flew into the air.

"Ah, oh, eee!"

"Jane!"

She heard Lord Motton shout her name just before she landed face-first in an overgrown bush.

Chapter 13

"Jane! Jane, are you all right?"

"Mmpft!" Thank God it wasn't windy or she'd be completely mortified. Her skirts hadn't flown up with her fall, had they? At least they were covering her lower half at the moment, but if an errant gust of wind caught her hem . . .

She struggled fiercely to right herself, but only succeeded in sinking down deeper in the damn bush's leafy embrace.

"Stop wiggling. I've got you." A strong arm wrapped itself around her waist and lifted, pulling her free of her prickly prison. "Are you all right?" Lord Motton set her on her feet and plucked a twig from her hair.

"Mmph." She removed a leaf from her mouth and rescued her bonnet from where it dangled on the back of her neck. "Yes. I think."

He held her by her shoulders and looked her up and down, a worried crease between his brows. "You look a mess."

"Thank you. You're not too natty yourself, you know." Though he must look far better than she. He'd lost his hat somewhere in their mad dash and one coat sleeve had parted from his shoulder, but other than that he looked remarkably unscathed. "Weston will be dancing a jig of delight at the tailoring bill you're going to be running up. That's the second coat you've ruined in as many days."

He shrugged. "It doesn't matter." He pulled out his handkerchief and dabbed at her cheek. "You've scratches all over your face. Are you certain you're all right?"

"Besides the fact that apparently my visage will be giving small children and the fastidious members of the *ton* nightmares, yes, I really am fine."

"My lord." Jem came up then, looking a bit worse for wear as well. He had a big scrape on his cheekbone and his livery would definitely need to be replaced. "Mrs. Hornsley sends word that she is very sorry for the trouble and would be happy to convey ye and the lady to yer destination."

Lord Motton ran his hand through his hair. "That would certainly help—I'd like to get Miss Parker-Roth home as soon as possible—but I don't wish to leave you alone with the wrecked curricle and the horses."

"I'll be fine, my lord. Ye can send help when ye get back to Motton House."

Edmund raised his eyebrows. "Given Mrs. Hornsley's equipage and coachman, that could take hours, you know."

Jem snorted. "Aye, I know."

"I can go by myself." Jane wasn't eager to leave Lord Motton—she still felt quite wobbly and his presence was very sustaining—but surely she could manage to sit in a barouche, especially Mrs. Hornsley's, without the viscount at her side and proceed at a snail's pace the few blocks to Motton House. "You stay and sort things out here, my lord."

"Begging yer pardon, ma'am," Jem said, "but I don't think that's a good notion." The man gave Lord Motton what was obviously a Significant Look.

The viscount hesitated a moment and then nodded. "I believe Jem has the right of it, Miss Parker-Roth. It would be wisest for me to accompany you. It can't take that long to—"

"Aye, it can."

Lord Motton and Jane both looked to see where the child's voice had come from. A young lad in livery stood patting one of Lord Motton's horses. He grinned at them. "Them old nags can't go above a walk—a slow walk. Not like these sweet goers."

"And this would be . . . ?" Lord Motton raised his eyebrows and looked at Jem.

"Mrs. Hornsley's page. She sent him to convey her apologies."

"Hmm. Do you think she would lend him to us for a little while?"

"I imagine she would." Jem turned. "Here, boy, Lord Motton wishes to speak to ye."

"Yes, my lord?" The boy gave the horse one last pat and wandered over—reluctantly, if one judged by the number of longing looks he gave the viscount's horses.

Lord Motton smiled at him when he finally had the boy's attention. "What's your name, lad?"

"Luke, my lord."

"Well, Luke, I have need of a quick, smart boy. Do you think you can help me?"

Luke threw back his shoulders and stood as tall as he could, which wasn't very tall. He must have been all of eight years old. "Yes, my lord. Mrs. Argle—that's Mrs. Hornsley's housekeeper—says I'm smart as a whip, and even Mrs. Hornsley says I can run like the wind."

"Splendid. Do you think Mrs. Hornsley will lend you to me just for the time it will take you to run to Motton House and deliver a message?"

"I expect so." He grinned, showing the big gap between his two front teeth. "She'll have ye instead, won't she?"

"Precisely. We'll make it a trade of sorts then. The message is simple—just tell Mr. Williams, my butler, that there's been an accident and he should send someone to help Jem with the horses."

"Right." The boy started to run off.

"Wait!" Jane couldn't believe that was all the message Lord Motton had given the boy. It was just like a man not to think of the truly important things.

"Yes, ma'am?"

"And be certain to tell Mr. Williams that the viscount and Miss Parker-Roth are fine and will be home shortly."

Luke snorted. "Begging yer pardon, ma'am, but if yer riding with Mrs. Hornsley, ye won't be anywhere shortly."

"Oh."

Lord Motton chuckled. "Too true, so tell Mr. Williams we are on our way. And you may wait for us there, Luke, in the kitchen. I imagine Cook can find something for a hungry boy to eat."

Luke's grin spread from ear to ear. "Yes, my lord, I 'spect so." With that, he took off across the grass at an impressive pace.

Lord Motton laughed. "I wager young Master Luke wants to increase the amount of time he has to enjoy Cook's handiwork."

Jane frowned. "Do you think Mrs. Hornsley doesn't feed him?" The boy had looked perfectly fit, but appearances could be deceiving. Mrs. Hornsley was quite elderly; perhaps she wasn't aware of a young boy's needs.

"I imagine she or the estimable Mrs. Argle is quite aware of how much a boy his age can eat. Have you forgotten what enthusiastic trenchermen your brothers were when they were young?"

She laughed. "Yes, you are right—and they can still eat me under the table; especially Nicholas, who is only twenty. Now that they are so much bigger than I am, I don't think it remarkable, but when just they were boys . . . I did wonder where they managed to put all the food they stuffed in their gullets. They never gained an ounce, of course."

"Of course." He looked over at Jem. "Will you be all right? I don't like leaving you alone."

Jane frowned. Why did Lord Motton sound so concerned? They were standing in Hyde Park in the middle of the day. Surely he didn't expect brigands or highwaymen or some other nefarious individuals to accost Jem? Why would they? They might make off with the horses, but Jem was a servant. He had nothing of his own to tempt them.

"I'll be fine, my lord." Jem shrugged. "Should anything odd happen, well, I'll not play the hero."

Good heavens, did Jem also think there was danger here? What was the matter with them both? Perhaps they'd gotten their heads knocked when the carriage had crashed. She examined them more carefully. They both looked unharmed.

"Good." Lord Motton clapped Jem on the back. "I know I can rely on you. Miss Parker-Roth?" He offered her his arm. "Shall we go?"

They walked down the lawn. "You don't believe what just happened was an accident, do you?"

Lord Motton gave her a long, considered look and then shook his head. "No, I don't believe it was an accident."

"Why?" Jane heard the strident note in her voice and took a deep breath to try again, more calmly this time. "Bad things happen, my lord. It is regrettable, but true. You can't be seeing bogeymen behind every bush." She shrugged. "It's a wonder, with all the noise and hubbub of London, that more horses don't bolt."

"A London horse grows immune to noisy crowds and large, unpredictable mobs, Miss Parker-Roth. My team is very well behaved under normal circumstances."

Oh, dear. She certainly hadn't meant to insult his horses or his handling of them. "But what about that up-ended vegetable cart? Or those dogs? You can't say it's a regular occurrence for horses to have to dash through wayward vegetables pursued by vicious animals."

"No, indeed. It's very unusual"—he looked ahead to where Mrs. Hornsley awaited them in her barouche—"but not unusual enough to raise suspicions."

She let out a short, impatient breath. "Now what do you mean by that mysterious remark?"

He looked back at her. "It's not mysterious at all. If we'd been injured or even killed just now, everyone would have thought the accident merely a tragic sequence of events—a twist of fate—bad luck. No one would have suspected it was planned—the vegetable woman placed just so, the dogs let go at precisely the right moment."

"Don't be absurd. How could that all have been planned?" She shook her head and tried to shake off the chill Lord Motton's words sent skittering down her spine. He must be wrong, because if he was right . . . how could someone have that much power and be capable of such careful, evil plotting?

"Satan has his fingers everywhere, Miss Parker-Roth. He has eyes and ears at every street corner and every social gathering, be it in Seven Dials or Mayfair. I think it's clear he wants us to stop looking for the pieces to Clarence's puzzle." His face hardened. "Or he wants us to stop, period. I assure you he would not have shed a tear if we hadn't survived our little adventure just now."

Jane kept herself—just barely—from looking over her shoulder. Soon she'd be imagining the trees and bushes had eyes. Lord Motton was wrong—he had to be. "I still think you are jousting at shadows."

He stopped, so she had to stop as well. "Do not take this lightly. I've dealt with Satan's handiwork for years. He is very clever and very dangerous. I'd wager he was behind all the problems we encountered going to and from the gallery—the reckless drivers, the toppled carts, our final crash—as well as the near collision with the dandy-horse yesterday."

"Oh." What was she supposed to say to that? Panic was settling into her chest. The viscount must be wrong. This was London, not the wilds of America. Certainly there was crime, but not such organized lawlessness. But he looked so dead serious. She glanced away—and saw Mrs. Hornsley waving from the barouche.

"I think Mrs. Hornsley is becoming impatient, my lord."

"What? Ah, I see." He waved back. "We should not keep her waiting."

"Yes, I would prefer not to walk back to Motton House."

Lord Motton snorted. "You might arrive sooner if you did, and with less aggravation."

"What? You don't find Mrs. Hornsley congenial company?"

Lord Motton gave her a look and paused just out of the woman's hearing. "I'm serious about the danger, Miss Parker-Roth. Do not take the risk lightly."

"I don't suppose I'll be able to, with you throwing the long shadow of doom over me."

"Lord Motton, Miss Parker-Roth, do come along," Mrs. Hornsley called. "Lady Snuggles wants her tea."

"Her tea?"

Jane choked back a giggle. "Mrs. Hornsley drinks the tea; the dog eats the cakes—off the good china."

"Good God." Lord Motton smiled at the elderly woman when they reached the carriage. "Good afternoon, Mrs. Hornsley."

"Good afternoon, my lord." Dear heavens, the woman was batting her eyelashes at the viscount. "I hope you don't mind letting yourself in. Usually my page would do the honor"—she frowned—"but he's gone missing."

"I'm afraid we borrowed him, ma'am. I needed a good, quick lad to take the message to Motton House that my tiger needs help with my horses. I hope you don't mind terribly." He gave her a blinding smile and opened the door to the carriage, folding down the stairs and helping Jane in. "I offer myself as his replacement until you can collect him at my home."

"Oh, well, I suppose we can make due." Mrs. Hornsley fluttered her eyelashes so furiously, Jane was sure she felt a breeze. "What do you think, Snuggy?"

Lady Snuggles barked what Jane assumed was her agreement as the viscount vaulted into the barouche and shut the door. The carriage lurched into motion.

"You know, my lord, you were driving far too quickly just now." Mrs. Hornsley tapped Lord Motton playfully with her fan. "You gave my poor coachman quite the start."

"My abject apologies, Lady Hornsley. I certainly did not mean to startle anyone."

Mrs. Hornsley shook her head, setting the assortment of plumes in her rather garish bonnet swaying. It looked as if she were hosting an ostrich soiree on her head. It was a very good thing the woman had a dog and not a cat, Jane thought, or she'd have a feline amongst the feathers. And few cats would let themselves be forced into the ridiculous outfit Lady Snuggles was wearing—a pistachio coat and tiny bonnet to match her mistress's.

"You young men, always showing off with your fast carriages!" Mrs. Hornsley tittered. "Why, even my dear departed husband was known to 'spring 'em' on occasion."

Mrs. Hornsley was fond of attributing all sorts of interesting behavior to her deceased spouse, and since the man had shuffled off this mortal coil close to fifty years earlier, few members of the *ton* could dispute her. Frankly, more than one person doubted the gentleman had ever existed.

"Lord Motton did not intentionally drive so recklessly, Mrs. Hornsley," Jane said. "His team was chased by two large, vicious dogs."

"Really?" Mrs. Hornsley blinked at her, smiled vaguely, and then returned her attention to the viscount. "Your valet will not be very pleased with you, sir." She tapped him again with her fan. "Your coat is much the worse for wear."

"Yes, well, my curricle did end up in pieces."

"Oh, you poor thing. Mr. Hornsley was so unhappy if one of his carriages got even the smallest scratch. You must be in a terrible fit of the dismals." She patted him on his knee. "How can we cheer up Lord Motton, Snuggy?"

Well! Jane glanced at Edmund; he was being remarkably stoic about Mrs. Hornsley's attentions, though she thought he did look slightly nauseated. She might have been a seat cushion for all the notice Mrs. Hornsley paid her.

She turned to Lady Snuggles. The stupid poodle pulled back her lips, showed her teeth, and then turned away, giving Jane the cold shoulder like her mistress.

All right. She could take a hint. She would observe the people passing on the walkway. The damn carriage was moving so slowly, she could have a conversation with any one of them if she so desired.

Hmm. That man with the large nose. Hadn't she seen him outside the gallery today? And the fellow with the hideous waistcoat . . . wasn't he the driver of that high-perch phaeton that had almost hit them pulling out of Brook Street? She should ask Lord Motton.

She turned to get his attention, but he was too busy listening to Mrs. Hornsley. And when she turned back, the men were gone.

She was letting her imagination run away with her. The curricle crash had shaken her, that was all, and then Lord Motton had done his best to frighten her with his tales of Satan. She would have a nice bracing cup of tea when she got back to Motton House and all would be well.

"Here we are. So nice to have had the chance to visit with you, my lord." Mrs. Hornsley waved her fan in front of her face instead of using it to hit Lord Motton as the barouche rocked to a stop. "Quite takes me back to my salad days, having a handsome young man to converse with."

"It was a pleasure, ma'am." Lord Motton let himself out of the carriage and extended his hand to assist Jane. "Thank you again for conveying us home."

"You're quite welcome." Mrs. Hornsley shifted back and forth so Jane's departure wouldn't block her view of the viscount. "Any time—though of course I hope you don't find yourself in such a situation again."

Jane reached the pavement and turned to try to bid farewell to Mrs. Hornsley. "I add my thanks to Lord Motton's, ma'am."

Mrs. Hornsley smiled vaguely in her direction. "Yes, well . . ." She turned back to the viscount. "We will have to chat again, my lord. Oh, and Lady Snuggles wishes to say adieu as well." She picked up the poodle's paw and made the stupid dog wave.

Lord Motton nodded and took Jane's arm as Luke

came bounding out of Motton House. "Ah, and here is your valiant page. I hope Cook treated you well, Luke?"

"Aye, she did, my lord. Thankee." He hopped up on his perch, grinning.

"Good day, then." The viscount stepped back so the coachman could put the barouche in motion.

As the carriage pulled away, Lady Snuggles, her ridiculous bonnet askew, looked back over Mrs. Hornsley's shoulder. Jane couldn't resist. She wrinkled her nose and bared her teeth—and caused Lady Snuggles to so forget herself as to bark and lunge.

Lord Motton raised his eyebrows. "Wasn't that a little childish, Miss Parker-Roth?"

"Yes, it was, and I don't regret it. You probably didn't notice, but Mrs. Hornsley ignored me completely."

"Believe me, I noticed and thought you very fortunate. I'm sure I'll have a bruise on my knee from her blasted fan."

Someone cleared his throat and they looked over to see Williams standing in the open doorway.

"Yes, Williams? What is it?"

Mr. Williams stepped aside as Motton led Jane into the house. "My lord, the ladies are anxiously awaiting your and Miss Parker-Roth's arrival in the drawing room. They were quite distressed when the Young Person arrived to say there had been an Accident."

"Williams, I don't want to be fussed over by the aunts."

"They have been waiting most impatiently, my lord"—Williams looked at Jane—"as has Mrs. Parker-Roth."

"Then I imagine there's no escaping?"

"I think not, my lord."

The question was moot. The drawing room door flew open, and Aunt Winifred and Jane's mother came rushing toward them.

"What 'appened to you, matey?" Theo, perched as

usual on Winifred's shoulder, examined Motton from one eye and then the other.

"You look a complete mess," Aunt Winifred said.

"Are you all right?" Mrs. Parker-Roth looked worriedly from him to her daughter.

Aunt Winifred and Theo had given him the perfect excuse to avoid the aunts. "We had a slight accident with my curricle. We are both perfectly fine, but, as you can see, our raiment is in serious disrepair, certainly not appropriate for the drawing room. If you'll excuse us?"

"Absolutely not." Winifred stood solidly in front of the stairs.

"Jane, you have scratches on your face." Mrs. Parker-Roth stepped closer to her daughter. "Are you certain you're all right?"

"Yes, Mama. They are only scratches, truly."

"Brandy, that's wot they needs." Theo bobbed emphatically up and down. "Whisky. Blue ruin."

"How about a nice cup of tea," Aunt Winifred said, "and a few biscuits and cakes?"

"Biscuits?" Theo stretched to his full height. "Theo likes biscuits."

"And I'm sure Cook has plenty, though not as many as she had before Luke came by."

"You met Luke?" Motton asked. Why would the ladies have encountered Mrs. Hornsley's page? He should have gone straight to the kitchens.

"Indeed we did. Cecilia and I were going for a little stroll when we saw him run up."

"I see." Why the hell were Aunt Winifred and Mrs. Parker-Roth going out for a stroll together? Planning his wedding to Jane, no doubt.

"He was clearly a boy with an important errand," Mrs. Parker-Roth said. "So we helped him find Mr. Williams and deliver his message; then we sat with him in the kitchen while he recovered his energy."

"Cecilia was very good at drawing the boy out, you know."

"Well, Winifred, I do have six children." Mrs. Parker-Roth smiled. "Boys can be a little harder than girls to pry information from—I mean, to talk to—but if you go about it the right way, you can usually discover what you need to know."

Poor Luke. Motton had had no idea what a trial he'd sent the boy to. But perhaps the lad hadn't minded. He must have made serious inroads on Cook's sweets.

"Luke is quite a bright young boy, my lord," Mrs. Parker-Roth said. "I doubt his skills are fully utilized in the Hornsley household. An inquisitive lad can get into trouble if he's bored, you know."

Aunt Winifred nodded. "Indeed. Idle hands are the devil's workshop."

What did the ladies want him to do? Hire Luke away from Mrs. Hornsley? Given her behavior this afternoon, he was afraid the woman would be all too happy to discuss the issue. He'd be lucky if all that got bruised on his person was his knee. "I—"

"When are you going to bring those two in here?" Aunt Gertrude called from the drawing room door.

"Oh, that's right. The other aunts are waiting. Come along." Aunt Winifred gestured for him to follow her.

"We didn't mean to keep you standing in the entry, especially when you've had such a shock." Mrs. Parker-Roth put her arm around Jane. "Come in and be comfortable."

"I'm fine, Mama. I really would like to go up to my room, have a bath, and rest."

"First a cup of tea, dear."

Motton eyed the door to his study longingly as they passed it. He could reasonably take refuge there, pleading business—he certainly had letters from his estate manager to answer—but it would be cowardly to throw poor Miss Parker-Roth to the aunties. Cowardly and unwise. The aunts would politely tear her limb from limb, extracting every detail of their outing—including exactly what they were doing while Mrs. Parker-Roth was in the gallery—if he wasn't there to prevent it.

The aunts were almost sitting on the edge of their chairs when they entered the drawing room. Unfortunately, all the pets were elsewhere—he suspected that shortly he'd be eager for a lively distraction or two.

"Sit here, Miss Parker-Roth"—Aunt Winifred indicated a red striped chair in the center of the room—"and I'll get you some tea and a biscuit or two."

Mrs. Parker-Roth chose the seat closest to Jane. Aunt Winifred, after depositing Theo on the back of a vacant wing chair and getting Jane her tea, chose to share the settee with Aunt Gertrude—leaving the only unoccupied chair the one whose back was occupied by Theo.

"Do sit, Edmund." Aunt Winifred smiled at him. "I know you don't mind Theo."

"Thank you, Aunt, but I prefer to stand."

"You look like you should sit," Gertrude said. "You're a mess. What happened to your coat, for God's sake?"

"I'm surprised you're in the drawing room in all your dirt, sir." Aunt Louisa frowned at him. "It is not what I am used to."

"I'm quite aware of that. Miss Parker-Roth and I both wished to retire to our rooms and make ourselves more presentable, but we were advised that our presence was required here."

"And it is," Gertrude said. "Don't be silly, Louisa."

Louisa sniffed and sat back while Dorothea muffled a snigger. Gertrude shot them both a glare and then turned to Miss Parker-Roth, damn it. Gertrude knew she'd much better odds at getting information from Jane than from him. "Do tell us what happened, dear."

Surely Jane wouldn't do that? At the moment she was gripping her teacup and a biscuit, looking warily back at Aunt Gertrude.

Mrs. Parker-Roth leaned forward to touch Jane's knee. "I was worried, Jane. I stopped by the gallery to look for you. Mr. Bollingbrook said you'd been there. Where did you go?"

Damn. Jane flushed scarlet, looking guilty as hell, and stuffed the biscuit in her mouth.

All the feminine eyebrows in the room—except Jane's, of course—shot up, and all heads swiveled as one to stare at him.

"Yer in big trouble, matey."

Leave it to Theo to state the obvious. Of course, he *was* a parrot. Deep insight was not part of his makeup.

Mrs. Parker-Roth's brows snapped back down into a scowl; he had to squelch the involuntary urge to protect his privates. The woman would not attack him in his own home—or at least not with witnesses—would she?

Whom was he fooling? All these women would support Jane's mother. He stepped behind the vacant wing chair. Theo moved over to give him room.

Aunt Winifred was smirking, damn it.

"We went for a drive," he said. "It's such a fine day, it seemed a shame to spend it all inside." Thank God the weather was pleasant—he'd be hard-pressed to come up with another excuse.

Mrs. Parker-Roth's scowl relaxed slightly. She obviously suspected there was more to the story, but she was willing to accept his explanation for now. Her children may have sharpened her ability to detect verbal evasiveness, but he'd had years of practice perfecting his technique.

"But how did you lose control of your team?" Winifred asked. "Luke said you came tearing down the carriage-way at Mrs. Hornsley's barouche as if you were being chased by demons."

"We were." Jane had managed to swallow her biscuit and take a sip of tea. "Two vicious dogs attacked the carriage on Oxford Street. Lord Motton should be commended for his handling of his horses. We could have ended up . . . we might have . . . we almost . . ." Her tea cup rattled in her saucer and she put it down quickly on a side table. "If Lord Motton hadn't been so skilled, we might have crashed in the traffic on Oxford Street and been trampled."

Blast. Jane was now white as a sheet. She'd been so brave all day—hiding in the closet, riding in a runaway carriage, facing his aunts—of course it would all catch up to her eventually.

"Jane, dear, perhaps you would like a sip of brandy," Mrs. Parker-Roth said.

Brandy was all very well. He would like a glass of the stuff himself—hell, he'd like a bath of it—but what Jane needed was a little peace. He stepped over and touched her arm.

"Would you like to retire now, Miss Parker-Roth?"

She looked up at him—the poor girl appeared to be completely exhausted—and smiled. "Yes, thank you."

He helped her rise. "If you'll excuse us, ladies?"

"Huzzah!" Theo squawked as Edmund opened the door for Jane. "You show 'em, matey."

Chapter 14

"Is there anything more ye'll be needing tonight, Miss Jane?"

Jane could tell Lily's fingers were itching to braid her hair, but it was still a little damp. "No, Lily, thank you."

"Are ye *sure* ye don't want me to do yer hair?"

"Yes, I'm sure. I hate going to bed with it damp—it will dry better loose." Jane looked at herself in the dressing-table mirror. Most of her scratches had already faded; if the one on her forehead was still noticeable by tomorrow night, Lily could dress her hair in a slightly different style to cover it. And if she went out during the day, her bonnet would conceal the problem.

If she went out . . . She glanced at the door connecting her room to Lord Motton's. Hmm. Where would the next piece of Clarence's puzzle take her? There was no time to waste . . .

Lily frowned at her in the mirror. "Ye'll be a disaster in the morning if ye don't do something with yer hair now, ye know."

"I'll braid it myself when it's dry." Was Lord Motton in his room? Lily would know—but Jane couldn't ask. She didn't want Lily speculating as to why she was interested in the viscount's whereabouts.

Lily headed for the door, muttering "tangled mess" and "knotted past saving" and "scissors."

"Lily?"

The maid stopped with her hand on the doorknob. "Yes, miss?" Her face lit up—she must think Jane had reconsidered the braiding issue.

Jane hated to disappoint her, but she hated the notion of damp hair more. "Did everyone else go to Lord Fonsby's musical evening?"

Lily's face collapsed into a scowl. "Yes, miss, they did."

Ah. She bit her lip so she wouldn't grin. She could slip into Lord Motton's room while he was out and see if she could find the part of Clarence's sketch they'd discovered at the gallery today. She'd been too exhausted when they'd got home to discuss it with him. After they'd left the drawing room, she'd taken a nap. Then Mama had come up with a dinner tray and had tried to pry information out of her. She thought she'd managed moderately well—she hadn't told Mama anything incriminating and Mama had been somewhat appeased, at least enough to leave her in peace and let Lily help her with her bath. Now she was in her nightgown, ready for bed. But first she had a little poking around to do. She'd—

"The ladies, that is. Lord Motton stayed home."

Damn. "I suppose he must be tired from our adventures." He should be. He'd had the physical and mental strain of handling his runaway team. "He's gone to bed, has he?"

"Oh, nay. He only stopped in his room to change his coat after he saw ye to yer door. He's been too busy to rest. Had his dinner on a tray in his study, poor man. He's still there, I expect."

"Ah." She tried to sound properly sympathetic while her gut was doing the fandango. Hurrah! If she was quick about it—and stayed alert—she should be able to search the man's room. He'd put the sketch in the pocket of his coat, hadn't he? If she was lucky, he hadn't yet removed it. Or if he had, he hadn't had much time to hide it. "I hope he finishes his tasks"—*but not too quickly*—"and can get some rest." *When I'm finished looking around.*

"Aye." Lily nodded. "Ye know, yer mama thinks his lordship would be a good match for ye."

Oh, Lord. She did not need to listen to this, though how was she going to free herself? Lily had a determined, almost mulish, expression.

And she would *not* look at the door to Lord Motton's room. Lily would notice. But she didn't have all night to listen to a lecture. The clock was ticking. The viscount might come upstairs at any minute. "At this point, Mama thinks almost anyone in breeches is a good match for me."

Lily nodded. "And she's right."

"Lily! I am not that desperate."

"Well, ye should be. Yer not getting any younger. Each year yer just that much older than the new crop of girls."

"Those debutantes look like children. Reasonable men can't be interested in them." Though many men married those young girls each year.

Surely she hadn't appeared that young when she was seventeen? She examined her face in the mirror again. And she didn't look old now . . . did she?

"Year after next Juliana makes her come-out," Lily said.

"No, Juliana is only . . ." Good God, surely her little sister wasn't . . .

"Aye. She's fifteen. And Lucy, the baby, is thirteen. Are ye still going to be a spinster when Lucy comes to Town?"

Lily snorted. "Ye can chaperone Juliana and Lucy and save yer mama dragging herself to all the social events."

Damn. She did not want to sit with the chaperones. "Well, that's four years away. A lot can happen in four years."

"Not much has happened in the last eight, has it? Yer still as virginal as ye were when ye were seventeen. And if ye don't bestir yourself, ye'll die a virgin." With that pronouncement, Lily left, slamming the door behind her.

Well. There was nothing the matter with being a virgin. John would let her stay at the Priory once Mama and Da passed on. It was large enough she could stay out of John's way—and his wife's way, if he ever had a wife. Perhaps something interesting *would* happen at Lord Tynweith's house party.

Why couldn't Mama focus solely on John, at least until she got him into parson's mousetrap? She should want Jane to stay single, so Jane could be her companion in her old age.

Gaa! Jane wrinkled her nose at herself in the mirror. Da was Mama's companion, and she hoped that wouldn't change anytime soon. When—if—something happened to Da, she couldn't imagine Mama wanting her permanently underfoot. Nor did she want to be the spinster aunt to her siblings' children.

And did she want to be a virgin forever?

She might have said yes once. The mechanics of deflowering sounded painful and messy, and no gentleman had ever made her doubt that assessment—except Lord Motton. And their encounters in the last few days . . .

What was she thinking? She had a puzzle to solve, and, if she wasn't very alert, she'd wager Lord Motton would cut her out of the search in the misguided notion he should protect her from the danger he saw around every corner. She'd best get into his room and see if she could find that new piece of Clarence's sketch. She only hoped the man hadn't taken it downstairs with him.

She snuffed all her candles and cracked open the door to the viscount's bedroom. Then she held her breath and listened. It would be beyond embarrassing if she walked in on his valet.

She didn't hear a thing. Either the room was empty or Mr. Eldon moved as quietly as a ghost.

She would move as quietly as a ghost. She opened the door farther—thank God the viscount kept the hinges well-oiled—and slipped through.

She was in a dressing room area. There was a clothespress to her right, a wardrobe to her left, a small table, and a chair with Lord Motton's damaged coat thrown over it.

She pounced on the coat. Could this really be so easy? Mr. Eldon must be busy elsewhere, or ill—she wasn't questioning God's grace here—because surely otherwise he would have dealt with this ruined garment immediately. She didn't know him well, of course, but she couldn't imagine the viscount keeping a valet who was incompetent or inefficient.

She shook out the coat. It weighed down her hands. Mmm. It still held the viscount's scent—eau de cologne, linen, leather, and . . . man. Edmund. She closed her eyes and buried her face in it. She'd had her cheek pressed against this cloth all those minutes they'd been hiding from Mama and Mr. Bollingbrook in the gallery closet. She'd felt so secure then, so protected. It had been more than a physical sensation, though it had been very physical, too. Edmund had been so hard and big—she flushed. His body—*all* his body—was so much harder and bigger than hers.

He wasn't noticeably larger or stronger than John or

Stephen or Nicholas, but the sense of safety he gave her was so different. Her brothers would guard her from harm—at least, she thought they would—but . . . well, there was an . . . excitement with Edmund. Being pressed up against one of her brothers in a closet would have been very annoying. She would have been scrambling to put more space between them—and she surely wouldn't be sniffing their dirty old coats afterward.

And she should not be sniffing Lord Motton's. He could be on his way upstairs even now. She did not have an unlimited amount of time to find the newest part of Clarence's sketch.

She searched all the pockets quickly and then again, more carefully. Nothing. They were completely empty. Damn. The viscount must have taken the paper out and put it somewhere else. Where? Perhaps he'd hidden it amongst his socks.

There was something rather intimate about going through a man's clothes.

She looked in the wardrobe and clothespress, pushing breeches and coats aside, lifting socks and shirts, cravats and waistcoats and—she blushed and put that particular stack of clothing down. Nothing. Where else might he hide a scrap of paper quickly? He hadn't had much time. Lily had said he'd just taken off his coat and then had gone back downstairs.

She peered around the door to the bedchamber proper. Hmm. The desk was the most obvious place to look. Too obvious? Perhaps, but she'd start there and then move on to the drawers of his cabinets and the bedside table. She might get lucky. After all, he was in his own home. He had his men guarding the place. He must feel secure, maybe secure enough not to go to great lengths to hide something. The paper might even be lying on the desktop.

It wasn't. Jane slid into the desk chair. She shivered. This was where Edmund sat to write at least some of his correspondence—perhaps his private letters. Whom did he write to? He had no parents, no siblings. Did he have friends with whom he shared the events of his days, his thoughts? Did he perhaps keep a journal?

He didn't keep a terribly neat desk, though. The surface was gritty—he must have sanded a letter and not cleaned up properly afterward. She brushed the residue into a basket and opened a drawer. Paper. Could he have hidden the sketch here? She ruffled through the sheets—nothing. She opened another drawer—penknife, quills, sand, blotting paper, sealing wax, magnifying glass—nothing of interest here either.

She peered in every drawer, even the very small ones, and looked in every nook and cranny. She found a few balled-up bits of paper, some stray blobs of sealing wax, a broken stub of a pencil, and lots of dust.

There was no sign of a journal; no letters to answer; no bundle of missives saved to be reread. The desk was completely impersonal. Why even have a desk in your room if you were going to ignore it like this? The man must do all his correspondence in his study.

She sighed and got up. Perhaps he'd stuck the paper in one of the drawers of the cabinet in the corner. She looked there and in the pages of some books on a shelf. No scrap of paper. Where in the world had the man hidden it? Could he have just put it in the pocket of his new coat? She'd look in the drawer of his bedside table and then she would have to give up in defeat. Surely Lord Motton was planning to share the drawing with her anyway, wasn't he? He wouldn't really cut her out of the hunt.

She didn't believe that for a moment. If his silly male

brain thought keeping her in the dark would protect her, that's exactly what he would do.

She pulled open the drawer by his bed. It made a scraping sound . . .

Wait. Had that sound come from the drawer or from . . . ?

She whirled around. Damn! The doorknob on the door to the corridor was turning. In a second someone else would be in the room. She had to hide, but where?

The door was opening. Her time was up. She had only one choice.

She dove under Lord Motton's bed.

"My lord, you should have come up hours ago." That was Mr. Eldon's voice. Jane heard him sniff. "I regret to inform you that you . . . ahem . . . stink."

"I was hoping that might keep you and other people from interrupting me." Lord Motton's voice sounded muffled, almost as if he were taking off his shirt.

There was more commotion from the direction of the door. Then a procession of feet passed by her hiding place, stopping on the hearth. A copper slipper tub appeared with a dull thud and then there was the sound of water splashing.

"My lord, it is my duty—my pleasure—to serve you even when you smell like a pig."

"Oh, surely I'm not *that* ripe, Eldon," Lord Motton said as the footmen departed and he moved to the chair by the fire. "Though I suppose my feet might be. Help me off with my boots and then you can go to sweeter-smelling climes."

"Very funny, my lord." Mr. Eldon's hands appeared and grasped Lord Motton's right boot. They yanked it off and moved to the other. A heavy, musty smell wafted Jane's way. She pinched her nose closed. "Of course I will stay to assist you with your bath."

Lord Motton's fingers made short work of his stockings. "You will not. I can bathe myself, you know."

"I do not know. I'm sure your back was wrenched in the accident."

"Why the hell do you think that?" Lord Motton stood. He had blunt, strong-looking feet.

"It might have been. You should have come up right away and soaked it. I will have Cook prepare—"

Lord Motton's breeches dropped to cover his feet. He stepped out of them, and his hand swooped down to scoop them up. It sounded as if he threw them at Mr. Eldon.

"You'll get your sorry arse out of here, Eldon. I do not want you fussing around me like my old nurse."

"Now, my lord—"

"Now, Eldon, if you have this sudden desire to put your hands on my naked person, you can just walk out that door and keep going."

"My lord! Of course, I have no desire . . . that is not my intent at all . . . I merely wished to . . . how can you imagine—"

"Stubble it and just leave me be, all right?"

"Yes, my lord. Of course." Eldon's voice had just the perfect mix of subservience and wounded feelings as he gathered Motton's soiled clothes and shut the door behind him.

Damn. It wasn't his valet's fault he was so edgy. Motton stared at the closed corridor door and then glanced at the other—the door connecting his room with Jane's.

Was Jane already asleep? Should he peek in to see?

Not dressed— Ha! Exactly—as he was or, more to the point, wasn't.

He stretched. Faugh, he *did* stink.

He padded over to the tub and climbed in. Ah! It felt

wonderful. He slouched down, laying his head against the back of the tub, and let the wet heat loosen his muscles. He wasn't worried that he'd hurt his back this afternoon, but his body did feel tight—and not just due to fighting runaway horses. One particular body part was aching for an entirely different reason.

Jane.

What was he going to do about Jane? Satan obviously had him—and therefore her—in his sights.

Bloody hell, how could he keep her safe? Satan had his eyes and ears everywhere. At a minimum he should forbid her looking for the last piece of Clarence's puzzle.

He snorted, sending a small ripple spreading out across the tub. He could imagine her reaction. Jane would not care to be told "no."

He dunked his head and started lathering his hair.

It wasn't just Satan's interest he'd brought on her, though; it was society's as well. She'd managed to spend seven Seasons in London without getting her name on every gossip's tongue, and now? Their sudden and marked interest in each other had the old gabble-grinders flapping their lips fast enough to generate a small wind storm. The aunts had definitely noticed. They were probably mentally decorating the chapel at his country estate—unless they planned for him to marry in London.

And if society knew exactly what he and Jane had been doing . . . He must have compromised her several times over.

How *had* he overlooked her all these years? Well, he'd been in no hurry to marry—why would he want to repeat his parents' disaster?—so he hadn't been looking, at least not for a wife. And he couldn't very well look to John and Stephen's sister for dalliance.

But once this puzzle and the Satan problem were solved . . .

He dunked his head again to rinse the soap out. He surfaced, wiped the water from his eyes, and—Was that a cough?

He spun around, rapidly checking every corner of the room. Nothing. Was he starting at shadows now?

This was Motton House. He had men guarding all the entrances. It would be hard for anyone to sneak in here . . . hard, but not impossible.

He held his breath, listening.

Silence.

It must have been his imagination.

He rubbed the soap cake into a lather and scrubbed his arms.

He didn't usually have an overactive imagination, but he didn't usually have a female involved in his business. He'd always worked alone. But now . . .

He blew out a long breath and moved on to rub his feet and legs. It wasn't just having Jane involved that was putting him on edge; it was being near Jane. It was her scent and her figure; her smile, her eyes, her independent streak, the way she tasted . . .

Was she interested in him or was she only interested in Clarence's puzzle? Surely she wouldn't have let him kiss her—and she wouldn't have kissed him back—if she didn't care for him. Or maybe she was just curious . . . but if that was all it was, she'd best be careful. The aunts could be very determined when they'd got the bit between their teeth. And Jane's mama seemed inclined to fall in with them. If Jane didn't keep her wits about her, she was liable to find herself swept up the church aisle—and then into his bed.

His cock poked its head out of the water at that

thought. He would definitely like to have Jane hot and naked in his bed. Mmm. He'd been imagining that scene in exquisite detail these last two nights while she'd been sleeping soundly in the viscountess's room.

He put his head back against the tub and ran his soapy hand down his poor, aching cock. He'd start with her spread out on his sheets, on her back, her small sweet breasts with their delicate nipples crying for his touch, her legs open, her—

His hips bucked up, sending a small wave of water splashing over the sides of the tub. Damn, just one stroke of his hand and the image of Jane had almost caused him to spill his seed.

His cock throbbed, begging for release. If he ever did have Jane in his bed, he would have to go much more slowly. Women needed time, careful tending, whereas men—he, at this particular moment—could—

"A—Achoo."

Bloody hell. He was out of the tub in one motion, hunched over slightly as his cock struggled to resume more appropriate dimensions. That sneeze had come from under his bed. Who would have thought Satan would have one of his minions hide there? Was he waiting till he slept to slip out and kill him? And then go next door and kill Jane?

Ice filled his veins and the last wisps of lust cleared from his brain like hoarfrost in the sun. The creature under his bed would rue the day he was born.

He swiped his hand over his desk. The sand he'd left there to alert him to an intruder was not merely disturbed, it was gone. Had he a tidy villain? Odd, but he'd seen stranger things. His sword cane was still where he'd propped it, however. He jerked the sword free and directed its point toward the bed. "I know you're under there. Come out slowly."

Jane bit her lip. Damn it. If only she'd been able to muffle that sneeze. What was she going to do now? The glance she'd stolen of Edmund told her he was very angry—and very naked.

Watching him bathe had been shocking. And well, yes, she had inched over to the edge of the bed to get a better look. He was so lean, yet had such muscles in his upper arms and chest and such broad shoulders. And how could she have guessed he had a dusting of light brown hair over his chest, down his flat belly to . . .

She'd seen her brothers naked, of course, but when they'd been children, before they'd had muscles and hair and such an impressive . . . Mmm.

Edmund quite put Pan to shame.

She'd wanted to touch him. And when he'd had his hand around his shaft, she'd wanted it to be *her* hand.

The place between her legs felt swollen and damp. It ached for something—and she had a very good idea exactly what it ached for.

"Come out now." Edmund sounded very angry. She should move. He had a sword. He might do something drastic if she didn't show herself soon, but her nightgown was all tangled up.

"In a moment." She tugged on her gown.

"Good God!"

She swiveled her head around. His voice sounded very close . . .

It was. He'd squatted down and was now peering at her. "What are you doing under there, Jane?"

He had his sword on the floor, pointing in her direction. As she watched, something else of his rose to point at her.

Would his penis be hard like Pan's if she touched it?

She would find out. Edmund would think she was shameless—a complete light skirt—but Lily was right, she wasn't getting any younger. She did not want to die a virgin.

"I'm hiding." She'd wager her chances of persuading the man to relieve her of her virginity would increase if she were naked, too, but how could she free herself of her nightgown?

"Who are you hiding from?" His voice was hard, as if he were ready to skewer whoever was to blame. She smiled.

"You. I'm hiding from you." But she wasn't going to hide any longer. Oh, no. She was going to show him everything.

Was she being foolish? Perhaps. He might reject her, though she had little fear of that. Men were not too choosy when offered bed sport. Look at John. He went regularly to visit Mrs. Haddon in the village, and she bore a striking resemblance to a goat. An attractive, pleasant goat, but a goat nonetheless.

"Why?" He sounded quite taken aback. "Surely you aren't afraid of me?"

"No." She wasn't. He was much larger than she and much stronger, but she knew he would never hurt her. "I was merely startled. I didn't want to be found out. I'm not supposed to be in your room."

She was not worried she'd become enceinte. Women did not conceive every time they shared a bed with a man. It often took months of dedicated effort—and probably took some practice as well. Her womb must need to become accustomed to the procedure before it could produce a child. Edmund's parents had been the exception.

Her womb—and other nether organs—shivered at the

thought and produced more dampness. Her lower body was certainly in favor of seduction.

"That's true." His voice sharpened again. "Why are you here?"

And what of her mind—and her heart? Did it matter that she loved Edmund and he only lusted after her?

No.

"Jane, why are you here?"

She would rather he loved her, of course, but she was not going to wait for love or marriage. She could have been killed today. If she'd gone headfirst into a stone wall instead of a bush, or gone flying out of his curricle and under the horse hooves and carriage wheels on Oxford Street . . .

"I was . . . I wanted to, ah . . ." She could have died.

She started to shake.

"Are you stuck?"

"N—no." She bit her lip. She couldn't cry. Edmund would never take a weeping woman to bed. And she would look terrible, as well, with red eyes and a dripping nose. Not seductive at all.

He was down on his hands and knees now, sword shoved aside, squinting, obviously trying to see her in the dim light under the bed. "Are you crying?"

Thank God she was hidden in the shadows. She swiped at her nose with the back of her hand. "W—Why would I be crying?"

She took a deep breath. Better to concentrate on clothing removal. He was already perfectly dressed— undressed—but she . . . she would just have to slip the nightgown off when she got the opportunity. There was no way she could manage the feat underneath a bed.

"I don't know." He frowned—he was in the light; she could see him perfectly well. Oh, not perfectly. He was too scrunched down to be viewed in all his glory. "*Will* you come out of there? Carrying on a conversation like this is completely ridiculous. I've got my naked arse in the—damn."

He stood up. She watched his feet move away. Damn, indeed. He'd finally remembered he was naked.

She scooted out from under the bed. Yes, he'd gone back to the bathtub and was reaching for a towel. This was her opportunity. If she pulled off her nightgown now, when he wasn't looking, he couldn't deter her. It would be a fait accompli.

She grabbed her hem and pulled it up and over her head in one motion. Then she dropped the nightgown on the floor and kicked it under the bed.

She wouldn't have thought the thin cloth provided any warmth, but the sudden touch of cool air on her bare skin turned it to gooseflesh—and caused other things to pebble as well.

Should she try to cover her womanly bits with her fingers? That felt overly coy. But where *did* a naked woman put her hands? She had no skirts to hide them in, and placing them on her hips felt too bold.

She should not have removed her nightgown, but it was too late to rectify that. Edmund had picked up the towel now and was turning.

She clasped her hands together at her waist and smiled.

Chapter 15

Good God. The towel he'd just picked up slipped to the floor from his nerveless fingers. Miss Parker-Roth was standing by his bed stark naked.

Had he died in the curricle crash this afternoon? He must have, since he was now in heaven.

She was exquisite. Her lovely warm brown hair tumbled over her delicate shoulders, begging his fingers to comb through its silky length; her perfect small breasts made his palms itch to feel their soft weight. He wanted to run his hands over her graceful waist and flaring hips and part her beautiful milky thighs to find the treasure he knew was nestled in the thatch of curls there.

All the blood left his head and rushed to his cock. Damn. He grabbed the towel back off the floor and held it in front of him.

"Oh, don't be shy," Jane said. She giggled and held out her arms. "I'm not."

He heard the nerves in her voice, the mix of excitement, defiance, and fear, and his heart turned over.

She'd had a hard day, full of shocks and upheavals. She'd seen that damn painting of her father, hidden from her mother on the floor of a closet, and been thrown out of a runaway curricle. Finally, to add insult to injury, she'd had to endure Mrs. Hornsley, her mother, and his aunts. She must be worn to a thread. "You should go back to your own room, Jane."

"No." He watched the candlelight shimmer over her hair as she shook her head. "I don't want to."

He should insist. He should take her arm and escort her to her door.

If he took her arm at this moment, he would escort her to his bed.

At least he should put on a dressing gown or nightshirt or breeches or something to bring a little sanity back to his overheated brain, but all he could do was hold the damn towel in front of his cock and stare at Jane like a lust-crazed noddy.

"I don't want to go to my room, Edmund."

He knew it was mad, but he couldn't stop himself from asking. "Then what do you want, Jane?"

She wet her lips. "Y—you." Her voice shivered.

God. The word when straight to his cock. It jumped with eagerness to present itself to her.

He grasped the towel more tightly and tried to grasp his suddenly elusive self-control. She was tired. She was upset. She was not in any state to make life-altering decisions. He should put her in bed—her *own* bed. She was a virgin, for God's sake. She had no idea what she was asking for.

But he was not a virgin. He had a painfully detailed picture of exactly what she was requesting, and he would so like to give it to her, again and again, slow and gentle, soft and teasing, hard and fast, any and every way she'd like it.

She had—they both had—narrowly escaped death this afternoon. They should celebrate life in the most elemental way possible. Skin to skin, breath mingled with breath, his body deep in hers.

She was compromised past saving; they would have to marry. Did it matter so much if they anticipated their vows?

She was coming toward him. He could see fear and uncertainty in her eyes, but under that, determination.

"I could have died today, Edmund, and, if you are correct about Satan, I might die tomorrow."

He had not meant to give her that much fear. "I'll keep you safe, Jane. Satan won't hurt you."

She shook her head, ignoring his words. "I always thought I had the future, but this afternoon, when I was thrown from your curricle and had that sick, helpless moment of being tossed through the air, I realized I don't. The future is just a dream. Nothing but this very moment—this *now*—is real."

She was close enough to touch, but he kept his hands on the towel. He knew if he touched her, the faint voice of propriety, the whisper of his conscience, would be shouted down by far more urgent exhortations.

"I don't want my life to end before I've lived it. I don't want to die a virgin, Edmund." She put her hands on his shoulders; her fingers burned like a brand. Her breasts taunted him. They were so close.

"We'll have to marry." He waited for the heavy knot of dread to twist his gut. It didn't. The hot tide of lust washing through him must have drowned it, and his already weakened notions of propriety were sinking fast.

And it wasn't just lust he was feeling. There were other currents in the flood—protectiveness, tenderness, admiration. He'd never felt this way before.

Of course, he'd never felt as though his cock were literally going to explode, either.

"That's the future," Jane said. "I can't think about the

future." She started moving her hands from his shoulders down his arms.

He was having a damn hard time thinking about the future as well, or anything besides the soft slide of her touch over the muscles of his upper arms and her lovely naked breasts just inches in front of him. He drew in a deep breath, and the musky scent of her need wafted up from the hot place between her thighs . . .

Hell, his cock *was* going to explode. Her hands had slipped down his forearms, over his wrists to his fingers, which still clutched the towel.

"Please, Edmund? Will you please show me what I've been missing?"

"Ah." God! Her fingers bypassed the towel and wrapped around his cock, just like she'd wrapped them around Pan's prodigious member. He thought his eyes would roll back in his head and he'd pass out with pleasure. He dropped the towel and put his hands on her shoulders to steady himself.

Normally he took the lead in the bedroom. Hell, normally he paid for what he was getting, so his partner did what he wished when he wished as he wished. He had one specific goal; once that was achieved, he took his leave, forgetting the woman as soon as the door shut behind him—if not sooner. It was a physical and a financial transaction, nothing more. He'd never had a long-term mistress; he'd never wanted one. He didn't want to live a life anything like his father's.

But this was different, so different that he felt almost the virgin Jane was.

"You are hard like Pan," she murmured, "but soft, too, and warm."

Warm? Hot, more like. His temperature must have just shot up a hundred degrees with her words. Her hand moved, sliding up and down his length. Her touch was soft, tentative—teasing. He sucked in his breath.

"Do you like that?" He'd leaked a drop of fluid; she found it and spread it over his tip, slipping her finger around his sensitive skin.

"Y—yes." He couldn't manage more words—he could barely manage that one.

She stepped closer, cradling his aching cock against her belly. Her nipples teased his chest. He slid his hands from her shoulders to her back, but didn't pull her against him. Soon, but not yet. He'd let her keep the lead for a little while longer—she was going in so many interesting directions.

Her hands moved down to his arse while her mouth moved up his chest. She laved a nipple, then trailed her lips over his skin to his collarbone, his neck, his jaw. As she stretched, her body rubbed against his.

Sweat trickled down his back. Letting Jane do what she wished was torture—wonderful torture. Rational thought fled—lust clouded his poor brain.

He needed her as he needed food and water and air.

And then her lips reached his mouth and he couldn't hold back any longer. He pulled her tight against him, leaving no breath of a gap between them.

She was his now. They might not have spoken vows before a minister; they hadn't even made promises to each other—in words. But their bodies were promising everything.

This was not just the need to erase their brush with death; it was the need to affirm life. To begin a life together . . .

And a new life? A child?

Good God.

He expected a flood of dread, but felt only anticipation.

He *wanted* a child. A son—or a daughter—with Jane. He wanted a family, a future, with her.

That cleared the lust from his brain. He needed to slow down. Jane was a virgin, after all.

Damn. He'd never taken a virgin to bed.

He ended the kiss and lifted his head so he could see Jane's eyes. "Are you sure you want this?"

"Huh?" She looked so beautiful, her mouth soft and open, her gaze unfocused. Her tongue touched her lips; she blinked. "Y—yes."

His heart sank. "You don't sound sure." He relaxed his hold, and stepped back. The air on his damp body chilled him—or was it the disappointment? He couldn't take her to bed if she was uncertain.

Jane swallowed. Damn it, why did Edmund suddenly have to have an attack of scruples? She didn't want to think or talk—she just wanted to *do*. Yes, she was nervous; of course she was nervous—she'd never done this before—but that didn't mean she didn't want to do it. "I *am* sure. Very sure."

"No, you're not."

Oh, dear God, he was going to prose on and on and then convince himself to do the right—the noble—thing and return her to her room. She would never get to sleep if he did—she was *aching* for him. Desperate for whatever he would do to her. And she would never find the courage to do this again. How could she persuade him?

There had been that very odd part of Clarence's sketch. It had looked rather disgusting, but Clarence had drawn an extremely happy expression on the man's face. Perhaps Edmund would like it, too, and be moved to stop talking and proceed to his bed with all due haste.

She dropped to her knees and fastened her lips around his male member. The poor organ had shriveled to a limp shadow of its former self, but it perked up nicely the moment her lips touched it.

"Jane!"

Was he appalled? He sounded . . . she couldn't decide how he sounded. His fingers buried themselves in her hair, but he didn't pull her away.

If his morals were horrified, his body was not. She smiled and ran her tongue over the bit of him between her lips. She heard him suck in his breath. His hands clenched in her hair, and his hips flexed toward her. His penis grew even thicker. She leaned back slightly to admire its sturdy length. Another drop of moisture glistened on its tip. She licked it.

Edmund made an odd sound, a combination of sigh and moan and laugh. He tugged gently on her hair. He clearly wanted her to stop playing and stand up. She wasn't about to do so. "I'm not done." She licked him again and watched his organ almost jump in response. "I think you like it."

"Of course I like it. I like it so much my knees are about to give out."

"Really?" She could bring this strong man to his knees? She rather liked that thought. She licked him once more. What would happen if she took him in her mouth again and sucked? She would see . . .

He wasn't letting her. He held her head immobile and moved his hips back, taking her prize beyond her reach. "Enough," he said. "It's my turn."

She'd thought he *was* having his turn. Well, at least he wasn't trying to send her back to her room. This time when he tugged on her, she stood up. He pulled her against him, hugging her so tightly she could barely breathe. Then he stooped slightly, put an arm behind her legs, and scooped her up.

"Ack!" She threw her arms around his neck. She wasn't certain she cared for this new position. The floor looked much too far away. What if he dropped her? She wasn't large, but she wasn't light, either. Stephen had tried to pick her up once, and had made a great show of groaning and complaining before giving up. Of course, they had been children then . . .

Edmund's arms felt very strong, but she was used to standing on her own two feet. Giving her body into his complete control was distinctly unsettling . . . though that would be what happened anyway when he laid her in his bed.

No, she would have some control there. She'd just demonstrated that.

"Are you all right?" A slight frown formed a line between his brows. Oh, damn. She didn't want to get him thinking again.

"I'll be better when you put me down on your bed."

He grinned. "I couldn't agree more."

Thank God. Finally she would get what she wanted.

Was this all she wanted?

No. She wasn't going to think, either. She was just going to feel. She'd deal with tomorrow tomorrow. Life was too uncertain—and she was certain she didn't want to wait another moment to learn what Edmund could teach her.

He lowered her to the sheets; they were soft against her skin. His mattress was large and firm. Had generations of viscounts been conceived here?

She wouldn't think of the past either. The present was all she had; all she wanted.

Edmund followed her onto the bed, covering half her body with his. She felt the length of his erection heavy along the inside of her thigh. She was so damp, aching for him.

His mouth explored hers, his tongue stroking, soothing, promising mysterious delights, while his hand cupped her breast and his thumb rubbed back and forth, back and forth, teasing her nipple to a hard, tight peak. She arched up, but all she could do was press against him. His body was as unyielding as a stone wall, trapping her close to the mattress.

Did she feel trapped—or protected? Whichever, she did not want to escape.

His mouth left hers and trailed over her cheek to her jaw, while his fingers kept playing with her nipple.

"Ohh." She spread her legs farther apart. She was so hot, all of her, but especially there, between her legs.

"Do you like that, Jane?" His words tickled her ear.

"Mmm. Yes."

He chuckled. "Good. Perhaps you'll like this as well."

His lips moved to her collarbone and then down to her breasts. Wonderful—but his clever fingers had abandoned their play. She frowned. His mouth and hands teased, touching everything else. Her poor nipples pouted at the neglect, tightening into hard, aching points. She arched and moaned, but Edmund refused to take the hint. Could she thread her fingers through his hair and pull him to where she needed him? She was desperate enough to attempt it.

He laughed, sending a tiny current of air over her skin. "Patience, Jane. That's the way the game is played. The longer you wait, the more the need builds until finally it explodes." He drew a lazy circle around her nipple with his tongue, still not touching the point. She made a little sound—not quite a growl, not quite a whine. She felt his mouth pull into a smile against her breast.

"Skeptical, are you?" he said. He leaned over and finally flicked her nipple with his tongue.

She squeaked, jerking as a flash of exquisite sensation shot to the ache between her legs. Oh, my. And then he sucked the nipple into his mouth, and another bolt of liquid need surged through her. Her hips twisted on the bed. She required his attention *there.*

His hands gripped her, holding her still, as his mouth moved lower. The room's air chilled the wet nubs he'd left behind, but that was all right. That other part of her was demanding his attention—crying for it, if the growing dampness was any indication. But what would he—

Oh! Who would have thought it? She would never have imagined . . . His *mouth* was on her. His *tongue.* It touched one particular spot, flicked over it . . . She grabbed the sheets with both hands and arched her back.

Her world narrowed to that tiny point of flesh. Edmund had no pity—each slide of his tongue wound her tighter and tighter. She was going to fly off into a thousand pieces; she was—

She caught her breath, bit her lip. She was on the edge now. It—whatever *it* was—was almost here. She was going to . . . do something in just an instant . . .

Edmund's tongue touched her one last time.

"Ohh." Her hips jerked and then wave after wave of drenching pleasure swept through her.

Mmm. She felt satiated, every part of her body heavy and relaxed—boneless. Wonderful, but . . . she frowned. Something was missing. She looked up at Edmund. He appeared to be exceedingly pleased with himself, but also a little . . . tense.

Because he *was* tense, of course. He moved and she felt his erection brush against her leg. He was still very hard and thick—that didn't seem right. He'd given her release, but he hadn't taken it himself.

"We aren't finished." She ran her finger over his cheek; it was rough with the faint shadow of his beard. "You aren't finished."

He smiled, though the expression was definitely strained. "No. I'm not."

He *should* be finished, he thought. He should kiss her quickly and lift himself away from temptation. The bathwater was still in the room. It might be chilly enough to cool his ardor a little. But, dear God, he wanted to be inside her so badly he could taste it. He swallowed. All right—he could taste her. She was still sweet on his tongue, and her scent filled his every breath.

He would send her back to her room, and use his hand to ease his discomfort. Or he could show her how to give him release. She did not have to give up her virginity to save him pain. They could wait. They *should* wait.

He didn't want to wait. Jane was here in his bed—the bed where generations of Smyths had been conceived. She would be his wife before God and the law soon. He wanted—needed—to make her the wife of his body now.

He felt her hands running down his back, pulling him closer. She arched her hips and pressed her wet heat against his leg. "What are you waiting for?" She gave him a saucy smile. "A personal invitation? I thought I'd already extended that, but if you need another . . ." She shifted so she found his tip and rubbed herself against it. "Please, Edmund. Please come inside."

She didn't need to ask twice.

He kissed her, slow and deep—the last thing he was going to do slow for a while, though deep . . . yes, he would be as deep inside her as he could be. Mmm. And he would stay there, and give her his seed and, God willing, a child.

But first he had to get inside, and that would not be so pleasant for her. Best get it done as quickly as possible.

He thrust his hips forward.

"Ow!"

He held still and kissed her forehead. "I'm sorry. It will only hurt this first time."

She made a disgruntled little sound. "I suppose it didn't hurt you the first time you did it?"

"N—no. I don't believe it did."

"It's not fair. Men should have to experience the same trials women do."

"Um." He was not capable of an extended conversation at the moment. His mind was overwhelmed by his cock, by the exquisite sensation of being buried deep in Jane's lovely, tight, wet heat.

"We will have to do it again," she said, "so I can see what it is like without the pain."

"Um." His cock throbbed in agreement. "Yes. Indeed." *Many times.* But first he needed to finish this time. His body was clamoring for him to move. "Are you all right?"

"I suppose so."

"Hold on, then. I'll be quick." He pulled back and then surged forward. Once, twice, and once again, holding deep inside her as bliss slammed through him and his seed spurted into her, into the woman he loved.

He collapsed; he couldn't have moved if Satan had burst through his door that very moment.

He'd never before felt such complete, such utter peace. Normally he spilled his seed on the bed—he wanted no by-blows—paid his money, grabbed his breeches, and left. But this time he wanted to stay, wanted Jane to stay and sleep in his bed all night.

But she couldn't. Her mother and the aunts would be home shortly.

"Mmm. That was nice," Jane murmured by his ear, "after the part that hurt, of course." Her hands slid down his back to hug his arse closer. "When can we do it again?"

His traitorous cock started to swell eagerly. "Not now." He flexed his hips backward, breaking her hold and lifting himself off her. "You have to be sore." He stretched out next to her.

"Maybe a little." She snuggled against him. "Will I be better tomorrow?"

"I think so." He ran his hand over her hip. The minx lifted her leg and draped it over his. He removed it. "But you have to go back to your own room now."

"I don't want to." She snuggled closer. "I want to stay here."

He brushed her hair back from her face and ran his hand down her side. "You don't want your mother to find you here, do you?"

She stilled. "No." She threw a worried look at the door. "Do you think they are back from Lord Fonsby's yet? Mama might stop to check on me."

"It is probably too early, but we'd best not take any chances."

She sighed. "I suppose you're right."

He kissed her quickly. "I wish you could stay. I know you came to . . ." He paused. Wait a minute. When he'd first seen Jane, she'd been hiding under his bed. He frowned. "Why *did* you come to my room?"

"Er." Jane looked extremely guilty.

Chapter 16

"I came looking for the piece of Clarence's sketch we found at the Harley Street gallery this afternoon." Edmund wouldn't get angry, would he? Not after the wonderful activity they'd just shared. Though perhaps it wasn't quite so wondrous for him—he *had* done it before with other women.

She found she did not care for that thought at all.

"I'm sorry for invading your privacy," she said, "but I got the distinct impression you weren't planning on showing me the drawing."

"I wasn't."

"What?" She sat up, and his eyes dropped to her chest. "Stop that!" She hauled the coverlet up to block his view— and uncovered his splendid chest and waist and . . .

She tore her gaze back to his face. "How could you think not to show it to me? I was the one who found it. I found every single piece of that sketch. You can't keep it from me."

"I can. I have." His face looked like the cliffs of Dover. All warmth and tenderness had vanished. She wanted to grab him, shake him, knock some sense into him.

She wasn't stupid. She knew banging her head against

a rock would only give her a colossal headache. Still, she had to try. "Be reasonable, Edmund."

"I am being reasonable. Satan is involved, and, as you discovered this afternoon, his involvement is not to be taken lightly. I will not allow you to put yourself in danger"—he covered her belly with his hand—"especially now that you may be carrying my child."

His child? Oh, dear God. The man wasn't just being overly protective because he was a man and she was a woman, but because he saw his line endangered. Surely she wasn't enceinte.

"So if we hadn't"—she waved her hand at the bed—"you know. If we hadn't done this, you'd let me see the sketch?"

"Of course not. I want you safe. The possibility of a child just strengthens my resolve."

He really could do a fine imitation of the cliffs of Dover; in fact, they could take lessons in impassiveness from him.

"But what harm can it do just to show me the paper?" She dropped the coverlet to spread out her arms; Edmund's eyes didn't move from her face—a bad sign. "Look around. We are the only ones in the room. Satan will never know."

"No."

"But I helped you with the other clues. I might be able to help you with this one, too. Have you looked at the drawing yet?"

Edmund glared at her. "No, I didn't have time."

"Then you don't know if you need my help or not."

A frown creased his brow and his mouth took on a mulish line. "I don't need your help."

She leaned forward and poked him in his lovely, naked chest. "Remember, you had to ask Stephen to identify the

Magnolia grandiflora in the first part of the sketch, and I had to help you find the tree in Lord Palmerson's garden."

He shrugged, making his muscles move in a very interesting way, and pushed her hand away. "That was the first part." He wouldn't meet her eyes; he obviously realized the power of her argument.

"And you would never have discovered the second piece had anything to do with the Harley Street gallery if I hadn't puzzled it out."

He shrugged again.

"So why do you think you'll be able to make sense of this third part of the drawing by yourself?"

Had he growled? He looked frustrated enough to have done so. "Let me see it, Edmund. Please?"

He let out a long, annoyed breath. "Oh, all right." He swung out of bed and walked naked to his desk. Mmm. With his strong legs and muscled back and buttocks, he looked like a statue of a Greek god come to life.

She scrambled off the mattress and found her nightgown under the bed. "I already looked in your desk."

"I know. The sand I left on the top was disturbed."

"Oh. And here I thought you were just not very tidy." She slipped the nightgown over her head and went to stand next to him. How could he be so casual about his nakedness? She couldn't look anywhere but at him. She ran her hand over his arse and around toward—

He stepped out of her reach. "I thought you wanted to see Clarence's sketch."

"I do." His penis had gone from dangling by his legs to standing straight out from his body in a matter of seconds. Fascinating. She reached for him, but he dodged her hand, stooping quickly to pick up his towel and wrap it around his waist.

"You have an odd way of showing your interest."

"Oh?" How could she show more interest? He kept dancing away from her.

"In the sketch! Your interest in Clarence's sketch." He made an exasperated noise, half sigh, half laugh. "*Will* you stop looking at me like that?"

"Hmm?" The towel didn't do a very good job of hiding his penis. It looked rather like he'd affixed a small tent to his front. "Like what?"

"Like you wanted to eat— Oh, never mind." He opened one of the desk drawers—a completely empty drawer, she knew since she'd looked in it earlier—and fished around inside. She heard a little click. Then he pulled on what she'd thought was merely some decorative carving on the back of the desk. A section of the desk swung open, revealing a narrow space behind it. Edmund pulled out a piece of paper.

"How clever! I never would have found that."

He raised an eyebrow. "I hope you wouldn't. I paid a man a hefty sum to build it so even a person used to looking for such hidden places wouldn't find it."

He spread the paper on the desk. This was the lower left corner of the sketch. More members of the *ton* were behaving shockingly. Lord Easthaven knelt on the floor under an unruly potted tree while a footman wearing Baron Cinter's livery—oh, dear. She averted her eyes only to encounter the ancient Duke of Hartford. At least he was engaged with a woman—well, two women and neither was his wife. A balloon coming from his mouth said, "I love a lusty wench—the more, the merrier!" And in what would be the center of the picture . . .

"Do you have the other sketches?"

"I do. I brought them up from the safe downstairs. I'd intended to look at them all after my bath." Edmund went over to the chair where he'd left his coat and pulled the papers from his pocket. He arranged them so they fit together. Jane studied the area where the pieces met.

"Damn." She scowled at the drawing. Why had Clarence even bothered sketching this figure? All one could see was the man's—or woman's—long cloak.

"There's not much to go on, is there?" Edmund said.

"No." She traced the intricate pattern around the cloak's hem. There was something familiar about it, but she would swear she'd never seen a cloak like this. "Do you think this pattern is actually embroidered on Satan's robe—if this is Satan—or is it something Clarence added?"

"I don't know. It *is* distinctive, isn't it?" He pointed to the torn edge of the new sketch piece. "We may finally learn something when we have the last section. See, the robe is pushed back slightly. It looks like he or she is holding something."

"Faugh!" Jane straightened. "There's not enough here to give us any indication of Satan's identity." She would gladly have strangled Clarence at the moment if he weren't already dead.

Edmund nodded. "Unfortunately we do need that last piece. Now let's see if Clarence has given us a clue as to its hiding place." Edmund got a magnifying glass out of a desk drawer and examined the new sketch piece. "Damn!"

"What?"

Edmund held the magnifying glass over the bottom corner, by a man riding a goat. Hmm. Perhaps not precisely riding the goat . . . well, all right—riding but not *riding*.

Did people really do that with animals? Surely not!

Jane focused on the other magnified bit. A man and a woman—rather a tame pairing for old Clarence—were wearing hooded robes like the shadowy partial figure in the sketch's center, but, except for their faces, there was nothing shadowy or indistinct about these people. Clarence had drawn all their bits in loving detail.

Loving—or rather, just happy swiving. The woman was sprawled on what looked like a marble casket, her robe fallen open so her body was completely on display. The man's body was covered except for his enormous cock sticking out of his robes. The couple was surrounded by an army of randy Pans, their prominent penises echoing the robed gentleman's. One of the Pans was even grinning.

"What does this mean?" Jane pointed to the words in the bubble by the woman's head: *"Fay ce que voudras."*

"'Do what you will.' It's carved above a doorway at Medmenham Abbey, which was the site of a sort of hellfire club about sixty years ago."

"Sixty years ago?" Jane frowned. Was Edmund joking? None of the members of that club—or, at least, very few—could still be alive. But Edmund looked completely, unpleasantly serious. "Why would Clarence care about something that happened sixty years ago?"

"That's the question, isn't it? My guess is Satan has started a new hellfire club—or taken an existing club in a new direction. At the Palmerson ball, Stephen said he'd heard rumors to that effect."

"Oh. And what do hellfire clubs do?" Jane gestured at the papers. "Engage in various forms of debauchery?"

"Yes. Hopefully that's all they do. But there is a strain of devil worship that can infect these groups. Put a number of drunken men—and women—together and sometimes people get hurt. Add someone like Satan and I would wager people get killed."

"Oh." Jane felt the same chill she'd felt when she'd

realized how close she'd come to death this afternoon. "Like your runaway carriage."

"Precisely."

"And Clarence's odd demise."

Edmund nodded. "I expect so."

She turned back to look at the small picture. "But what can we do? We have to find the last piece of the drawing and Clarence hasn't left us a clue."

"But he has." Edmund pointed to the casket. Clarence had drawn a rampant griffin—and its wings and claws were not the only things in the air. The creature was very obviously male, its dimensions rivaling the Pans'.

"That's rather obscene." Jane wrinkled her nose. She'd never be able to look at heraldic devices in the same way again.

"And the Pans aren't?" Edmund snorted. He did have a point. "And look here. On this side of the griffin, he's drawn the planet Saturn three times, and on the other side, a clock showing eleven with a crescent moon above it."

Jane rubbed the back of her neck. "That's all very well, but I have no idea what it means, do you?"

"Unfortunately, I believe I do." Edmund did not look happy. "The griffin represents Baron Griffin—"

"The sweet old balding man who is such a philanthropist?"

Edmund grunted. "There are some who think his good works are merely penance for his sins—and the more he sins, the greater penance he does."

Jane's eyes widened and her eyebrows shot up. "I believe he just gave a very generous donation to the Foundling Hospital."

"Exactly." Damn. Was that for something Griffin

had just done—or was about to do? He didn't like this situation at all.

"So what do the other pictures mean?" Jane ran her finger over the casket.

Should he tell her? She'd want to be part of it if he did—and the most damnable thing was, he probably did need her help. "The three Saturns mean the third Saturday of the month; the clock and moon, eleven at night. Griffin is known to host a masquerade then."

"Really? I've never attended. I've never even heard of it."

"Of course not. It is not for respectable women. Even many of the male members of the *ton* choose not to go. At best it's a drunken orgy; at worst—" He shrugged. There had been rumors for years of bestiality and animal sacrifices. Stephen had told him a few of the darker, more recent tales before he left England, stories about prostitutes and children from the Foundling Hospital going missing. Many influential people were concerned, but no one had any proof atrocities had been committed or could identify the perpetrators.

Damn. He would much prefer to have nothing to do with Griffin's gathering, but it very much looked as if he had no choice—nor any choice about Jane's involvement. Men said if you didn't come as part of a couple, you'd be paired with one of the extra whores.

Perhaps Jane would see reason and refuse to come, but then who would he find to take her place? He definitely didn't want to be burdened with a light-skirt.

Jane frowned at the sketch. "How could Clarence have been part of all this? I only met him once, but he certainly didn't appear to be a monster. And his sister is one of Mama's friends."

"I'm sure he wasn't a monster. People get drawn all the time into situations they don't like."

She leaned back to give him an extremely skeptical look. "Would *you* have gotten involved with this group?"

His gut twisted. He was far too particular to be part of Griffin's set. "Good God, of course not."

"So you admit there was something wrong with Clarence?"

"I admit there was something odd about Clarence." He had a good idea what that was—Clarence must have had unusual sexual proclivities—but he wasn't about to share that with Jane. "That doesn't make him a monster. I imagine he was appalled by what was going on, and that is why he went to all this effort to reveal it."

Jane frowned. "For heaven's sake, why didn't he just tell Cleopatra?"

"Perhaps because he knew the knowledge would put her in danger. Who knows? He might even have known his life was at risk. At least he did this much."

"Yes. So are we going to this masquerade? Tomorrow is the third Saturday."

"I know." He paused. He wished he could come up with a way to keep Jane far away from Griffin's house.

"You're not going to try to tell me I can't go, are you?" Jane glared at him. "I might not have solved this puzzle, but I'm sure I can be useful once we arrive at this gathering. And you can't leave me home. It wouldn't be fair."

"Fair has nothing to say to the matter. If I could, I would indeed leave you here. I'd lock you in your room and set Jem to guard you." He sighed and ran his hand through his hair. "But I'm very much afraid I do need your help."

Jane grinned. "Of course you do, but I'm surprised

your thick male skull allowed that thought to settle in your brain."

Bloody hell. He grabbed her shoulders and shook her slightly. "Jane, this is not a game. You will be forced to rub shoulders with some of the most depraved members of the *ton* and likely women—and men—from the roughest sections of London as well. You may see and hear things that no one—not a gently bred woman or the lowest slut—should see or hear."

Jane's face paled. "Edmund, you are scaring me."

"Good." He did feel an acid sense of satisfaction. If she was frightened, perhaps she would be cautious, and if she was cautious, perhaps she would get out of this damnable situation in one piece. "You need to be scared."

She lifted her chin. "And where will you be?"

He sighed. "Chained to you, my love. Chained to you."

"Did you sleep well last night, Miss Parker-Roth?" Edmund's aunt Louisa looked up from her kippers and *The Morning Chronicle.*

"Yes, thank you." Blast. Jane felt her face flush. Could anyone tell just by looking at her that she was no longer a virgin?

Louisa's greyhound padded over to sniff a very embarrassing location. Jane pushed her head away.

"Diana!" Louisa said. "Behave yourself."

Diana returned to her place by Louisa's chair. Jane fled to the buffet.

She would have stayed in her room to have chocolate and toast in solitary splendor—if she'd been solitary. But she'd wanted a bath after the night's activities, and then Lily had discovered a red stain on the back of her nightgown. Since her courses weren't due for another couple weeks, Lily was ready to call a doctor or her mother, or both, immediately. She was finally able to persuade Lily she must have cut herself—and then Lily wanted to inspect the cut. She'd put her foot down at that—and then had bolted for the breakfast room.

Oh, dear, how was Edmund going to explain the blood on his sheets?

"You do look very flushed." Cordelia, the only other aunt in the room, took a bite of her strawberry scone and washed it down with some tea. "I don't believe it's exceptionally warm in here. Are you sure you're feeling quite the thing?"

"Yes. Yes, I'm fine." Jane selected a few slices of toast—her stomach did not feel up to anything more substantial—and took a seat as far away from Diana as possible.

Cordelia gave her a concerned look and then shrugged, turning back to her paper. "I was just perusing the gossip column in *The Morning Post.* There's—"

Louisa snorted. "Why do you read that twaddle?"

Cordelia rolled her eyes and smiled somewhat acidly at her sister. "Because I enjoy 'that twaddle.' I like to be au courant."

"Pshaw!" Louisa turned to the next page of the *Chronicle.* "Who cares what the ninnyhammers of the *ton* are doing?"

"I do. And we are members of the *ton,* you know, Louisa."

"Well, of course we are, but not *that* part of the *ton.*"

"*That* part?" Cordelia's eyebrows rose. "Which part would that part be?"

"The young and scandalous part, of course." Louisa looked up from her reading. "*Is* there anything about us in there?"

Cordelia frowned. "No, and I find that rather surprising. I would have thought Edmund's runaway carriage would have merited a mention."

Jane's stomach sank, and she put the piece of toast in her hand back on her plate. "Perhaps no one saw it. The park was rather deserted, and we weren't in the fashionable section."

That comment earned *her* an eye roll. "You tore down Oxford Street—not some little byway—in great commotion, Miss Parker-Roth, and then rode back at a snail's pace with Elvira Hornsley." She tapped the paper. "I would have thought half this column would have been about your antics, but no, there's not even the briefest mention. Very odd."

Jane took a gulp of tea to try to moisten her throat. It was too hot; she spat it—as discreetly as possible—back into the cup. The roof of her mouth and her tongue would be sore for days. She tried to smile. "I don't believe I've ever made the gossip column before. Why should I start appearing in it now at my advanced age?"

Louisa laughed. "Even I know the answer to that question, Miss Parker-Roth—you'd not caught Edmund's eye before."

"Exactly." Cordelia nodded. "Edmund's sudden interest in you at the Palmerson ball was recounted in rather great detail, but since then, silence, even when you two darted out onto Easthaven's terrace the next night. I don't know what to make of it."

Jane was afraid she did. No, she must be wrong. Satan couldn't have that much control of what happened in London that he could keep something out of the newspaper, could he? "Perhaps there was too much other, more interesting gossip."

Cordelia stared at her for a moment, her mouth slightly

agape, apparently speechless. Then she took a breath and shook her head. "Miss Parker-Roth, I know you have not lived under a rock your whole life. The possible matrimonial interests of a wealthy viscount are *always* news. I'm sure half a dozen or more young—and not so young—ladies are checking this space daily to see if they must give up their hopes of catching Edmund in parson's mousetrap."

Louisa snorted again. "Silly chits. They don't need a newspaper to tell them he's been well and truly caught. All they need do is open their eyes and look."

Jane was certain her face was as red as fire—it was certainly as hot. This conversation was headed in an extremely awkward direction. She had to deflect it. "Er, had you found something interesting in the paper, Miss Cordelia? I thought you were about to read aloud when I sat down."

Cordelia's left eyebrow rose, but she forbore to comment on Jane's desperate change of topic. "Yes, actually. There was a very interesting note in the gossip column—well, on the same page." She looked down at the paper. "Ah, here it is: *The Earl of Ardley and Miss Barnett were married yesterday at the bride's home. The happy couple sailed on the evening tide and will tour the Continent on their honeymoon. They plan to return to Town in a few weeks.*"

"The Earl of Ardley married Miss Barnett quite precipitously." Louisa put the *Chronicle* aside. "Whyever did he do that? It's not as if he's a young buck caught up in passion, surely—he won't see fifty again. How old is she?"

"Louisa! I thought you weren't interested in hearing the *Post*'s twaddle." Cordelia smirked.

"No, I don't care to hear it, but now that I have heard it, I am curious. How old is the woman?"

"Considerably younger than Ardley—about your age, wouldn't you say, Miss Parker-Roth?"

Poor Miss Barnett—Jane had completely forgotten about her predicament. "I believe she's a year or two older than I. Perhaps twenty-five or six."

"Ah," Louisa said. "So that explains why she married Ardley. Her papa must have been getting desperate, as, I imagine, was she. Is she a fright, then?"

Jane bristled. How could Louisa make that assumption? There were many reasons why a woman would choose not to marry—as Louisa must surely know as she and her sisters were all unwed. And twenty-five or six was certainly not the age of desperation.

Cordelia laughed. "She does bear a striking resemblance to a horse."

"Hmm. Ardley is no Adonis by any means, but he *is* an earl. One would think he could get a more attractive female, if he wished, so he must have wished for something else. He has an heir by his first wife, doesn't he?"

"Yes, but no wealth. The first countess managed to keep him in check," Cordelia said, "but she died three years ago and the man has run wild ever since, gambling and whoring, spending money as if it were water. The poor heir stands to get only a mortgaged estate and debts when Ardley cocks up his toes. This marriage will solve that problem—assuming Miss Barnett can also exercise a restraining hand. Barnett is as rich as a nabob."

Jane stared at her plate. She'd hardly touched her toast, yet she had even less appetite than when she'd sat down. Would Louisa and Cordelia and the other aunts wonder why Edmund had chosen her? She didn't have money to bring to the union and she certainly had no great beauty. He could definitely do better. Heavens, he could choose just about any unmarried woman in England. He was titled, wealthy, handsome, and young.

She cautiously took a sip of tea. It had cooled down considerably, but her mouth was still sore from her scalding drink earlier.

At least now she knew Lord Ardley would not be at the masquerade tonight. Who would be there? Satan? She shivered.

"Are you sure you're feeling all right, Miss Parker-Roth?" Cordelia was frowning at her, a look of concern in her eyes. "You were markedly flushed just a few moments ago and now you are shivering. Perhaps we should send for the doctor—or at least tell your mother."

"Oh, no." She definitely didn't want a doctor examining her. He might be able to tell . . . No, how could he? She was being silly. He'd have to look *there,* wouldn't he, to ascertain whether she was a virgin? And he would have absolutely no cause to look anywhere near that part of her anatomy for a mere chill. And Mama . . . She didn't want Mama looking at her too closely either. "I'm fine."

"Perhaps you should stay home tonight and rest," Louisa said. "Though it would be a shame to miss the theater. I'm quite looking forward to it."

Cordelia laughed. "Oh, Louisa, you always say that and you always complain bitterly afterward about the chattering lobcocks who ruined the play for you. When will you learn that people in London go to the theater to be seen, not to see a performance."

Louisa's brows descended into a deep vee; she looked extremely disgruntled. "Hope springs eternal, Cordelia, though you are correct; London contains a shocking quantity of fools and Philistines. I remember—"

"Excuse me." Jane stood. She didn't care to hear another of Louisa's diatribes, and her appetite had long since fled—it was past time for her to follow. At least the aunts had presented her with the perfect excuse to stay home from this evening's excursion—Mama and the aunts' excursion, that is. "I think you are correct—I should rest."

"You poor thing." Cordelia patted her hand—and made Jane feel like a worm, but it couldn't be helped. She certainly couldn't announce she'd have to miss the theater because she'd be accompanying Edmund to a shockingly scandalous masquerade. "I'm not surprised you're feeling a bit out of curl. You had a terribly upsetting day yesterday."

"Yes, well, I'm sure I will be better tomorrow." Assuming she survived her visit to Lord Griffin's.

Ridiculous! Now she was truly letting her imagination run wild. Of *course* she'd survive the masquerade. She wasn't a character in some gothic novel. The gathering would probably turn out to be very staid, no more alarming than an evening at Almack's.

On the other hand, Clarence's sketch had certainly not depicted a scene one would ever encounter at Almack's.

"If you'll excuse me, I think I'll go sit in the garden for a little while." If she was going into one of Satan's dens, she might be wise to enjoy the sunshine while she still could.

Chapter 17

"How did you manage to avoid escorting the ladies to the theater?" Jane hoped her voice didn't sound as breathless as she felt. Edmund had just stepped through the connecting door into her room, his arms draped in brown cloth. It was the first she'd seen him since last night, and she felt such an astonishing mix of love, mortification, and lust, she'd swear her heart stuttered.

He dropped a kiss on her mouth. "I hid at White's all day, and then sent word I was, regrettably, unable to attend. It's far easier to deal with the aunts in abstentia." He grinned and laid what he was carrying on her bed. "I got Lord Wenthrop, an old friend of Louisa's, to take my place. He's happy to use my box, and Louisa will be delighted to have another intellectual in attendance with whom she can critique the play."

"Yes, I can see where she would like that." She felt unaccountably shy and unsettled. What they had done last night had been so . . . momentous. And so odd. Had she dreamt it? No, she didn't have such an imagination—and the place between her legs was still slightly sore. She looked at the things on the bed rather than at Edmund.

"What is all this?" She picked up a bit of the brown cloth. Was it a sleeve?

"It's your disguise for tonight. I got it from an . . . associate who sometimes attends." He lifted the fabric and shook it out. It was a robe like the man and woman in Clarence's sketch had worn. "Here, let me help you put it on."

He held it so she could stick her arms through the sleeves and then he lifted it over her head. It dropped down to cover her completely.

"At least now no one can see I'm not wearing an evening gown. I had a hard enough time convincing Lily she didn't have to help me into my nightclothes." And for some stupid reason, she felt herself flush. Edmund had seen her in her nightclothes—he had seen her without any clothes at all. And if truth be told, she was hoping he'd help her undress tonight.

The flush burned brighter, she was certain of it. Fortunately, Edmund's face was covered with cloth as he put his own robe on, so he couldn't see her embarrassment.

"I was afraid your robe might be too long," he said as he emerged and straightened his costume. "Are you certain you can walk without tripping?"

"It's fine. If I have to hurry, I can pick up the front a bit."

"Good. I hope you won't have to hurry, but it's best to be prepared." He took her hands in his and held her gaze. "Jane, you do realize you must be very careful, don't you?"

He paused, obviously waiting for an answer. Did he think she was a complete ninny? "Yes, of course. I'll be careful."

He squeezed her hands. "You must be. This isn't a game or a lark; it's very dangerous. If I could do it by myself, I would, but unfortunately I need your help."

She tried not to smile. "Of course you do."

He sounded like he was grinding his teeth. "Yes, damn it." He let her go and picked up two black masks and a cloth bag. He handed her one of the masks. "You'll need to keep this on the entire time we're in Griffin's house. And pull your hood up so it shades your face. I don't want anyone recognizing you."

"Yes, of course." This could be a very long evening if Edmund was determined to be so overbearing. She followed him out of her room, through the corridor, and down the back stairs. When they got outside, Jem was waiting with a closed, anonymous carriage.

"Why aren't we taking one of your vehicles?" she asked, as she settled herself on the rented carriage's exceedingly hard squabs. They appeared to be clean, though it was hard to tell in the dim light. At least there was no unpleasant odor.

Edmund sat next to her, putting the cloth bag on his knees, and knocked on the roof to give Jem the signal to start. The carriage rocked into motion. "Because my coaches all have my crest emblazoned on the door, and the last thing I want is to advertise my presence at this dreadful gathering."

That made sense. Secrecy was the theme for the evening. She waited for him to open the bag, but instead he leaned over to light the lamp and draw the curtains.

She'd never been alone in a closed carriage with a man before. She breathed in his scent—shaving soap, eau de cologne, and . . . him. It was very intimate.

What was she thinking? She'd been far more intimate with Edmund than merely sharing a closed carriage. They'd shared a bed, for God's sake—a bed *and* their bodies. She looked down at her gloves. She wasn't going to spend the entire evening blushing, was she?

Yet sitting here with him, fully clothed . . . perhaps she *had* dreamt last night. Her behavior had certainly borne no resemblance to her usual way of conducting herself.

She tried to sit a little straighter. She had to think about something besides bodies and beds. She looked over at Edmund. "What's in the bag?"

"You're not going to like it." He loosened the draw-string, reached in—and pulled out a pair of handcuffs.

She scooted as far from him as she could get, which in the coach's confines wasn't very far. "What are those for?"

"The party. Give me your right hand."

She whipped her hands behind her back. "No."

"You have to. I wasn't joking last night when I said I'd be chained to you. It's the only way I can be certain we won't be separated."

"Won't that look odd?"

"Unfortunately, no."

Jane was staring at the handcuffs as if they were live snakes. "What if I have to go to the ladies' retiring room?"

He almost laughed. "I'll close my eyes." No need to tell her there would be nothing as civilized as ladies' retiring rooms at this gathering.

Jane shuddered. "That's disgusting."

Perhaps he should have hired an actress or a whore for the evening. He'd considered it to spare Jane's sensibilities, but such women were not well-known for their intelligence, resourcefulness, or discretion. He'd also considered slipping in through the servants' entrance or one of the windows, but Griffin guarded his house almost as well as he'd been guarding Motton House since this all started. A mouse couldn't slip into the party.

Maybe if he had an inkling where in the house to look . . . but he didn't. He just hoped they'd find Pan in one of Griffin's public rooms; if he and Jane had to start searching the bedrooms, Jane might never recover from the shock. *He* might never recover; more than one of the people he expected to see this evening were reputed to have some *very* odd preferences. He did hope there were no livestock on the premises.

"All right." Jane stuck out her arm. "If there is truly no alternative."

"I'm afraid there's not. You do not want to be caught alone tonight." He put the manacle around her wrist. "The cuffs are thickly padded, so they shouldn't rub your skin or dig into your hands." He snapped it closed. "How does that feel?"

She lifted her hand. "It's heavy, but otherwise I suppose it's fine."

"Good. And it looks like your hand is thin enough you can pull it free if you need to." That was a relief. He snapped the other manacle onto his wrist.

"I thought you said I shouldn't leave your side." Jane was still lifting her arm and turning her hand this way and that, studying the handcuff. "Why would I need to get free?"

"If something happened to me. I'd hate for you to be chained to a deadweight." Her gaze flew from the manacle to his face and her mouth dropped open. Hmm. Perhaps he could have chosen his words more carefully.

"Are you still trying to frighten me, Edmund? I've already promised to stay by your side and"—she lifted her arm again to show off the handcuff—"you've made certain I will."

"I just think it's wisest to be prepared for anything that might occur." He didn't like the feel of the handcuff on his arm—he didn't like having his movements restricted. He'd put the cuff on his left wrist to free up his right, but he'd still not be able to fight effectively with Jane locked to his side. He had the key, of course, but he couldn't very well ask an assailant to wait while he freed himself.

"I see. So do you—we—have a plan?" Jane shook her arm, making the chain rattle. "Perhaps it will work better if I pretend to be a ghost."

He was going to throttle her—once they were free of Griffin's damn party, and after he'd taken her to bed again.

"No, we do not have a plan—at least not a detailed one. We will pretend we are there for the party; we'll stroll through all the open rooms, keeping our wits about us and our eyes open. Hopefully we'll stumble upon Pan."

Jane raised one eyebrow in an extremely skeptical manner. "You have no idea where Lord Griffin might keep it?"

"I'm happy to say I'm not familiar with Griffin's house."

"And men don't gossip about such things?"

"No." There were too many other, far more scandalous things to gossip about concerning Lord Griffin's gatherings.

"I see. And when—if—we find Pan, what do we do then? Relieve him of his penis in the middle of the party?"

"We'll cross that bridge when we come to it."

Jane snorted. "So you haven't the vaguest idea."

"No, that's not true. What I'm hoping will happen is we'll come upon the statue in a deserted room shortly after we arrive, remove the sketch, and leave, but I've been at this long enough to know what I hope will happen rarely does." The coach was slowing; they were almost there. "Here, I want you to have this—just in case." He took a smooth black cylinder out of his pocket.

"What is it?"

"A folding knife I had made to my specifications. You

push this button—" He suited action to word, and the blade snapped out. Jane drew in a quick breath, jumping back. He chuckled, folded it up, and handed it to her. "Now you try it. You have to press firmly, but the button shouldn't be too stiff for you to manage."

She took the knife from him gingerly. "I've never seen anything like this before."

He grinned. "Let's just say I had a special need for such a tool. Can you press the button?"

"Yes." The blade snapped out again. "It's very smooth."

"And very sharp." He closed it for her. "Keep it in the robe's pocket. I hope you won't have to use it, but at least you'll have it should something unforeseen occur. Now let me tie on your mask."

She handed it to him. He made certain it was on securely and her hood was pulled down to hide her hair and as much of her face as possible; then he tied on his own mask and pulled up his hood. When the coach stopped, he opened the door, let down the—

"Ow!" Jane hit his back. "Be careful. I'm attached to you, remember?"

"Damn. I'm sorry." He examined her wrist. This being physically linked to another person took some getting used to. "Are you all right?"

"Yes—if you ignore the fact I almost had my arm ripped off."

"You're exaggerating."

"I am not."

"My lord." Jem's voice floated down from the coach's driver's seat. "The horses are getting restless." He coughed significantly.

Edmund glanced around. "Blast it, we're attracting some attention. Come on. We have to go. Hold on to my arm so I don't move too quickly and jerk you again."

"All right." Jane grasped Edmund's forearm as she maneuvered down the stairs. She glanced up when she reached the pavement. A man in a purple coat, yellow waistcoat, and elaborate wig was examining them through his quizzing glass. His companion, a very large, unattractive woman, her garish, wide-skirted dress the same shade as the man's waistcoat, giggled. She . . .

Jane blinked and looked more carefully. Then she leaned close to Edmund and whispered, "Is that woman . . . I mean, she's wearing a dress, but, well, she looks like—"

"Yes, he's a man. Don't stare."

Jane dropped her eyes to her slippers and clung to Edmund's arm as they entered Lord Griffin's house. Edmund didn't sound at all shocked; had he seen men in dresses before? Well, it was true women had not been allowed to perform in plays even in Shakespeare's time, so perhaps men in women's clothing was not so terribly odd.

"Welcome," someone said. "I see you are ready for the evening's devotions." Jane stole a quick glance—Lord Griffin, dressed in hose and doublet with a huge golden codpiece, smirked at them. And by his side . . .

She looked down at her feet again. There was no doubt as to the gender of his companion. The woman wore a golden collar and golden slippers and nothing else. The poor thing must be freezing.

"Of course."

Jane kept herself from looking this time. She knew it was Edmund speaking—the sound was right by her ear—but his voice was very different. It was higher and thinner, with a slight French accent.

"We must see how the spirit moves us," he said.

Lord Griffin laughed. "Splendid. Until then, do enjoy yourselves. There are rooms upstairs if you prefer privacy, but, as you'll see, many of my guests don't. You may find yourself inspired, eh?"

Edmund laughed in a decidedly nasty fashion. She did look up then and unfortunately caught the baron's eye.

"And you, madam, are you also eager for inspiration?"

How was she supposed to answer that question?

"Your pardon," Edmund said, still in that odd accent, "but my companion is mute. We have a wager, a game, if you will. She swears she will not make a sound all evening. I say I shall make her scream before the new day dawns."

Lord Griffin grinned. "A delightful wager. I wish you luck in winning it." He leaned toward Jane. "And, madam, I'm sure you know you will win most if you lose this bet, eh?"

Did Lord Griffin never clean his teeth? His breath stunk worse than Lord Wolfson's. She forced a smile and then ducked her head again.

"What a well-behaved pet you have, sir. When you tire of her, let me know, hmm? I'll be happy to take her." Lord Griffin's voice was disgustingly unctuous and male. She'd like to kick the toad in a very sensitive location— wearing spurs. It would be a cold day in hell before she had anything to do with him.

"I'll keep that in mind." Did Edmund's words have a slight glaze of ice? Good.

They moved away, into a small room that held a large punch bowl and not much else. At the moment, it was deserted.

"That man is a pig," Jane hissed. "A revolting, odious, repulsive, repugnant worm."

A corner of Edmund's mouth turned up. He did have a very nice mouth. The mask rather emphasized his lips. "I guess you don't like him."

"Of course I don't like him. How dare he talk that way about me?"

Edmund pulled her a little closer as a man dressed in flowing robes and a turban, leading a woman by a gold leash, passed through. The woman's clothes were so gauzy Jane could see the freckle on her oversized arse.

"He didn't know who you were," Edmund whispered. "He thought you were a whore."

She glared at him. "He shouldn't talk that way about any female. And he had a woman standing right next to him. Did he think she was deaf? I can't imagine she was flattered to have that oaf make salacious insinuations about me."

"She *is* a whore, Jane. This is all a business arrangement to her. As long as she gets paid, she doesn't care what Griffin does. If he's busy with someone else, she earns her fee for less work."

She wasn't an idiot; she knew the woman was a whore, and she knew whores got paid to do certain things with gentlemen. But now that she'd done those things—or at least some of those things—herself, her understanding had changed. "So she gets paid for doing what I did last night?"

He stiffened, and his mouth turned sharply down. "No. It is not the same at all." Another couple passed through the room. "And this is not the place for this conversation."

"How is it different?" Jane looked at him. He could be anyone with that mask on. She looked away. "Have you been with whores?"

"I am not a monk"—he snorted—"notwithstanding my current garb, but what a man does with a whore . . ." He shrugged. "The physical act may look the same, but it isn't—just as the man we saw outside looked like a woman, but wasn't. Now can we please concentrate on the problem at hand? If we linger here any longer, we will cause talk."

Two couples came in together then and stopped by the punch bowl. They were laughing—and staring at Edmund and Jane.

Edmund grinned and whispered, "We'd better give them something to see."

"What do you—oh."

He caught her chin with his free hand and tipped it up. Then his mouth covered hers, his tongue slipping past her lips to plunge deep. She couldn't help it—she sagged against him. His hand left her chin to slide down her back and grasp her bottom, bringing her tight against him.

"Huzzah! Have another cup of punch, Albert, ladies, and let's watch the show." That was a man's voice.

Jane stiffened. He was talking about her and Edmund, of course.

A woman with the rough accents of the street laughed. "Do ye suppose they'll take the robes off?"

"It would certainly improve the entertainment, wouldn't it, Betty . . . Bessy . . . oh, hell."

"Just call her Breasty, Rafe. That's why you chose her, ain't it?"

Edmund put his tongue back in his own mouth and whispered, "Remember, we are acting a part tonight. Just keep your head down and don't speak."

"All right." She couldn't resist a quick glance to see who the idiots were—Sir Raphael Flindon and Mr. Albert Isley. In normal company, they were rather bland. Sir Raphael was thin and spotty and had a marked tendency to swallow his words; Mr. Isley was portly and chinless. Here they were dressed rather spectacularly in matching red velvet tunics and green tights. The "ladies" wore Grecian style draperies that ended at their knees—

and silver sashes tied around their waists and their escorts' wrists.

Sir Raphael grinned at Edmund and Jane. "Have some punch, Brother Mystery—and here's a glass for your lady." He sniggered. "If that is a lady in there. Rather hard to tell; would have thought a different costume would've been much more, er, decorative."

"How about you give us a peek, sir?" Mr. Isley said, reaching toward Jane. She stepped quickly behind Edmund. She did not want to be touched by the disgusting snake—and she certainly didn't want her identity revealed.

"My apologies, but the lady is very shy—and I'm extremely possessive." Edmund smiled, but there was a clear threat in his tone and stance. Mr. Isley and Sir Raphael stepped back.

"All right, then." Mr. Isley cleared his throat. "No offense meant, of course. Merely trying to be pleasant. Do as you will." He cleared his throat again. "Believe we'll go see what's what in Bacchus's temple. What do you say, Rafe?"

"Splendid. Excellent idea. Come along, girls." He shot Edmund a wary look as he and the others left the room.

Edmund sniffed his drink, took a sip—and put both glasses back on the table. "I think we'll skip the punch. It's mostly gin." He put his right hand over Jane's where it rested on his arm. "Let's start searching for that statue."

They stepped into a room with wine-colored wallpaper and a wine-colored carpet—obviously the temple of Bacchus. A statue of the god graced a fountain in the center of the chamber, pouring wine from a large jug to fill a pool at his feet. A riotous crowd held their glasses under the stream or dipped them in the basin. Sir Raphael, Mr. Isley, and their female companions had apparently finished their punch and were now enjoying the fountain.

As Jane watched, one gentleman in a toga leaned over

backward to catch the wine flowing from Bacchus's jug in his mouth. His companions hooted with laughter, and then pushed him. He landed with a splash.

"Damn it, Clarden!" The man shook his head like a wet dog, spattering wine everywhere. "I borrowed this bloody toga from Genland. He's going to have my arse."

"Genland's wanted your arse for years, Dattling."

Everyone laughed but Dattling, who roared, scrambled out of the fountain, and flung himself at Clarden. The two crashed to the floor and started hitting each other as the spectators took bets on who would be the victor.

Jane flinched at the sound of fist meeting flesh. "Shouldn't someone stop them from hurting each other?"

Edmund shrugged. "They're too drunk to do much damage. They'll forget why they're fighting in a moment and be best of friends again."

Just then Dattling hauled Clarden up and threw him into the fountain. Clarden whipped around, grabbed Dattling, and pulled him in after him. One of the women laughed and jumped in to join them—naked except for the red leash around her wrist.

The crowd cheered and more people shed their costumes to wallow in the wine.

"I'm suddenly not at all thirsty, are you?"

Jane looked at the bodies splashing in the fountain. "No, I can't say that I am."

"Let's look for Pan here while everyone is otherwise engaged."

They strolled the room's perimeter, being certain to stay outside the range of wine drops, but, besides a sad little ficus tree, they found nothing.

"Blast. I was hoping we'd find the statue immediately and leave before the gathering got much more out of control." The fountain frolickers were now spitting mouthfuls of wine at each other.

"Perhaps things are more sedate in the other rooms."

Edmund gave her a long look. "You're kidding, right? The farther in one goes, the worse it becomes, if this is like any other gathering of its ilk."

"And you've been to many of these gatherings?"

"Not when I could avoid them. Come along."

The strains of a waltz enveloped them as they crossed the threshold into the next room. An orchestra played at the far end and couples crowded the dance floor, but what they were doing . . . the Almack patronesses would have a collective apoplexy if they witnessed this ballroom behavior. A few were waltzing, but their bodies were pressed so tightly together it was amazing they didn't trip over each other. Most ignored the music altogether. Two women— not Lady Lenden and Lady Tarkington, surely?—were kissing each other while a knot of men encouraged them, and off to their right, two men and two women were—Jane couldn't quite figure out what they were doing, but whatever it was, they were all pressed very closely together.

She glanced at Edmund. Was he titillated by what he saw? She couldn't tell. His hood and his mask hid his expression.

"Coming through." A man with his shirttail hanging out and his fall partly unbuttoned dragged a woman with rouged nipples past them. They disappeared behind a red velvet curtain just a few steps to Jane's right.

"Where do you suppose that leads?" she asked.

"It's probably just an alcove. I imagine Griffin has a number of secluded places for men who have difficulty—" Edmund stopped and cleared his throat. "Who prefer privacy for amorous matters."

"Oh." She looked at the curtain again. "Do you suppose Pan might be back there?"

"It's possible. We'll look in a moment."

There were increasingly enthusiastic grunts and groans emanating from the alcove.

"Perhaps we should wait somewhere else."

"Oh, no—that's Paddington. He'll be done in just a second." Edmund cleared his throat again. "He's known to be rather quick about these things."

"How do you—"

"Ah!" A roar erupted from behind the curtain.

"Quick and loud." Edmund's voice sounded tight.

Jane put her hand on his arm. "Are you all—"

The curtain billowed, and Paddington emerged with his companion. "You've got quite the nimble tongue, you know," he said. "I—" He looked over and saw them standing there. He grinned and jerked his head toward the alcove, his hands being busy with his shirttail and fall. "It's all yours. Do enjoy yourselves." He waggled his eyebrows. "A little warm-up before the ceremony, eh?"

"Quite." Edmund nodded and swept Jane behind the curtain. He would like to enjoy himself. Hell, watching everyone else, listening to that fool, Paddington—his cock throbbed and his bollocks felt like rocks.

"What did he mean about 'the ceremony'?" Jane asked.

"I don't know." But he had a bad feeling about it. He'd wondered why Bantle had snickered when he'd given him the robes. He took a deep breath. He needed to think with his brain, not his cock.

But the deep breath had brought Jane's scent into his lungs. It was shadowy in the alcove; private. Surely he could take a moment for a brief kiss.

He touched his lips to hers. She made a small sound

and put a hand on his chest. He wrapped his arms around—

"Eep." She twisted as her arm moved with his.

"Sorry." He brought his hands back to his sides. There were definite disadvantages to being chained together. "Are you all right?"

"Yes, of course." She stepped back and stopped abruptly. "Something's poking into my, er, hip." She looked behind her. "It's Pan!"

"It is? Let's see." He moved next to Jane. Yes, it was indeed one of Clarence's lascivious statues. Thank God! They could get the last puzzle piece and get out of here before this ceremony, whatever it was, occurred. He felt quite certain they did not want to be present for that event.

"You'll have to twist Pan's penis," Jane said. "I'm right-handed."

Another disadvantage to being handcuffed. Well, they'd be done with that very shortly. He grabbed the god's member, twisted it, reached inside, and . . . Damn.

"There's nothing here."

Chapter 18

"What do you mean there's nothing there? There has to be something there." Jane snatched the penis from Edmund and peered inside. "Maybe your fingers are just too thick." She raised her right hand to probe the member's interior and dragged the chain and Edmund's left hand up with it. "Oh, bother. Here, you hold it."

Edmund took the penis back, and she stuck her fingers into it. Blast, Edmund was right. There was nothing there. Perhaps the paper had been left behind in Pan's body. She knelt down and looked there, too, fishing around in the cavity as far as she could reach. "I suppose it could have fallen farther in. The whole statue is hollow."

"If it has, the only way to get it out is to break the god open."

"Hmm." It would make a bit of noise, but the orchestra, not to mention the guests, were loud, and in any event they needed that last piece of the sketch. Doing nothing was not an option.

She gave Pan a trial shove to see how easy it would be to upend him. It was very easy, perhaps because the god was unbalanced, having parted company with his manly member. Her tentative push sent him toppling backward.

He shattered on the marble floor the second after the orchestra played its last note. The sound was startlingly loud.

"Oops."

Edmund sighed. "Never mind, it can't be helped now. Do you see the paper?"

Jane looked carefully over the floor. Lord Griffin had equipped the alcove with a wall sconce, but some of the shattered Pan had slid beyond the circle of candlelight. There wasn't room in the alcove to push past the now-empty pedestal, especially with her right hand chained to Edmund. "No, but maybe it's in the shadows." She needed some way to extend her reach. If only she had a pole or . . . "Here, give me the penis."

Edmund handed her the lonely member and she used it to push the bits of plaster around. "I don't see anything, do you?" She looked up at him. "Could someone have got to this Pan before us?"

Edmund frowned. "I don't think so. How would they have known where to look? I don't believe we left them any clues."

She tried to brush her robe off with her left hand. "The first Pan was shattered and the second we put back the way it was, but the third one . . . Do you suppose someone found its incomplete body in the Harley Street gallery closet?"

"Doubtful, though I suppose it's possible." Edmund straightened her hood and tugged it down so it concealed more of her face. "Still, I don't see how they would realize its significance. There was a lot of rubbish in that closet. Why focus on a broken Pan?"

"True." But the sketch was missing . . . or was it? Perhaps it had never been here. "Clarence drew a group of Pans in the clue, and Mama said he'd made a lot of them."

"Hmm." Edmund looked back at the mess on the floor. "So you think this is the wrong Pan?"

"I think it must be." She certainly hoped it was. "We need to keep looking."

Edmund's mouth drew into a tight, thin line. "I'd hoped we were done."

"Well, we're not. Come on." She pushed the curtain aside and stepped out of the alcove—right into Mr. Paddington's obnoxiously knowing gaze.

"Got a little carried away, did you?"

Thanks to the robe and mask, her blushes were invisible. Edmund didn't dignify Paddington's observation with a reply, but took her arm and headed for the next room.

"I'd be happy to take a turn when he's done with you, mistress," Paddington yelled after them. "I'm as lusty a man as you'll find."

"Lusty?" the woman with him said. "Aye. Lusty and hasty."

The people standing around them erupted into laughter.

"What are you complaining about?" Paddington said. "You don't have to wait, do you?"

The woman snorted. "Ye nodcock, I'm *still* waiting."

Motton wanted to go back and shove Paddington's teeth down his throat, but he couldn't allow himself that luxury. One would think the ridicule the coxcomb was being forced to swallow would prove almost as indigestible, but the man was such a blockhead, he probably didn't comprehend the insults.

He guided Jane into the next room and stopped. Oh, Lord, this was the orgy room. Couples were engaged in various forms of sexual congress on the many chaise longues scattered throughout the chamber. A quick glance didn't reveal any especially peculiar practices, but the night was still young.

"No one will make us do that, will they?" Jane asked in a small voice. She stepped closer so she was almost pressed against him.

"No." Though could he swear to that? "We'll leave. There must be another way to find the missing paper."

Jane shook her head, but her voice sounded less certain. "N—no. We need to—"

"Oh, good, there you are." A portly, balding man in a robe and mask like theirs grabbed their elbows. "I heard we had two initiates here tonight, but I haven't had time to find you." He shrugged sheepishly. "Ate something that didn't agree with me, don't you know. Been just about glued to the jakes. Most inconvenient to be in the convenience so much." He let go of Jane to cover his mouth. A nasty smelling belch emerged . . . unless the source of the miasma was the orifice at the other end of his person. "Best get you settled now, before I have to run out again. Come along."

He didn't give them an opportunity to decline, but hustled them through a door, up a flight of stairs, and around a corner. He stopped at a set of double doors. "Here you go. You may as well wait in the ceremonial chamber—that way I won't have to go looking for you when it's time."

"When will it be time?" Motton asked. Best to know how long they had before they needed to flee.

"At midnight, of course." The man hauled his watch out of his pocket. "Which would be in about twenty minutes." He pulled the doors open. "Just don't forget to—" He slapped his hand over his mouth again and his face assumed a distinctly green cast. He gave them a frantic wave and bolted.

Jane wrinkled her nose. "Poor man." She frowned and

glanced at Edmund. "I wonder what we weren't supposed to forget to do?"

"I have no idea." He turned to survey the ceremonial chamber. "Ah!" He blinked. "I have some good news and some bad news." His voice sounded slightly strangled.

"What?" Jane finally turned as well. "Oh!"

The room was designed like an amphitheater, seats rising to their right and descending to their left. At the bottom was a small stage, and on the stage sat the casket from Clarence's drawing.

But that was not the only notable thing about the chamber—not at all. There were at least a hundred, probably more, randy Pans on display. They were everywhere—marching along the walls on both sides of the room, standing guard at the doors, crowding around the stage. "No wonder Cleopatra thought Clarence had become obsessed," Jane said. "How will we ever find the right one?"

Edmund was fishing in his pocket. "We can just smash them all. We've got twenty minutes." He pulled out the key to the handcuffs, and then checked his watch. "Fifteen to be safe. I want to be out of here before anyone else arrives." He freed Jane's wrist. "You take that side of the room, and I'll take this."

"No, wait." She put a hand on his arm as he unlocked the cuffs from his wrist. "If we do that, they'll know we were here."

"They'll know we were here anyway. Our digestively challenged guide will tell them."

"Not if he's still in the"—Jane blushed and waved her hand vaguely—"you know, when the ceremony begins."

"Perhaps, but we still need the sketch and we don't have time to carefully unscrew and rescrew all these damn penises."

"We don't have time to search through the debris breaking them will produce, either."

Edmund blew out a short, annoyed-sounding breath. "So what do you suggest?"

"I'm thinking."

Edmund rolled his eyes, and then consulted his watch again. "Think fast. You've got about three minutes while I check to see if there's another exit to this room." He hefted the handcuffs. "Then I'm going to start an extreme form of castration." He strode across the room to a smaller, single door half hidden by a phalanx of Pans.

Jane rubbed her forehead. She had to ignore the mental ticking of Edmund's watch, marking off the seconds until he started separating the gods from their jolly genitals.

Clarence had been so careful in his other clues to provide a clear way to find the next Pan—he'd drawn the *Magnolia grandiflora* so they could locate the statue in Lord Palmerson's garden, and then he'd included Cleopatra's painting to point them toward the Harley Street gallery. He must have given them a way to find the right Pan in this instance as well. He knew the room was full of the gods—he'd sketched a crowd of them.

He'd also included that casket on the stage. He must have had a reason to do so. She would begin there. She started down the incline.

Edmund stepped back into the room. "One minute before I start swinging this chain."

"Then spend that minute helping me." She walked around the casket, running her hand along its sides. There were no griffins or Saturns—Clarence must have added those for the sketch.

Edmund grumbled, but joined her on the stage. "Half a minute now."

"Oh, do be quiet." Clarence had fabricated the markings

on the side of the casket, but he wouldn't have invented everything, would he? What would have been the point of that? He wanted them to find the rest of the sketch.

Mama often droned on about seeing like an artist—choosing a subject, studying it, noticing all its details, how the light played over its surface . . .

She paused and looked out over the rows of seats. Clarence had painted the view from one side of the casket, but this wasn't it. This was the view of the particÁipants. The audience would see something else.

There was only one other choice.

She turned around. A group of Pans stared at her. One of them was smiling.

"Time's up," Edmund said. "Let's go." He swung the chain as if to get a feel for it. "We'll start with these—"

Jane grabbed his arm. "Wait. I know where the sketch is."

"You do?"

"I think I do." She grabbed the smiling Pan's penis and unscrewed it. *Dear God, please let the sketch be here.* If it wasn't, she'd have to give up and help Edmund break open as many gods as they could. She lifted the massive member free.

"That's it!" Edmund plucked a scrap of paper out of the penis and put it in his pocket. "Well done. Now let's put this organ back and get out of here before—damn."

Jane had heard the door open, too. Edmund's hands imÁmediately joined hers on Pan's penis, helping her finish screwing it in place, but making it look as if he were showing her how to stroke a man's member—*his* member.

"Like this, mon amour." He was using his high, thin, faintly French voice again. "From the base to the tip, firmly—ah!" He turned, making a show of being surÁprised. She looked as well—it was their earlier guide, back from the convenience. "Yes? What is it, monsieur?"

"Getting the lady ready, are you? Good, good. I'll be sure to be first in line—after you, of course." He covered his mouth and belched. "Ahem. Assuming I don't have to run off."

First in line? Did he mean . . . ? Jane's stomach lurched. *She* would have to run off to the convenience in just a moment.

"Of course." Edmund consulted his watch. "But it's not yet time, is it?"

"Oh, no. You've got five minutes at least. I just wanted to remind you, because, what with all my, er, issues, I think I forgot to tell you that you can put your clothes in the bin behind the stage."

"Ah. The bin." Edmund nodded calmly as if he knew exactly what the man was talking about and wasn't disturbed about it in the slightest. Jane clenched her fists and breathed through her nose. She was *not* going to swoon. At least, she hoped she wasn't, but the thought of shedding her clothes and doing something that might involve this unpleasant, ill gentleman and penises . . . She bit her lip to keep her moan from escaping.

"Yes. You'll see it if you just look behind that statue there." The man grinned. "Unless you've already come naked under those robes? Some do, but it's a bit cold out, especially for the ladies." He nodded at Jane. "Don't worry—if you've brought any finery, you'll get it back later."

Jane looked up at Edmund. Could he tell how desperate she felt?

"Bon. The lady, she must get ready." Edmund gestured toward the door. "If you would be so kind?"

The man laughed. "Of course. They're all shy at first, but once they get a swallow or two of the devil's brew, there's no stopping them, eh?" The man headed for the door. "Don't dally, though." He looked at his watch again. "The servants will be bringing in the brew any moment now."

"Ah. We will hurry, then. Thank you."

The man closed the door behind him, and Edmund grabbed Jane's hand. There was no way in hell he was going to let her get caught in this obscene situation. "Come on. That door leads to some servants' stairs and from there to an alley. We should be able to find Jem and the coach quickly and be free of this place."

Jane picked up her hem in her other hand and hurried to keep pace with him. "Do you think we'll run into the men bringing up the drink?" He could hear the tension in her voice.

"I hope not, but if we do, they'll probably be burdened with jugs or casks. We should be able to slip by them easily." He paused before opening the door. "If there is any need to fight, stay out of the way. If you must, use the knife I gave you."

Jane nodded. Good. He hoped she would be sensible. He opened the door and ushered her through it.

It was two flights down to the outside door. They made it safely down the first flight, but as they reached the small landing before the second, they encountered two of Griffin's burly servants hauling a big, open vat of some liquid. It looked and smelled like ale but with something pungent added. A third servant, who seemed to be supervising the first two, carried a large, ornate chalice. He rested the chalice on his hip and glared at them. "The initiation's upstairs."

Bloody hell, this wasn't just a servant, it was Helton— Beelzebub himself. "Initiation?" He'd try his Scots accent instead of the French—perhaps that would confuse them if the man upstairs and Helton compared notes. "We're nae here for any initiation." He pulled Jane forward, pushing her ahead of him so she could make a dash for freedom. The odds weren't horrible. Three to one, yes, but two were burdened by the vat.

He wrapped the chain around his hand, hidden in his robe. Flight would be preferable to confrontation, but if flight wasn't possible, he'd best be prepared.

Helton looked him over. "You're dressed for the initiation."

"That's a mistake." He shrugged, smiling in a conciliatory fashion, he hoped. He wished Jane would keep going. He gave her a nudge, but she didn't move. "These are the only costumes I could get—I just found out about the party today."

Helton grinned in a most unpleasant fashion. "Oh, well, a mistake. My master won't mind as long as he has someone. Come on."

"Nay. I"—Motton gestured toward Jane—"we have another appointment." He waggled his eyebrows. "If ye know what I mean."

Helton narrowed his eyes. "I don't give rat shit about your appointment. More to the point, my master will make me eat rat shit if I don't give him someone to initiate. You're coming with me now."

Everything happened in a blur then. Helton grabbed Jane's arm and jerked her across his body, but she stumbled and fell heavily against him. He screamed and let her go. She caught the side of the vat as she tumbled toward the floor, tipping it and splashing the brew all over.

Motton didn't need an engraved invitation to take advantage of this situation. He swung his chain, hitting Helton square in the head. The man went down like an oak—and Motton saw the knife he'd given Jane protruding from his side.

"Good girl." He yanked it out and turned to the servants,

but they'd already decided the situation was far beyond their duties. They'd dropped the vat, squeezed past the bodies on the floor, and bolted down the stairs as if all the hordes of hell were after them—which they probably would be once Satan got wind of what had just happened.

He folded the knife up, stuck it in his pocket, and stooped down next to Jane. She was a bedraggled mess, reeking of Satan's brew. "Are you all right?"

She pushed her hair out of her face. Her hood had fallen back, but surprisingly her mask had stayed on. "Yes, I think so. My elbow and ars—er, seat—are sore, and I hope there was nothing poisonous in this liquid because I swallowed a mouthful, but other than that, I think I'm fine." She frowned and peered over at Helton. "How is he? I didn't k—kill him, did I?"

"No, more's the pity. He—" Motton heard the door at the top of the stairs open and someone—several some-ones—come into the stairwell.

"Bloody hell!" some man shouted—probably the man plagued with intestinal problems. "Satan will string me up by my bollocks if I've lost those two. Do you suppose they went this way?"

"You'd think Helton would have run into them if they had," someone else said. "But I guess we'd better look."

Motton grabbed Jane's hand and breathed by her ear, "Come on, and be as quiet as you can."

She nodded. He dropped her hood back over her head and started swiftly and silently down the stairs. It didn't hurt that the fellows looking for them were making so much noise he could have set off a rocket and not been heard.

They reached the door—and heard shouts up above. The men had found Helton, and even these idiots would be able to deduce where his attackers had fled. There weren't that many options. They had only seconds left.

They slipped outside. "Ooo." Jane put her hand to her head. "I feel so odd."

"It's probably the cooler air. Just hold on a little longer. We're almost out of danger." At least, he hoped they were. Perhaps they could hide in the foliage, get rid of the robes, and try to leave undetected after the first wave of searchers went by, but it looked as if there wasn't much greenery and Jane was beginning to look rather green herself.

"Ohh." She moaned again and started rubbing her chest. Hmm. Not rubbing so much as . . . fondling. What *was* the matter with her?

They had best leave immediately. He looked around. Ah, thank God. Luck had smiled on them. They were right by the gate to the alley where Jem waited with the coach.

He grasped her hand again and ran. They crossed a small gravel yard and darted out the gate. Jem was ready; the carriage rolled slowly toward them. Motton jerked open the door, grabbed Jane around the waist, threw her inside, and vaulted in after her, slamming the door shut the moment his feet cleared the opening. Jem picked up the horses' pace so by the time the servants' door opened again, the carriage was already turning out of the alley.

"Damn, that was close, but I think we're safe now." He pushed himself off the floor onto one of the seats, and then took Jane's hand to help her up. He tugged—and she flew into his lap.

He hadn't thought he'd pulled that hard. "Sorry, I didn't mean to—"

Her mouth came down on his, and her hands tore at his robe. She shifted on his lap as though she wanted to climb into his skin. What was this all about? Not that he didn't appreciate her enthusiasm; it just felt too much like desperation.

He flinched. If she wasn't a bit more careful, he wouldn't

be able to help her at all. Her knee had been much too close to a very sensitive part of his anatomy.

He took firm hold of her shoulders and pushed her back far enough that he could speak. "What's wrong, Jane?"

She was panting; she struggled against his hold, trying to plaster herself against him again. "I need you. Now. Inside me. Can't wait."

His cock, already quite interested in the proceedings, snapped to full attention. "Er, yes, well, I'm delighted you are so, ah, enthusiastic, and I would be even more delighted to assist you, but wouldn't it be better to wait until we are home? We should be at Motton House in just a few minutes."

She tried to lurch toward him again. "No. I can't wait another moment."

Good God, she was almost wailing. Something was definitely amiss. What? She'd been fine until . . . oh, God. "How much of Satan's drink did you swallow?"

"I don't know. Why are you talking about that? Why are you talking at all? Get your clothes off."

His cock was pleading with him to follow Jane's orders. He couldn't very well decline, could he? She was obviously in a very bad way.

He wasn't normally one for copulating in exotic locations, and while a carriage might not be that unusual, he'd never tried it. He'd never seen the point. A bed was so much more comfortable. But Jane couldn't wait for a bed.

"Ohh, I'm so hot." She was actually moaning. "My skin is burning. The place you were last night is hot and swollen and so wet." She fidgeted on his lap, bouncing a little. "I need you now. Please?"

Well, there was a first time for everything. "All right, but I have to tell Jem not to go to Motton House." That would be awkward, having Jem open the door as they were in the midst of a passionate encounter. "Can you keep quiet while I speak to him?" He would rather not give Jem a crystal clear idea of what activity they were engaged in.

"Yes, but make it quick."

"It will only take a moment." He knocked on the roof, and Jem slowed the carriage. Motton detached himself from Jane long enough to lean out the door.

"Miss Parker-Roth and I need to discuss a few matters, Jem. Drive around Town until I give you the signal to proceed to Motton House, will you?"

"We're almost there, my lord."

"Yes, I know, but it can't be helped." Did he hear another moan coming from the interior of the carriage? Surely there was too much noise outside for Jem to hear it.

"Very well, my lord. As ye wish."

"Splendid." He'd swear he heard the sound of fabric tearing behind him. "Carry on, then." He closed the door and turned around.

Good God. Jane was sprawled on the squabs, completely naked, legs spread wide, hands rubbing her breasts. He had never seen a more beautiful, more wanton sight. "How did you get your clothes off?"

"Quickly." She moistened her lips and ran one hand down her body. She wasn't going to touch herself, was she?

She was. She ran her fingers over herself and then held her hand out to him. "My skin is so hot, and I'm so wet."

"Er." He struggled out of his robe as quickly as he could.

"Get your pants off." She drew her damp fingers slowly over her belly and then played with the curly patch of hair between her legs. "If I do it, you'll lose all your buttons."

"Uh, huh." He was having trouble with his buttons as well. He fumbled with them, opened his fall and jerked his breeches down.

"Yes!" Jane launched herself at him, knocking him back to sit down abruptly on the other seat. Then she straddled him, grasped his cock, and lowered herself onto him. "Yess."

She rested her head on his shoulder for a moment. He stroked the sides of her breasts. Her skin *was* hot; she was like a little furnace.

He waited; he would let her take the lead. The aphrodisiac in Satan's brew was driving her, not her own desires, and he didn't want to make her do anything she might regret—or blame him for.

Thank God they'd gotten away safely. To think of sweet Jane forced to be like this with all those other men—

"Oh." She rocked back and forth. "Oh."

"What is it?" He rubbed his thumbs over her nipples, and she sucked in her breath, arching her back. Then she dropped her head back to his shoulder.

"I don't know what to do." He heard the frustration in her voice. "I don't know how to make the ache stop." She rocked her hips again. "Help me."

He slid his hands to her hips. "Rub yourself up and down on me, Jane. Like this." He lifted her hips, and then pressed them back down. Up and down. Up and down.

"Ah."

"Find your own rhythm now."

"Yes." She rose and fell, head back, hair streaming over her shoulders. She was beautiful, and her tight, wet passage felt wonderful sliding over his cock. He'd almost reached the point of release—but she hadn't.

"Ohh. I can't . . . why won't . . ."

"Shh. Here, let me." He grabbed her hips to stop her increasingly frantic motion. Then he touched the small, sensitive place just in front of her opening.

"Oh!" She looked at him. She was panting, desperation yet hope in her eyes. "Oh."

He smiled and rubbed his thumb lightly, teasingly, over the hard little nub.

She panted faster and squirmed, making little breathy, needy noises that got higher and higher. He thrust up sharply with his hips, pressed with his thumb—and she stiffened and screamed. He felt her body contract around his cock as he poured his seed into her.

"Oh." She collapsed, sweaty, boneless, into his arms.

"Better?" He ran his hand down her back.

"Mmm." She kissed his jaw. "Much better."

They lay that way for a few moments. He listened to the clop of the horses' hooves, the rattle of the carriage wheels. He should tell Jem to turn for home. He would in a minute.

Or maybe he wouldn't. Jane was fidgeting . . .

"Again." She sat up. "I need to do it all again."

Chapter 19

Jane hunched over her teacup and breathed in the fragrant steam. Her head throbbed, her brain felt cloudy, and her mouth tasted evil, like cheese someone had forgotten and left sitting in the sun for days.

Last night hadn't really happened, had it?

Ohh. She squeezed her eyes closed. It must have. The place between her legs was so sore. And the memories . : . Some were hazy, but many were startlingly clear. She'd begged him to take her again and again, and he had—on his lap, on her back, from behind, with his mouth, with his fingers.

What must Edmund think of her? Thank God her mother and the other ladies were off visiting by the time she finally dragged herself out of her room and down to Edmund's study. She must have "jezebel" written all over her.

She took a sip of tea in the hopes it would quiet her stomach and help the pounding in her head. Where was Edmund? He'd told Lily he wished to see her, but he wasn't here—something she was quite thankful for. How could she bear to face him? But she would have to face him— she was living in his house.

Ohh. She put down her teacup and rubbed her temples.

He had been so kind to her in the carriage; he could have been rough and demanding, but he'd been as thoughtful and gentle as possible in the circumstances. If she'd been forced to drink that nasty stuff in Lord Griffin's ceremonial chamber—

She swallowed quickly and pressed her hands over her eyes. No, she couldn't think about what would have happened then. It was far too horrifying. She'd never have—

"Are you all right?"

"Eek!" Jane screamed and threw up her hands, almost knocking over her teacup and the teapot.

"Sorry," Edmund said. "I thought you heard me come in."

"No." She glanced up at him and then dropped her head back into her hands. "I, ah, d—didn't."

He'd never seen Jane so despondent. During this whole crazy situation, she'd been determined, optimistic, energetic.

She'd certainly been energetic in the carriage last night. He grinned. He'd tried to rise to the occasion, but by the fourth time, he couldn't rise at all. She'd worn him out.

The damn aphrodisiac hadn't made her ill, had it? "*Are* you all right?"

She shook her head, keeping it buried in her hands. "I'm so m—mortified." She sniffed twice and then burst into tears.

"Jane." He'd swear he felt his heart twist in his chest. The poor, sweet girl. He grasped her shoulders and pulled her out of her chair and into his arms. "Don't be embarrassed. No one knows what happened except me." Well, he'd wager Jem had an excellent idea, given the knowing look the man had shot him when they'd finally stopped at Motton House and he'd carried Jane, sleeping and disheveled, out of the coach. And, truth to tell, he'd been more than a little disheveled himself.

"But you do know. How can you bear to touch me?"

"Jane." He led her over to the settee and sat down with her, gathering her back into his arms once they were settled. "You're not making sense. Why wouldn't I want to touch you?" He kissed her forehead. "I very much enjoyed touching you last night. I thought you were magnificent."

She *had* been magnificent. Their time in the carriage had been a fantasy he hadn't had the imagination to conceive before—but now he could. "I'd be delighted to do it all again"—he chuckled—"though perhaps not all at once again. I was quite exhausted by the time you fell asleep."

She buried her face in his shoulder. "I was so wanton."

"You weren't." He grinned, remembering in vivid detail exactly how she'd behaved. The thought was reenergizing his poor, tired cock. "Well, perhaps you were."

"Ohh." She tried to pull away, but he wouldn't let her.

"It wasn't your fault, Jane. It was the drink you swallowed when the vat got dumped on you. It must have contained a powerful aphrodisiac. Once it took hold of you, you no longer had control of your, er, urges."

She relaxed a little. "No?"

"No." He stroked her back. Last night in the carriage, her skin had been so soft. His cock stirred again. He'd so like to have her now, but slowly this time. Fast and frantic had its place, but slow and thorough . . . mmm. He would definitely enjoy that.

But it was out of the question. She must ache from all their activity last night, especially as she'd only just got over losing her maidenhead. And they did have other, more pressing matters to attend to. Satan must be furious his ceremony at Griffin's had been ruined; he would be out for blood and likely be happy to take theirs, whether he knew they were responsible for the mêlée or not. They'd best solve this puzzle immediately before he dealt with them in an unpleasantly permanent fashion.

Motton would like to keep Jane out of it, but she was in too deep now. "Let me get the sketch pieces out of my safe, and we'll see what the completed picture looks like."

Jane took out her handkerchief, blew her nose, and raised her chin. "Yes, of course. I'm very eager to solve Clarence's puzzle."

Edmund arranged all four pieces of the drawing on his desk, while Jane took a steadying breath. She could do this. She would focus on the puzzle and not last night. Once her body stopped aching, it would be easier.

She was so aware of Edmund. Perhaps it was a residual effect of the wretched brew she'd ingested. When he'd held her just now, she'd wanted to rub her body against his. If she hadn't been so sore, she might even have done so.

The moan escaped before she could clamp her teeth on it.

"Is something hurting you, Jane?" Edmund laid his hand on her upper arm, and she felt the imprint of each of his fingers as if she were as naked as she'd been in the coach. If he moved just a little, he'd graze her breast.

She would *not* moan again. And she would not tell him what was hurting—her breasts now as well as the place between her legs. She stepped a little away from him, pretending to get a slightly different angle on the sketch, but mostly just so he had to drop his hand. "I think I'm still feeling a little ill from that nasty drink."

"Would you like more tea?"

"No, thank you." She'd like him to be quiet. His voice was torturing her, too. And his scent. Damn. If she didn't stop being so sensitive, she would go mad.

She tried to concentrate on the sketch. It was disappointing, to say the least. The last piece hadn't added much at all. It completed the shadowy figure, but kept his—or her—identity secret, hidden behind a grotesque mask. "Oh, blast it all. Why didn't Clarence draw Satan's face?"

"That would be too simple, wouldn't it?" Edmund leaned over to look at the sketch more closely. "I wonder if Clarence even knew Satan's identity."

Jane's stomach lurched. She pressed her hand to her mouth and swallowed to be sure the tea she'd just drunk stayed down. They couldn't have been on a wild-goose chase these last few days—especially last night.

Had Clarence merely sketched another bawdy picture to hang in print shop windows, giving the *ton* something else to laugh and gossip about?

No, it *had* to be more than that. Why would he have torn it up and hidden the pieces? "He *must* have known who Satan is."

"Maybe not. Very few people can know Satan's identity—and many people know of this sketch. Ardley, Mousingly, Lady Lenden, and Lady Tarkington are all looking for it. Likely Satan knows of it, too—and he'd never have allowed Clarence to draw an identifiable portrait."

Edmund shook his head. "Maybe there's no point to this. Clarence was known to be an odd bird. He could have designed this all as a game—or a joke—and maybe one he thought he'd be here to see. If he's in a position to observe our efforts now, I'm sure he's completely delighted at how he's forced us to go all over London, searching out his ridiculous Pans."

Jane scowled at the sketch. Damn it, it was possible Clarence was laughing his arse off in heaven—or, more likely, hell. Even Mama had thought the man exceedingly peculiar, which was saying a lot coming from a fellow artist.

No, she was not ready to—she could not—accept that all her and Edmund's efforts had been for naught. "Satan must be worried we might learn something or he wouldn't have devised our disaster on Oxford Street."

Edmund shrugged. "I suppose that could have been a bizarre confluence of coincidence."

She was far too stubborn to accept that. She'd scrambled in the greenery, hidden on a closet floor, been tossed into a bush, lost her virginity, and attended a shocking party with even more shocking results, all because of Clarence's bizarre sense of humor? No. She would never swallow that willingly—she'd have to have the evidence that it was true shoved down her throat.

"Clarence was just being devious. I'm sure if we look closely, we'll find more clues to Satan's identity." She jabbed her finger at the picture. "Why would Clarence have drawn Satan holding this peculiar staff? It has the same pattern as the robe." A pattern that still looked maddeningly familiar. It was like having a word on the tip of her tongue—she could almost remember where she'd seen it before . . . almost, but not quite. "And why did he draw this dog by Satan's feet? It's just sitting there. All the other animals are—" She flushed. She wasn't about to say what activity the other animals were engaged in. "Doing something."

"Hmm." Edmund nodded and leaned closer. "It is a rather large and unpleasant-looking animal."

"I'm sure Satan would only have a vicious dog. Do you suppose that's a clue?"

"Perhaps. We'll have to ask Aunt Louisa. She's certain to have identified every London pet." He pulled a magnifying glass from his desk and examined the right lower corner. "Hmm. Poor Clarence apparently suffered from an attack of Gothic fantasy."

He passed the glass to Jane and she peered through it. This little part of the sketch *was* rather grisly. A skeleton dangled from a wall, and in the skeleton's bony fingers was a quill. Next to the quill was a book.

"See? The book has the same pattern as the robe and the staff," Edmund said. "Clarence has added what looks to be some sort of stone in the center. It would help if he'd used color—"

"A ruby." Jane sucked in her breath. No, it couldn't be, but it looked like—

"What?"

"I think the stone is a ruby." She stared at the picture. "But it can't mean anything. It's too unbelievable."

"What can't mean anything?" Edmund sounded exceedingly exasperated. "What's unbelievable?"

"The pattern. It must be something Clarence saw once and duplicated by accident. Or perhaps it's just a decorative touch."

"Jane." Edmund leaned on the desk and pinned her with a very pointed look. "I sincerely doubt Clarence was aimlessly drawing a pretty pattern. He included everything else in this sketch for a purpose. Why do you think when we get to this crucial detail Clarence went on a mental holiday?"

"Er . . ." It did sound ridiculous when Edmund put it that way.

"So do you recognize this pattern?"

"I—I think so. But I'm probably misremembering. I must be. It can't—"

"Jane!"

"You don't have to shout."

"My apologies." Edmund took a deep breath, obviously trying to hold on to his temper. "Why don't you tell me where you think you might have seen it?"

"Very well." She wished she hadn't said anything; she had to be wrong, but clearly Edmund was going to insist she tell him her nonsensical notion. "In Baron Wolfson's cravat."

"What?"

"You're shouting again."

"Sorry." He straightened and ran his hand through his hair. "So you saw this pattern on Baron Wolfson?"

"Yes. In his cravat pin. It's very distinctive. A ruby surrounded by gold filigree in this pattern. But it can't mean anything. Lord Wolfson is old—he must have at least sixty years in his dish. He couldn't be involved in anything like what we saw at Lord Griffin's last night."

"Jane, he's old—he's not dead."

"Yes, but . . . Lord Wolfson?"

"If Satan walked around with horns and a tail, he wouldn't be hard to spot, would he?" Edmund tapped his finger on the sketch. "I'll wager this animal isn't a dog, but a wolf."

"Oh." The creature *did* look rather wolfish.

Edmund gathered up the sketch pieces and put them back in his safe. "It was at Wolfson's estate Clarence met his unfortunate end, remember. And there have been vague rumors about the man for years."

"But he's so . . . boring." Perhaps Satan wouldn't wear horns, but surely he should appear at least a little dangerous. "And he's accepted everywhere. I was dancing with him at Lord Easthaven's just the other night."

"You were?" Edmund frowned as he closed the safe's door. "I thought Wolfson was as wedded to the refreshment table as Spindel. Have you ever danced with him before?"

"N—no, I don't believe I have. I'm not sure I've ever even spoken to him before."

"And what did you talk about?"

What *had* they talked about? She'd been more focused on his breath than his words. Eew. She could almost smell

the garlic again. And then she'd been studying his pin . . .
he'd been somewhat perturbed that she'd not been listening to him . . . "He wanted a tour of Clarence's house."

"Hmm. Amazing how the *ton* have become so fasci-
nated with Widmore House, isn't it?"

"Y—yes." Jane pushed a wisp of hair behind her ear.
Her face was pale, and she had dark circles under her
eyes. The poor girl looked almost burnt to the socket.

He gathered her into his arms. She stiffened slightly,
but then relaxed against him. She felt so good. He rubbed
his hand up and down her back, and then cupped her jaw
so he could study her face. "You should rest today. Tomorrow we'll brave Lord Wolfson's weekly soiree along
with your mama and my aunts and see what we can discover, all right?"

"All right." He watched her swallow. "Yes. I—I think
that is a good idea. I am still rather tired."

He frowned. "Are you certain you have no lasting
effects from that dose you swallowed last night?"

She wouldn't meet his eyes. "Y—Yes. I am completely
recovered. I will never behave that way again."

He grinned. "Oh, don't say that. I liked the way you behaved last night." He laughed. "Though I'll admit, it was
slightly too much of a good thing."

She groaned and tried to pull away, but he wouldn't let
her go. He kissed her. She tasted so good. Like home—
a home he actually wished to have, not the home he'd
grown up in. With Jane, he would never have his parents'
cold disdain. He'd have love and passion and laughter.
And arguing, too—Jane was not a namby-pamby miss—
but they'd always make up afterward, perhaps with a few
of the activities they'd engaged in last night.

He whispered by her ear, "Wantonness is a good thing
between husband and wife, Jane."

"But we aren't husband and wife," she said.

"We will be. As soon as this mystery with Clarence and Satan is resolved, I'll get a special license."

She pushed away from him to look him in the eye. "You don't have to marry me."

He almost laughed. "Of course I do. I've compromised you beyond redemption."

"No one need know—"

"People are going to suspect something when your belly swells with my child."

Jane shoved harder, and he let her go. "I—I don't know that I'm ah, er . . . you know."

"True, but it is certainly a strong possibility. Lord knows I sowed my seed in you enough times to have fathered an heir and a few spares." He hoped she *was* increasing. The thought of her, round and heavy with his babe, was surprisingly satisfying.

Jane's face was now beet red. "I will let you know if I am in the family way—"

The door swung open. "*What* did you say?" Aunt Winifred actually looked startled.

"In the family way. In an interesting condition." Theo flapped his wings. "Breeding."

Jane's face was now ghostly white, and her mouth hung uselessly open. Aunt Winifred's gaze moved to him.

"Miss Parker-Roth was urging me to let her know if she were in my family's way—and I was about to assure her she wasn't. She and her mother are welcome to stay here as long as they wish. Don't you agree, Aunt Winifred?"

"Yes, of course." Winifred looked skeptical, but wasn't certain enough to call him on his lie—though she did keep throwing glances at Jane's middle.

Jane found her voice; it sounded unnaturally high and thin. "Thank you so much, Miss Smyth. Lord Motton is all that is g—gracious. My brother John should be in London soon, and then we can remove to the Pulteney. I'm rather tired now, so if you'll excuse me?"

Jane rushed out of the room as if Satan were indeed on her heels.

Lord Wolfson's soiree was surprisingly crowded. Jane was trapped in the baron's green parlor between the exceedingly stout Lady Blessdon, Lady Blessdon's good friend, the emaciated Miss Canton, and a potted palm. Jane had often thought if the ladies' weight could somehow be averaged, the result would be two normal-sized women. They were gossiping about some *on dit* she'd missed by avoiding the social scene—the *polite* social scene—these last few days. She let their words flow over her; her attention was on Edmund on the other side of the room. Lady Lenden and Lady Tarkington were talking to him, while some beautiful young debutante stood far too close to his side.

Jane curled her hands into fists. Fortunately her gloves kept her fingernails from digging deep gouges in her palms.

Edmund was hers. Except . . . oh, botheration. Her life was such a mess. Should she marry him? If she really was increasing, she'd have no choice; she was not so selfish as to condemn a child to bastardy to suit her whims. But if it turned out she wasn't—she pushed aside the disappointment that suddenly appeared like a rock in her stomach—should she say no? She loved him, but did he love her? He hadn't said so. And his father had been trapped into a loveless marriage by similar circumstances . . .

"Don't you agree, Miss Parker-Roth?"

"Er . . ." Lady Blessdon was looking at her expectantly,

but she had no idea what the woman had said. "I'm sorry, I was woolgathering."

Lady Blessdon and Miss Canton exchanged a significant look. "It wasn't wool you were gathering." Lady Blessdon lifted a brow and tilted her head toward Edmund. "Will we be hearing an interesting announcement soon?"

Jane felt a hot flush flood her face. Damn. She hadn't blushed so much in her entire life as she had since encountering Lord Motton in Clarence's study. "Announcement? I don't know what you mean."

Lady Blessdon's other brow rose to match its mate. "Miss Parker-Roth, surely you realize all of society has watched with interest your sudden, intense . . . friendship with the viscount. Dashing into the bushes at Lord Palmerson's, taking in the exhibit at the Royal Academy, disappearing onto Lord Easthaven's terrace—if there is not an announcement soon, your reputation may suffer."

Miss Canton nodded vigorously. "Sorry to say it, but you'll be thought no better than you should be."

Jane's stomach twisted. And the truth was, she *was* no better than she should be. After her performance in that rented carriage, even the most notorious light-skirts might consider her too soiled to associate with.

She forced a smile. "But I'm not some young debutante. I've been on the Town for years; surely the gossips will allow me a bit more latitude."

"A bit, but not *that* much," Lady Blessdon said.

"I had it from Mrs. Eddle who had it from Lady Iddleton that you had twigs in your hair when you came in from Lord Palmerson's garden." Miss Canton's eyes were large with horror . . . and a touch of envy, perhaps.

"And grass on your skirt." Lady Blessdon gave Jane a knowing look.

Jane glared at her. "The gossips are wrong." While she

might have had a stray twig about her person, she most definitely did *not* have grass on her skirt—Lady Blessdon's sly way of intimating she'd been doing . . . exactly what she *had* been doing with Lord Motton in his bedroom and that damn hired coach.

"Don't worry, Miss Parker-Roth." Miss Canton smiled. "I'm certain you can bring the viscount up to scratch."

Lady Blessdon nodded. "Indeed. A few of us have placed a friendly wager or two, and the odds are much in your favor."

Miss Canton giggled. "Truth is, no one will bet against you getting him to pop the question, so we've changed the terms. Now we're guessing which day the announcement will appear in the papers."

"Ah." Jane would like to scream or kick someone's shins. Since neither activity was appropriate for a soiree, she cleared her throat. "Very interesting. I'm quite parched. If you'll excuse me, I believe I'll go in search of Lord Wolfson's refreshments."

"They're set up in the dining room, but don't get your hopes up," Lady Blessdon said. "Wolfson is a shocking nipcheese. The lemonade is worse than what's served at Almack's."

"Oh. Thank you for the warning." Jane nodded, smiled, and hurried off, trying to close her ears to the whispering that started the moment her back was turned. Would Edmund hear the gossip, too? She snorted. The females monopolizing him at the moment wouldn't tell him. They—

A large male hand wrapped itself around her arm, jerking her to a stop. "Well, well, well, look who I've found."

Chapter 20

"Lord Wolfson." Damn, that had come out rather weak. She cleared her throat and tried not to appear as terrified as she felt. The baron looked . . . different. Oh, his face was the same, of course, but something in his expression had changed. Now she could very easily believe he was Satan.

"Miss Parker-Roth." He smiled and a chill slithered down her spine. "Just the woman I most wish to have a comfortable coze with." His smile broadened. "Well, I will be comfortable. You? Perhaps not."

He pulled her toward the door he'd just come through. She dug in her heels. Where was Edmund? Probably still looking at that blasted debutante. She opened her mouth to scream, but Lord Wolfson clamped his hand over her lips before she could do more than inhale. He was far stronger than she would have guessed.

"Now, now, Miss Parker-Roth," he murmured by her ear. "You know a proper lady doesn't scream . . . in public."

He still smelled of garlic and dirt and, given her current proximity to him, sweat and other objectionable body odors. The man would benefit greatly from a bath, fresh clothing, and a new diet.

He jerked her over the threshold and slammed the door closed behind them, cutting off the comforting sounds of the crowded party. Then he released her, and she backed away, putting as much space as she could between them as she struggled to get her breathing under control.

She was trapped. On the other side of the heavy door were freedom and the normal, everyday world of the *ton*; on this side . . . on this side, she strongly suspected, was hell.

She swallowed. She couldn't panic. He hadn't locked the door. Perhaps she could escape or Edmund would rescue her.

"What are you doing?"

She jerked her head around. A tall, thin man stood by a large desk; he was glaring at Lord Wolfson. Would he help her?

Her heart lurched. No. It was unlikely Mr. Helton had forgiven her for stabbing him.

"Have you met my, er, associate?" Wolfson asked, coming to stand too close to her again. He chuckled. "Some wags have dubbed him Beelzebub."

Mr. Helton's glare deepened to a scowl. "Have you completely lost your mind?"

The baron shrugged and smiled down at Jane, ignoring his henchman. "They've named me Satan. Isn't that amusing?"

Mr. Helton slammed his hand down on the desk. "Bloody bollocks, that's torn it. Now you've got to kill her."

Lord Wolfson tried to run his finger down Jane's cheek, but she flinched away. He laughed. "Of course I'll have to kill her. I'm quite looking forward to it."

Oh, damn, this was definitely not good. She glanced around, hoping to find some means of escape or at least a weapon. She was in the baron's study, a rather gloomy room with blood red curtains . . .

Blast it, she did *not* want to think about blood.

Books lined the walls. On her right, Lord Wolfson had hung a skeleton, perhaps belonging to someone who'd displeased him—

No, that thought wasn't helpful either. As it was, her knees were almost knocking against each other, she was so frightened.

"Are you mad?" Mr. Helton was saying. "She's not a whore no one will miss; she's got a father and brothers—and the second brother is a damn dirty fighter."

Lord Wolfson shrugged. "Stephen's off in Iceland or some heathenish place."

"But Motton's not—and he's as dangerous."

The baron laughed again. "Even better. I don't like Lord Motton. He's been a thorn in my side for years, spoiling my fun. I would take great delight in spoiling something of his." He smiled at Jane. "Are you his, Miss Parker-Roth?"

"No. Of course not." She backed toward the skeleton. Something about it was familiar. What? She didn't make a habit of observing skeletons—this might be the first time she'd been in the same room with one.

"You're not a good liar, you know. Motton guards you like a dog guarding his favorite bone. I was quite surprised—delighted—to find you without him at your side." He looked her up and down, and she clenched her hands in her skirt. She felt as if he'd stripped her naked with his eyes. "Are you still a virgin, Miss Parker-Roth?"

She flushed. "Ah . . ." *Why* couldn't she lie convincingly?

"What a pity." He sighed and opened a cabinet by his desk. "I was hoping you were. They say swiving a virgin cures the pox and a multitude of other ailments." He shrugged and took out a flask. "I suppose I can't have everything." He smiled again—an extremely repulsive expression. "There will be plenty of blood anyway. I'm quite rough, you know, and Helton here has an enormous cock."

"I'm not going to rape the girl." Mr. Helton actually snarled. Unfortunately, he also seemed unwilling to do anything to stop Lord Wolfson.

She backed closer to the skeleton. There was a staff there, too, attached to the wall. Now she remembered—she would have recognized it sooner if her brain wasn't frozen with terror. This was the scene Clarence had drawn in the last piece of the sketch. Dear God, what did it mean?

Lord Wolfson walked toward her, unscrewing the flask. "I was exceedingly . . . displeased that all the drink I'd carefully prepared for the initiation at Lord Griffin's was spilled, but you'll be happy to know I have some here, just for you."

"No." If she swallowed that vile drink . . . if she behaved as she had with Edmund in the coach, mindlessly, frantically rutting . . .

She looked at Mr. Helton. His expression was a mix of disgust and pity, but he made no move to save her.

Lord Wolfson was close now. He grabbed her arm and jerked her up against him. "Are you going to help me dose her, Helton?"

"No, damn it."

"Suit yourself." He backed her against the wall, holding her still with the weight of his body. "I can manage perfectly well alone." He smiled unpleasantly. "The struggle is quite . . . exciting."

She felt the hard ridge of his excitement digging into her stomach. She had to do something to save herself—

He pinched her nose closed and held the flask to her lips. "I'm betting you'll give in to the need to breathe,

Miss Parker-Roth, and open your mouth, but if you don't I'll just pour the drink down your throat when you pass out. You won't be out long—you won't miss any of the fun." He thrust his hips against her. "And yes, I know this from experience. You are not the first female who's been less than enthusiastic about the process." He chuckled. "But they are all *very* enthusiastic once they get a little of this brew in them."

She tried to breathe through her nose, but it was hopeless. She didn't want to faint. Perhaps if she didn't swallow—

She gasped, and he splashed the liquid into her, holding her mouth open with his thumb. She felt as if she were drowning, but she knew this was her best chance while both his hands were occupied.

She grabbed his cravat pin—the one that echoed the pattern on the robe and the book—yanked it out of his linen, and stabbed it as hard as she could into the bulge digging into her belly.

He screamed, dropping the flask and loosening his hold on her. She spat the drink in his face—she'd swallowed some, so she knew she'd only a little time—and lunged for the staff. Damn. It was attached to the wall. She pulled on it with all her strength and weight . . .

A section of the bookcase slid away. A very ornate book—the book Clarence had drawn—sat in solitary splendor on a shelf. Its cover mimicked Lord Wolfson's cravat pin exactly.

"Bloody bollocks." Mr. Helton gaped—and then flung himself across the room to grab the book off its perch. Lord Wolfson, unfortunately recovered from his piercing, roared and leapt on Helton's back, causing him to drop his prize.

That damn book must be *very* important. Jane scooped it up before she rushed toward the door and freedom.

"No!" Lord Wolfson must have vanquished Mr. Helton, because he grabbed Jane from behind, causing *her* to drop the book as he swung her around. "You bitch." He lifted his fist.

The door crashed open. Edmund stood there, looking like an avenging angel.

"Damn." Lord Wolfson jerked Jane around again so her back was pinned to his chest. She heard a *snick* and felt something prick her neck. Edmund must not be the only one to have had a special folding knife made for him.

"Don't come a step closer, Motton, unless you want to see the lady's throat slit," Wolfson said, backing away with Jane.

Someone in the corridor screamed, and Edmund closed the door behind him, shutting out the crowd. He did take a step closer. "It will only go worse for you if you hurt the girl, Wolfson. You know your carefully guarded secret is out now. You can't escape."

Lord Wolfson stiffened, causing the knife to dig deeper into Jane's skin. The pain was good—it would help keep the aphrodisiac's madness at bay. She would rather die than behave here as she had in the rented carriage.

She saw Mr. Helton had recovered his senses. He'd inched quietly across the floor and had picked up the book from where she'd dropped it. Had Lord Wolfson or Edmund noticed? Apparently not. They were too focused on each other.

Perhaps if she brought Mr. Helton's actions to Lord Wolfson's attention, he would let her go.

"Ah—uk!" The knife stabbed deeper; she felt blood trickle down her neck. So perhaps she wouldn't mention Mr. Helton's activities. The man was moving toward the fireplace now. What was he going to do?

She glanced at Edmund. His eyes hadn't strayed from

Lord Wolfson. He looked like murder. She could almost feel sorry for the baron—if he weren't digging a knife into her throat.

"Let her go, Wolfson," Edmund said. "Now."

"I don't think so. I still have the book."

"Urk." Jane tried again, but just got more pain for her troubles. If Lord Wolfson took his eyes off Edmund long enough to look at the floor where she'd dropped the blasted book, he'd see it was gone. And he must know Mr. Helton would take it at his first opportunity; hadn't he heard the adage about there being no honor among thieves?

"Ah, yes, the book." Edmund snorted. "It won't get you out of this mess."

"But it will. Do you even know what's in it?"

Edmund shrugged. She knew he hadn't a clue as to the book's contents—they hadn't even known there *was* a book half an hour ago. But Edmund was brilliant. He came up with an excellent, vague guess.

"Names," he said. "It's always names, isn't it?"

"Yes." Lord Wolfson sounded as if he were gloating. "It's names, lots and lots of names—the names of half the bloody *ton*. A list of every lascivious action, every perversion, every salacious sin they've committed. A list of all the whores and waifs that have gone missing over the last years and what each of my disciples has done to and with them. As long as I have the book, I am untouchable. No one dare harm me."

"Urgle." If she couldn't get Lord Wolfson's attention, she'd try for Edmund's. She opened her eyes very wide and moved them in Mr. Helton's direction. She couldn't quite see, but she thought the man had just held a candle to the pages of Lord Wolfson's precious book.

Edmund frowned at her and then darted a glance at Mr. Helton. He grinned, though the expression was a bit, well, malicious. "You mean that book Helton is feeding to the flames?"

"What?" Lord Wolfson spun around, digging his knife farther into Jane's flesh. If she survived this night, she would have to wear high-necked gowns for the next few weeks.

"Yes, *my lord.*" Mr. Helton dropped the burning book facedown into the flames in the fireplace. "I've destroyed it. I'm free. We're all free—Ardley, Mouse, everyone. And you laughed at Widmore and his odd little sketch, didn't you, you—"

Lord Wolfson screamed, fortunately drowning out Mr. Helton's colorful description of the baron's sexual preferences and the baron's mother's peculiar habits that had resulted in Lord Wolfson's birth. Also fortunately, Wolfson shoved her out of his way so he could leap for Mr. Helton's throat.

She should bolt from the room—no, if she rushed out into the crowd, she might attack the first male she encountered. The aphrodisiac was definitely beginning to take effect. She wrapped her arms around her waist and hung on tightly as she watched Lord Wolfson and Mr. Helton battle each other.

"Jane." Edmund's hands were running up and down her arms. "Your poor neck." He brushed his lips over one of her cuts.

Damn. It was as if she were the pages of that blasted book and Edmund was the lighted candle—she exploded with a need that was going to consume her if Edmund didn't put it out immediately. She didn't care if Lord Wolfson and Mr. Helton killed each other; she half hoped they did. She just wanted Edmund—now. Sooner than now, if possible.

She pressed herself against him, locking her arms around his back. She straddled his leg quite by accident, but the pressure of his thigh against the throbbing spot between her legs was beyond wonderful. And if she rocked against him—

"Jane." Edmund caught her hips and shoved them back. "I'm happy to see you, too, but—"

There was a loud crash as if someone had gone through a window. Edmund glanced up, so she took the opportunity to assess his interest—splendid. There was a sizable bulge beneath his fall. She stroked it as the door to the room was flung open and the *ton* poured in.

"Jane." Edmund grabbed her hand and pulled it away. "We are in a rather public place."

She flung her arms around his neck and rubbed her body against his to a chorus of gasps and other shocked sounds. "Lord Wolfson gave me some of that devil's brew. I'm going to strip you naked in about three seconds if you don't do something drastic."

She licked his neck to underline her determination. She thought she heard two or three ladies swoon, and a few more called for their vinaigrettes. Some of the men resorted to whistles and rude encouragements.

"Jane!" That was Mama's voice. It loosened the aphrodisiac's grip on her for a moment.

"Help?" she whispered. Edmund was her only hope of salvation, whatever salvation might be.

He did not desert or disappoint her. He gave her a swift kiss and then threw her over his shoulder, pushing through the crowd and out into the night.

Motton stretched, careful not to disturb Jane. She was sleeping on her back, snoring slightly. A strand of hair twisted close to her eye; he brushed it out of her face.

She grunted softly and turned away from him. He

studied the gentle curve of her neck and shoulder. He wanted to kiss her there, and on her delicate back, following her spine to—

He slipped out of bed to find the chamber pot behind the screen. He hadn't bothered putting in plumbing—he didn't use this house much anymore—but he'd been happy to have it last night. Taking Jane home would have strained her mother's and his aunts' tolerance. And there would have been little chance of hiding what they were doing—Jane had been very loud and enthusiastic.

He grinned. *Very* loud and *very* enthusiastic. But he would like to make love to her slowly, without the aphrodisiac driving her. Perhaps when she woke up.

He headed back to bed, but stopped when he saw a sheet of paper on the floor. What was this? He picked it up. Someone—Henry, this house's butler, was the most likely person—had slipped it under the door. Why? He'd sent the man to Motton House last night to let the ladies know Jane was fine and they'd be back today. He hadn't wanted them to worry. Though what they were thinking . . . they must realize he and Jane were planning to marry.

At least, he was planning to marry Jane. She might need some persuading. He grinned again, looking over at her. She'd turned onto her back again. The covers had slipped to her waist, revealing the mounds of her lovely small breasts, their pink nipples just waiting for him.

He glanced down at the paper again. Henry'd written that Wolfson had broken his neck when he'd landed on the pavement under his study's window; Helton had slipped out a secret door during all the commotion and got away scot free.

Motton shrugged. He felt certain without Satan, Beelzebub would not be a threat—it sounded as if he'd been an unwilling pawn for Wolfson all these years. In any event, he'd pose no further danger to Jane.

And what was this? He read farther down Henry's missive. Jane's father and brother John had arrived in London and were none too happy with him. They had, in fact, been on the verge of searching him out last night, castration apparently on their minds. He had Aunt Winifred and Jane's mother to thank for the fact he'd remained intact.

"What's that?"

Ah, Jane was awake. She was leaning up on her elbow, holding the coverlet to her chest. He put the paper down on his desk and walked toward her. "Why are you covering yourself? Are you shy this morning?" He laughed. "You weren't at all shy last night."

She turned bright red. "It was the damn devil's brew."

He watched her eyes dart to his growing cock and back to his face. She grew even redder.

"Really? Is that all it was?" He stopped next to her, close enough to touch her, but he didn't touch her . . . not yet.

Her glance dropped from his face to his cock again, and then skittered away to stare at the boring pastoral he'd hung on the wall years ago when he'd first bought the house.

Where was his sharp-tongued, prickly, demanding Jane?

Mmm, he'd like to feel her tongue again.

He reached out and gently pulled the coverlet down to her waist. She didn't resist; she let go with a small sigh and flopped back on the pillows, closing her eyes. He studied her pale, beautiful breasts for a moment—and watched their dusky pink nipples pebble. Did anticipation thrum through her as it did through him?

He looked at her face. Her eyes were still closed, her top teeth biting her bottom lip.

Yes, he thought it did. He'd wager if he touched her between her legs, he'd find her already wet and ready for him—and his cock swelled even more at the thought.

He skimmed his fingers lightly over her breasts, and she sucked in her breath, arching slightly.

Then he dropped his hand. "*Was* it only the devil's brew, Jane? Do you feel no passion for me without that driving you into my bed?" He grimaced. "Or my carriage."

She peeked at him and then squeezed her eyes shut again as if she were afraid to look at him. "The first time I shared your bed had nothing to do with drugs."

"No, but that time you were reacting to a brush with death. Relief can be another kind of drug."

Jane frowned. It was hard to think—her breasts ached; the place between her legs throbbed. Her body was almost vibrating with need. Why wouldn't Edmund just climb into bed and do all the wonderful things he'd done last night? Why was he torturing her with talk?

Because he was uncertain. She struggled to control her lust long enough to think about his words. There'd been a thread of vulnerability in his voice. She finally looked up at him. There was vulnerability in his eyes as well. How could that be? Hadn't she been spectacularly obvious in her lust for him?

But lust was for a body; *love* was for a person—body, soul, heart, mind. He needed her to say she wanted *him*. She leaned up on her elbow again and met his gaze. "You must know it was never the urge to find Clarence's sketch that drew me into this search."

"No?" He looked surprised. Men could be so stupid at times.

"Of course not. It was you. I've loved you for years, Edmund, even when you didn't know I existed, and I love you more now. I wouldn't be here if I didn't."

His smile lit up the room, and she could almost see the tension flow out of his body. He reached for her breasts, but she slipped away from him.

"Not yet." She had uncertainties, too. "Do you lov— care for me? Or am I just another woman to find comfort with in bed?"

He laughed then. "I'm not sure I've found comfort with you, Jane. You've made me work far too hard."

She scowled at him, then dropped her eyes to his enthusiastic male member. "You seem no worse for wear."

"Apparently I'm not. I'm even eager to get back to work."

He touched her breast and this time she didn't have the self-control to pull away. The pleasure of it shot like an arrow to the part of her most in need of his attention. She whimpered and shifted her hips. She should wait, insist he answer her question, but her body didn't want to wait.

But then he removed his hand—and she almost wailed with frustration.

"Jane." He cupped her face so she had to meet his eyes. "I never sought you out before, because you weren't a candidate for anything but marriage—and I wanted to put marriage off for as long as I possibly could." He grimaced. "You know my parents didn't have a pleasant association."

"I know. And that's why I don't want you to feel compelled to marry me. I don't want to trap you as your mother trapped your father."

He laughed. "Believe me, I don't feel trapped in the slightest. I'm very, very eager to get a special license as quickly as possible." He grinned. "Though I do believe your family and my aunts will insist as well."

She frowned. He said he wasn't trapped, but he was. "I don't want them to force you to marry me. I—"

He covered her lips with his fingers. "Our relatives would have to use force to keep me from marrying you. You are maddening and annoying—and amusing and intelligent and strong and beautiful. You have wormed your way into my life so I cannot imagine living it without you. Of course I love you."

Happiness bloomed in her heart—but need was still blooming elsewhere. "Then come to bed and show me."

"Again?"

"Yes." He didn't look as if he needed encouragement, but she would offer it anyway. She threw the rest of the covers off, so she was completely naked—body and heart. "Please, Edmund?"

"I wouldn't be a gentleman if I refused such a delightful—and polite—request," he said, leaning over to kiss her forehead. "But slowly this time."

Slowly was torture. His tongue explored every corner of her mouth and his fingers teased her nipples. His lips trailed a lazy path down her jaw to her neck and then to her breasts. He lingered there, even when she moaned and wiggled, trying to encourage him to move on. She loved his lips—and tongue and teeth—on that sensitive flesh, but there was other, more sensitive flesh that required his urgent attention.

He finally took her hints and proceeded in the correct direction, down over her belly through her nether hair to—

"Oh!" The wet flick of his tongue was exquisite. The second stroke shot her to the edge of release. She tugged on his hair. She needed him inside.

"I thought we were going slowly this time?" he said. Did his voice sound a little breathless?

She yanked again and growled at him. He grinned.

"Or perhaps next time. I take it you are ready now?"

"Yes. Now."

"Very well." He slid inside and she shivered with delight. "As luck would have it, I am ready, too." His voice was as strained and tight as she felt. He withdrew and stroked in again.

"Ah!" It was all she needed. She shattered, and as she did, she felt Edmund's warm seed pulse deep into her.

They lay tangled together as their hearts slowed; then Edmund lifted himself off her. The cool air chilled her damp skin before he covered them with the blanket. She sighed and snuggled close to him.

"I'm afraid it may take a lot of practice to master the slow approach," he said, smoothing her hair off her face. She smiled. She felt relaxed—and pleasantly wanton. "But we'll have years to perfect our technique."

"Mmm." Years with Edmund. That sounded lovely. And to think, just a few days ago she'd been bored and wanting adventure, certain this Season would be like every other.

"But we don't have years before we have to face your parents and brother and my aunts," Edmund was saying.

"What?" Jane sat up abruptly. "Da is in London?"

"He is, as well as your brother John. I cannot think they'll be happy you spent the night in my company."

"Da and John hate London." Her eyes widened. "You didn't tell them what we were doing, did you?"

Edmund laughed. "Do I look like I have a death wish? No, I didn't give them any particulars, but after the scene at Wolfson's, I don't believe I had to. All of society must have a very good idea what we've been up to. I merely sent round a note telling them you were well and with me so they should not worry. I doubt that put their minds completely at rest, however."

Jane snorted. "It should. Your aunts and my mother have been throwing me at your head all week."

He grinned. "True. So shall we go tell them their efforts have been successful?"

Jane looked down at the naked man lying beside her on the sheets. It was hard to imagine this scene was real. She should pinch herself . . . or maybe touch him . . .

"Jane, we'll never get to Motton House if you do that or, ah, mmm, yess . . ." He flipped her onto her back. "I'm afraid your poor family will have to wait a little longer for our news."

Dear Readers,

  The Naked Viscount is the seventh "Naked" story I've written. New readers—and even fans of the series—sometimes ask me if the books need to be read in order. I don't think so—in fact, I didn't *write* them in order. I found as I went along, I discovered new characters that intrigued me—and then I'd have to figure out what *their* story might be.

  However, for those of you who are interested, here's a chronology of the stories—the year in the parenthesis is the year the book was published.

  1816—*The Naked Duke* (2005)
         The Naked Baron (2009)
         "The Naked Laird" in *Lords of Desire* (2009)
         The Naked Marquis (2006)
  1819—*The Naked Earl* (2007)
         The Naked Viscount (2010)
  1820—*The Naked Gentleman* (2008)
  1821—"The Naked Prince" in *An Invitation to Sin* (coming in February 2011)
         The Naked King (coming in June 2011)

  I hope you enjoyed *The Naked Viscount*. Thanks so much for being a "Naked Reader"!

                                                    Sally

And here's a selection from Sally's
next sexy Regency romance,

THE NAKED KING,

to be published by Zebra Books in 2011.

Stephen Parker-Roth landed in a large puddle. Mud and water splashed into the air, soaking his breeches, spattering his coat, and decorating his face with flecks of dirt. He wiped a blob off his right cheek with a clean corner of his cravat and frowned at the perpetrator of this sartorial disaster. "You have deplorable manners, sir."

The miscreant blinked at him, tongue lolling. He looked not the slightest bit abashed, damn it.

"This wouldn't have happened if I weren't very, very drunk, you know."

The fellow tilted his head to one side.

"You doubt me?" Stephen leaned forward and poked his finger at the beast to emphasize his point. "I warn you, I'm an exceedingly dangerous man. I've won brawls from Borneo to Buenos Aires to Boston. More than one blackguard has rued the day his path crossed mine."

The dog barked, a rather startlingly deep, ringing sound, and put his head down on his front paws. His hindquarters remained in the air, tail waving like a flag in a stiff gale.

Stephen unbent enough to scratch the creature's ears. "Ah, well, I won't hold your ignorance against you. You're just a . . ." He frowned. "No, you can't be a homeless cur—you're far too clean. How is it you're roaming Hyde Park by yourself?" His fingers found a collar in the dog's deep fur—and then he noticed the leash dragging in the grass. "Oh ho, you're not alone. What have you done with your master, sir?"

The dog's ears pricked up. A woman's voice, rich and incredibly alluring, called out, "Harry!"

"Or mistress . . ." Stephen found himself addressing empty air. Harry was already bounding across the grass to a figure about a hundred yards distant. Stephen squinted in the sun. The female wore an enormous bonnet and a dress that looked like an oversized flour sack.

Pity. A voice that evoked twisted sheets and tangled limbs should not belong to an antidote.

The woman stooped to reclaim the leash, and Harry promptly began towing her back toward him. He'd best stand, then, like a gentleman should.

He struggled to his feet. The mud didn't want to let him go. MacInnes was going to have an apoplexy when he saw him. Why his valet, who didn't blink at tending his gear in the Amazon or the wilds of Africa, got as priggish as a damned dandy when they reached England's shores was beyond him.

Eh. The change in altitude was not felicitous. He bent over, resting his hands on his knees, and swallowed several times until the landscape stopped whirling and his last meal agreed to remain in his stomach. It would be shockingly bad form to greet the lady by casting up his accounts all over her slippers.

"Harry! Slow down!"

Even sharp and breathless, her voice sent a jolt of pleasure through him. He leaned forward a bit more to shield any obvious evidence of his interest.

Rein up, you cawker. She might have buck teeth and garlic breath; she might be toothless and eighty years old.

He glanced up. Well, not eighty. She was moving too quickly to be that ancient.

The dreadful bonnet slid back off her head as he watched. Ah! Now he saw the purpose of that hideous headgear—it hid her riot of bright red curls. They glinted in the sunlight like dew-kissed roses.

She had spectacles, too, that looked to be in danger of falling off her rather prominent nose, and delightfully full lips, currently twisted into a grimace. She wasn't beautiful, but she was definitely attractive.

Who was she? A maid assigned to walk the family dog? No sane butler or housekeeper would assign this girl that task—the dog was walking her, not she the dog. A lady of the night? Unlikely. It was now an awful hour in the morning, and he'd never heard of a dasher with an obstreperous dog, the voice of a siren, red curls, and spectacles. A fallen female with those striking attributes would be the talk of the male *ton*. Perhaps she was a widow.

Or married. Damn, he hoped she wasn't married. He didn't dally with married ladies.

He shook his head. Was he insane? How the hell had dalliance crept into his thoughts?

He was drunk. That was it. Very, very drunk.

And she was very flushed and very annoyed. She was glaring at him.

He *was* covered in mud—his shoes squelched with the stuff—but that wasn't his fault. Her dog was to blame.

Harry dragged her the last few yards and plopped down at his feet. The girl's brows were the same shade as her hair. She looked more like a flame than a rose, actually. Was she as fiery in bed?

He closed his eyes briefly. If he could remember how many glasses of brandy he'd had, he'd vow never to have so many again.

He regarded her glowering countenance. "Er, good morning." He sounded perfectly sober, if he said so himself. "It's, ah, a lovely morning, isn't it?"

"No, it's not." She blew out a short, sharp breath and pushed her hair back out of her face. Her green eyes were as stormy as a wind-tossed ocean, full of passion . . .

Perhaps he should swear off brandy entirely, though drink had never made him so lustful before.

"I mean . . ." She swallowed, obviously trying to get her spleen under control. "That is, yes, it is a lovely morning. How nice of you to say so after Harry caused you to fall into the mud. I apologize for his behavior."

Mmm, that voice. He'd so like to hear it threaded with need and desire, panting his name—

Definitely no more brandy.

"He's a sheep dog," the woman said. "I imagine he was trying to herd you away from the puddle, not into it." She reached back to reclaim her bonnet.

Oh, no. He couldn't let her cover her beautiful curls again with that monstrosity. His hand shot out, plucked the millinery mistake from her fingers, and dropped it into the mud. He mashed it down with his foot for good measure.

"My bonnet!" Lady Anne Marston gaped down at her poor bonnet, flattened under this rude person's shoe. What sort of gentleman attacked a woman's hat?

No sort of gentleman. The man might be handsome as sin with his startlingly clear blue eyes and shaggy, sun-streaked hair, but handsome is as handsome does—she had learned *that* lesson beyond hope of forgetting—and destroying a woman's bonnet was not handsomely done.

She drew in a breath to tell him exactly what she thought of such behavior—and stopped. Was that brandy she smelled? Certainly the man wasn't foxed at 10 o'clock in the morning!

"Your bonnet is an abomination," he said.

"It is not!" And now he was insulting her as well. That was her favorite bonnet under his foot. It might not be stylish—*she* wasn't stylish—but she liked it. She'd had it for years.

"You didn't buy it in London, did you?"

She gritted her teeth. "Of course not. London bonnets are frilly, silly dabs of straw and feathers and gewgaws. I need something serviceable."

She should leave. Yes, the man had landed in the mud, but it was probably more his fault than Harry's. Drunkards were notoriously unsteady. She tugged on Harry's leash, but the idiotic animal stayed where he was, at this human animal's feet.

"Serviceable?" He ground her poor hat deeper into the muck. "How could this atrocity be the least bit serviceable?"

"It protected me from the sun"—*and kept critical eyes off my disreputable hair.*

She would admit that last only to herself, certainly not to him. What did this fellow know of the matter anyway? He didn't have red hair—though, being a man, he probably wouldn't care if he did.

He snorted. "It protected you from the sun and every male who saw you in it, I'll wager."

Oh, she'd like to kick the cod's-head exactly where it would hurt him most. He didn't think she was some silly miss on the catch for a husband, did he? "I'd hoped it would protect me from annoying men"—she sniffed, giving him her best pretention-depressing look—"such as yourself."

He chuckled. "Now that's put me in my place, hasn't it? And here I just rescued you from the ugliest bonnet in Britain." He leaned forward slightly, sending another whiff of brandy her way. "When you go looking for a replacement, try Madam de Fleur's on Bond Street. Fleur's hats are far more attractive."

Of course this fribble would be an expert in female fashion. She jerked on Harry's leash again; Harry merely yawned. "You are drunk, sir."

He nodded, looking not the least bit repentant. "I'm very much afraid that I am."

"Did you rise early, then, to begin your debauchery?" It was a shame—in an academic, aesthetic sense only, of course—that such a handsome man was so dissipated.

"Er, no. I haven't yet been to bed."

"You haven't?" She looked at his clothes more closely. Under all the mud they were indeed evening wear.

And under the clothes were exceptionally broad shoulders, a flat stomach, narrow hips . . . She flushed. Damn her coloring. She squeezed her eyes shut and drew in a deep breath—still tainted with the scent of brandy. What was the matter with her? She was not interested in men, certainly not this man.

"I don't believe I've engaged in any debauchery yet this morning . . ."

He paused suggestively, and, damn it, she couldn't keep her eyes shut. She looked at him.

". . . but I'd be willing to attempt some now, if you'd like." He waggled his eyebrows.

Surprisingly, she had to swallow a laugh instead of a gasp.

His eyes gleamed and his lips slid slowly into a smile—
with dimples, blast it all. "Care to tuck me into bed?"

"No!" This man was the very worst sort of London
coxcomb she could imagine—had imagined when she'd
worried about this unfortunate trip these last few months.
Only, he didn't seem so bad. He seemed . . . amused and
amusing.

The horrifying truth was part of her did wish to tuck
the handsome rascal in. "Behave yourself."

Hadn't she learned her lesson ten years ago? Apparently not if the odd warmth in her belly—lower than her
belly—was any indication.

She would not let herself be taken in again. This man
might not seem like Lord Brentwood on the surface, but
his heart was likely as black. His heart and another,
specifically male organ.

"Oh, well." He shrugged. "I'll be off to bed straight-
away then once I've seen you home." He raised his brows,
looking ridiculously hopeful. "If you're certain you'd not
like to read me a bedtime story at least?"

She turned another laugh into a cough. The fellow was
indeed an accomplished seducer if he could charm her
well-armored heart. She must be sure to keep her half
sister away from him. At eighteen, Evie was too young to
have learned to be suspicious of handsome scoundrels.
"Quite certain. And there is no need for you to escort me."

"Oh, but there is. You know I wouldn't be a gentleman
if I didn't see you safely home."

She turned her nose up at him. "You are not a gentleman—and I am quite all right by myself."

"No, you're not. A gently bred woman needs a male
to protect her."

She glared. "I have Harry—he is both male and
protective."

"And you have no control over him."

"Oh, and I have more control over you?"

The moment the last word left her lips, she froze, as if she'd shocked herself, and then bit her lip and flushed. Her eyes dropped in apparent embarrassment—and focused on his crotch.

Damn. He wasn't about to hide behind his hands like a bashful virgin, but if she stared at him much longer, she would get quite an education in male anatomy.

"I assure you, I can find my way home by myself." Her eyes moved on to her dog, thank God. "Forgive me for not apologizing earlier for the state of your clothing. I intended to immediately"—her eyes came back up to scowl at him—"and would have if you hadn't accosted my bonnet."

"I wouldn't have accosted your bonnet," he said, stepping on it once more and twisting his foot to grind it farther into the grime, "if it hadn't so vilely accosted my eyes and my male sensibilities."

She pressed her lips into a tight line, obviously wishing to brangle with him, but equally obviously restraining herself. Too bad. He found sparring with her surprisingly stimulating.

She took a deep breath, causing her formless bodice to swell in a rather interesting fashion. "In any event," she said, "Harry was at fault." She dropped her eyes to his muddied cravat. "Your clothing is likely irreparably damaged; my father will wish to make it right. Please have your bills sent to Lord Crane."

"Ah." That was why he didn't know her. Crane spent even less time in London than Stephen did. "So you're Crazy Crane's daughter."

He was sober enough to notice her flinch, but she must be used to hearing the nickname. Everyone called Crane crazy. His passion for finding antiquities was even greater than Stephen's for discovering new plant species. The word at White's was the earl had come to Town—briefly, as it turned out—to fire off his daughter on the Marriage Mart. Stephen frowned. He was drunk, but he wasn't completely disguised. This girl was too old to be a debutante.

"So you're here to find a husband?" he asked.

Her brows snapped down as her eyes snapped back to his face. "Of course not." She curled her delightful upper lip slightly. "Were you quaking in your boots?"

"Don't have boots." He lifted his foot to show her and almost left his shoe in the quagmire. "And you don't scare me. I've been dodging debutantes for years—though you do seem a little long in the tooth to be just making your bows."

"I am twenty-seven"—it sounded as if she were gritting her teeth again—"not that it is any of your business. It is my half sister who is being introduced to the *ton*."

"Ah!" He nodded. Now he remembered. "You're Crane's older daughter, the one by his first wife. The bluestocking as opposed to the—"

A sliver of sobriety wormed its way into his sodden brain. He coughed.

"As opposed to the beauty." She sounded indifferent, but he saw the hurt in her eyes before she turned abruptly and started walking briskly toward Grosvenor Gate. Even Harry gave him a reproachful look as he left.

Damn. That hadn't been well done of him. He should let her go. She would not want to spend another moment in his presence.

He couldn't let her go. He did *not* break hearts, nor offend anyone, at least unintentionally. He had to apologize. He took off after her.

Crane's daughter—what was her name? Damned if he

could remember. No one at White's had talked much about the bluestocking—who had a long stride, but she was hampered by her skirts, and Stephen was used to walking long distances. He caught up to her quickly.

As he feared, she was crying.

"Go away." She wouldn't look at him.

"Look, I'm sorry. I didn't mean that quite the way it sounded."

She snorted—and then had to sniff repeatedly. He offered her his handkerchief.

"Thank you." She glared at him briefly, her eyes quite red behind her spectacles. He took Harry's leash, so she could blow her nose, which she did rather defiantly. She looked anywhere but at him.

He felt an odd pain in his chest. A bout of indigestion, most likely. He'd certainly had too much to drink. Once he saw Lady . . . Lady . . .

"Er, you never told me your name."

She shrugged. "And you never told me yours."

"So I didn't." He inclined his head. "Stephen Parker-Roth, at your service."

"What?" She stumbled on a crack in the pavement. He reached to grab her, but she avoided his hand. *"The King of Hearts?"*

"Ah, well, yes, some people call me that." He cleared his throat. "I'm rather good—or lucky—with cards."

Cards? Anne sniffed. "It's not *cards* you're good with."

"It is."

The rogue looked like a blasted choir boy, as sinless as a cherub, but she knew through long association with her half brothers not to trust that mask of innocence. "Oh?" She allowed her skepticism to show in her voice.

He had the grace to laugh. "I grant you my skill with cards is not the only reason I got that dam—er, unfortunate nickname." He raised his brows. "How do you know it, Lady—" He frowned. "Devil a bit, I *still* don't know your name."

She might as well tell him. He would learn it soon enough once the Season got underway. "Anne. My name is Lady Anne."

"Lady Anne," he said.

Her name sounded like someone else's when he said it—someone beautiful, or at least someone interesting. Someone he was interested in.

Idiot! Only a complete noddy would think the King of Hearts could have the slightest interest in a red-headed, bespectacled bluestocking. She was *glad* he wasn't interested in her. She wasn't interested in him.

She was a terrible liar.

"So how is it, Lady Anne, that you know my nickname when you have so recently arrived in Town? If gossip is correct, the earl dumped you—" He coughed. "I mean *deposited* you at Crane House just yesterday."

Dumped was the correct description. Papa could barely stand to pause the coach long enough to let her, Evie, and the boys out. He certainly hadn't waited for their baggage to arrive; he and Georgiana were far too anxious to get to the docks and board their ship for Greece. Fortunately Cousin Clorinda, being in London already, had moved in the day before, but things were still very much at sixes and sevens.

"The London papers come even to the country, you know."

He raised one eyebrow and looked annoyingly superior. "So you can peruse the gossip columns?"

She glared at him. "So I can read the entire paper."

And, yes, perhaps she had paid particular attention to gossip concerning the K— of H—. She'd taken an interest—a *scholarly* interest—in him. She'd come across an article in Papa's *Gentleman's Magazine* a year or two ago, an account Mr. Parker-Roth had written describing one of his plant hunting expeditions. He'd sounded exceptionally intelligent and rather intrepid—obviously he'd learned how to be as cozening in print as in person.

She flushed. She'd dreamt about him once or twice, too. She was lonely on occasion—well, most of the time. He'd caught her fancy—what harm was there in a little romantic woolgathering? She was never going to meet him.

Except she just had.

One would think a twenty-seven-year-old spinster would have more sense, especially a woman with her experience.

Apparently, one would be wrong.

Traffic was beginning to pick up. The streets and walks had been deserted when she'd left Crane House earlier— a very good thing as she'd had to run to keep up with Harry. Of course now the stupid dog was walking sedately at Mr. Parker-Roth's side.

"The *ton* is always making up nicknames for people," he was saying. "They'll probably christen you and your sister as soon as you attend your first social event."

"I sincerely hope not." Blast it, how was she going to navigate these treacherous social waters with only Cousin Clorinda to help her? She bit her lip. It was just like Papa and Georgiana to go off to dig in the dirt, leaving her in charge of the children. Not that Evie was a child any longer. Of course not. They wouldn't be in this mess if she were.

She swallowed a sigh. Thankfully, Evie was a sensible girl—but Anne had considered herself sensible once, too. All it had taken was one experienced, London beau paying her a little attention—

Dear God, what if Brentwood was here in Town?

She struggled to take a deep breath. No, she couldn't be that unlucky. She'd been reading the gossip columns very carefully for weeks and had not seen his name.

But if he *were* in London—

It didn't matter. The . . . event had happened so long ago and been such a small occurrence in his life, he must not remember a bit of it.

"A penny for your thoughts, Lady Anne."

Her heart thudded into her throat. "I, ah, wasn't thinking about anything."

"No? You looked—"

"Oh, yes, look, here we are at Crane House already." *Thank God!* "What a surprise. I don't know how we got here so quickly." She was blathering, but if she kept talking, he couldn't ask her questions she didn't want to answer. "Thank you for escorting me and for taking charge of Harry. If you will just give me his leash, you can get"—she hadn't been about to say he could get to bed, had she?—"that is, you can be about your business." She smiled, or at least tried to, and held out her hand. If she was lucky, she would never see him again.

Ha! She might hope she wouldn't see him, but she was here for the whole cursed Season. She couldn't hide in her room and send Evie to the parties and balls with only odd, elderly Cousin Clorinda as chaperone.

Perhaps Mr. Parker-Roth would leave London tomorrow to hunt for greenery in some exotic—and very distant—location. She would add that thought to her prayers tonight.

"Lady Anne," he said, looking far too serious all of a sudden.

"Mr. Parker-Roth, I should go. Cousin Clorinda and my sister must be wondering where I am—"

She glanced up. What if someone looked out a window and saw her conversing with Mr. Parker-Roth? She and he would be quite recognizable—neither was wearing a hat. Their faces were evident for any curious spectator to see.

Whom was she kidding? It wasn't only her face she had to hide—her unfortunate hair was a blazing beacon, proclaiming her identity to anyone not colorblind.

Perhaps no one would look. It was early for most of the *ton* . . . but Lady Dunlee lived next door and she had a nose for even the faintest whiff of scandal. Cousin Clorinda had warned Anne about the woman the moment Anne had crossed Crane House's threshold—and Lady Dunlee herself had already stopped Anne to let her know the boys had been teasing her nasty gray cat.

"But I never properly apologized," Mr. Parker-Roth said. Harry sat calmly at his feet. Why wouldn't that dog behave for her?

"No apology is necessary. Now, please—"

He touched her lips with his gloveless fingers. She froze.

Oh.

His skin was slightly rough—he clearly used his hands for more than raising a quizzing glass or shuffling cards—and warm.

All of a sudden, she didn't care about the windows overlooking the square.

"I don't want you to think you aren't beautiful." His fingers slipped sideways to cradle her jaw; his thumb moved back and forth over her bottom lip. "You are."

He was an enchanter, that was it, weaving a spell around her. Faintly, very faintly, she heard the voice of reason warning her about gossip and Lady Dunlee, but for the first time in a decade, she ignored it. Her hands crept up to rest on his broad, solid chest.

She smelled the brandy on his breath again. "You're drunk." She spoke to him, but she was reminding herself.

"Yes." His words whispered past her cheek. "But I'm not blind."

His mouth brushed hers. Her lips tingled, feeling suddenly swollen. This kiss—if you could call it a kiss—was nothing like the hot, wet, slobbery affairs she'd endured from Brentwood. Being kissed by Brentwood had been an attack—this was something else entirely.

Comfort, not lust. An invitation, not a command.

"Anne."

She loved the sound of her name in his voice. A little shiver slithered through her and she sighed, tilting her head more, like a sunflower seeking the sun.

He made a small, satisfied sound and nibbled on her bottom lip while his free hand, the one not grasping Harry's leash, slid to the back of her head.

An odd warmth gathered in her belly. Something hard and frozen began to melt. She leaned into Mr. Parker-Roth's strong body, wanting—needing—more of his heat.

And then she heard the hiss of an angry cat and Harry's answering bark. Mr. Parker-Roth jerked backward. She felt herself wobble and grabbed his coat.

"Hold tight," he muttered. His arm locked around her waist as they lost their battle with gravity and tumbled toward the pavement.

"*Oof!*" He flinched as he took the brunt of the impact. She was not a featherweight. "Are you all right?"

"I'll live." His voice had an edge of pain.

"I'm so sorry!" She relaxed against him for a moment. His body was so hard under hers. Pleasantly hard. And something else of his was getting hard as well . . .

Her face burned. What had she been thinking? Here she was, sprawled across a man's body in a public square and from the feel of the sun on the back of her legs, her skirt was up around her knees. And from the feel of the man below her, he was having the expected reaction. How mortifying. And if anyone saw them . . .

She started to scramble off him. He grabbed her and held her still.

"Let me go." She tried to twist free. "Think of the scandal if we are observed."

He flinched again and tightened his hold on her back . . . well, a bit lower than her back.

"Mind your knee, love."

"Oh." Her leg was now between his. Her knee was indeed very close to— "I'm so sorry."

"That's all right. No permanent harm done." He smiled a little tightly. "I hope. Now, we'll just have—"

That's when she heard the sharp intake of a breath.

"Trouble," Mr. Parker-Roth muttered.

Anne looked up. Lady Dunlee stood ten feet from them, a look of delighted horror on her face.

"Lady Anne—and Mr. Parker-Roth! What in the world are you doing?"